Published by Sourcebooks Casablanca, an imprint of Sourcebooks
P.O. Box 4410, Naperville, Illinois 60567-4410
(630) 961-3900
sourcebooks.com

Cataloging-in-Publication data is on file with the Library of Congress.

Printed and bound in the United States of America.
SB 10 9 8 7 6 5 4 3 2

The Lady He Lost

FAYE DELACOU

sourcebooks
casablanca

To my Grama Martha, who first made me want to become a writer when I was eight years old. This is probably not the book either of us had in mind at the time! I'm not sure you would've approved of the racy chapters, but I hope you would have been proud that I got here.

One

1839

LIEUTENANT ELEAZAR WILLIAMS WAS RESURRECTED ON A Sunday—which, though fitting, proved terribly inconvenient for his family.

The Williamses were just getting ready to attend church (where, it so happened, they intended to light a candle for their departed son, now some two years in his watery grave), when their butler announced a visitor.

"It's the young Mister Williams!" he gasped, his face white. "Returned to us!"

This statement produced some confusion, for Eli's younger brother was away on his grand tour, and therefore a more likely candidate for an unexpected return.

"But he's just reached Rome," protested Mrs. Williams. "Why should he have come home now?"

"Not Jacob, ma'am," the servant amended. "Eleazar."

At that moment, Eli himself walked into the room, looking

nothing like a man long-drowned. He was breathing, his flesh was a healthy tan, and he wasn't even wet.

"Hello," said Eli.

Mrs. Williams screamed and fell into a dead faint. Her daughter barely managed to catch her before she hit the ground. With a stagger and a grunt, she tipped her mother toward the settee. Hannah was a sturdy girl.

"Good God!" cried Mr. Williams. "We thought you had drowned."

"No," replied Eli. "Terribly sorry to have frightened you."

Needless to say, no one made it to church that morning.

"The most important thing," Jane Bishop began, with an earnest look to the pair of ladies before her, "is never to wager more than you're prepared to lose. Both in life and in card play."

It might seem self-evident, but a remarkable number of people couldn't grasp this principle. They left more than they could afford on the table, or took risks with their hearts or their reputations that no sensible person would counsel. Not Jane, though. She knew exactly what her odds in life were (poor, especially in the financial sense), and how to best safeguard against future risk (don't play a losing game). It had served her well thus far.

"Wait a minute." Miss Reva Chatterjee frowned and tilted her head, her long lashes shadowing her dark eyes. She was several years younger than Jane, and spoke with the sort of innocence only a debutant could muster. "I thought you said the most important thing was to always hold if you reach seventeen."

"No, no, I said you must always hold if you reach *nineteen*. If you have seventeen, it depends on the other players and whether you have an ace or not. If you memorize my chart, you'll see how it all works."

Another thing most people didn't seem to understand was that gambling wasn't actually a risk if you understood maths. At least, not for the house.

Miss Chatterjee shot an uneasy look to the large piece of foolscap on the table between them. Jane had written out every possible combination the dealer might draw relative to the players and indicated where one should hold or seek another card to maximize the chances of winning, shrinking her neat script to the most miniscule proportions to fit everything in. What better way could there be to show their newest helper the ropes? All she needed to do was to follow it perfectly, and profits were guaranteed.

Cordelia Danby—Della to her friends—cleared her throat delicately. "Jane, dear, I thought we agreed that the chart was a bit much to start with and we were just going to focus on the other rules for now." It had been Della's idea to invite Miss Chatterjee to join them this morning.

They'd agreed that they needed to train a third dealer if they were to have any hope of expanding their card club, and Miss Chatterjee was the logical choice. She was a regular member and a trusted friend of Della's, but she was already starting to look a bit overwhelmed by the vast array of possibilities listed on the page. Jane loved the numbers best, but not everyone shared her enthusiasm. *Oh dear.* Della was going to be cross with her if she scared the poor girl off. They'd managed well enough on their own thus far, but they were starting to have too many guests to continue without help. They needed this to work.

"You're quite right," Jane conceded with a last, regretful glance at her chart. "We can cover that next week. Let's get back to not wagering too much. That was the part I wanted to tell you about. It isn't just yourself you need to keep in check, it's the guests as well. You'll need to step in if they're being too extravagant."

"But isn't it good if the ladies wager a lot?" Miss Chatterjee shot a hesitant look to Della. "Then we'll win more."

"That's what I've been saying," Della agreed. She had a cherubic face and laughing brown eyes that lit up when she was excited. That, combined with her short, plump figure and high-pitched voice, gave her an almost childlike appearance, though her character was anything but innocent.

"*No.*" Jane pressed her palms to the table. They'd been over this a hundred times. Della might be her dearest friend, but they held opposite views on what constituted an acceptable level of risk. It probably came from being born to such different circumstances. Della had never needed to worry much about how her life would turn out, with her parents as wealthy as they were. "The goal of our card club is to make a steady profit, not a quick one. If we have to explain to an angry father how his daughter came to lose the family rubies over a game of vingt-et-un, we'll be shut down within a week."

Miss Chatterjee considered this a moment before she nodded, and Della wilted a bit at the loss of her ally.

Before Jane could savor the victory, a rap on the door interrupted them.

Drat, not Edmund! I told him I was using the study this morning.

But it wasn't Jane's brother who entered the room a moment later; it was her uncle.

"Good morning." He nodded to their guests. "Jane, darling, I'm so sorry to interrupt your callers, but I'm going out and I simply *must* know what sort of fabric you'd like me to order or we won't have time to make you a new gown for Cecily's rout. You've been putting me off all week."

Jane suppressed a sigh. *Not this again.*

Some people suffered the trials of the matchmaking mamas of the ton, those tenacious, indefatigable creatures who flitted from one ballroom to the next, ensuring the reproduction of the upper classes with only marginal inbreeding. Jane had no such figure in her life. Instead, she was blessed with a matchmaking uncle. Though he might not have seemed the most likely choice for the role, Uncle Bertie had risen to the challenge of conquering the London season with remarkable enthusiasm. Almost—dare one say it—*too* much enthusiasm.

"Thank you, Uncle, but I really don't need anything new." They couldn't afford anything new, truth be told. But Bertie believed that Jane's wardrobe expenses should be dictated by his affection rather than his finances. "I was planning to wear that cream gown with the gold flowers on it."

"*Jane.*" He stomped one foot so sharply it made her jump. "You've worn it twice already. How shall we ever find you a husband if you won't make an effort to look your best?"

Jane risked a glance at Della, who understood her anguish and was trying valiantly not to laugh.

Uncle Bertie followed her gaze, adopting his most inviting tone as he addressed their guests. "Girls, you'd love to go to the modiste together, wouldn't you? Talk some sense into my niece. Wouldn't she look lovely in a new gown?"

"Um." A look of mild panic flitted across Miss Chatterjee's face. She obviously hadn't counted on being thrust into a family squabble when she'd called this morning.

Indeed, Jane had been quite safe from this sort of thing only last year when Cecily was still at home to serve as the center of Bertie's universe. But now that his own daughter was happily married, he had fixed his sights squarely upon his niece.

She loved Uncle Bertie, but being the sole object of his enthusiasm could be a bit exhausting.

"What is it you girls are doing in here, anyway?" Bertie had finally noticed the chart of all the vingt-et-un hands stretched out on the table between them. Jane might have shoved it out of view, had she been a bit quicker, but she couldn't bear to crease the page. She'd worked so hard on it.

"Nothing," she blurted out. "We were just…"

Oh goodness. What feminine pursuit could this giant list of numbers possibly resemble? Calligraphy practice? Dance steps, perhaps?

"It's a ranking system for eligible gentlemen," Della supplied without missing a beat.

How does she come up with these ideas of hers?

Unlike Jane, who never had a fib ready when she needed one, Della's silver tongue was the solution to (or the cause of) many a scrape.

"Beg pardon?" Uncle Bertie drew his graying brows together in confusion. "How would one rank gentlemen?"

"Yes, Della. How *would* one rank gentlemen?" What a thing to choose!

"It's simple, really. You just assign a value for attributes such as income, good manners, temperament, and so forth, and then you add up the total to see if the gentleman in question would be a good match."

Bertie stared at the paper for so long that Jane began to worry he'd seen through their trick. When he finally spoke, there was a hint of disappointment in his tone. "I know one must consider practicalities, but in my day, young people used to hope for a *love* match. Ah, well. I suppose I should be happy you're taking an interest in your future." His index finger traced the first column on the page. "Tell me, which gentleman does this one represent? Who's your best match?"

Oh Lord.

With three seasons behind her already and nothing to show for it but a split sole on her favorite dancing slippers, Jane had all but given up on attracting a husband. Only Bertie's steadfast faith kept her from voicing her thoughts aloud. He'd been so good to her and

Edmund after their parents died; surely she could muster a better effort for his sake. But no matter how Jane tried to follow the path that was expected of her, the task proved impossible.

No one wanted an orphaned lady without any dowry for a wife. Much less one who aspired to run a clandestine gambling club.

Even if she could find a gentleman willing to overlook her poverty, marriage would be nothing but a losing game for her—the sort of risk she couldn't afford to take. Without any funds to settle on herself or her future children, she would be entirely dependent on her husband. If he mismanaged his fortune or died unexpectedly, she would be left with nothing all over again, a poor relation shuffled from house to house, forever unwanted.

She couldn't endure that.

Far better to make her own way in life, if Jane could manage it. Once she and Della had earned enough money to prove their club could work, she would explain everything to Bertie and make him understand.

"Er...that's—that's Mr. MacPherson," her friend offered when Jane hesitated too long.

Mr. MacPherson had spoken to Jane for ten minutes after the opera last month, and then danced with her exactly twice the following evening. That had propelled him to the status of her most promising suitor, at least in Uncle Bertie's estimation.

"How lovely!" His mood brightened once more at this news. The prospect of a match always had this effect, no matter how unlikely. "I *did* think he took a particular interest in—Jane, you're frowning. We've talked about this, darling. You cannot afford to wrinkle your brow at three-and-twenty."

"I'm not frowning, that's just my face." Jane sighed, though she endeavored to turn the corners of her mouth upward instead of down. It cost her some effort, given that she was fairly certain her uncle would be on the subject of her future marriage to Mr. MacPherson for the rest of the day, all thanks to Della. There was no chance they would finish preparing Miss Chatterjee now. "Do you know something, Uncle? I've had a change of heart. I believe we *shall* go to the shops this morning."

"Lovely. I'll have the carriage prepared."

"No need. We'll stop by Della's first and get a few things, then we'll take hers."

Della and Jane lived on the same street, so close they were practically neighbors. They were in the habit of dropping in on one another this way.

She shot her friend a look, trusting her to understand. The excuse would satisfy Bertie and give them the freedom to continue their work undisturbed.

Her uncle looked so pleased, Jane almost felt guilty. She didn't like to lie to him, but how else was she supposed to accomplish anything? Their plans were too important to put off.

The ladies stood to go, when Bertie suddenly produced an envelope from his coat pocket. "I almost forgot. There was a letter for you." Jane glanced down as she took it. Her name and address were scrawled in the center by a neat hand, but the sender's name was absent. Odd.

She gently tore open one edge, unfolded the short missive, and read.

Dearest Jane,

I am alive and recently returned to England. Allow me to come to you to explain things in person. I am so very sorry for the grief I have caused.

Eli Williams

Jane's heart was pounding by the end as her eyes struggled to make sense of the words. It was impossible. Eli had died nearly two years ago; everyone knew that. Was this someone's idea of a cruel joke?

Unbidden, her mind flashed back to his funeral service. Cecily wailing dramatically over an empty coffin, drowning out his mother and sister. Jane hadn't felt it was her place to weep openly in the face of all that. What was she but a friend? Instead, she'd swallowed the lump in her throat a hundred times and held herself together by force of will until she was back in the privacy of her bedroom, at last free to indulge in her own grief.

She read the letter a second time, but it refused to transform into anything like a coherent explanation under her gaze. She felt sick to her stomach.

Everyone was staring at her.

"Well, Jane, is it a billet-doux from Mr. MacPherson? What's the matter? You're frowning again."

"No." She folded up the letter and assumed a neutral expression for Uncle Bertie, who was watching her expectantly, a glimmer of hope in his eyes. She couldn't share this with him; it was too vile. "No, it's just a letter from..." She searched for something plausible and uninspiring, dropping her attention to the envelope. The only clue of its origin was in the postmark, indicating it had been paid for in Plymouth. "From Cousin Henrietta. She writes that everyone is well and the weather is very fair in Devon." There, that was good. It was from the right part of the country. The Williamses and their cousins were neighbors. Although she may have been pressing her luck to say the weather was fair in Devon.

Uncle Bertie gasped. "Has Mrs. Bishop had her *accouchement*?" *Drat.*

Not such a good fib after all. She hadn't been thinking.

"Not that they mention. I must presume she is still unaccouched."

"It should be soon now," he continued, a crease marring his brow.

The subject of his older brother's offspring was a sensitive one. While John Bishop was blessed with the whole of the family fortune and an entailed country estate, he had never been blessed with a son. Every few years, he attempted to remedy this, and Bertie waited on pins and needles to learn if another girl would join the ranks of her sisters.

The whole business was of no concern to Jane, of course, but Edmund stood to be a good deal richer one day if the much-anticipated baby turned out to be the right sex.

Or the wrong one, depending on one's point of view.

"Anyway, we must be off," Jane said briskly. If she'd been eager to escape before, the letter had lit a fire beneath her.

Bertie saw them on their way down the road before he bid them farewell and went to attend his own errands. They had only to walk five minutes past the series of white stucco town houses—identical save for the curtains on their sash windows or the contents of their flower boxes—and then they were at the Danbys'. It was considerably larger inside and more richly furnished than the rest, a reminder of her family's fortune.

Still, Jane didn't suffer any pangs of envy. She and Edmund were extremely fortunate to have a relation willing to take them in and look to their comfort after their parents' deaths. Though Uncle Bertie's income was limited, he treated them like his own, and Uncle John supplemented their welfare with the occasional gift or invitation for a summer visit when he was feeling charitable. She was lucky to have this much.

"We're not really going to the modiste, I expect," Della said the moment they were safely indoors.

"Of course not."

"Good. Let's go upstairs. My rooms are the only place we're sure not to be disturbed." This was most likely true, as they could already hear her siblings quarreling somewhere down the hall.

They followed Della to a large room cluttered with papers, a neglected watercolor that had stood half-finished since last Christmas, and several boxes of quilting supplies—her most recent passion. The maids were powerless to impose order on the space in the face of Della's insistence that she had a method to her madness. In a perfect demonstration of said method, she kicked a box under her bed to clear a path to the armchairs and gathered up all the odds and ends on the table to tuck them in a corner, most likely never to be thought of again. "There. Now then, where were we?"

"Don't let anyone gamble the family rubies, I believe," Miss Chatterjee supplied.

They spent another half hour preparing their newest helper for her responsibilities, but to Jane's horror, she found her mind kept wandering back to the letter as they spoke.

It was a prank, of course. It wasn't worth another minute of her time. Not when they had Miss Chatterjee before them and had finally escaped the distractions that threatened their progress. She had money to make, and precious little privacy in which to do so.

"Is anything the matter?" Della murmured once Miss Chatterjee had departed, Jane's borrowed copy of *Hoyle's Games* tucked under one arm and a promise to read it on her lips (the opening chapters on probability in games of chance were quite good, if less detailed than Jane might like). "You don't seem quite yourself. You didn't even *mention* your chart again."

Jane produced the letter from her reticule and handed it over. It seemed easier than explaining. As Della unfolded the small note and read, her eyes grew rounder and rounder.

"By God, Lieutenant Williams is *alive*?" Della was not prone to uttering oaths, so this was no small sign of her shock.

"Of course he isn't. This has to be some malicious person's idea of a joke." Jane fought back a touch of impatience. It was obvious that this was a hoax. Wasn't it?

"But..." Della bit her lower lip. "Who would ever joke about something like that? And why would they want to target *you*?"

Jane had no answer to that. It wasn't as though she had enemies. The most offensive thing she'd done was step on a dance partner's toes (or perhaps frown, if one asked Uncle Bertie). She couldn't think why anyone would be so cruel as to fake a resurrection.

"It might be someone from our ladies' club," Jane said hesitantly. "Mrs. Muller lost quite a lot last week."

Three pounds two shillings, to be exact. Jane kept the tallies stored carefully in a ledger on her bedside table, but she could recall each one down to the last penny. Those numbers were her future.

"You don't really think she's the sort to try something like this, do you?" Della looked back to the note, her lips pressed together in disbelief.

In truth, none of the ladies in their card club seemed a likely culprit. Jane and Della curated their list of invitees carefully, passing over those who might speak too freely of their endeavor or start a scandal. They only admitted people they could trust. But if the note wasn't from an angry debtor, what explanation was there?

"Lieutenant Williams is dead," Jane said firmly. She was sure of it. Not so sure as she had been an hour ago, admittedly, but still at least ninety-eight percent sure. Ninety-seven at the worst.

"But they never found a body," Della said with some hesitation. "And some of his crewmates survived the shipwreck, didn't they?"

"Yes," Jane admitted. That was what she'd read in the papers, at least. The HMS *Libertas* had been wrecked in shallow waters during a skirmish with pirates off the coast of Greece. Most of her crew had escaped safely before a great wave dashed the ship against the rocks and dragged the last few men under. Poor Eli had never washed ashore. She shuddered. "But it's been nearly two years. If he *had* survived" —she couldn't believe she was saying that— "there would have been some sign of him sooner than this. And I doubt I'm the first person he would write to."

Della glanced back at the note she still held in her hand, raising one eyebrow pointedly at the salutation. "*Dearest* Jane."

Jane snatched the note back, her face growing hot.

"I didn't realize you two were on such intimate terms."

"This isn't *from* him, so it says nothing whatsoever of what sort of terms we are—*were*—on."

Della had a point, though. Whoever had written the letter must have known that she'd granted Eli permission to use her given name, which they had only done in private. Not to mention the presumption of a gentleman writing to her while she was unmarried.

Who could possibly have the means to know she and Eli were so close?

"I wonder if he calls Cecily his 'dearest,'" Della mused. "Do you think she received anything?"

Cecily.

Jane made a regretful sound halfway between a sigh and a harrumph. "It's none of my concern if she has."

In truth, Jane hadn't even thought of her cousin. She would have to ask, though. Or perhaps she wouldn't. Cecily didn't exactly keep secrets. If she'd had a dramatic letter, the whole ton would know soon enough.

"If he *is* back—"

"He is not."

"But if he is," Della continued doggedly, "he and Cecily aren't... well...you know. She's gone and married someone else now."

"Yes." Jane pressed her lips together, not quite certain of what she might say next if she kept talking. Better not to say anything.

Five years later, and she was still nursing that wound. When would it heal?

Della was staring at her expectantly. When it became apparent that Jane was not going to speak, her friend took up the task. "He would finally be free for you."

"He was free for me *before* he formed an engagement with Cecily, you will recall. He made his choice."

Her cousin. Not her.

Cecily was everyone's favorite. A touch prettier, a great deal more amiable, and endowed with that nameless ability to draw every eye in the room. Jane didn't expect the eligible gentlemen Uncle Bertie ferreted out to pay her any attention when Cecily was nearby, even now that she was married. But Eli had been different. They'd become friends when Cecily wasn't around. They'd been close enough that she'd imagined an attachment there. Imagined that she might be first in his heart.

She'd been wrong.

"But Jane, you aren't going to hold that against him, are you? It's all in the past now that she's married and he's..." Della was obliged to pause here, searching for the correct term.

Jane supplied it for her. "Miraculously restored to life with no explanation after two years unaccounted for?"

"Well..." Della sighed. "When you put it that way, I suppose it does seem ill-done."

"Precisely." Even if Eli was alive (a possibility which Jane was now willing to fix at a generous five percent), he had whittled away his time while everyone believed him dead, never bothering to set ink to paper and put an end to their grief.

Never bothering to put an end to *her* grief.

She may not have been the one he'd promised to marry, but Jane had mourned him all the same.

It was unforgivable.

"The man I knew would never have shown such disregard for other people's feelings. If Lieutenant Williams really is alive, I can only conclude that I gravely mistook his character."

Della made no reply to this, but only looked back at her with a regretful sort of softness in her eyes. She took Jane's hand into hers and pressed it gently, and after a long moment suggested they take some tea downstairs, where they would speak no more about Lieutenant Williams and this mysterious letter.

And that was why Cordelia Danby was her dearest friend.

Two

"Remarkable," said Mr. Filby, the Williams family's solicitor, at their meeting five days after Eli's reappearance. "Simply remarkable. Never, in all my career, did I imagine that I would have the opportunity to bring someone back from the dead." He clapped his hands together gleefully. "The estate should be easy enough, as the entail on the property remains in favor of the eldest son. Once we have your death certificate annulled, you'll be right back where you were."

The turn of phrase startled Eli. *Right back where you were.* He'd only been home a few days, but nothing seemed as he'd left it.

All his savings were gone, his family having seen no need to preserve them after his apparent death. His ship was destroyed, and the navy was still trying to decide where to assign him next. Those of his friends who survived the wreck had been dispersed to new posts, far beyond his reach.

Nor had any word come back from Jane. Only Cecily had replied to him, her letter full of gushing proclamations of joy and closing with an invitation to a rout at her London town house next Thursday.

He couldn't help but think that if he'd had nothing from Jane yet, it was because she didn't intend to write. He'd posted her and Cecily's letters on the same day, after all.

What a mess. He might have made a few mistakes, but Jane would still be happy he hadn't drowned, wouldn't she? It really was the bare minimum.

Maybe the mail coach had misplaced her reply.

"How long will it take to annul the certificate?" he asked.

"Oh goodness, I haven't any notion," Mr. Filby replied. "This might be the first time that the General Register Office has received such a request since they started recording deaths. Just think, you'll set the precedent for anyone who comes after you!"

"How wonderful," said Eli. "I've always wanted to start a new trend."

His mother smiled, but his effort to lessen the grimness of the subject didn't reach his father, who approached this meeting the same way he approached all things—with much grumbling. "I don't see why we have to bother registering anything. In my day, the parish records were good enough for everyone. You knew your rector and he knew you. No need to report your doings to some office of meddlers."

"Let's not start in on that please, Mr. Williams." Mrs. Williams sighed with a less-than-affectionate roll of her eyes.

"It's none of their business who's dead or alive!"

A familiar tension crept up Eli's back. Must they squabble in front of company? In spite of himself, he'd hoped that something might have changed in his absence. That they might have been forced to come together without him there to keep the peace.

"All the same, sir, I'd prefer not to leave any room for doubt." Eli focused on his father, usually the more recalcitrant of the two. "When everyone thinks you're dead, it's deucedly hard to get theater tickets."

He succeeded in shocking a breathy chuckle from his mother, almost against her will. *Be serious, please,* her eyes scolded him.

But she'd forgotten her quarrel, which was all that mattered.

"More importantly, Mr. Williams, it could cause confusion when your son wishes to marry or should there be a dispute in the estate," the solicitor added. "His death was reported by the ship's captain, leaving a record we must correct."

"Thank you, Mr. Filby," Eli said, grateful for the support. "I want to get this all sorted out quickly so I can resume my life."

He'd lost enough time.

His father grunted his assent, still muttering to himself about privacy and meddling bureaucrats as Mr. Filby continued. "It might help if you could gather up several written statements from your friends and family, to attest that you're undead—"

"Undead?" Eli echoed. That really was too much, even for him. "I'm not Frankenstein's monster."

"Oh no." Mr. Filby looked up in surprise. "I didn't mean to offend. I should've said *not* dead. Now that you're not dead—"

"Might we simply say 'living'?" Honestly, everyone was behaving as though his return to England was some sort of supernatural event instead of an unfortunate mix-up. Townspeople who'd known him since he was a boy now whispered and stared. It had been amusing enough at first, but lost its novelty when old Mrs. Adams crossed herself as he'd passed.

"Well, yes, but *everyone* is living, Lieutenant Williams," Mr. Filby explained. "You're quite another matter. Legally dead, though factually alive. Shall we say quasi-deceased? Oh, I have it! *Pseudomortuus.* Latin always comes through in a pinch, doesn't it?"

He paused to flip open a leather-bound notebook and jot the word down, his pencil skipping excitedly across the page.

"It makes me sound like an exotic species in a botany text," Eli said. "Is that the impression we wish to make with the General Register Office?"

"A little Latin can never hurt," Filby replied, undeterred. "In any case, let me handle the registrar. All you need to do is gather up some letters from those who might vouch for your good character and confirm your identity, and we'll send everything off to Somerset House to explain how you survived. Speaking of which…how *did* you survive?"

"I was able to cling to some of the wreckage, and I washed ashore on a neighboring island, but I had no way to return to my crew."

"And after that? Where have you been all this time?"

"Kidnapped by Greek pirates."

"Pirates? Goodness." This pronouncement caused Mr. Filby to blink owlishly, though he seemed less impressed than he had been by the coining of a new term in Latin.

"Yes."

"Well." Mr. Filby turned back to his notes and continued to scribble at a more leisurely pace. "Kidnapped…by…pirates. How did you ever make it back?"

"Eventually they came to harbor near Corinth and I managed to escape, and from there found passage back to England on a merchant vessel." It was nearly the truth. As much of it as he was going to share with the family's solicitor, at any rate.

He'd made some mistakes these past two years, but he was no fool.

"Most fascinating. There is still the matter of your naval service. Since you're not dead, and you were never discharged, you could be accused of desertion for the period you were missing. I cannot represent you if they bring a court-martial, you understand."

"A court-martial?" Mrs. Williams's voice took on a shrill edge. "But he was *dead*."

"I wasn't dead, Mother." A trace of his fatigue snuck into his voice before he could catch it. *Don't be selfish.* After all the grief he'd caused them, the least he could do was keep his chin up.

"Yes, yes, *pseudo*-whatever it was," she continued. "Surely a man can't be expected to report for duty while he's presumed dead *and* captured by pirates."

"I would think the latter impediment is the most likely to convince the court-martial," Mr. Filby observed sagely.

"I wish you would stop saying those words. Really, no one would court-martial our boy. He's a hero."

The praise hung uneasily upon Eli's head. He was no hero, but neither was he a traitor. Would the navy truly convene a court-martial? He'd reported his survival as soon as he'd arrived, and had no trouble obtaining a brief shore leave to sort out his affairs. Their reaction had been one of astonishment, not suspicion. Surely once the death certificate was cleared up and a suitable assignment could be found in keeping with his rank and experience, he would return to sea.

Wouldn't he?

"Can you tell me more about your captivity, Lieutenant? I don't suppose there are any witnesses who might produce an affidavit?"

"No, I'm afraid the pirates are the only ones who can confirm where I was, and they aren't the most helpful lot." Eli cleared his throat. He hated these questions. What was the use in dwelling on the past? Self-pity never helped anyone. "And as to the details, you'll forgive me if I don't wish to relive them, since you can't handle that part of my case."

"No." Filby sighed. "Quite understandable. Well then." To Eli's relief, he rose to his feet and set his hat back upon his balding head. "You know where to reach me. Send over the character references as soon as you're able, and I'll handle everything from there. It would be prudent to have several from outside the family, to eliminate any possible concern that your return is a hoax."

Eli rose from his chair and took the opportunity to see their solicitor out.

He stood in the stillness of the entranceway for a long moment after Filby had shut the door behind him, unable to put a label on the feeling crawling over his skin. A vague sense of...wrongness.

What would he do if the navy laid charges? He needed his post, needed the income and freedom it brought him.

And then there was his family. He couldn't lay a scandal at their door after all the pain his disappearance had caused.

He should go and see Captain Powlett, his commanding officer on the *Libertas*. That was the answer. They'd gotten on well. If he could be found in England now, he'd surely help smooth things over. Or if not, then some other connection toward the top of the ranks. He would go to London and make some inquiries and resolve this whole problem before it could hurt anyone he cared about.

Now that his course was decided, Eli's body hummed with nervous energy. He would fix everything, not only with the navy.

Jane was in London too.

He would accept that invitation to her cousin's rout. She was sure to be there. Perhaps she hadn't written to him because she was so surprised, but if he had the chance to explain himself in person, he could mend things between them. She'd once been the first person he turned to for advice, the one he trusted without hesitation. Whatever else his reckless choices had cost him, it couldn't erase that.

He wished he were already there.

Eli walked back into the parlor, where his parents were still debating the usefulness of a government bureaucracy. He interrupted them without any compunction.

"I've decided to go to London."

"But you've only just come home!" His mother looked up, startled. "We've scarcely had the chance to see you."

"If you like, you could join me. Shouldn't Hannah be attending the season?"

"Oh, I couldn't persuade her. Her coming out went rather badly last year." His mother sighed, a familiar worry line creasing her brow. "I don't know *how* we'll find her a husband at this rate."

"I am sorry to rush off, but what Mr. Filby said about the court-martial makes me think I might visit a few connections from the navy and ensure there's no confusion about my return. Better not to put it off."

"You don't really think it's a risk, do you?" She brought a hand to her breast. Eli could practically see the images unfolding in her head—her son's name splashed in the papers, branded a deserter or worse.

"Of course not," he said quickly. Why had he shared his fears with his mother? He should have made up some pretext for the journey. "I'll take care of this in no time. Don't think of it another moment."

She had enough to deal with without Eli adding to her burdens.

"Well, if you're sure." The lines on his mother's brow faded into smoothness at his words, and he breathed a little easier. "Maybe I can persuade Hannah to come along for the rest of the season. It's rather late to go about renting a town house, but your aunt's place should be free while she's in Bath."

"Never understood why everyone makes such a fuss about going to London," muttered Mr. Williams. "Too crowded. Too noisy. And you see all *kinds* of people filling the streets. At least in the country, you know what sort of stock your neighbors come from."

Eli bit his tongue. His father took the wrong view on just about everything, but arguing only worked him into a state. It was one of the reasons Eli had been eager to get away when he'd joined the navy. That, and Cecily.

"You're welcome to stay at home, Mr. Williams," Mrs. Williams suggested mildly.

"If you're all going, I'll have to come," he grumbled. "People would talk."

And with that, their plans were made.

$\mathcal{J}$

On Thursday evening, Jane was obliged to attend Cecily's fête. Only a few hours earlier, she'd stood before their little medicine cabinet, spoon in hand, contemplating whether a small dose of purgative might mimic illness and free her from the evening. But Cecily had promised there was a surprise in store, and Uncle Bertie would have been disappointed if she missed it.

It's probably another illusionist, she reflected as they were ushered inside. Maybe if she slipped him some coin, he would let her be the lady who disappeared into the sarcophagus and never returned.

Her cousin's house was at the center of the ton's social scene, bordering Berkeley Square near the residence that the new Earl of Leicester had rented, and only one block down from the Countess of Jersey. The interior was just as fashionable as the exterior, with its vaulted ceilings, wainscoting, and various portraits and trinkets adorning the walls. Just as the sparkle assaulted the eyes, the scents of perfume from a hundred different guests assaulted the nose.

This was nothing unusual, but tonight felt worse somehow. It was that stupid letter. Ever since she'd seen it, she couldn't stop thinking about Eli. She felt like she was back in that time five years ago. When he was still alive and her greatest heartbreak was the knowledge that he'd chosen Cecily.

Goodness, no. She wasn't going to spend the whole evening comparing herself to her cousin. They weren't children anymore, squabbling over a poppet. This was silly.

"There you are." Della had to shoulder her way through the crush to reach Jane's side, pausing to smooth her hair once she'd made it. She was dressed in a crimson gown with tiny silk roses embellishing the neckline, sure to draw the eye. "Even busier than usual tonight, isn't it? How are you?" She dropped her voice to a whisper before adding, "You haven't had any more letters?"

"No. I would've told you if I had. I'm sure it was just a malicious prank."

Della raised her brows as if she would've liked to argue this, but she let it pass. "I suppose we'll know soon if Cecily's had one as well."

Dread curled Jane's insides into a knot, like the chain of a pendant too tangled to work loose. She'd avoided her cousin all week, afraid of what it would mean if there'd been a second letter.

Not that it would prove anything. Even a prankster would think to write a fiancée before a friend.

"What shall we do first?" Della continued. "Find ourselves some punch, or some dance partners?"

Jane looked out over the sea of faces before her, feeling adrift. She normally tried to make the best of these events. Though she didn't enjoy forcing smiles and kind words for the eligible gentlemen Bertie nudged in her direction—nor hearing Cecily's insights on why she failed to ensnare any of them—there *were* certain advantages to be found here for one determined enough to look. Chiefly, the number of ladies in attendance who had vast sums of money to lose at her card table. Cecily had wealthy friends.

But tonight, even the prospect of finding new members didn't hold her interest as it normally did.

"Della, do you—" She stopped herself, half doubting what she would say, but then decided to continue on. She could tell her friend anything. "Do you think I'm too severe?"

"Pardon?"

The question must have seemed to come from nowhere.

"It's only…I've been out for years and I haven't had any offers. The closest thing I've had to an admirer was Eli, and even he picked Cecily over me."

The reminder had shaken her confidence.

They'd grown close when she'd gone to stay with Uncle John the summer she turned sixteen, and they'd been neighbors. Jane had been terribly lonely in that grand manor house with its portraits of long-dead ancestors, reminding her of everything she'd lost. Eli had been all too happy to escape the bickering in his own house, and he'd soon taken to exploring the country with her, wandering up the hillside and finding ways to make her laugh until her problems were forgotten. When she worried that Edmund was falling behind in his education because Uncle John refused to support the expense of a tutor, he'd dusted off the texts he'd studied at Eton and explained his lessons to Jane until she could instruct her brother herself. Long after Eli was gone, that knowledge had laid the foundation of what she hoped would soon be a successful money-making endeavor.

She'd never shared that kind of intimacy with a gentleman before.

But despite her adolescent hopes, he'd never taken her into his arms and confessed his undying love. Not then, nor any of the times they'd crossed paths in London in the years that followed. While Jane waited and waited for Eli to declare his intentions, Cecily had swooped in and accomplished the task in a single evening.

The injustice of it still stung.

"He didn't pick her over you," Della scolded. "He suffered a lapse in judgment that had the misfortune to be uncovered. I doubt very much he wanted to marry her."

"He shouldn't have gone out in the gardens alone with her then."

Really, what were gardens even for, except to compromise young ladies at house parties? Everyone knew that.

"You're too unforgiving," said Della. "I'm not sure if that's the same thing as severe, but there you are."

This conversation wasn't making her feel any better. It was foolish to let this business about the letter distract her from what mattered. She was wise enough now to understand that she was better off as a spinster anyway. If she had been the one Eli loved, he would only have left her a widow.

He'd been young and strong, and still all it took was one stroke of ill-luck to erase him from the world. Just like her parents. They'd seemed immortal, until illness swept through their house without warning.

A husband might leave her just as easily, though he would force Jane to give up everything she was building with Della before he did. And then where would she be?

No. If she was to find real security in this life, she would have to build it herself. A woman without fortune couldn't risk relying on anyone else.

"Let's forget about Eli." Jane waved away his specter with a brisk motion. "Have you spotted any fresh prospects for us this evening?"

Della's eyes lit up at this. "Cecily bragged that she'd invited Lady Eleanor Grosvenor tonight; she would make a handsome addition to our club. Or else one of the Countess of Jersey's daughters.

The eldest is out, isn't she?" It was tireless work, building the right connections at every event, but it was the only way they could gather the numbers they needed to ensure a steady profit each week. Then she would never need to worry about money again.

Della nodded. "I saw them earlier in the retiring room."

"Let's find them directly, before—"

"There you are, my darlings!" Cecily's girlish voice carried above the buzz of the crowd as she bustled forward with outstretched arms. Jane clapped her jaw shut. She'd made it through half the season without letting her cousin discover her club, and she wasn't about to slip up now. "It's been too, too long."

It had been ten days.

Everyone always commented on the resemblance between Jane and her cousin. Both had dark hair and pale eyes, though Cecily's vivid blues drew comparisons to a summer sky that Jane had never inspired. And while both women had wide cheekbones in a heart-shaped face, only Cecily's might have launched a thousand ships. Jane might manage a tugboat on a good day.

Jane summoned a tardy smile as Cecily planted an excessive amount of kisses on her cheeks, then on Della's. Jane tried not to squirm under the onslaught.

Sir Thomas Kerr, Cecily's husband, waited patiently to greet them until her enthusiasm had subsided, a practice he employed often. He was a quiet fellow, content to let his wife talk most of the time, and recently knighted for his service to the empire, which allowed Cecily the satisfaction of being called "Lady Kerr" for the rest of her days. In short, he was everything she could want in a husband.

"Good evening, Cecily. How are you? How's the baby?" At least he would be kept upstairs tonight. Though Jane liked babies well enough as a rule, Cecily's son was the exception. It wasn't that he'd done anything wrong—he couldn't do much but lie there looking sweet, at his age—it was the degree of fawning his presence commanded from everyone.

"Oh, he's wonderful. He can nearly crawl!" This seemed an egregious claim, as the child in question was only three months old. Cecily hadn't wanted a long confinement, eager as she was to enjoy the season. "But never mind that," she gushed. "You'll never believe the news I have for you."

Jane's heart missed a beat. She tried to feign nonchalance. "Oh, what is it?"

"I've had a letter! From Eli Williams!" Cecily flung this information before them with the thrill of a child throwing seeds before sparrows.

Oh Lord.

Della was trying to catch her gaze, but Jane didn't dare look.

"Really? That seems quite a feat, as he's dead."

Cecily was too excited to be put out by Jane's sharp remark. "He's *not*. It was all a mistake. Just listen."

She immediately produced a piece of parchment from her reticule, so worn from folding that she must have read it a thousand times since its arrival.

Cecily cleared her throat delicately and began. "Dear Sir Thomas Kerr and Lady Kerr, I hope you will not think me too forward in writing to you, but I am recently returned to England after a long absence for reasons outside my control, and I did not wish for you to suffer the unpleasant surprise of hearing the news from another source. Please accept my deepest apologies for any distress that mistaken reports of my death may have caused, and my congratulations on your marriage and the birth of your child. I trust that you will also convey my regards to Lady Kerr's family. Yours truly, Lieutenant Eleazar Williams."

Cecily lowered the paper from her eyes to gauge their reactions, though she still gripped it in her fist, lest it be needed again.

Jane couldn't summon any reply. Sir Thomas still stood silently at one side, unmoved by his wife's display.

Good God, could Eli truly be alive? Or was the prankster merely committed to his game?

"Goodness." It was Della who broke the silence, in the brisk voice of someone not quite as surprised as she was supposed to be. "What an incredible turn of events. He must have survived the shipwreck somehow."

She cast a pointed glance to Jane at this last comment. No one seemed inclined to question the tale. Was she too cynical, or were they all too trusting?

Very well, she would have to be the wet blanket.

"But there's no mention of *how* he survived. Nor of where he's been for two years."

"I know!" Cecily replied with a sulk. "He doesn't tell us any of the interesting bits. That's why I wrote back to invite him here."

She motioned vaguely to her surroundings, already filled to the brim with guests.

"Do you mean...tonight?" Jane struggled to keep up. Everything was happening so fast. Five minutes ago, she'd still been certain Eli was dead. Now he was expected to join their company this very evening.

How could this be real?

"Yes! And he's sent a card this morning to accept. Quite tardy, but forgivable in the circumstances. He must have raced to London just to see *me*. Think what a tremendous coup it will be to host a naval hero who's returned from the dead!"

Jane's head was spinning. She tried to focus on the facts, winnowing them free of Cecily's assumptions. If Eli had truly written Cecily twice, once from his family's home and once from London, it seemed impossible that this was a hoax. An impostor wouldn't promise to attend tonight, surely.

Eli must really be alive. Had been alive this whole time, without her even knowing it. But how?

"I invited all the officers I know," Cecily continued, oblivious to Jane's turmoil. "I even found his former captain! Though most of the others are overseas. The problem with the navy is that it takes the men away from all the parties."

Jane finally hazarded a proper look at Della, who took in her struggle without the need for any further explanation.

"What an amazing turn of events," Della said. "We can't wait to see him. We're just going to get some of your delicious champagne before the excitement begins. Excuse us, please."

They hurried, arm in arm, to the refreshments. There were so many people they had to form a queue. The smell of their various perfumes overwhelmed Jane's senses. "Are you all right?" Della whispered.

Jane didn't reply. Nothing felt right.

How was it possible? Why hadn't he tried to contact her sooner? Even if they'd only been friends, they were *close* friends. He should've known his reported death would hurt her. Or if she didn't warrant his consideration, then why not write his family, at least? He must not have done, for if his survival had been known in Devon before now, she would've heard the news from Uncle John.

They hadn't even managed to get their hands on some glasses when Della clutched her arm. "Jane, look there."

It was him. Mercifully far away, near the opposite wall. He was talking to a gentleman she didn't recognize as the crowd swirled around them, suddenly dizzying.

Jane had the sense that she was watching a memory, or an actor moving across the stage. A fantasy layered over reality.

Eli looked every inch a navy man. Tall and fit, with a quick confidence in his bearing that inspired trust. The sort of man who knew his course. He had classically handsome features—dark hair and eyes, with a strong brow and an aquiline nose—but it was none of these things that made him so captivating. Rather, it was the animation that came over his face when he spoke, opening a window to his sentiments for all the world to see. His eyes and his smile brimmed with energy, lighting up a conversation at the slightest invitation. Whatever your troubles, he could make you forget them.

Though Eli's features were unchanged, he looked somehow

different than Jane remembered. It had been five years since he'd joined the service and sailed out of her life, shortly after announcing his engagement. Not so long a time as to put lines on a man's face. It must have been something else. He'd taken too much sun, perhaps, or he'd grown leaner. Or there was nothing different at all, and her memory was simply faulty.

They'd once kept company nearly every day. She'd known his face as well as her own. How could she have forgotten anything about it?

Stupidly, inexplicably, Jane felt as though she might cry.

Della placed her fingertips upon Jane's arm. "Do you want to go over?"

"No." Not now. Not like this. The last thing she wanted was to make a spectacle of herself in front of everyone. She lowered her tone and chose cowardice. "Let's hide, please."

"Hide?" Della repeated.

Eli looked their way. Not *at* them, exactly, for there was no sign of recognition in his eyes. But he was scanning the crowd. It was only a matter of time before he spotted her. And then he would want to come over and pretend everything was fine between them, just as he had after he proposed to her cousin. She turned her face away, fleeing from that possibility.

"Yes, and quickly."

They settled on the library, as it had served as a traditional hiding place for many a guest at many a party such as this. It was, in fact, already in use for this purpose by a young couple who occupied the love seat near the far wall. Neither of them was reading. They stared uncomfortably at Della and Jane, waiting to see who would back down first.

"Your chaperone is looking for you," Jane addressed her warning to the lady, whom she had never seen before in her life.

Della hid a smile behind her gloved hand, though it was only after the couple had vacated the room that she allowed a laugh to bubble out.

"It's probably true," Jane reasoned. "And besides, I've saved her from a terrible mistake."

Many an inopportune match began with a moment of seclusion. Like Eli and Cecily.

"Ah, but suppose they were star-crossed lovers, trying to escape their families' opposition." Della smiled, evidently judging her assessment of the situation to be preferable to Jane's.

It was a nice fantasy, but reality didn't often match one's hopes. Jane walked to the bookcase, tracing a hand along the spines as she breathed the earthy scent of paper and leather bindings.

"You know we can't stay here forever," Della said gently. "We shall have to go back out. And when we do, Lieutenant Williams is sure to see you."

"I know." There was no escape. Jane turned away from the books, wishing her galloping heart would slow its pace. "I won't hide forever. Just...ten minutes."

She would have herself back in hand by then. She didn't know why she was overwrought to begin with. Eli had no longer been her dear friend when he'd gone off to sea. He'd been the selfish cad who'd broken her heart. She shouldn't care half so much what became of him.

But try as she might, she couldn't erase the memories of how patient he'd been, sitting with her on a bench in the gardens at Ashlow Park, heads bent over an algebra text, as if there was nothing he'd rather do with his time. Every smile or joke they'd shared had made her feel cherished. Like she belonged.

It was nothing but a childish fancy. How could Eli admire her if he were the sort of man who admired Cecily? The two of them were as opposed in character and temperament as it was possible to be, like the ends of a magnet. Attraction to one meant repulsion from the other.

Even if one made allowances for a difference in taste, Cecily was also perfectly vile to her half the time, and Eli knew it. He could've chosen any other woman to compromise and marry, and she would have accepted it. Would still have called him a friend.

Just not that one.

A set of footsteps in the hall interrupted her thoughts. A heavy tread, belonging to a man. *Drat.* It had been too much to hope for a minute of solitude in a house this crowded. She and Della should go, before they found themselves subjected to unwanted company.

She had barely drawn a breath to say so when the intruder rounded the doorway and came into their sight.

It was Eli, and he'd clearly come in search of her.

Three

"By Jove, I can't believe you're really alive. We all thought you'd drowned." Eli's friend, George Halsey, raised a hand to touch his arm, but recalled himself before completing the gesture. His eyes were full of wonder.

Halsey had served with Eli on the *Libertas*, though he'd changed since the shipwreck. His jawline had lost the leanness of youth and gained a beard.

"What are you doing back in London?" It was a relief to see a friendly face at Lady Kerr's fête. Most of the other guests had been staring at him as if he were a carnival oddity since his entry was announced. A pair of ladies huddled to his left, trying to disguise their whispers behind their fans, but he caught snippets of their conversation.

"Missing for two years. Can you imagine?"

"I heard he was stranded on a desert island."

"I'd have gone mad if it were me."

Eli suppressed the urge to toss a quick retort in their direction. Halsey might enjoy the sport, but it wouldn't solve anything. He would have to get used to this sort of thing.

"I was recalled home after the wreck," his friend explained, tugging the glove from his left hand to reveal two missing fingers. The remainder was bent as though the bones hadn't set properly. "Got it crushed against the foremast. Though at least it wasn't my good hand. I'm secretary to the third naval lord now." A comfortable position. Halsey came from an old, monied family, with an uncle in politics. No doubt it had helped him secure it. "But never mind me. Where were *you* all this time?"

"It's a long story." Eli glanced around, conscious of how many observers were fixated on his every move. This wasn't the place. "Come by the house later this week and I'll share it with you. It will be good to catch up."

I should hurry and find Jane. So far, there was no sign of her.

Eli scanned the room again, sifting through the sea of curious faces to find one that was familiar. His eye was drawn to a dark-haired lady whose quick, resolute stride set her apart from the figures milling aimlessly about the edges of his vision. Eli's heart lurched in his chest even before his mind had time to recognize her. She vanished through a doorway barely a second later, making him question if she had really been there at all. Perhaps he was so eager to see her that his mind had drawn her portrait upon some other woman.

No. It must have been Jane. Even at this distance, he couldn't confuse her with anyone else. She carried herself with a purpose that belied her slight frame, each shift of her limbs an edict. No one else moved like that.

Eli turned back to Halsey. "Would you mind if I left you for a moment? I've...just seen an old acquaintance I must catch up with."

"Was it that lady you were staring at?" Hal's face split into a sly grin. "Left behind a string of broken hearts, have you? I'm sure they'll all be *very* moved to see your heroic return. Women love a tragic story."

"It's nothing like that," Eli said quickly. "She's just a friend."

That was all she'd ever been, no matter how he might have wished otherwise.

Hal looked undeterred as he took his leave. "Good luck all the same."

Eli left Halsey and plunged into the crowd. The people swirled around him, every head turning to follow his path. More than one acquaintance (and several strangers) tried to catch him in conversation, but Eli pressed on.

By the time he reached the doorway where he'd last seen Jane, she was gone. He set off down the darkened hall, following the sound of voices until he reached the library. It was dimly lit, and nearly empty, the evening still too young to have spilled guests to all the odd corners of the house. But here was Jane.

She looked exactly as he remembered. Her dark hair was pulled up into a mass of curls. Her eyes, a muted shade caught between blue and gray, were turned away from him. Her mouth was set in a line he knew well, the corners tipping down of their own accord, so that she seemed to be perpetually frowning no matter what her true sentiments might be.

She wore a gown of violet silk with the low, wide neckline that was in fashion, cut in a deep V to expose the lace chemisette she wore underneath. Eli always felt vaguely as though he were looking at a woman's undergarments when he saw a gown cut that way, which was probably the point. Tonight, it made his throat turn dry.

Jane looked up at the sound of his footsteps, and the expression on her face cut through him as cleanly as a blade. There was no surprise in her eyes, so she must've been expecting him. But no joy either.

He'd hoped she would be glad. When he'd imagined this moment—as he often had those many months in his lurching bunk or while on watch, with nothing but his thoughts for company—she'd always been happy.

Of all the disappointments his return to England had brought him so far, this was the worst.

"Hello," he managed. His voice was pitched low, but it seemed too loud for the stillness of the room.

He finally realized that there was another lady with them, sitting on the love seat. He hadn't even noticed her.

"Forgive me," he said quickly. "I don't believe we've been introduced. I didn't intend to surprise you."

He'd meant the explanation to reassure the young woman that he was no threat to her reputation, but upon closer inspection, she didn't seem worried in the least.

"Cordelia Danby." She inclined her head gracefully.

With a speaking look to Jane, she rose to her feet. "I'll leave you two to talk."

Jane raised a hand, as if to call her friend back, then let it fall without voicing her objection. She acted as though she had reason to be wary of him. What had he done to deserve that? They'd often stolen time alone on her uncle's estate or his parents' adjacent property, and he'd never abused her trust. They'd been at ease in each other's company.

Before he went to sea. Before Cecily.

And now she was standing four feet away, rigid and remote, as though to move one inch closer would bring certain doom. She still hadn't said a word, though she'd had more than enough time to compose a response to his greeting.

What had he expected? That Jane would throw herself into his arms?

Actually, yes, Eli realized with keen discomfort. *I was hoping for that.*

He took a deep breath, and found the air tinged with her scent. Light and sweet, with faint notes of lilac. The same as always.

"I hope you aren't so silent because you're overcome with shock," he tried. "I don't have any smelling salts."

He'd thrown the words out in jest, to break this unbearable tension and pry open a window into Jane's thoughts. But she merely replied, "I don't faint."

Of course she didn't. One arch of her brow left him feeling utterly foolish.

"I've offended you." If levity wasn't getting him anywhere, Eli would try being forthright. "My apologies."

He wished she would give him some hint of how they were supposed to act. At least when his parents were quarreling, or Hannah had been hurt by some childish disappointment, he always knew the words to set things right. He hated being suspended this way, unsure of the path forward.

"Why should I be offended?" she asked mildly, in a voice that spoke of complete indifference. It was worse than anger somehow. "I'm very happy to learn you're alive. It's remarkable; everyone says so. Welcome back."

She fixed him with a look from those cool, gray eyes that seemed to lower the temperature of the air. He almost expected his breath to fog. "I wish you would speak to me plainly," Eli insisted. "You never stood on ceremony before."

Jane was always direct. It was one of the things he admired about her. She never hesitated to speak her mind or worried what others thought. He sometimes envied her ability to separate her own wishes from the obligations others imposed—a skill he'd never mastered.

"Perhaps I should have," she said. "Our acquaintance was inappropriate for two unmarried persons, particularly once you were engaged." She smoothed down her skirt and looked to the door, as if preparing to leave already. "In fact, it's inappropriate for us to be alone like this. We should go back to the party before Cecily misses us."

Cecily. Was she still angry about his engagement, five years later? He had only himself to blame, of course, but that didn't make it any easier to accept this punishment.

"Jane, look at me," he commanded.

She obliged, though her gaze was less steady than it had been a moment before. He studied the liquid whorls and flecks of her irises, searching for…something. A trace of understanding.

"I'm not engaged to her any longer," he said. "There's nothing between us."

"Yes, I'd gathered. You have my sympathies."

"Oh, for—" Eli bit back the rest of his retort, wishing he could remain as cool as Jane. "I was eighteen. I made an impetuous decision. Can't you forgive me for that?"

What else could he say without bringing Cecily's reputation into disrepute? He wasn't going to blame her for their entanglement. No one had held a pistol to his head and forced him to go out into the gardens that night. But he certainly wished that her father hadn't discovered them and forced him to turn an impulsive decision made under the influence of a few too many drinks into a proposal to bind them forever.

His fate had been sealed, and all for a few kisses and an ill-placed hand. Ten minutes of his life, at most, had determined everything that followed.

"Yes, I trust you've matured a great deal since then," Jane shot back in a tone that betrayed significant doubt. "But there's nothing to forgive. You were entitled to form whatever attachments you wished. Then, as well as now. Excuse me, please."

She made as if to return to the rout, turning her back on him as neatly as if he'd been a stranger.

"Wait." Eli wanted to stop her. To pull her into his arms and force her to face him. But it would have been ridiculous, so he had little choice but to call after her. "It's been years. Can't we talk about this?"

Jane paused at the door, finally looking back at him over her shoulder. "Silence is contagious, it would seem."

With that, she disappeared from the door frame, leaving Eli alone to contemplate his mistakes.

Jane wasn't sure how she put one foot in front of the other without stumbling as she fled the library, shaky as a newborn foal. She'd held her composure before Eli only through supreme force of will, but now it threatened to leave her. Where had Della gone to? The crush was so great it would take half the night to find her friend now. Instead, Jane tucked herself in a corner of the ballroom and pretended to admire a landscape on the wall. If she stayed here long enough, perhaps Eli would leave.

How could he seek her out as if they were old friends, after all this time? He should have been a stranger to her by now. Yet she hadn't been able to stop herself from drinking up the timbre of his voice and the mannerisms that marked him as the man she'd known—the way he spoke with his hands when he was trying to make a point or tilted his head when he was listening. Everything about him was as familiar as if he'd never left England, and only yesterday they'd been sitting in the shade of the oak tree on Uncle John's estate. As if his long absence had been nothing but a story they'd told to pass the time.

"Is it a Turner, do you know?"

Jane jumped at the sound of a woman's voice behind her. The painting. She must be asking after it, and here Jane was studying her own memories, heedless of the image on the canvas.

She opened her mouth to admit she had no idea which painters graced her cousin's wall, until she realized that the young lady had been talking to her companion.

"I expect so," the other woman replied. "You have a discerning eye, Lady Eleanor."

Lady Eleanor.

Jane did a quick assessment of the woman's appearance, her mind leaping through the possibilities. She was quite young, perhaps eighteen or so, and trussed up in so much lace that her ruby pendant was in danger of being swallowed whole. Could this be Eleanor Grosvenor, daughter of the Marquess of Westminster? If only Della were here. She knew how to enchant people with her conversation, whereas Jane was liable to say the wrong thing, especially in her current state.

But she couldn't let this opportunity escape her. Increasing their club's numbers was a delicate balance. They needed to grow their base of invitees to assure steady profits, but they had to be careful to remain exclusive so that women would be begging them for an entrance instead of the other way around. What a coup it would be to secure Lady Eleanor's patronage!

"A lovely piece, isn't it?" Jane ventured, as if it were perfectly natural to approach two ladies vastly above her station with whom she had no prior introduction. Never mind. They'd been invited tonight and they'd chosen to come, which meant they knew Cecily, which was only one step away from her, really. "I believe Lady Kerr has more of Mr. Turner's work in the study, if you're an admirer." This was a shameless fib, but it seemed to pique Lady Eleanor's interest, so it served its purpose.

"Does she, really? Oh, but I wouldn't want to intrude."

"Nonsense. I'd be happy to give you a tour of the house, if you like. I'm Jane Bishop, Lady Kerr's cousin."

"Lady Eleanor Grosvenor." The woman extended a dainty, bejeweled hand. "And this is my friend, Mrs. Harriet Duff."

Jane scarcely had time for an obligatory curtsy and a "How do you do?" before Mrs. Duff interjected, "Her cousin, you say? Why, you must know all about it then!"

The "it" in question was obviously something more exciting than the landscape on the wall, for Mrs. Duff was practically bouncing on her feet as she continued, "Lady Kerr was just telling us that her former fiancé is here tonight, after two years missing and presumed dead. Is it really true?"

Not again. Must Eli hound her all evening?

But Jane suppressed her wince as she gave the answer the pair wanted. She was off to a promising start, and she wouldn't let Eli spoil it for her. "It *is.* I believe I caught sight of Lieutenant Williams earlier, alive and well."

Much as she would've liked a fine story for her audience, Jane was hardly going to reveal they'd shared a tête-a-tête in the library. Uncle Bertie had already proven his willingness to force a proposal under such circumstances, should word get back to him. She had no desire to be the second woman in the family Eli pledged to marry under duress.

"Which one *is* he?" Lady Eleanor dropped her voice to a whisper, casting curious looks about the crowd. Though she held herself in check a bit better, she was clearly as enthralled as her companion by the tale.

Jane hesitated. She needed to impress these women and keep them talking long enough to casually inquire, first, whether they held any moral objections to gambling, and second, whether they were free on Monday evenings to join a select group of friends with heaps of money to wager.

For the profits that Lady Eleanor would bring her, Jane could endure the sight of Eli again.

"Why don't we take a turn about the room together, and I'll point him out if I see him?" With any luck, she could steer the conversation where she wanted before they even found him.

"What a dear you are," Lady Eleanor accepted on behalf of them both, and the trio set off together.

They found Eli in precisely two minutes.

He'd been cornered by Bertie, who spotted Jane and began waving her over, his motions too enthusiastic to ignore. So much for her plan to discuss her club before they found him. When he caught sight of her, Eli stiffened, his jaw growing tight.

If Jane had known she would meet him again with Lady Eleanor watching, she might have parted ways on a better note.

"I've been looking *everywhere* for you," Bertie gushed, heedless of her reluctant approach. "Where have you *been*?"

"I was just admiring some of Cecily's artwork." She tried not to look at Eli as she made her excuses, but it was quite impossible. Her uncle was so excited, he hovered over him like a bee on a honeycomb.

"Look who it is! Isn't this *remarkable*?"

Though one might presume that Bertie would harbor some dislike for the man whom he'd surprised in the hedges with his only daughter five years prior, one would be wrong. Jane had been a reluctant party to many conversations between Bertie and Cecily in the course of her cousin's engagement, and the tone of their discussions (prior to his reported death, at least) was always one of unbridled glee.

Cecily is to marry a lieutenant! How jealous your friends shall be. When will he get shore leave for the wedding, my dear?

And so on, and so forth. For the better part of three years.

Uncle Bertie knew no greater desire than to see his charges married, and Eli had won him over by agreeing to perform the task within a neat ten seconds of having been caught with his hand upon Cecily's décolletage.

"Quite remarkable," Jane agreed. By this point, she couldn't keep track of whether she was meant to feign shock or joy. She hurriedly presented Eli to Lady Eleanor and Mrs. Duff so that they might provide a distraction. They were all too eager to take up the task, spouting breathless questions and forgetting Jane entirely. With each one, she felt her chances of getting them alone again to discuss her club slip further from her grasp. *Drat.* Eli had ruined everything.

Barely a minute had passed when Cecily burst into their circle on the arm of an older gentleman with a large, handlebar mustache whose tips defied gravity. "Here he is, you see? Oh, Lady Eleanor, how good to see you again. May I present Captain Powlett?" She narrowed her eyes when she finally noticed Jane. "And you're here as well, darling."

The mustachioed man greeted each of the ladies in turn before he explained, "Retired captain, lately of the *Libertas.* I never thought to lay eyes on this one again after how I saw him last."

Eli's former captain. That's right, Cecily had mentioned inviting him.

"I couldn't believe it when Lady Kerr told me you were here," he said. "How the devil did you survive?"

All eyes turned to Eli expectantly. He shifted in his evening jacket, looking ill at ease.

"I was just telling Mr. Bishop that the story really isn't as interesting as you might expect."

He's stalling.

Jane wasn't sure if it was the crowd or Eli's nearness, but there didn't seem to be enough space for all of them. He was close enough that she caught a faint hint of his scent: something woodsy and clean—cedar, perhaps—with a warmth at its core. It flooded her senses with longing, at once familiar and unexpected. How had she forgotten that scent?

"Nonsense." Cecily reached out and laid a hand lightly upon Eli's forearm. "You're being too modest. We're hanging on your every word."

Where had her husband got to, anyway?

"Well, you must already know that the *Libertas* was wrecked in pursuit of some pirates off the coast of Greece."

Captain Powlett nodded along, his brows drawn together as if revisiting the memory.

"The last of the crew was still boarding the lifeboats when the wave hit and I was pulled under," Eli continued. "I managed to get hold of some flotsam and make it to an island, but when I tried to signal an English ship, the pirates spotted me first, so..." He shrugged, as if this was a complete explanation for his absence.

"*Soooooo...?*" prodded Cecily.

"They took me captive. I spent my time watching for a chance to escape, and then I finally did, and here I am."

After nearly ten seconds of silence, it became apparent that this was the end of the tale.

Mrs. Duff shot an accusatory glance at Jane.

"And the pirates just...kept you. For two years." Jane broke the silence, as no one else seemed inclined to.

"I can't even *imagine!*" Cecily gripped Eli's arm again, as if she feared rampaging pirates were likely to invade her town house. Why did she have to keep clinging to him? "Would you describe your confinement as a harrowing ordeal, or would that be going too far?"

Eli blinked, the strangeness of this question disrupting his habitual good cheer. "I...try not to describe it as anything, I suppose," he finally answered. "No good can come of dwelling on bad memories."

"But how did you escape?" Captain Powlett pressed.

"They kept me in irons at first." Eli's speech was almost stilted, each word deliberate. It reminded Jane of something, but she couldn't quite decide what. "But after a time they let their guard down. They made me work the ship, but sometimes the watch was lax in his duties. Eventually, there came a night when we anchored near Corinth and I had an opportunity to jump overboard and swim for my life. I found passage on a merchant ship bound for France, and from there it wasn't difficult to get back to Devon."

It's the same tone he uses when he's trying to get his parents to stop arguing, Jane finally realized. He had a certain way of speaking when he wanted them to forget whatever subject had disrupted the peace of the house. She'd heard him use it a dozen times. A practiced nonchalance, as though their quarrel didn't truly bother him. And then he would usually make some lighthearted remark to—

"I suppose I should count myself lucky there were no sharks about."

There it was. There was a rehearsed quality to all of it, a falseness that rubbed Jane the wrong way. This wasn't how he spoke when he let his true thoughts show.

"Incredible." Captain Powlett ran a thumb over the tip of his mustache. "You've the devil's own luck, to survive that."

Incredible, indeed.

Jane knew she should keep her suspicions to herself. After all, what reason would Eli have to lie about such a thing? She was probably mistaking a perfectly natural hesitation to revisit bad memories for something more.

But sometimes her mouth seemed to open of its own accord and words fell out. Usually awkward ones. This was one of those times.

"It's a bit odd that they wouldn't try to ransom you, though, isn't it?" She heard herself say. "Why do you suppose they didn't?"

Everyone turned to stare at her. As if she'd started listing a man's faults at his funeral. *Oh goodness, why did I do that?*

Eli clearly had to search for a moment before he could summon a reply. "I'm afraid I didn't ask them. On account of my not speaking Greek."

"Honestly, Jane," Cecily intervened. "Poor Eli can't be expected to know what the pirates were thinking. They're *criminals.* Who can imagine what goes on in their minds?"

There, she knew she should've kept her mouth shut. Now she looked horrid for asking, and in front of Lady Eleanor too.

Cecily pressed on over Jane's faux pas.

"What has it been like, returning to British soil after such an absence? Has it been very difficult for you?" She leaned a bit closer in her sympathy, though her eyes slid toward Jane.

Is she trying to make me jealous of her flirtation? What a tired, old trick. If Cecily thought she had any interest in reigniting their competition for Eli's regard, she was sorely mistaken. Jane never repeated the same mistake twice.

"The greatest difficulty at present is the fact that the General Register Office still considers me dead, and the navy doesn't know what to do about me until that's resolved. I'm working on annulling the death certificate."

"Oh, but I'm sure that Sir Thomas and I could help you with that," Cecily proclaimed. "We're very well connected, you know."

"Er...thank you, Lady Kerr, but I'm sure that won't be necessary. It's a simple enough matter. I just need to provide some letters of support, attesting that I'm myself and not an impostor, and the registrar will take care of the rest." He turned to Captain Powlett. "Could I trouble you for it, sir? You can speak to the circumstances of the shipwreck."

"Of course, of course," he said readily.

"We could write one too," Cecily insisted. "Sir Thomas is a knight, you know. That's sure to carry some weight."

"Oh, is he a knight?" Jane murmured. She immediately regretted it when Eli suppressed a smile, his eyes sparkling with mirth even as his jaw held firm. It almost felt natural, him laughing at her jokes again.

"Us as well," Uncle Bertie offered. This was turning into quite the fashionable thing. "I was nearly your father-in-law, and Jane has known you for—what is it, now? Six years? Seven?"

She could just imagine it. She would spend an hour searching for the right words to set out her knowledge of Eli's good character and convince the registrar that there was nothing suspicious about his return when she wasn't convinced of either point herself. No, thank you.

"I simply couldn't write one, Uncle," Jane said coolly. "It's been so long since we've had any word from him, I wouldn't know what to say."

Eli was in too foul a mood by the end of the evening to provide good company to his parents and Hannah on the coach ride home. He fixed his gaze out the window and watched the familiar sights of London roll by, noting the changes of the last five years while they discussed which guest had been the most fashionably dressed and who might make a favorable match this season.

When they arrived at the town house, he excused himself to his room and dismissed his valet for the evening, unwilling to inflict his ill humor on anyone else.

Five years since he'd last laid eyes on Jane. Nearly two years since the *Libertas* had been wrecked and marked him for drowned. He'd thought of her constantly since then. Particularly those first few months of his capture, when he'd been in irons and had no way of knowing if he would ever come home.

She wouldn't even give him the time of day.

Eli paced the room as he unbuttoned his shirt and pants, stripping down to his drawers. The cool air on his skin did little to calm his thoughts.

How had he ruined things so completely?

It was his proposal to Cecily, of course. He would've liked to call it jealousy, but that seemed optimistic, given the circumstances. Jane had never seen him as more than a friend. She'd been so businesslike when they studied together, her attention locked on their equations. Even when their talk strayed to more personal matters, she'd held herself strictly within the limits of propriety, never granting him a word or lingering look to suggest that another type of attention would be welcome.

If not jealousy, then it must have been a keen disappointment. A betrayal, even. That he would prove to be the type of man to succumb to base lust and take advantage of a member of her family. Never mind that Cecily had been more than willing, and they'd both indulged in too much champagne that evening. He should've known better.

But she was married to Sir Thomas now, and with a child to boot. If that couldn't smooth over his transgression, what else could be done? He couldn't turn back time, much as he might wish to.

Perhaps Jane would never forgive him. He would just have to accept that their connection was ended. He wouldn't feel the thrill that came with breaking through her serious demeanor when she laughed at one of his jokes. He wouldn't be the one she trusted with her fears and hopes.

The thought depressed him.

Eli continued to pace, too restless and angry with himself to attempt sleep, though it was well past two in the morning. Beyond the confines of his bedroom, the house was still. Everyone else had gone to bed.

Jane was probably in her own bed by now too, not so very far from here. It was as close as he'd been to her since he left England. He walked to the window and leaned his brow against the cool glass.

How many times had he imagined their reunion on the long nights at sea? He'd been friendless and helpless, reduced to the status of captive without even the comfort of knowing anyone was searching for him. His memories of Jane were one of the few things that had made him feel less alone. She would miss him. She would care what became of him.

He could have stopped her when she'd stormed from the library. Could have pulled her into his arms and kissed her as he'd longed to, if only to make her look at him with something other than ice in her eyes.

Eli drew a long breath, watching the glass fog over as he exhaled. He would add the idea to his list of regrets.

Four

Everyone woke late on the morning after Cecily's rout. The family took breakfast together in the solar, as was their habit. Although some mornings it was only Bertie and Jane, if Edmund was disinclined to emerge from his adolescent cocoon. He had come down today though, looking more rested than either his sister or his uncle. It probably came of not having any responsibilities beyond meeting his tutor and horseback riding.

In contrast, Bertie was already in a state of nerves when Jane came down.

"It's half ten," he complained when he saw her. "Hurry and eat something, then go curl your hair. You need to look presentable before your callers arrive."

"Are we expecting callers?" Jane paused in the act of spreading marmalade on her bread, an orange glob dripping from her knife.

"Well of *course* we are," he said. "It's the day after a party. That's exactly when gentlemen will look in on you."

Jane said nothing to this, for she had no desire to confess that she'd spent more of her evening trying to win over Lady Eleanor and other prospective guests for her club than any eligible men. Normally she remembered to engage a few friendly regulars in conversation long enough to reassure Uncle Bertie she hadn't yet abandoned the war on spinsterhood, but last night had passed in a blur. She couldn't recall speaking to a single gentleman.

Except for one.

"Lieutenant Williams is sure to come. Did you speak to any others? There were so many officers."

Jane's heart skipped a beat. Had he read her mind?

"I doubt Lieutenant Williams would call on us, Uncle Bertie," she said, willing the pronouncement to hold true.

"But of course he will! I've invited him. And if he forgets, I shall go and leave my card as a reminder."

Jane set down her bread. *Why would he do such a thing?*

She'd been doing very well without Eli around. She was supposed to be moving forward. Focusing on her financial independence, not childish hopes she'd long since outgrown.

But Bertie meant well, so she forged ahead gently. "Should we be so eager to see Lieutenant Williams again? His connection to this family is ended. And we've heard the whole story of his survival now."

Even if she still had questions on that subject. She would let them go, so long as he disappeared from her life once more.

"But of course we must see him again. He's *famous*. This is all so exciting. Just look at the morning post."

He nodded toward Edmund, who was reading silently at the other end of the table. Edmund looked up at their mention of his newspaper and obligingly pulled out the page of interest for Jane. He mostly read the racing section, anyway.

It was a large story, a full quarter of a page.

THE LADY HE LOST   53

BACK FROM THE DEAD!

On Sunday last, Mr. and Mrs. Robert Williams of Egg Buckland parish, Devon, received a frightful shock to find their departed son returned to them! The young Lt. Eleazar Williams having been lost at sea without a trace in the service of Her Majesty's Royal Navy two years prior, and being presumed dead by all, has provoked considerable interest by his return. Lt. Williams was seen last night in attendance at the home of Sir and Lady Thomas Kerr, of Berkeley Square, in the company of some two hundred guests of the most distinguished society, to whom he recounted the tale of his miraculous survival. A confidential source tells us the gentleman was held hostage by pirates until he could make his escape from this harrowing ordeal. The story does not end happily, however, for upon his return to native soil, the brave Lt. was heartbroken to discover that his once-intended bride had married another, and is now the Lady Kerr.

Jane's eyes lingered over the description of Eli's "harrowing ordeal."

"Doesn't it seem odd that the article devotes so much attention to Cecily?"

There could be little doubt who the confidential source was.

"Hmm?" Uncle Bertie said absently. "Oh, I don't think so. It's the tragic part of the story, isn't it? Love lost, and all that."

Never mind. There was no point in trying to illuminate Cecily's faults. Perhaps an appeal to caution would serve her better.

"I think we might consider letting our connection to Lieutenant Williams lapse, Uncle," she counseled. "Cecily is married to another man. It might give people the wrong impression if her former fiancé is seen lingering over our family."

"Oh nonsense. No one will think anything amiss. Cecily adores

Sir Thomas, and she doesn't even live here anymore. What gossip could it possibly cause if Lieutenant Williams calls upon *us*?"

Jane bit her lip. She was still trying to think of a counterargument when her uncle continued, "Besides, weren't you two rather intimate friends at one time? I thought that was how he met Cecily in the first place. I should think you'd be happy to see him again, alive and well."

Jane winced.

It wasn't that she enjoyed keeping things from her uncle. In fact, she confided in him quite often about other subjects. But not this.

He had a blind spot where his daughter was concerned. If she tried to explain her feelings for Eli, Bertie was sure to say something that would only make her feel worse, in spite of his best intentions.

"I suppose we saw one another fairly often that time Edmund and I stayed at Ashlow Park while you and Cecily went to Bath with the Lindens. But that was ages ago. I hardly remember it now."

Edmund studied her from across the top of his paper. He was in a position to betray her, if he wished, for he'd seen exactly how much time she'd spent walking with Eli that summer. But he returned to his reading.

Perhaps it was a show of loyalty, or perhaps he simply didn't care enough about the subject to be lured out of silence. Either way, Jane made a mental note to be kind to him.

After breakfast, Jane did as she'd been bid and had her maid curl up her hair, though it was probably for nothing. She would've rather spent the morning with Della than wait around in the hopes of a caller. She was dying to tell her how close she'd come to snaring Lady Eleanor, and they still needed to plan another meeting with Miss Chatterjee to put her skills as a dealer to the test. If she proved up to the challenge, Jane wanted her leading a third table by Monday. It felt urgent, all of a sudden. She needed to prove to herself they were serious, that all those memories were behind her and *this* was her future.

But at quarter past eleven, the much-anticipated knock sounded at the door and the butler showed Eli into their drawing room, where the family greeted him with refreshments.

It felt like the floor lurched out from beneath her feet when Jane saw him. Every time, the shock of his presence hit her afresh, and she had to look twice to check if he was truly there. When would she get used to having him back?

Her eyes were drawn to the hundred little details she hadn't seen in years. The way his cropped hair was mostly straight but formed stray curls at the base of his neck. The way his warm brown eyes lit up with his smile as he greeted them, though their spark was subdued this morning.

He must have realized that only Uncle Bertie wanted him here. She'd made that clear enough last night.

Still, they traveled in the same circles and seemed doomed to see one another again. She would have to learn how to control these feelings. It had been so long, they should have died out by now, like any other passing fancy.

"The weather is very fair this morning," Jane began, once everyone was seated and had received their tea.

"Yes," he agreed stiffly. He studied her, no doubt searching for a safe topic.

Jane had brought her work out for the call, and she dropped her gaze pointedly to it now, ignoring how her hands trembled. She hated petit point. She had, in fact, been embroidering the same handkerchief for years, for she only touched it when she needed an excuse to ignore a visitor while appearing genteel. But those neglected little lilacs on the edges of her linen were a great help in keeping her eyes off Eli.

Bertie was immune to any awkwardness in the room. "Have you seen the papers, Lieutenant? There's a quarter page on your return!"

"Ah." Eli's smile was strained about the edges. "Yes, I saw. I wish they hadn't printed that."

"Why on earth not?"

"I don't see why it should be of such an interest to everyone." Though he was trying to appear unbothered, Jane detected a subtle tension in the set of his shoulders. He normally carried himself with more ease. "Aren't the Chartists up to something more exciting they could write about? All I did was get captured."

Odd that the article bothered him so much. Did Eli dislike being reminded of his experience, or was there more? Had he suffered greatly in his captivity? He hadn't said anything about it, except that he'd been in chains, but pirates probably weren't the most humane captors.

Jane didn't like to think of him that way—cold and alone, surrounded by enemies. The idea pinched at her heart, until she reminded herself that she didn't even know how much of his story could be trusted. Her only source of information was Eli.

Wait. Now *there* was an idea. Jane froze, her attention shifting from her petit point to the possibilities before her.

Would it be so hard to set her doubts to rest? His former captain was in London, and there must be other witnesses to the shipwreck, if she could dig them up.

It was an intriguing possibility, and only one thing held her back: a nagging voice in the back of her mind that said playing detective wasn't the best way to prove that she'd moved on with her life.

"You're too modest," Bertie insisted. "It's heroic. Isn't it, Jane?"

She looked up from her stitch. "I don't feel I have enough information yet to determine what it is."

Perhaps more information was just what she needed to banish Eli from her thoughts. If she proved he was lying, surely that would kill this lingering attachment she suffered.

Her uncle sighed, obviously put out. "Don't mind her, Lieutenant. We've had a late night, and are perhaps not in the best of tempers."

"I should let you return to your day." Eli stood. "I only wanted to stop in and give my good wishes."

He cast an apologetic glance to Jane, his meaning clear. He wouldn't have come if Bertie hadn't invited him.

"Oh no," Bertie assured him, rising to his feet to mirror Eli. "I didn't mean to rush you off. You've only just arrived. And I wanted to ask you about those letters you mentioned to correct your death certificate. What is it that we're meant to include?"

"You really don't have to do that. I can ask someone else."

"Not at all. We're happy to."

We, he'd said. Jane supposed she was included then, in spite of her protest last night. She punctured the linen with her needle a bit too hastily and pricked her finger, sucking in a breath as blood beaded up a moment later. It was all Eli's fault. He'd distracted her.

"Here." Somehow, he was at her side before she realized he'd crossed the room, holding out his handkerchief.

She didn't take it. "Don't be silly. I've got one right here if I need it."

"Yes, but yours has embroidery on it," Eli pointed out with a faint turn of his lips. They looked very kissable at this proximity. Her heart did an awkward tumble at the sight. "It's too nice to actually be used for anything. Whereas a man's handkerchief can mop up blood without misgiving."

"I don't want yours." Jane lifted her digit to her lips and sucked away the offending spot while Eli followed the motion with his eyes, his expression darkening. Did he feel it too, or was it only polite concern that prompted his attention?

Flustered, Jane lowered her hand again, and fresh blood welled up.

"You have to apply pressure."

Yes, I know that, she would have said. But the words died in her throat as Eli took her finger into his own hands and pressed the handkerchief round the pinprick. He was *touching* her. As if he had any right to such an encroachment on her person. And she was letting him.

Worse than that, she was acutely aware of the small point of contact between them. The warmth of his skin. The rough calluses on his palm, no doubt from lashing sails or whatever it was naval men did. She couldn't think clearly through the heat that flooded her.

"You're being contrary for no reason," he murmured, too low for Bertie to hear.

Even so, her uncle was watching them with no small measure of surprise upon his face.

The sight finally jolted Jane into reacting. She snatched her hand back, her cheeks growing hot.

"Thank you. I have it."

What was wrong with her? She must be a pathetic sight, so starved for attention that she would lose all composure at the simple touch of his hand.

Eli withdrew, turning back to her uncle and the matter of those wretched letters as if nothing had transpired. Perhaps for him nothing had.

"Very well. If you're sure it's no trouble. I am eager to set this all to rest so I can resume my career. Just explain how we met, and that you recognize I'm myself and not some impostor. Nothing more." He still hadn't resumed his seat, so he must intend to leave soon. Jane drew a shaky breath. Another moment and this would be over. "I can collect them for my solicitor once you're done."

"Very good." Uncle Bertie was brimming with enthusiasm, as if it were the prime minister who'd asked him to perform this favor rather than his erstwhile almost son-in-law. "We'll call on you in a few days to drop them off."

Jane frowned, still pressing Eli's handkerchief to her finger. Another call. Was there no end to them?

As long as Bertie still hoped to find her a husband, they would be obliged to make the rounds at all the same parties. If that article in the paper was any indication, Eli would be a prized guest in every house.

As if summoned by her desire for an end to this, a knock on the door and the murmured greeting of their butler alerted them that another caller had arrived. Thank goodness.

"I should let you see to your visitors." Eli retrieved his hat from the hook and turned the brim between his hands. "Thank you for offering to write the letters. It was good to see you again."

In a show of great restraint, Jane didn't even point out that she hadn't offered anything. Uncle Bertie saw Eli to the door, and it became a bit easier to breathe in the empty room. She could endure this. It was only the surprise of Eli's return that moved her. In another week or two, he would have sorted out his affairs and returned to sea, and everything would be as it had been before.

When her uncle returned, he had Mr. MacPherson in tow. Jane rose to greet him, summoning a bright smile that she hadn't managed for his predecessor. MacPherson had a bland sort of face and temperament, unlikely to provoke passion in anyone, which was exactly how Jane liked it. She breathed easy in the knowledge that he could never tempt her to trade her future for his.

It was only after she took a step forward to greet him that Jane realized she was still clutching Eli's handkerchief. Still clinging to some small piece of him, in spite of her best efforts.

Five

"I DON'T SEE WHY I SHOULD HAVE TO TRAVEL ALL THE WAY OVER to the Kerrs' town house to spend ten minutes telling them how remarkable their party was," Mr. Williams grumbled as the family carriage rolled them through Mayfair. "The sandwiches were too dry, and the crush so great that I couldn't manage to get any punch for half the evening."

"You have to be willing to elbow a few guests out of the way," Eli said. "It's how they make sure the punch goes to those who need it most."

"Please don't joke," his mother said, her voice strained. She was the one who'd insisted on a thank-you call to Lady Kerr, though she didn't seem to be enjoying the journey. "Your father might actually try it, and then where will we be? We must *all* make a good impression if we're ever to find Hannah a match."

The object of his mother's hopes was nowhere to be found, having had the good sense to call on friends this morning instead of listening to her parents bicker.

"I don't see why she can't meet a husband in Devon," Mr.

Williams retorted. "All this matchmaking is just an excuse to waste my money on new dresses, if you ask me."

"We didn't."

"I hear Dickens wrote a new novel while I was away," Eli interjected. "Have either of you read it?" He rather wished he'd ridden up top with the coachman instead of with his parents. They made him look back fondly on the pirates.

The Kerrs' town house was bustling with activity when they arrived, as expected. Several empty carriages awaited their masters on the road down Berkeley Square.

Perfect. They would pay their dues quickly and move on. There was no reason to spend any more time with Lady Kerr than strictly necessary—she was a reminder of everything he'd done wrong.

He would be back at sea as soon as this business with the death certificate was resolved, and once he was, it wouldn't be hard to let the connection lapse.

The butler begged them to wait in the entryway as his employers were still with the previous callers. He disappeared for a minute and returned with instructions to admit them to the drawing room to join the group.

Eli's heart sank as the door opened to reveal who it was.

Jane, her brother, and her uncle occupied the left half of the room, her friend from the library the other night and several strangers (the lady's parents, no doubt) occupied the right.

Sir Thomas and Lady Kerr held court from the center, on a velvet couch perched atop a Persian carpet, framed by an assortment of glittering bric-a-brac on the wall behind them. She was smiling at Eli before his gaze had even found her.

"I hope you don't mind sharing your call, but we're all on intimate acquaintance, aren't we?"

"Of course," Eli replied, though he wasn't sure Jane would agree.

She turned toward him a moment later than the others, and he had the keen discomfort of seeing her large, gray eyes grow cooler as she recognized him. She looked away quickly, the gentle lines of her profile turning stern.

Why must he make her miserable when he wished to make her happy?

With some rearrangement, they found space for Eli and his parents, though he was obliged to take the seat next to Jane, wincing as his knees brushed hers and their shifting brought her faint lilac scent to his nose. She was going to think he'd done this on purpose.

She looked well this morning. She wore the same day dress she'd had on during his earlier call—a green and blush print that was cut modestly, but cinched in a wide sash at her waist to accentuate her figure. Eli studied her from the corner of his eye, trying not to betray how easily she drew his attention. He could still feel the softness of her fingertips beneath his when they'd touched this morning. Even that brief contact exerted a hold over him.

"I'm so happy you've come." Though Lady Kerr's words extended to everyone, her smile lingered on Eli as she added, "A number of my guests have been asking about you. I daresay you'll have a king's welcome wherever you go."

"Everyone has been very kind."

They were drowning in calling cards at his aunt's town house, overrun with visitors he'd never met in his life. It was that blasted story in the papers. Everyone wanted to say they knew the man who'd come back from the dead. Never mind that he had no interest in being their latest bit of gossip.

People were going to start asking questions he didn't care to answer.

"We have you to thank for his introduction back into society," Eli's mother said. "Thank you so much for inviting us to your rout last night. It was delightful."

Eli took in the house as they spoke. The decor, much like yesterday's fête, spoke of extravagance. Her husband must have money, for though Lady Kerr's dowry had been of healthy proportions, it couldn't have paid for this.

We should have made each other very miserable if we'd married.

If he'd known it then, there could be no doubt now. A lieutenant's income wouldn't have allowed her to play the society hostess as she dreamed, and she was clearly suited to the role. Sir Thomas seemed affable enough. They even had a son. It seemed she'd gotten all she wanted.

Eli hadn't realized he'd been carrying a weight until the moment it lifted. He'd always suffered an acute sense of responsibility toward others—perhaps it came from being the firstborn. If he'd returned to London to find her new husband was a profligate gambler or a drunk who'd trapped her in a poor match while she was still reeling from news of Eli's supposed death, he would have blamed himself. A sense of obligation would always have linked them. Now, he could rest easy in the knowledge that their entanglement hadn't had any consequences.

At least, not for her.

His attention strayed back to Jane, so near him it was hard to look away. What did she want? Nothing that he could give, certainly. She wanted nothing to do with him. But if he was to return to the navy and have no news of her again for years, he would like to know that she was well before he left. Perhaps there was some service he could do for her.

It was the closest he could come to putting things right.

"Have you selected your gowns for Ladies' Day yet?" asked Lady Kerr. "I cannot decide if I should wear sleeves *en gigot*, or if the style is on its way out." The question must have been aimed at all the women in the room, but it was her own father who answered.

"Jane has *not*, and I am growing concerned that the dressmaker won't have enough time to fit her for something new."

"If there isn't time, I shall wear something I already own."

Lady Kerr clucked her tongue. "I know it's your fourth season, Jane, but you mustn't stop making an effort. Poor Papa puts so much time into finding you a match. We really can't let him down *again*."

Jane, who hadn't been blessed with a card face, looked as though she might strangle her cousin. She dropped her gaze pointedly to her lap, her cheeks pink.

I shouldn't have come. He didn't want to listen to a discussion of whom Jane should marry.

There had been a gentleman at the door when he left her uncle's town house this morning. Was he a suitor? Were there others? A trace of resentment burned in Eli's chest, entirely inappropriate for his position.

He was no one to her. If he'd once hoped she would look at him with affection, it was impossible now.

Lady Kerr turned to him so sharply that for a moment he feared his dismay had shown on his face. But she only asked, "You *are* coming to Ascot, I trust?"

"To be honest, we haven't had time to discuss it," Eli replied.

"We weren't planning on attending the season this year," his mother added. "But when Eli came back to us, he was eager to see his friends in town while he had the chance."

The glimmer in her eye caused Eli a pang of guilt. He didn't like to think of what she must have suffered, believing him dead for so long. It sometimes felt as though he'd summoned the wave that had dashed the ship against the rocks and led him to captivity. Hadn't he been desperate to avoid his vows? Though he knew it was utter nonsense, it felt like the sea had answered him.

"You *must* come with us," Lady Kerr said. "We're planning a picnic luncheon on the journey there. And they've just built a new grandstand on the heath. Have you heard?" When Eli shook his head, she continued. "This is the first year it's open to the public. They say it will hold three thousand."

It was the last thing he needed, to be thrust into a crowd with Lady Kerr drawing attention to him, just as she had last night. It seemed every time he told his story to someone, a dozen more listeners popped up like fairy rings from the earth. They weren't content with the part of the tale he had no qualms about sharing—that he'd been shipwrecked, held captive, and eventually made his escape (all quite true). Everyone wanted *details*.

Details were where mistakes could arise. All it took was one careless word, one accidental reference to the ship that had brought him safely to France, the exact timing of his escape, or the fact that he hadn't been traveling alone, and his world would come crashing down. No one would care about his reasons. They would see a small stretch of unmarked time and brand him a deserter.

Worse than that, he might put Geórgios in danger. Eli owed him his life; he couldn't risk exposing him.

"Thank you so much for the invitation," he began, "but I'm afraid we haven't lodgings at Ascot, and it's too late to find something suitable."

Less than two weeks out from the event, every accommodation would be full up.

But Lady Kerr brushed his excuse aside without missing a beat. "Oh, don't worry about that. We're all staying at the Lindens's house. Mr. Linden is a particular friend of our family and he has a place in Sunninghill. I'm sure he'd be happy to make room for you."

"We wouldn't want to impose," Eli maintained, trying to signal his mother with his eyes.

But instead of echoing his protests, she smiled broadly. "How kind of you, Lady Kerr. Are you sure he wouldn't mind the addition?"

Jane would mind, if the set of her lips was any indication.

Damn. He should've warned his mother beforehand not to accept any invitations.

"Of course not," Mr. Bishop said. "They're two people in a large house, and some of us can pair up for rooms, if need be. It's only four days."

"Is Hannah with you?" asked Lady Kerr. "I should love to see her again."

"Yes, and she'll be thrilled to attend. We have high hopes for her this season."

If Eli had entertained any notion of changing his mother's mind, it evaporated the minute their outing was linked to Hannah's marriage prospects.

"Then it's settled!" Lady Kerr favored them with a dazzling smile. "I can introduce her to all the eligible gentlemen. How exciting! I daresay we might even have her married before Jane."

This call had been the longest half hour of her life. Jane was ready to murder someone—most likely Cecily—by the time it came to an end. Why couldn't her cousin pass a simple visit without dredging up her every flaw? Ever since they were young, she'd behaved as though they were in competition. Jane didn't even know what they were competing *for.* By any measure that would matter to Cecily, she'd already won when she made it to the altar first.

Earlier than that, even. She'd won on the night she'd thrown herself at Eli, for no other reason than to prove she could take the one gentleman Jane cared for.

And now he was back to provide a walking reminder of her humiliation.

Eli and his parents were the first to go, Mrs. Williams still proclaiming her gratitude for the invitation to stay at the Lindens' house as they donned their hats and cloaks. Della's parents rose to follow, and Jane seized the opportunity.

"We should really be leaving, Uncle Bertie. Cecily and Sir Thomas must be expecting other callers this morning."

She issued a hasty goodbye to her cousin and hurried out to catch Della, who was lingering on the steps. Happily, the Williamses were already at their carriage, a dozen feet away. Eli's father climbed in without a backward glance to anyone, but as Eli held out his arm to help his mother inside, he cast a final look toward the house, and his eyes met Jane's.

It felt like a pinch, or the little zap of current one got touching someone who'd been walking on a carpet. Something sharp and unpleasant, at any rate. She wished very much that she felt nothing at all.

Jane turned away from him without waving goodbye.

"You've cut the poor fellow," Della murmured. Her parents were chatting with Uncle Bertie by now and paying no attention.

"I haven't cut him," Jane protested. What a strange accusation. "We just spent the entire call together."

"I think he might've liked you to lift a hand, even so."

"I don't care terribly what he would like." In spite of her pronouncement, Jane's cheeks were growing hot. Why should Della's words make her feel guilty? Eli hadn't spared much thought for her until now. "Will you come back to our house for some tea? I want to chat about our preparations for Monday."

"I promised Mrs. Davis that I'd call on her today. Why don't you join me and we'll talk on the way?"

They explained their plans to the others and set off through Berkeley Square, for their destination wasn't far. Jane tugged her cloak tight around her arms; it was still chill on this May morning.

Once they were out of earshot, Della spoke very quickly, her words coming out in a rush. "What happened last night? I couldn't find you again once I left the library."

"I spoke to Lady Eleanor and Mrs. Duff, but I didn't have the chance to invite them to join our card party before Uncle Bertie interrupted me. Did you have any more luck?"

"Not *that*," said Della impatiently. "I meant, what happened with Lieutenant Williams?"

What was that supposed to mean? She asked the question too eagerly, as though she expected the reply to be something scandalous.

"Nothing at all. I didn't think it was appropriate to be alone with him, and I went back to the party."

"You didn't."

"Of course I did."

"*Jane.*" Della piled heaps of disappointment onto her name. "I can't believe you. He's so handsome, and he's always staring at you. Don't you at least want to hear his explanation?"

"I've heard it. I ran into him again later on."

"And?" It was apparent that Della was infected with the fever for news of Eli that had gripped the ton overnight. It was bad enough that he'd captivated everyone else. Did he have to ensnare her friend, as well?

"You'll have seen the article in the post this morning?"

"Yes."

"It was much the same thing. Abducted by pirates, etc., etc."

"So it's true." Della placed a hand over her breast. "The poor man. A prisoner for two years."

Yes, she'd definitely caught Eli fever. A more irksome affliction, Jane had not yet seen.

"That seems a bit of a leap. Something isn't true simply because the papers print it."

"But why would he lie? And if he wasn't really abducted, then where was he all this time?"

Good questions.

"I don't know, but something isn't right." He'd been curiously vague about his captivity. And everyone knew that pirates ransomed their prisoners, or else why take them in the first place? She and Eli might not be on intimate terms anymore, but she could still tell when he was hiding something.

"Well, if you truly believe he's lying, I suppose you'll have four days together to sniff it out."

Jane cast her friend a murderous look, though it did little to quell her grin.

"It isn't funny," she insisted. Cecily was going to be insufferable, fawning over Eli the entire time, even with her husband there. She didn't want to watch their flirtation. Particularly when her own sentiments weren't nearly as controlled as she would like. "Could you ask your parents if I may stay with you?"

Just think how much progress they might make on their plans for the club if they had four days together! It would be perfect.

But Della dashed her hopes immediately. "We're full up. We've only rented two rooms—I'm sharing with Annabelle, and my parents are sharing the other with Peter. Everything goes so quickly during the races, there wasn't much choice. You're going to be far more comfortable as guests in a proper house."

"I assure you, I will not."

Della laughed, then clapped up her jaw at Jane's look. "Sorry."

Enough of this. It was bad enough that Eli would intrude upon her privacy for four days, she didn't have to let him intrude any further on her thoughts.

"We're almost there. Let's focus, please," Jane said briskly. "Have all our guests confirmed for Monday?"

This was what really mattered.

"Everyone except Lady Baldwin. She sends her regrets and hopes to return next time."

"Oh no." Lady Baldwin was their biggest draw. The only titled guest amongst their number, and liberal with her coin, she served to lend respectability to the club and encourage the other ladies to spend freely. It had taken weeks of careful effort to secure her patronage. "Do we still have twelve?"

"I'll find someone, don't worry. Did you say you'd started on Lady Eleanor? My mother calls on hers often. Maybe I can finish the job."

"If you can manage it, I'll give you my firstborn child," Jane promised. "We *need* another aristocrat."

Why did it have to be Lady Baldwin who'd canceled?

"I was thinking..." Della slowed her step as they approached the Davis house. They were both rosy-cheeked from the cold, but she made no move to mount the steps and lift the knocker.

"Yes?"

"We might consider asking Lieutenant Williams to join us. *Everyone* wants to meet him. If people hear he's attending, they'll all be vying for an invitation in the hopes of gleaning some bit of inside gossip they can share with their friends. We could be the most talked-about club in town overnight."

Oh dear. Jane knew the note of excitement in her friend's voice all too well. Della tended to get carried away with her plans and could maintain her fervor for months before she ran out of steam. It was Jane's role to be the voice of reason.

"It's a *ladies'* club," she reminded her. "I don't think your parents will be so eager to lend us your house if we start inviting gentlemen."

Besides Della's parents, there were also their reputations to think of. A gambling club might be a risqué endeavor for two unmarried ladies, but if it was limited to a select group of women, they had only to conceal the sums they played for to keep trouble at bay. Gambling in mixed company was another kettle of fish.

"A special guest," Della retorted. "One night only. Let me worry about my parents." Maybe she had a point. Lady Eleanor and Mrs. Duff had lit up at the mention of Eli's name last night. If he proved willing to come, he might achieve in a single evening what they'd been struggling for all season.

She and Della had made fifty pounds so far to split between them. An impressive sum for a hobby, but hardly enough to live on should the worst happen. But if they could clear a hundred before August signaled the retreat of most of their members to the countryside—oh! Then she might feel brave enough to approach Uncle Bertie with her plans to rent out rooms next year and turn their little gatherings into a profitable business. She would have undeniable proof of her idea's potential. Proof that he didn't need to worry about finding her a husband; she could take care of herself.

All she had to do was rely on Eli.

Jane drew a deep breath as her dreams crashed back down to earth. It was madness to depend on him again. The man who'd won her over with his kind attentions, then run off to the gardens with her cousin. The man who'd disappeared without a trace and returned just as suddenly, as if life and death could be swapped on a whim. Would she really trust her future to someone such as that?

"It isn't worth the risk." Pushing down the regret in her heart, Jane marched up the steps and knocked.

She put her faith in mathematics, not men. The odds of turning up a given card could be measured and relied upon, her power of reason transforming seemingly random figures into a pattern. Eli was just the opposite—unknown and thus unpredictable. It would be foolish to depend on him.

Six

THE LADIES' VINGT-ET-UN CLUB MET EVERY MONDAY EVENING at ten, though the invitees might slip in a little earlier or later, depending on the timing of their dinner plans. Play usually began at half-past. They were obliged to hold their meetings in Della's drawing room at present—a fine enough setting for their numbers—though Jane hoped that by next year they might have enough members to rent out rooms. They may not command the numbers of White's or Brooks's, but there was a market in London for a ladies' club of a comparable nature. The women who came to their tables couldn't be the only ones interested in playing for higher stakes than pennies at a house party, and in a more discreet setting.

The Danbys were indulgent of their eldest daughter and generally went out for the night, leaving Della and Jane to their own devices. The fact that they admitted only ladies probably did a great deal to secure their trust.

That, and no one had informed Della's parents they played for large sums.

Jane arrived early, as she always did, in order to help Della set up. As soon as her cloak was hung and she came into the room, she noticed something amiss.

"Why are there so many tables?" She'd been expecting the third, as their run-through with Miss Chatterjee on Saturday had gone smoothly. The young lady's confidence had improved, and she had a solid grasp of the basic principles of probability, even if full mastery was still a few weeks away. But there were *four* card tables set up for play, which meant Della must have invited far more guests than they'd agreed upon. And who would their other dealer be?

"Now, don't be cross with me," Della began. This was never a good start to a conversation.

"What's going on?"

"It's only that everyone has taken such an interest in Lieutenant Williams, and by extension, your connection to him. Everywhere I go, I'm met with questions about what he's like, and what he's said to you about his captivity."

"Della." A chill trickled down Jane's back. "Please tell me what you've done."

"I ran into him at church yesterday, and I didn't intend to invite him—"

"You invited Lieutenant Williams here?" This was unacceptable. Her club was a fortress, the one place Eli couldn't intrude. She told Della this notion of a special guest was asking for trouble! Why couldn't she have listened?

"—but we got to talking about you, as it happens, and when he heard about the club—"

Why should Eli be talking about me?

"Why would you tell him about the club? You know I don't want details to get back to Uncle Bertie and Cecily yet." This grew worse and worse. If her cousin were to learn of the club, she would no doubt proclaim herself queen of their number and interfere with everything.

"Oh, it's hard to explain if you weren't there. I didn't *mean* for it to happen. He inquired about my plans for the week, and I couldn't very well lie."

Yes, you could have, Jane wanted to protest. This seemed exactly the sort of situation where a small fib was called for. But there was no turning back time. Better to determine the depth of their present suffering.

"So he invited himself along?" And after she'd made it clear she didn't want to see him again. What an intrusive, conceited man.

"No," Della admitted. "He only asked if there was anything he could do to help. And I said it would probably increase interest if he attended just this once." She brushed a stray curl back into place, then motioned a servant to set the chairs a little farther apart before turning back to assess the degree of Jane's anger. "Please don't be cross. As I said, I couldn't lie to him. It *will* be a help to us."

She didn't look the least bit contrite. She might even have done it deliberately, reckless meddler that she was.

"You should never have told him that. We already talked about this."

It was all very well for Della to take free rein in other matters. They were partners; they both had equal say in running the club. But this was different. Jane possessed a power of veto where Eli was concerned. Surely that went without saying?

"I know, I know, but you should have seen him, Jane. He was so considerate. He thought our club was a clever idea, and he took everything I said so seriously, not at all as if it was a girlish fancy, the way some men behave. He really is a remarkable gentleman, and he only wants to help you. I think you've hurt his feelings with how cold you've been."

"*I've* hurt *his* feelings?" Jane sputtered. "He disappeared for two years and didn't even tell me he was alive! Why are we so concerned with how Eli feels?"

A remarkable gentleman. He only wants to help you. Honestly, how did Eli get Cordelia eating out of his palm in such a short time? It was sickening.

"Lieutenant Williams," Della corrected. "You keep forgetting to pretend that you don't use his Christian name."

Jane made a sound that was half shriek, half growl. The footman stopped arranging the chairs and exited the room with a quick stride.

"Anyway, it's done now, and guests will be arriving any moment," Della continued, unaware of how near Jane was to upending the tables and stomping home. "Why don't you ask me who's coming tonight? I found a replacement for Lady Baldwin just like you wanted, and I'm sure you'll forgive me once you hear who it is."

"That's doubtful." Jane scowled at her friend. But after a prolonged silence made it clear she wouldn't know unless she asked, she added, "Who, then?"

"Lady Eleanor Grosvenor." Della all but sang the young lady's title.

This news succeeded in shocking Jane from her ill humor, even if forgiveness still hid beyond sight. "You really did it?"

"And she's bringing Mrs. Duff and Miss Anwar..." Della continued listing off the new names while Jane made a tally of their characters and incomes where such details were known. Several heiresses. More than one lady of influence. These were exactly the sort of members they'd spent most of the season trying to attract. Della had done it. Not that it made up for her greatest error.

"Have you forgiven me yet?" Della asked when she finished. She had a glint in her eyes that said she knew what a success the night would be.

"Humph." Jane pursed her lips. Annoyed as she was about Eli, it was impossible to stay cross when the daughter of a marquess would soon be joining them. Della sensed her victory, for she pranced around the room, humming as she fussed with the refreshments and the centerpieces on the tables until the first knock came at the door.

They welcomed each of their guests warmly with a well-placed question or two about their families or hobbies. The ladies poured in quickly, craning their necks at the other arrivals and failing to hide their disappointment when they realized the attraction they'd been promised wasn't there yet. Then he walked in, and everything changed. It would be wrong to say that the ladies were overcome by Eli's presence, for no one had to call for smelling salts, but the result wasn't far off. Everyone turned to stare as he stepped over the threshold. The conversation receded, exposing every sigh and murmur to the ears. It was as though Lord Byron had just walked through the door. (Also resurrected, of course.)

"Hello." Eli gave a faint, self-deprecating sort of smile as he took in the number of eyes upon him. Something shifted in the air, and without any further effort the women were no longer staring *at* him, but looking *to* him. The crowd was his.

Jane drew a shaky breath, wishing that she didn't feel it too. It wasn't fair that he should be blessed with such charisma without having done a thing to earn it.

Della stepped forward, a dazzling smile upon her face. "Lieutenant, thank you so much for joining us. I'm sure your calendar must be packed full these days."

"Not at all. I had to see this for myself."

Della signaled Jane from the corner of her eye. There was no way to avoid him without appearing to give slight, so she stepped forward to join in the greeting. "Welcome, Lieutenant. I hope you're well this evening."

"Very well, thank you." A trace of hesitation crept into his voice at her approach. "I'm grateful to Miss Danby for the invitation."

She took his meaning: he wanted some reassurance from her that he was welcome tonight. She couldn't very well tell him he wasn't—not in front of this adoring crowd. Jane drew a large breath and girded herself for the rest of the evening. Her feelings didn't matter now; she needed to make the most of this opportunity, even if she hadn't asked for it.

"We're happy to have you." With a look that encompassed the rest of the room, she added, "But I'm afraid you mustn't get too attached, for this remains a ladies' club. You must consider yourself our guest for one evening only."

She kept her voice light and friendly, but trusted that he would receive the message. He could be as charming as he liked; she still wouldn't yield.

There were small sighs of disappointment at her pronouncement from some of the younger members, but no matter. They might think her too strict, but Jane had the future of her club to protect. Their fledgling endeavor couldn't risk any angry fathers showing up on Della's doorstep when they learned their daughters were gambling in mixed company.

"How long have you two been hosting a card club?" Eli asked.

"Only this season," Jane replied. There was no point in letting herself be drawn into conversation with Eli about this. They weren't friends any longer.

But Della (quite predictably) failed to show any solidarity. "Jane had the idea last fall, when a few of us were playing cards at a house party, and a gentleman in attendance made a disparaging remark about our ability to strategize." She managed to avoid rolling her eyes, but her tone of voice conveyed the sentiment. "We decided we'd enjoy the freedom to play in a more discreet setting and quickly found others who shared our view."

"I didn't know that you were a card player, Miss Bishop."

She hadn't been, when she'd kept company with Eli. Certainly not for large sums. But in searching for ways to supplement her meager income, she'd done a few calculations and realized that gambling was terribly profitable, for the house.

Still, these weren't thoughts to share with her guests. Eli had no business making such a comment. At best, he made her sound inexperienced.

"There's likely a great deal you and I don't know about one another, Lieutenant." Jane added a smile to soften her reproach. Let the others think she was flirting with him. He would hear the warning beneath the words.

He might have fooled half of London with his tragic story and miraculous return, but he wasn't fooling her.

"Well." Eli tipped his head in mock surrender. "I promise not to make any disparaging remarks about your ability to strategize, so long as you promise not to clean me out entirely. I've been off the navy's payroll for a few years."

Always joking.

This provoked gentle laughter from the other women, but Jane only arched her brow. "You must forgive me, but I can promise nothing of the sort. You see, I have a prior obligation to our members who come here expecting serious play. You will be at their mercy, should they choose to show it. They may just as easily decide to take all your coin home with them."

The laughter increased, which gave Jane a particularly warm feeling in her chest. It wasn't often that she got to enjoy such camaraderie. Della was more often the amusing one, while she was the taskmaster.

"Let's see which it shall be then." Della jumped in, herding them toward the tables.

Crisp little namecards awaited them at each seat. That was new. Jane wasn't at the same table as Eli, who'd been given a place of honor amongst their highest-ranking guests: Lady Eleanor and the wealthier ladies in their number. It made perfect sense to keep them happy. Why should Jane feel any disappointment? She didn't *want* to see Eli.

The table was hushed as they took their seats, each member of the party straining to catch the conversation from Eli's table. Jane's attention was fixed there too, watching him laugh at something Mrs. Duff had just said. With dawning horror, she saw him reach for the deck of cards and begin to shuffle.

Della hadn't just invited him as a guest, but as a *dealer*. What was she thinking? They'd spent *weeks* training Miss Chatterjee, making sure she had a solid grasp of all their rules, but Eli had only to grace them with his presence to be judged trustworthy? They'd never even observed him play! Jane tried to catch Della's eye to better convey her outrage, but she didn't look her way.

If he botches things for us with Lady Eleanor, I'll never forgive this.

Jane broke the silence with the crack of her cards as she shuffled, the movements so familiar she was scarcely aware of them. This was normally her favorite part of the evening, when the night was young and full of possibility. Now she was too nervous to enjoy it.

"Stakes, please, ladies."

"Lieutenant Williams was engaged to your cousin, wasn't he, Miss Bishop?" Miss Anwar kept her voice low enough not to carry as she slid a counter from her pile. She was a dark-haired young lady with a prominent overbite and high brows that made her look perpetually quizzical. "How heartbreaking to think that she married another when he was *alive* this whole time."

"He must have been devastated." Mrs. Muller's lip actually trembled before she stilled it with the touch of her champagne flute.

Whether or not to serve drinks had been a point of contention. Jane had been against it, for fear that it would set a poor tone and inflame tempers when a lady suffered a losing streak, while Della felt that a little champagne was always a welcome lubricant for the fingers upon the purse strings. Della had won out.

Perhaps she'd been right. There were occasions when a drink was called for.

"I don't know that he was *devastated*," Jane replied, taking a long swallow from her own flute. Across the room, Eli was sliding a pile of chips toward Lady Eleanor. How high was he letting the bets run? "There may have been some initial disappointment, but Lady Kerr is very happy with Sir Thomas and Lieutenant Williams is back safe, so it all turned out well."

Why must everything be about Eli? Jane volunteered nothing else, and the conversation subsided for a long moment as she dealt everyone a second card.

"Has he found another sweetheart, do you know?"

Jane startled at the question, turning to Miss Anwar.

"I...I couldn't say."

It hadn't occurred to her. The period when he'd been presumed dead was entirely blank. He might have met someone else during that time.

Are there such things as lady pirates?

"I'm sure he has," Miss Anwar said knowingly, her voice dropping to a whisper. "Or soon will. A young officer with a heroic past. He'll have found himself an heiress before the season is out, unless he's one of those who's married to the sea." She pursed her lips, though it was difficult to say whether her displeasure was aimed at her cards or at gentlemen who failed to enter the state of matrimony.

Jane stole another glance at Eli as she turned up cards for those who requested them. He looked impossibly handsome, smiling at Lady Eleanor as he reshuffled the deck. Could he really just waltz back into town as though nothing were amiss and have beautiful heiresses fawning over him for it? Would she have fallen under his spell as easily as everyone else if it weren't for their history?

Jane had a sinking feeling she would have. Even now, she couldn't deny that he was charming, and handsome, and irritatingly likeable.

"Mrs. Muller." Jane turned to the lady on her left, struck by sudden inspiration. "Your husband is in the navy, isn't he? What does *he* think about the lieutenant's return?"

"Oh, the captain is off in Halifax," she replied. "Though I expect I'll hear his opinion on the matter in his next letter."

"Do you have any friends in town who were stationed in Greece around that time?" Jane persisted. She must know a number of naval officers. Surely someone could provide more information. "The lieutenant is far too modest to recount the tale properly himself, but I'm sure we would all love to hear more about his heroism."

"An excellent idea." Mrs. Muller smiled as she presented her hand, a natural, and won the round. "I'll see what I can find out."

Finally, she might regain the upper hand. And prove to Della and the others that Eli didn't deserve their admiration.

As the evening wore on, the champagne flutes emptied, the conversation grew boisterous, and the bets grew larger. The ladies were in such high spirits that it was nearing three in the morning when Jane finally called for an end to play, her purse seven pounds heavier. It was the most she'd made in a single night, though only a fraction of what she could do in time if they were to expand and set up more profitable games.

Her future premises would be large enough to hold tables for faro and baccarat, certainly. A room devoted to dice games such as hazard, if she had the space.

Even once Della's footmen began clearing away the cards and refreshments, their guests were slow to peel off from the group, lingering breathlessly over Eli before they went.

"Next Monday is canceled for Ascot," Della reminded everyone as they donned their cloaks and gloves. "We reconvene as usual the following week."

Without our unwelcome visitor.

He was lurking about, clearly hoping for a private word, but Jane slid into her cloak as soon as the entrance cleared out. Far safer to let Della deal with him.

"I'll see you to your carriage," he offered.

"There's no need." Free of their audience, she wasn't going to mince words.

But there *was* still an audience, for Della came rushing to his aid.

"I'm sure Jane only refused your kind offer because she's embarrassed to tell you she didn't bring a carriage. She's in the habit of walking home."

Traitor.

"You intend to walk?" He seemed unable to believe it. "It's three in the morning!"

"Thank you, Lieutenant, I can read the clock," Jane replied, struggling to rein in her exasperation.

"I'm sure she'd be grateful if you saw her back safely." Della pressed Eli's hat into his open hands, practically shoving them out the door. "Good night!"

"Please don't accompany me," Jane repeated as the door slammed shut. "There's really no need. I walk this path a dozen times a week."

"At three in the morning," he said again. "You can't possibly think I'll agree."

"You know it's only at the end of the street. You can already see our shrubbery from here, and no robbers appear to be hiding in it." She wouldn't have gone out alone at this hour if it were anywhere else, but the distance was so scant that it took more time to harness the horses than it did to arrive.

Eli sighed. Loudly. "You're being contrary for no reason again."

"I will own only the first half of that statement."

That silenced Eli for a long moment, though he still followed her, his footfalls far louder than her own in the still night. Jane tried not to notice anything about him, but it proved impossible. Even obscured in shadows, his tall, athletic frame took up all the space in her mind. Where she refused to look, her memory and imagination conspired against her to sketch his profile—the strong lines of his brow and nose softened by those rich, coffee-brown eyes. She caught glimpses of the stubble that roughened his jaw this long after his morning shave. It was no wonder her entire club had swooned over him.

In spite of herself, Jane *did* feel safer with Eli beside her.

"What do you do with your winnings?" he asked as they passed the third house on their path. Already halfway there. "Do they go toward your pin money, or are you saving up for something?"

"Who's to say we win much of anything?" It was too late to close Pandora's box, but she wouldn't grant Eli any more information than he already possessed. The less he knew about her club, the less influence he held over her. He had too much already. "Luck is fickle."

"Please give me some credit. You were never a gambler, and I doubt you'd have put so much time and effort into a card club if you weren't sure it would turn a profit."

It wasn't fair that he could read her so easily. Nor that he should remember such details about her life years after he'd walked out of it. Jane would far rather be a mystery. When he behaved as though he still knew her well, it made her long for the easy companionship that once linked them.

This was silly. She wasn't lonely when she had Della and her uncle and brother around. Why should she miss Eli's attention?

But there was something different about his company, and it wasn't only that he was so easy to look at. He listened in a way that no one else did, with a sympathy that said her triumphs and hardships were his own. He shared his light without even thinking of it. When Jane basked in the glow of his full attention, she felt as though she were the most interesting person in the room.

She had to fight this feeling. It had betrayed her once already.

"How mercenary you make me sound. I can do things for fun, on occasion." She struggled to keep her attention on the path before them, when it was tempting to seek out the invitation of his eyes. "But to answer your question, the money goes to my brother's bank account, at present. I hope to contribute something toward his studies at Oxford in the fall, if I'm able."

She would have preferred to hold the earnings in her own name, if only the banks would allow a woman to open an account. But with her choices limited to Edmund or Uncle Bertie, her brother was the safer bet. His assets weren't willed to Cecily.

"Don't you plan to reinvest any of it in your club? Miss Danby mentioned you were thinking of renting out rooms to start a more formal association next year."

Miss Danby talks too much, Jane reflected.

"If you already knew the answer, why ask me?"

"I only wanted to know what agreement you two have to divide things up. I've ten pounds five shillings in my pocket, and it seems wrong to keep it if you have an arrangement in place."

Ten pounds five shillings! For someone too concerned about robbery to let her walk home alone, Eli wasn't shy about announcing his wealth.

"Consider it yours now." Jane fought to keep the regret from her tone. Ten pounds was ten pounds, and it was money she could use. But she couldn't let Eli start doing her favors. It crossed a line. "Many of the ladies came to see you, so I suppose you've earned it."

Her uncle's house was next. He'd left a candle burning in the entrance for her as he always did, its light signaling the warmth of home through the windowpane.

"It belongs to you," Eli insisted. "I only came tonight to try and help. I won't have served any purpose if I take your money home with me."

They stopped walking as they reached her door.

"Go on," he said. "Think of it as an investment in your future business. It's a clever idea, to strike up something like White's and Brooks's for ladies. Half the aristocracy would be at your disposal. I'd be happy to support it."

"It wouldn't be like those," Jane replied before she could think better of it. She'd spent so much time running over the possibilities, with no one but Della to share her excitement, that the words tumbled out at the slightest provocation. "You can't apply the same rules to a ladies' club; we have to be far too careful about our reputations. If we let people make extravagant bets and ruin their families the way gentlemen do, we'll be shut down within a week. It would have to be more discreet, and more—"

Why was she talking about this? Why was she sharing her plans with Eli as though he could give her advice and encouragement?

She understood now what made Della abandon her promise not to invite him. What was it she'd said? *He took everything I said so seriously, not at all as if it was a girlish fancy, the way some men behave.*

It was easy to forget yourself when someone like Eli offered encouragement. Handsome, confident, intelligent—if he praised your ideas, they must be good. It was a heady feeling. Eli was plying her with reassurance, and she was imbibing too freely, likely to embarrass herself before the night was done.

"Never mind," Jane mumbled. "It's just a thought, at present. Probably nothing will even come of it."

And if something *did* come of it, she couldn't accept Eli's help. Even this—the knowledge that he had faith in her, that he could be her supporter—rebuilt a connection she was trying to snuff out. If Jane delighted in his praise, she would find herself wanting more from him.

"Don't say that," he began. "I'm interested—" But Jane interrupted before he could take the thought any further.

"Keep the money. Really. I don't need it."

"Jane." His shoulders fell a touch. He looked so downcast, she almost wanted to take back her words. Eli had always hated having someone angry with him. "I know it was Miss Danby's idea to invite me, but why not let me help? I'm not trying to be a nuisance. I only want to make amends."

What an impossible task. There was nothing to make amends for, by any objective measurement. They'd been friends, and then he'd proposed to her cousin. If Cecily and Uncle Bertie didn't harbor any resentment at the manner in which the proposal had come about, neither should she. It wasn't her concern who Eli lusted after. He certainly wasn't the only man to admire Cecily.

And yet, even as the matter was too trifling to warrant such pique, it was also too deep to ever be repaired. Maybe she simply had a bitter nature. Nothing else could explain why it still hurt.

"The best help you could give me would be not to tell anyone about the club. I haven't shared all the details with my family yet, and I don't want to attract attention until we're more established."

"Of course, but—"

"Thank you for seeing me home. Good night, Lieutenant." She turned and let herself in, keys at the ready, before he could make any further reply. She caught a glimpse of his face, the trace of hurt in his shadowed eyes, and then she was safely ensconced inside. With the door between them, Jane felt a good deal more sure of her resolve.

Seven

"I THINK IT MIGHT RAIN BEFORE WE GET TO EAT," HANNAH SAID, scanning the darkening sky. "We should ask the servants if they might hurry up a bit."

"Hush," her mother hissed, with a look to where Lady Kerr was descending from her carriage.

She spotted them on the roadside and walked over, a brilliant smile on her face. "How is everyone feeling? It's a beautiful view, isn't it?"

"It is, Lady Kerr," Mrs. Williams agreed quickly.

It was the day before Ascot, and they'd left London three hours ago, stopping only now to water the horses and set up their meal. Though it was twenty miles into their journey, Lady Kerr had been adamant that they should delay their picnic until they reached the Ankerwycke Yew, a popular attraction.

Now that it was before him, Eli had to admit the sight had been worth the wait. Its great and gnarled trunk resembled a dozen trees fused and twisted together, for it was over twenty feet around. It stood on high ground, and there was enough space amongst the surrounding greenery that one could see the river Thames below, meandering lazily in the sun.

Jane glanced his way as she descended from her family's clarence, but made no move to join them near the blankets the servants were spreading out before the yew's tangled branches. She turned her face deliberately away.

This was going to be a damnably awkward four days.

Though he'd crossed paths with Jane several times at society events, he'd managed to keep his distance since his ill-fated attendance at her gaming club, conscious of how unwelcome he was. That wasn't going to be possible while they slept under the same roof.

He let his gaze linger shamelessly on the curves of her figure, drinking up the sight, while her attention was turned away from him. His eyes wanted to linger on everything that was pleasing—those striking gray eyes, the rare smile she let transform her lips, the gentle slope of her hips. Why did he have to want what he couldn't have? It took constant effort not to stare.

"Lieutenant." Mr. Bishop's voice broke him out of his reverie, dangerously close to his side. *He's caught you ogling his niece.* Eli had just enough time to imagine the dressing down he might receive before Bishop continued. "I hope it isn't too late to give you these. I meant to catch you at home, but you were out when I called."

He pressed something into Eli's hands. The letters.

"Oh. Thank you. It's not too late at all; I'll send them to my solicitor once we're back in town."

"Don't hesitate to tell me if you think I should change anything. It's no trouble."

Behind them, the wet nurse had brought Lady Kerr's baby out for some air, and a circle of people was forming to coo while they awaited the picnic. With a little nod, Mr. Bishop went to join them, leaving Eli to read.

Jane's letter was on top, her neat, feminine script the only mark on the unlined sheet.

To the attention of the General Register, Somerset House

I have been asked to provide you with an account of my acquaintance with Lt. Eleazar Williams. I first met Lt. Williams in April 1833 while I was staying at Ashlow Park, Devon. He was at that time a neighbor. I have compared the appearance of Lt. Williams today with my memory, and they appear to me to be physically the same person.

I hope the foregoing will be of assistance.

Sincerely,
Miss Jane Bishop

Eli read it twice, trying to decide if it was intended as an insult, or if he was being oversensitive.

She hadn't wanted to write it; her uncle had volunteered her. He couldn't blame her for doing a rush job. But that last part: *they appear to me to be physically the same person.* How was he supposed to interpret that? That he wasn't the same person by some other measure?

The phrase seemed to invite the registrar to doubt him.

He turned to the second letter. It was a full page in length, in heavy, ordered handwriting. Mr. Bishop described his intimate acquaintance with Eli owing to his former engagement to Lady Kerr and a statement of his good character, followed by the circumstances of their meeting again in London last Thursday. It was in every way satisfactory.

It made Jane's letter look even more horrible by comparison.

With a flash of irritation, Eli slipped the pages into his breast pocket and glanced over at the rest of his party. They were all still caught up in the adoration of baby Tommy—all except for Jane, that is, who stood back from the others, wearing the expression of a woman thoroughly underwhelmed.

The servants had set out the blankets and dishes by now, and they soon turned to their feast. Lady Kerr had provided a cold roast, a leg of lamb, a pigeon pie, at least four types of sandwiches, a basket of salad, vinegars, sauces, cheese, stewed fruit and pastry biscuits to serve together, cold cabinet puddings in molds, a pound cake, lemonade, ginger beer, and tea. It was probably too much for nine people.

They sat down to eat in two neighboring clusters. Eli's parents took a spot next to the Kerrs, and Eli promptly steered himself toward the furthest possible point from them. Too late, he saw his mistake. He was near Jane and her family. She held herself stiffly in place at his arrival, not quite looking his way. When a footman began distributing plates, she snatched hers back the moment Eli reached out to accept the next one, as though the risk of brushing elbows was a mortal threat. *You'd think I was a leper.*

There was no reason it should be like this. Surely they could find a way to be friendly with one another in public, even if they were no longer confidants.

"Thank you again for the invitation." Eli addressed his gratitude in the direction of Mr. Bishop, but his eyes slipped to Jane. "I know you didn't plan to share your space with so many people, but we'll do our best not to step on any toes."

He'd hoped she might warm a bit to his peace offering, but she ignored him entirely, reaching for a walnut sandwich. "These look lovely."

So that was how it was to be. The faint lilac scent and the nearness of her were driving him to distraction, but she was made of stone.

He couldn't stand it. Irrationally, Eli wished nothing more than to provoke some reaction from her. Any reaction.

"You know what's lovely?" He turned to her uncle abruptly. "Your grandson, Mr. Bishop. I've never seen such a remarkable baby."

Her eyes narrowed a touch. Victory.

"Isn't he?" Bishop grinned widely. "Cecily tells me he almost said 'Mama' the other day. At only three months!"

Jane spoke so softly, the words appeared drawn out against her will. "How does one *almost* say 'Mama,' exactly?"

Eli talked over her as if he hadn't heard. "Is that exceptional? I don't know when babies are supposed to do things, I'm afraid."

"Oh, *most* exceptional. He's sure to be quite the little orator."

"Perhaps he has a future in Parliament."

Jane drew in a long breath, which made her breasts swell up above the confines of her corset. The gown she wore, a creamy yellow with golden lace at the neckline and sleeves, reminded him of butter toffee. He yearned for a taste.

Don't look at that. Eyes up.

She tilted her head in a slow, languid movement. "How did you like the letters we wrote for you?"

Point to Jane.

Eli twisted his wince into a smile. "Very well. I'm so grateful you found the time. I hope you didn't exert yourself overmuch on my account."

"Not overmuch."

"No, I thought not."

Mr. Bishop studied their exchange with a cautious eye.

As Jane continued, she seemed to address her musings to the greenery around them. "I keep thinking we probably aren't the best people to write about your absence, seeing as we have no firsthand knowledge of it. Do you suppose any of the navy men who were stationed in Greece at the time might be able to illuminate matters?" She fixed her attention back on Eli so suddenly it felt like a fencing thrust. "Strictly for the Registrar, of course. Perhaps we should help you ask around. I have several friends with naval connections."

Was that a threat? But to what end? They were already trapped together for the duration of the Ascot. Retreat was impossible.

"That won't be necessary, Miss Bishop," he said tightly. "You've already done more than enough to help. I would hate to see you trouble yourself any further."

"It would be no trouble at all." Jane took a long sip of her ginger beer, a trace of triumph in her eyes.

This was all a game to her. She had no idea how easily her inquiries might shatter his reputation and put Geórgios in danger. If his role helping Eli to escape were exposed, he'd be thrust directly into the navy's sights. But how was Eli to stop her? Controlling Jane was impossible, with her iron will.

She might destroy him, and there wasn't a thing he could do.

After a tense silence, Mr. Bishop braved the fray. "Tell me, Lieutenant, do you have any favorites for the races?"

"Hmm?" Eli struggled to follow the new thread of conversation, visions of a court-martial still clouding his mind. "I'm sorry, I'm afraid I've fallen out of touch with the racing circuits. All the names I recognized have retired now."

"Of course. How thoughtless of me!" Bishop was the picture of contrition. If only his niece had half as much concern for Eli's comfort.

"It's perfectly fine," Eli assured him.

"You're the very opposite of thoughtless, Uncle," Jane added with a barbed look to Eli. The implication was clear.

God help me. How will I endure four days of this?

By the end of the picnic, Jane was at her wits' end. Eli was deliberately antagonizing her; she was sure of it. Though she'd finally managed to silence him with her veiled threat to talk to his fellow navy men, his mere presence continued to vex her even after his words had died out.

She'd brushed fingers with him more than once as they passed plates and drinks around, formality dispensed with. Every contact set her nerves alight. The air carried his woodsy scent. His smile and his eyes drew her attention, even when he was talking to someone else.

Jane couldn't understand it. She was angry with Eli. She'd resolved to cut him from her thoughts. But her heart still raced when he was near.

"What time are Mr. and Mrs. Linden expecting us?" he asked.

"Around three or four o'clock," Cecily called back from her spot a few yards away. She must have been eavesdropping. "We've heaps of time."

"And it's Mr. and Miss," Jane corrected him. Though she'd been half-tempted to let him make an embarrassing blunder as punishment for his teasing, it wouldn't have been kind to the Lindens. "They're brother and sister, not husband and wife."

"Thank you." His gaze lingered on her for a fraction of a second before it flicked away. Even that was enough to make her skin prickle with awareness.

Stop, stop, stop. How would she get through this?

"Neither of them ever married?" Hannah asked.

"No," Cecily replied. "It's tragic, really, when one never manages to find a mate."

She cast a speaking glance toward Jane from across the mountain of sandwiches.

God, I could smack her.

The worst part about Cecily's little barbs was that they were always too subtle to be called out. A look here, a certain tone there. If Jane said anything, everyone would think *she* was the ill-tempered one.

"I'm sure they're very happy as they are, my dear," Uncle Bertie cut in smoothly. "Not everyone wants to marry. The Lindens enjoy their independence and get on well."

"You've been friends with the family for many years then?" Eli asked. He was doing it again. Listening with that keen attention that drew people out.

"Oh yes," Bertie replied, happy to bask in his glow. "We're old school chums, but we got back in touch about twelve years ago, after my wife passed away. The Lindens were a great help to me, raising Cecily without any woman in the house, and then Jane and Edmund as well. I daresay they're more like an uncle and aunt to the children than friends."

"I sometimes wonder if Papa shouldn't have made them proper family and married Miss Linden," Cecily said with a teasing smile.

Oh dear. Jane paused in the act of cutting her roast beef to watch her uncle's reaction.

Though he'd never said anything, Jane strongly suspected that if there were a romantic sentiment between Uncle Bertie and one of the Lindens, it was more likely to be the brother than the sister. Then again, she shouldn't presume knowledge of such a personal matter. If he wanted to confide in her, he would do so in his own time.

"Don't be silly, Cecily." Uncle Bertie laughed, but it came out stilted. "I'm far too old to remarry. All I want is to see my children happily settled."

He cast a warm glance to Jane and Edmund as he spoke. Cecily, watching them closely, forgot to put on her habitual smile when she replied, "I'm sure we can achieve it. This will *finally* be Jane's season."

"Thank you for your confidence," Jane said flatly. "But let's try to find a more engaging subject for our guests than my hypothetical marriage. Why don't you tell us what entertainments you have in store this week?"

She could always mine this topic when a distraction was needed, and today proved no exception. Cecily launched into a list of plans for her audience. If Jane hurried her meal, she might even escape before the subject exhausted itself. She devoured her selections in a manner that would've made Uncle Bertie scold her, had he been looking.

"I think I shall go for a walk around the priory ruins," she announced once she was down to clean china. "Would anyone like to come?" Eli's gaze was making her skin prickle again, so she quickly added, "Hannah?"

The girl rose to her feet and they walked arm in arm along the hillside toward the ruins, which stood nearby. No one else made to follow them, as most of the group were still picking at their desserts.

Saint Mary's Priory was once home to a group of Benedictine nuns, though it had fallen into disrepair since the dissolution of the monasteries. It must have been quite picturesque when it was still in use, standing as it did near the riverside. But over the years, the roof had given way to open sky and the ancient stonework had begun to crumble back into the earth or been reclaimed by local farmers. Jane was content to wander aimlessly around its perimeter with Hannah.

"How is your family faring?" she began. "It must have been such a shock, having your brother back after you thought him dead for so long."

Maybe it was only peevishness at how Eli had been antagonizing her earlier, but Jane was more sure than ever that he was hiding something about his absence. If she was going to be trapped with him for four days, she may as well see what she could uncover.

If the story about a pirate abduction was a hoax, he must have gotten word to his family during that time.

But Hannah dashed her suspicions against the rocks. "You have no idea!" she exclaimed, her dark eyes growing round. Like her brother, she had an expressive face. "We were all about to leave for church, and he just turned up on our doorstep. Mum fainted."

"He couldn't manage to get a letter to you first to warn you he was arriving?"

"It would have been hard for a letter to arrive before he did. He took the mail coach once he docked in England."

Hannah wasn't a liar. If she said he hadn't written, then he hadn't written. Perhaps he truly had been held prisoner. In which case, Jane was a terrible person for doubting it.

"Does he ever talk about his captivity?"

"Not really." Hannah shifted uncomfortably. "I don't want to pry. I think he's trying to forget it, poor fellow."

Poor fellow, indeed. Either Eli was an utter scoundrel who'd concocted the most elaborate ploy for attention she'd ever seen, or Jane was a bitter-hearted snoop for doubting him.

She wasn't sure which possibility she hoped for.

They walked in silence for a moment, Hannah taking in the view while Jane turned over this new information.

"How have you been enjoying your season?" Jane asked. "Is it your first?"

Hannah was seventeen, if memory served. An age where most girls were excessively preoccupied with their newfound access to society.

But Hannah seemed discouraged by this subject, hunching her shoulders and ducking her head as if to disappear. "No, I came out last year."

"And you haven't liked it?"

"All the gentlemen in London are horrid," Hannah explained. "Either they don't notice me at all, or they're unkind. I don't want to marry any of them. I wish we hadn't come to Ascot." She jumped slightly, as if startled by her own words. "Oh, I don't mean to be ungrateful! Your family had been very generous, it's only..."

"It's fine. I understand what you mean." The season could be unforgiving, especially to a girl just out, too green to have constructed any armor to protect her from petty slights like an empty dance card or an unkind word. Hannah had sparkling brown eyes and a warm smile like her brother, but the poor girl always seemed to be shrinking inward or tugging at her gown or shawl as if to hide herself. Looking at her, Jane was reminded of her own debut and how discouraging it had been not to receive an offer as her friends married off. On impulse, she said, "Don't let anyone make you feel obliged to be pleasing to people who don't please you."

Hannah's eyes widened at this. "My mother wants me to make a good impression on everyone. She's hoping that with all the invitations coming in for Eli, I'll secure a match this year."

Oh dear. She shouldn't undermine Mrs. Williams, but she hated to see a young girl thrust at a man for no better reason than to have her settled. Even if it was all too common.

"If that's what you want," Jane said delicately. "But you're still very young. It's important to be sure about such things. It's not a choice you can take back."

"I don't know that I'll ever be sure." Hannah scuffed the grass with her shoes as they walked. "Marriage only seems to make people miserable." They continued on in silence for a moment before

Hannah asked, "Is that why you haven't married yet? Because you aren't sure?"

"I suppose so," Jane replied. She had a sinking feeling she'd already proven a bad influence on Hannah. Probably best not to reveal her wicked plan to remain a spinster forever and run a ladies' gaming hell.

"That wasn't a very polite question, was it? Forgive me."

"No need." Jane gave Hannah's arm a reassuring squeeze. "I should like you to feel that you may speak plainly to me."

Jane had no desire to face Eli any sooner than strictly necessary, so she suggested they pick some wildflowers for the Lindens. They continued through the meadow until the yew tree and their families fell back beyond their line of sight.

A low rumble in the distance made the air hum, raising goose-bumps on Jane's arms. The women exchanged a look. Not ten seconds had passed when the sky darkened and cold droplets began to fall upon their upturned faces.

"Well I *told* Mother it might rain, didn't I?" Hannah sighed.

Eight

"Everyone get back inside the coaches," Lady Kerr called out. "Oh, my gown will be ruined."

"Where have Hannah and Miss Bishop gone?" Eli's mother squinted in the general direction of the priory.

"I'll fetch them," Eli offered. "You get inside where you'll be dry."

He snatched up one of the blankets they'd been using for the picnic as the servants raced to pack away the last few dishes. Though the priory wasn't far, the rain was coming down in earnest by the time he reached it. It had been a comfortable temperature all day, but the storm had turned the air chill again, and Eli shivered as droplets slid down his collar and back.

"Hello?" He made a quick circuit of the ruined walls, but only his own voice echoed back at him. "Jane! Hannah!"

Where the devil are they?

He pressed on toward the river, still running, though he had no idea if he was moving closer or farther from his prize. A great crack broke the sky, drowning out his calls.

A woman's shrieks filled the silence that followed the thunder, and he finally saw the ladies rushing toward him. By this point, the rain had formed a curtain over the earth that shrouded their forms in a blue-gray haze.

"Here!" he shouted, holding the blanket out for Hannah to use as an umbrella, for she reached him first. He should have brought a second blanket. Hannah snatched it up and flung it over her head without breaking stride, running back up the hill toward the priory. He pulled off his frock coat, already so wet that it clung stubbornly to his body, and draped it over Jane's shoulders as she drew near. Together, they turned and followed his sister.

By the time they reached the ruins, their clothes were so wet that it had become difficult to run. Jane's skirts were muddied and tangled about her legs, the crinolines bunching up and tripping her. Eli gripped her waist to prevent her falling, and she clung to his shoulder, the uneasiness between them giving way to necessity.

He pulled Jane under the first archway they reached, as it was thick enough to shelter them from the downpour. Hannah never stopped, and any words they might have tried to call out would be lost in the clatter of a thousand drops on stone. A moment later she was gone, presumably to the warmth and shelter of the carriages. Eli couldn't even see the yew through the sheet rain.

"It should pass soon." Eli was obliged to raise his voice to make himself heard. "Unless you'd rather press on to your clarence?"

"I don't think I can run any farther like this." Jane frowned at her ruined skirts, drawing his coat tighter around her shoulders as she shivered.

"We can wait out the rain here—"

Sweet merciful heaven.

Eli forgot whatever he'd been about to say, struck by the sight before him. Jane had leaned forward slightly to fuss with her skirts, and his coat had fallen open, revealing every detail of her form beneath.

When they'd set out this morning, her cotton gown had been a light, buttery yellow. Drenched as she was, the fabric was plastered to her like a second skin. The boning of her corset provided something of a barrier between her naked waist and Eli's view, but above that, her breasts were covered only by the gown itself and a chemisette beneath. Both were so light as to become practically transparent when soaked to this degree. The dark circles of her nipples were visible through the fabric. It was very, very close to seeing her half-naked.

His cock began to swell at the sight.

No. Unacceptable. Get yourself under control, man.

He tried to think of unpleasant things. Memorizing sonnets for his professor at Eton. That time he'd nearly been shot when some pressed men tried to escape the *Libertas*. The shipwreck.

It wasn't working. Probably because it was physically impossible to pull his eyes away from Jane's tits.

She took a deep breath as she tugged her skirts free of a spot of mud, straining her bodice tight against her chest.

To Eli's utter horror, a sound escaped him. It wasn't quite a moan, but something not far off. It certainly wasn't restrained.

Dear God, please say she didn't hear that.

The rainfall still roared around their ears. Maybe she hadn't noticed.

Jane stopped tugging at her skirts and looked directly at him.

$$\mathcal{J}\!\!\sim$$

What was that?

When Jane raised her eyes, the expression on Eli's face nearly stopped her heart. Something halfway between pain and hunger. He tore his gaze away immediately, turning so sharply to look out upon the hillside that he practically set his back to her.

She was so shocked by his reaction that it took her a moment to piece together what was happening.

Jane looked down at herself again, trying to see what Eli had. Her gown, once a light poplin, had transformed into gauze somewhere along their flight uphill.

Oh no.

She spun away, too humiliated to face him. Her heart was pounding in her ears, harder now than when they'd run from the rain.

Jane pulled Eli's frock coat tight across her chest, but it was a good five minutes too late for that. He must have seen everything. She might as well be nude. She wanted to run back down toward the riverbank and find a nice bog to sink into until she was never found again.

They passed several very long minutes this way, the silence punctuated by the rain and thunder.

Why hadn't she realized what would happen when this fabric got wet? If only she'd thought to hold Eli's coat shut, she would've been fine. He must have been appalled.

But then there was the matter of that moan he'd made.

It hadn't been the staccato pitch of shock or offense. Quite the contrary. It had been a low, aching noise. As if he were yearning for... something.

What, exactly? She wasn't sure, but she knew she could give it to him, if she chose to. Jane's heart began to race again.

That sound was for me.

She dared a glance over her shoulder. Eli stood rigid and tall, except for his head, which he was obliged to duck slightly under the low threshold of the archway. She could see the muscle in his jaw working from here.

She was imagining it, surely.

But she heard that moan again, echoing through her memory. She hadn't imagined that. It stirred a low, dangerous heat in her belly.

Me. He wants me.

At least right now, in this moment. She was the one who was beautiful. Desirable.

Eli cleared his throat, though he still didn't look at her as he broke the silence. "I'm sure it will stop soon. Rain that comes up this fast tends to clear fast."

His voice sounded strange. Too tight. He seemed to have forgotten that he'd already said something much like this when they first arrived.

"Yes. You're probably right."

Jane had a decision to make. She could pretend that she hadn't noticed the look on Eli's face before he'd turned away, or the way his breath had picked up speed. They could make strained conversation until the storm passed and then head back outside as if nothing were amiss. She would hold on to this memory afterward, perhaps pull it out from time to time and wonder what could have happened if things had been different.

Or she could do something very reckless.

No, not so reckless as all that, she reasoned quickly. Nothing that would have any lasting effect or divide her attention from her club. But she could allow herself a few minutes to explore this, couldn't she? It would be such a small risk.

How do other women do these things?

Had Cecily reached out and touched Eli, or had she merely invited him with her words and let him do the rest?

No, she wouldn't think of that now. This was her own time.

Jane released her hand from the coat, so that it fell open once more. She felt as exposed as if she really were naked.

It was no good. He wasn't even looking at her.

She took a step toward Eli. There was so little room in the archway, one step was all they needed to be practically touching. Her legs were trembling. She wasn't sure which was more frightening—the possibility that he might reject her, or that he might not.

He was as soaked as she was, the fine linen of his shirt clinging to the muscles and contours of his body. He looked every inch like a man in the service, driven hard by the demands of his ship and the struggle against the elements. More muscular than he'd been when he'd left England.

She reached up to rest a finger against the wet fabric plastered over his arm. One finger only, that was all she dared. Her throat had gone dry.

He jumped at her touch.

"What are you doing, Jane?" His voice was barely a whisper, but it made her tense.

"I—I'm not sure." No, that was all wrong. She should be confident. She forced herself to meet his gaze, and the hunger she found waiting in his eyes did a great deal to restore her nerve.

He wanted her. She wasn't wrong about this.

"I think I'm going to kiss you," she said. She had just enough time to watch Eli's eyes widen, and then she did it.

For a terrible second that seemed to hang in the air forever, he was frozen against her, unyielding. Then his lips parted, and suddenly he was coaxing and teasing her. Tracing her lower lip with the tip of his tongue, pulling her deeper. It happened so fast, she scarcely knew what to do. But the brush of his mouth on hers triggered an aching hunger. His hands clutched at her waist, twisting the fabric of the gown, as if in frustration. He made that sound again. Louder this time.

For me.

She didn't want it to stop. He surrounded her. His scent filled her lungs—something woodsy and green, but with an edge of salt that reminded her of the sea.

Jane rode high on the thrill of him. She wanted more. He was hers, finally. She wrapped her arms around his neck and grasped him tight, wriggling her body closer.

"Don't," he gasped, tearing his mouth free. "You shouldn't."

He'd braced his hand on her waist to keep some slight distance between their bodies. She yearned to breach it.

"Why not?"

"I—I don't want to shock you." Even as Eli said the words, his lips were parting, bending back toward hers, as if he couldn't stop himself from kissing her again. She leaned into it eagerly, and they gave and took in turns.

"I thought you were still angry with me," he murmured into her mouth, his confusion mixed up with lust.

Jane didn't answer. She didn't have time to examine that now. Whatever they were doing was too pressing.

By now the rainwater was no longer cold on their skin. They were both flushed, and the heat seemed to bind them. Jane pulled Eli toward her again, more firmly this time, and he finally relented, relaxing his grip enough to let them touch.

The bulge in his trousers pressed firmly against her, making her gasp. She'd been expecting something like this—Della had explained what happened when a man got aroused, after a very daring and educational encounter she'd had one night with a fellow in a closet at a fête. But Della had made it sound absurd and a bit amusing. She'd never said how *good* it would feel.

Jane arced her hips upward, craving more pressure. They were slick and hot where they touched, and he seemed to fit perfectly against her. Eli gripped her behind and pulled her tighter, moving his own hips in time with hers. He was rubbing his cock against her. It was so indecent she would never have imagined herself doing such a thing, but it felt so achingly good, she couldn't summon the presence of mind to stop.

Though their wet clothes (particularly Jane's skirts) were thick and clumsy, it made her long to try this after shedding a few layers. Was this what it felt like to go to bed with a man?

"Oh God." Eli moaned again, the sound far more urgent than when they'd begun. "Jane, stop. You have to stop."

"I like it," she gasped. "Just another minute, please." She was getting perilously close to the sort of release she'd only ever encountered in hesitant explorations at night in utter solitude. It was very different with another person. With Eli.

With a strangled noise, he wrenched free of their embrace and turned away again, gasping for breath. Her disappointment cut as keenly as a blade. He'd left her teetering on the edge. What was she supposed to do now?

She reached for him, but he shook his head. "I just...need to cool down a minute."

Before she could reply, he stepped out from the archway and into the rain.

"You've gone mad!" Jane shouted.

Eli grinned and cast his head back, water running over his profile and down his neck. The rain had already tapered off somewhat, though it was still enough to drench him, wet as he'd been. Watching him, Jane's breath caught in her throat. He was beautiful.

He stood there another few minutes until nothing fell from the sky but a fine mist. When he came back to her, he was shivering.

"You're going to catch a chill and be bedridden for the rest of the visit," she scolded.

"I'm a naval officer. I've been wet and cold before." Eli brushed her concern aside with a trace of amusement, but it couldn't stave off the question behind his eyes for long. "Does this mean you—"

Edmund's voice interrupted them, echoing from somewhere far beyond sight as he called Jane's name.

Eli craned his neck to assess the state of the path to the carriages. "It's half muck now. You'll never make it up in those." He motioned to her ruined skirts. "Let me carry you."

"What? You can't—"

Apparently he could, for Jane didn't even have time to complete her protest before he'd slid one hand beneath her shoulders and another beneath her knees, and hoisted her into his arms. She had little choice but to grip his neck to keep from sliding out of place, her mortification complete.

She couldn't bring herself to look Eli in the eyes while he had her in such a ridiculous state, so she fixed her attention somewhere around his jaw. A trace of dark stubble had appeared since they'd first set out this morning. Jane counted the hairs and tried not to notice the warmth of his chest. She was half-tempted to rest her head there and listen to his heartbeat.

Get ahold of yourself.

Whatever had come over her back there, it didn't make Eli her knight errant. He'd still chosen Cecily first, not her. Nothing could erase that.

But as his breath came faster as he carried her up the hill, Jane remembered the way he'd been breathing right before he'd moaned her name.

Oh God. Jane, stop. You have to stop.

She could have melted.

When they drew near the party, Edmund and two of the coachmen were waiting, every bit as soaked as she and Eli were.

"Has she fainted?" her brother hollered.

"Of course I haven't," Jane called back, insulted. She'd never fainted in her life. "My skirts got so muddy it was hard to walk back, that's all. You can put me down now, please."

Eli's arms tensed around her as if he intended to refuse, and her heart jumped into a panicked speed. But a second later, he set her safely back on earth.

Poor Edmund was white as a sheet and his teeth were chattering.

"What are you doing outside?" she asked him. "Why on earth didn't you get in the clarence?"

"Well someone had to calm the horses, didn't they? The thunder spooked them."

"We tried to tell him we had it under control, miss," said the first coachman, John. "But he wouldn't listen."

"Never mind, just go inside and dry off." Reason would be impossible where horses were involved.

Eli stepped forward and took his mount's reins from Edmund, who disappeared into the clarence.

"I...um...need to borrow your coat a bit longer."

"Yes, I should think you need it more than I do." He was obviously battling the urge to say more, but finally settled on: "Let's get moving so you can dry off before a hot fire."

"Won't you be cold riding in just your shirt? Let me get you a blanket, at least."

She fetched several from the servants' carriage, for Eli as well as the two coachmen who'd been out with the horses, then she took the last for herself and darted back inside to safety.

"Good heavens, Jane," her uncle exclaimed as she took the spot next to him on the bench. "You look like you survived Noah's flood. You'll catch your death!"

"I'm not the only one."

Edmund sat opposite, white and shivering from the rain.

"I don't know why you insisted on staying with the horses," Jane scolded. "You're the only one who *chose* to be drenched."

Edmund said nothing, growing lumpish beneath her scrutiny.

"Here." After a glance down to make sure Eli's coat still preserved her modesty, Jane handed the blanket off to her brother. "I've got Eli's morning coat. You should take it."

He must have been freezing, for he accepted the offer without any protest. Lately, he resisted Jane's attempts to fuss over him. He'd been so much easier when he was younger.

Uncle Bertie watched them with affection. "I do love when you two are kind to each other."

Edmund's only response was to roll his eyes.

The carriage lurched forward as they resumed their voyage. It was only another seven miles to Sunninghill, but the roads were now muddy and they had to stop partway when a wheel got stuck. The result was that Jane had plenty of time to sit and stew over what she'd just done. As they rode farther from the scene of her indiscretion, the spell that had held her and Eli hostage faded away, and the memory that remained seemed like utter lunacy.

Nine

AT FIRST, ELI WAS GRATEFUL FOR THE RAIN. IT HAD GIVEN HIM the most magnificent view of his life, and then done him the service of killing his cockstand (which would otherwise have made for a very uncomfortable ride). But by the time they reached the Lindens' house, Eli's gratitude was extinguished. He was cold, he was soggy, and he wanted nothing more than to get himself indoors.

The Lindens greeted their party with a great fuss for those who'd gotten wet, and Jane was immediately ushered from his sight toward a hot bath somewhere.

The house was a simple, cozy place with plaster walls painted in cheery shades of mostly cream, yellow, and blue. He and Edmund were sharing a narrow room at the end of the first story, as were the two girls. Both the married couples had only one room each. Only Mr. Bishop had a space to himself.

"We're terribly sorry," Miss Linden said as she showed him upstairs. She was a small, thin woman with graying hair and a high voice, who greatly resembled a sparrow. "I wish we could give you more privacy, Lieutenant. It's not a very large house."

"I'll be perfectly comfortable," he assured her. "It's kind of you to accommodate us on such short notice."

He was used to close quarters; his parents were the ones he worried about. Four days in the same bedroom would have them at each other's throats.

Eli let Edmund have the bath first, though his valet helped him strip off his wet things and get into a warm house robe while he waited. A maid brought his frock coat in, averting her eyes from his undressed state. Eli's attention lingered on the felicitous garment for a long time. He had the absurd urge to bury his face in it and inhale to see if it carried Jane's scent, but his valet spirited the whole pile of clothes away for cleaning before he could embarrass himself.

When it was his turn for the bathroom, Eli eased himself into the steaming, fresh water and relished the solitude.

His mind immediately returned to that kiss. Good Lord. He could hardly believe it had really happened. What had Jane been thinking?

She'd still been angry with him only an hour before. Something must have made her forgive him. More than forgive him. And if they could start afresh, how much more enjoyable would this trip prove?

He brought to mind the sight of her breasts through her gown, and his cock was hard again in an instant. He took himself in hand and began to stroke, a groan escaping as he did.

God, he needed this. He'd been going mad for the past hour, trying not to think of Jane's mouth against his, her hips rubbing against him shamelessly. She'd been so brazen. He never would have dared to hope for that. What else would she have done if they'd been alone in a proper bed instead of under open sky?

He imagined her slipping into the bath with him, easing herself onto his cock without any preamble, just as bold as she'd been amongst the ruins. He was so close already.

Eli rose from the water before he climaxed, gasping at the much-needed release.

Once he'd come back to himself, he felt better in every respect. He was clean, warm, clear-headed, and for the first time in two weeks, he felt hopeful. This time was no longer a trial. It was an opportunity. By the end, he would have mended things with Jane, and they would see exactly how far this newfound warmth extended.

Jo

Once she was cleaned up and dry again, Jane got ready for dinner. She hadn't brought her maid, as space was too limited, and Cecily had offered to share hers.

She should be grateful for the generous gesture. She was *meant* to be grateful, certainly. But watching stern-faced Biddy comb her chestnut hair out in the mirror, it was hard not to miss her own maid.

"What will you wear to dinner, miss?" Biddy opened the wardrobe where Jane's clothes had only just been hung.

"There should be a blue silk evening gown in there. The striped one, with a pleated yoke."

"Oh." Something in Biddy's tone hinted at disapproval as she pulled out the gown in question. It had been the height of fashion when Jane had it made for her debut season, though in retrospect, maybe she shouldn't have let the modiste talk her into so much lace. It was too late to do anything about it now; she couldn't afford to have new clothes made when the old ones were still serviceable.

"Don't you think it suits?"

On another night, Jane might not have let it bother her, but she was questioning everything this evening. Down felt like up, and up felt like down.

"Certainly, it suits, my lady," Biddy said, a bit too quickly. "Miss,

I mean. Beg pardon. I'm so used to saying my lady." She began the laborious task of getting Jane's corset and underskirts on, which took a good twenty minutes. It was only once Jane was finally in the gown and it was far too late to change course that Biddy added, "Though it's such a bright shade."

"What's wrong with bright?" Jane asked. Wasn't bright good?

"Nothin' t'all, miss. Lady Kerr has one very much like. It looks well on her, almost a perfect match to her eyes." She closed the last button, removing any chance for Jane to change her mind. "Alike as two sisters, you are. But different, all the same."

"Yes," Jane agreed, her voice flat. The differences in character, she was thoroughly grateful for. The differences in appearance, though... Jane sometimes wondered how the same face could make Cecily stunning, and her forgettable. It was probably something to do with her downturned lips. "Is my cousin wearing her blue gown tonight, do you know?"

"Not sure, miss." Biddy gave a broad shrug. "I'm to dress her soon as you're done wi' me. Shall I go ask?"

"No, thank you, Biddy." She didn't care what Cecily was wearing. Two ladies could both wear blue gowns in the same evening without anyone minding.

She shouldn't be fretting over her appearance, in any case. It was an intimate dinner. Only the Lindens and their party, this first night. Nothing had changed. Except that everything had.

Her face heated at the memory of how shameless she'd been. She was half-tempted to pretend that she was unwell, just to avoid facing Eli. How could she have convinced herself it was a harmless risk? She had to look him in the eye again, somehow.

Biddy watched her carefully as she curled her hair into ringlets. "We were awfully worried about you in the rain, miss. Are you feeling quite well now?"

"Very well. Thank you for asking."

"'Twas kind of Lieutenant Williams to go out to fetch you," she continued, pausing only to adjust a stray curl. "He was gone so long, we worried you'd both washed away in the Thames! Particularly when Miss Williams come back alone."

Jane swallowed. She had the uncomfortable suspicion that Biddy could see right through her, but she forced herself to reply. "Hannah had the only blanket. We had no choice but to take shelter in the priory ruins until the worst of the downpour passed."

Had Cecily sent her maid to sniff out gossip, or was she simply making conversation? In any event, Jane kept her mouth clamped firmly shut until her hair was done and she could send Biddy back to her mistress with a message of thanks.

Unfortunately, dinner was not so easy to navigate. To start with, she couldn't send Eli away if her composure started to slip. And it was impossible to make idle talk of the sort that was expected before they went in to dine. She found him waiting with the others in the drawing room when she came down, and her tongue fused to her jaw at the sight. He'd exchanged his wet clothes for proper evening attire—a white shirt and cravat with a black waist and tailcoat—and his jaw was freshly shaven. Even his hair was perfectly in order, not a strand out of place. Though he'd always worn it short, there was just enough to make gentle, dark waves that begged for the touch of her fingers. There was nothing so unusual about his appearance that it should have affected Jane greatly, and yet she was outmatched by the sight of him. She couldn't see him dressed up like a perfect gentleman without remembering how ungentlemanly he'd been only a few hours before.

She knew what was underneath all the polish. What was in her too. Something unspeakably exciting and dangerous. If she wasn't careful, it would break free again.

When they finally went in to dine, it was Eli who escorted her.

"You're quiet tonight," he murmured. Even the soft notes of his baritone set her nerves alight. She couldn't seem to relax her hand atop his forearm. "How are you feeling?"

"Perfectly well." Her voice came out tight. She said nothing more, but as Eli pulled her chair out for her, a stray finger brushed the back of her arm and drew goosebumps from her skin. She shivered, unable to stop herself.

Jane spent the meal trying to decide where to look, and finally concluded that no place was safe. Not Eli, clearly. She couldn't even set her eyes upon the lapels of his tailcoat without blushing up to her ears. His coat had been over her shoulders right before she'd seduced him. It had started the whole mess.

Well, not *that* coat, exactly. The frock coat from this morning had been fawn colored, and this was black evening wear. But her humiliation was such that it extended to include all of Eli's coats as a class.

Nor could she look at any of her family or the Lindens, for they were sure to detect in an instant what she'd done. It must be written plainly on her face for anyone who knew her.

She finally decided that the best course of action was to stare at her plate for the entire meal. Her spring lamb chop with mint sauce seemed unlikely to catch her out.

"We're so glad you all came," Mr. Linden said brightly. "It's been too long since your last visit."

"You're quite right," Bertie agreed with an apologetic smile. "But you know how busy the season gets for Cecily. We might visit again in the fall if you like, once things quiet down."

While chopping her meat into smaller and smaller portions, Jane alternated between elated highs and agonizing lows.

She was desirable. Adventurous. Eli had wanted her so badly he'd barely been able to contain himself. He'd touched her as if she were precious.

She was foolish. Wanton. She'd thrown herself at a man and left herself vulnerable to rumor or worse. She was so desperate for his regard that she'd debased herself without so much as an invitation.

"How was your picnic?" Miss Linden asked. "Aside from the rain, that is."

"I'm not satisfied with myself," Cecily sighed. "I forgot to tell cook to pack horseradish for the beef. It wasn't the same without it."

"Nonsense, Lady Kerr," Eli assured her. "Everything was perfect. And the view was stunning."

Jane nearly choked on her lamb.

"Yes, I do love that spot," Miss Linden agreed, oblivious to the fact that Jane was one careless word from suffocation. "Did you know it's where Henry VIII courted Anne Boleyn?"

"Not the most auspicious place then, is it?" Eli replied with a laugh. "Let's hope the yew brings better fortune to any other couples who steal an embrace in its shade."

Though he looked to Cecily and Sir Thomas as if his words were meant for them, he might as well have called Jane out by name. He was *teasing* her. In front of everyone!

Never mind that they wouldn't catch it. *She* knew what was meant.

She still couldn't bring herself to look across the table and meet Eli's gaze, lest she find amusement there. She almost tried, but her eyes snagged on the sight of his hands upon his knife and fork. Those hands had clutched at her as if he were a man drowning, and she was the last thing keeping him afloat. They'd twisted the fabric of her gown as if to tear it open. Finally, they'd cupped her rear and pulled her tight against his swelling—

No, she couldn't even think it. It was too indecent.

"Dear cousin, are you quite all right?" Cecily asked. "Your face has gone as red as a stewed tomato. I hope you've not caught a fever."

"Oh dear," Uncle Bertie joined in. "It's being out in the rain that's done it. I told you you'd catch your death."

They know.

Or if they didn't yet, they soon would. She couldn't possibly hide something of this magnitude. It took all her effort not to look straight at Eli, which would be sure to give her away.

Jane was so horrified, she couldn't even take offense at the comparison to a tomato.

Enough of this agony. She'd tried her best. It was time to exit with whatever dignity she could salvage.

"I—I am feeling a bit warm. I think I might be catching a cold."

"Straight to bed with you," Uncle Bertie ordered, as she'd known he would. "If you're to have any chance to get well, you need your rest."

"I'm very sorry," she said to their hosts. "It's a lovely meal."

"Not at all, my dear girl," said Mr. Linden. "Please go and rest. We'll send up some broth for you."

She rose from her chair and made her escape. It took some effort to walk when she would have run. She only breathed easy again once she made it to the safety of her room, surrounded by the familiar sight of damask wallpaper and the plush feather bed that was always hers when they stayed here.

What had ever possessed her to do such a thoughtless thing?

Jane collapsed onto the bed and buried her face in the pillow. No amount of pleasure could be worth this—the knowledge that she'd ruined herself with a man who was keeping secrets from her, and even worse, who saw her as his second choice.

For that's what she was: second. Even if she'd felt like she was first for that stolen bit of time in the priory ruins, it had ended, and now reality was back.

He wanted Cecily. He'd only shown an interest in Jane once the prettier cousin was married off.

Ten

Jane and Hannah took breakfast in their room the next morning, then dressed with care for the opening day of the races. Biddy was nowhere to be found, her mistress requiring her full attention for such a public event, so they took turns lacing up each other's corsets. Much like Jane, Hannah hadn't brought a maid of her own and had to share with her mother.

"What are you wearing?" Jane asked. "We may as well finish getting dressed."

Hannah selected a pink taffeta gown with too many flounces to count, and Jane wore an outfit in a thick, red-and-blue-checked serge that was sure never to become transparent, no matter how wet it got. The sky was clear, but she wasn't taking any chances.

She managed to avoid Eli completely in the general chaos of organizing eleven people for departure, breathing a sigh of relief once the door to the carriage was shut and they rolled away. Now she just had to keep doing this until Friday.

It was scarcely a quarter hour to the heath from the Lindens' house, though it took a little longer owing to the crowd. Jane and

Edmund pulled back the curtains on the carriage to peer at the new stand as they drew near. They approached from the rear, but even at this angle it was an impressive construction.

The grandstand towered over fifty feet in the air: three enormous tiers of white-columned pillars meant to resemble the amphitheaters of ancient Rome. The gentlemen and ladies descending from carriages in their finest clothes looked like ants in its shadow. Once they arrived and stepped inside the grand floor that served as a sort of drawing room for the structure, Jane could appreciate its full size.

It housed ten long rows of ascending benches with windows extending from floor to ceiling from which twelve hundred people were supposed to be able to view the races, as well as a sheltered promenade with refreshments, amusements, and retiring rooms for those more interested in viewing society than horses. The balcony above the grand floor extended the entire length of the building and held at least as many people as the lower level. In front of the building, a space of about fifty feet before the heath was reserved for the makeshift stalls of betting men and others who plied their trades here.

The final effect was a sea of color, noise, and movement.

"Our tickets are for the balcony," Cecily informed them. "We still have time to explore the promenade before we go up to see the Royal Procession."

The group splintered apart to take in the sights that pleased them most, and Jane quickly saw her dilemma. Cecily walked on her husband's arm, Mr. and Mrs. Williams followed suit (with a great deal less enthusiasm), and the Lindens claimed Uncle Bertie. Only Edmund and Eli were left to escort her and Hannah. She tried to grab her brother's arm first, but it was too late—he had already aligned himself by age over blood. *Drat.*

Was this how it would be the whole time? The two of them paired together despite her best efforts?

She slid her hand atop Eli's forearm reluctantly, remembering the last time they'd touched. He looked as handsome as ever this morning. His dark hair was combed back neatly, and he wore a blue shirt with a gold silk cravat knotted around his collar and a brown frock-coat overtop. Not the same one he'd worn at Ankerwycke yesterday.

"Did you sleep well?" he asked as they set out. In her charged mood, it didn't seem an innocuous question. She hadn't been able to settle last night, still dwelling on their kiss at the priory.

"Very well," she lied. "And you?"

"Fine."

She had goosebumps again. They were barely even touching. How could he exert this sort of effect over her? Her body was a traitor, yearning for pleasures she should know better than to want. If only it hadn't felt so *good*. If Eli had been a clumsy, pawing brute, she could've dismissed the incident as a single lapse in judgment. Conversely, if they'd been able to finish what they'd started, Jane might have found some release from the hold he exerted over her.

"Do you think that we might find a way to have a word in private sometime today?" he murmured.

"In private?" Jane echoed. She didn't dare press her luck. Private meetings could turn into forced proposals at the drop of a hat, as they both knew. "I don't believe there's any privacy to be found at Ascot."

"Back at the house then."

"We can't risk being caught together."

Why did he have to be so persistent?

She scanned the crowd for something to save her from this uncomfortable discussion, and found the perfect thing. A familiar, dark-haired young lady was sampling taffies at a stall near the edge of the crowd.

"Jane, you can't—"

"Della!" she called, heedless of how rude it was to shout. With a belated glance to Eli, Jane slipped her arm free. "Excuse me. I'll see you later."

Then she fled to safety.

Della would know what to do. Jane clutched her hand so tightly that surprise illuminated her round face.

"You cannot imagine how happy I am to see you."

"Is everything all right?"

"No," Jane admitted, her tone low. Della's sister was just a few steps down the promenade, and she was a notorious snoop. "I've done something terribly foolish, and I can't take it back, and now this visit has become a torture. You *must* let me come stay with you. I'll give you all my winnings from the vingt-et-un club if you only rescue me."

"What happened?"

"I can't tell you here."

Della shot an irritated glance over her shoulder to Annabelle, who was doing a passible impersonation of someone engrossed by the trinkets on display rather than straining to catch their every word. "Just whisper. She can't hear us from over there."

"I really can't," said Jane. She would've loved nothing more than to unburden herself to Della before the secret consumed her, but the risk was too great. If even one person should overhear how she'd compromised herself, it would be the end of her, at least socially.

"You can't tell me something like this, and then *not* tell me something like this," Della complained. "That's teasing."

"Very well." Perhaps there was a way to convey the information discreetly. "The very foolish thing I've done is similar in principle, if not in precise details, to something you once did."

Della's brow scrunched up even further than it had been, until it resembled a folding fan.

"You know I love puzzles, but I'm afraid I need you to narrow it down a bit. I've done more foolish things than you have."

With a nervous glance to either side, Jane whispered, "In a closet."

"*No.*" In spite of this protest, Della looked as though someone had presented her with a thousand pounds. "Is the individual in question who I think it is? I'm *so* proud of you."

"Of course it's who you think. Who else could it be?" Jane's face had gone completely red; she just knew it. She had to stop talking about Eli, or people would begin to stare. "Never mind that. I'll tell you everything later. For now, you have to help me get out of the Lindens' place."

"Why on earth would you want to leave?" Della's eyes clouded with worry as she added, "He didn't hurt you, did he?"

"No, of course not," Jane assured her quickly. "I was willing. That's the whole problem. I've been making some very rash decisions, and I'm worried I might continue to do so."

Perhaps more frightening than the threat of discovery was the loss of her own good sense.

"Wonderful." The joy had returned to Della's face. Couldn't she see that this was serious? "In that case, I'm afraid I can't help you. My greatest wish is that you should stay exactly where you are, see this through, and tell me all about it afterward. You could use an adventure."

"Adventure!" Jane repeated. "That's a fine word for it. You'll be sorry when I'm—" She cut herself off. She'd been about to say *When I'm ruined.* But no. Surely she had more self-control than that.

Della's eyebrows jumped so high they almost disappeared into her bonnet.

"Never mind," Jane muttered. "Forget I asked you for help."

"I shall," Della agreed happily. "Though if it's any consolation, I am *dying* of envy." Her eyes dancing with excitement, she mouthed, *He's gorgeous.*

Jane rolled her eyes and turned away from her friend to look out at the crowd. "I shall never forgive you for abandoning me like this."

"Yes, you shall." It was exactly the tone that the cat who'd been at the cream would use, if cats could talk. "Farewell for now. I must join my family, and I'm afraid you can't come because I don't want you using me to hide. We'll see you for dinner at the Lindens' tomorrow, and I'll expect to hear your report then."

With a jaunty little wave, Della left her on the promenade.

Things were very bad indeed.

Eli watched from a distance as Jane spoke with her friend, trying not to stare.

Had he done something wrong? He might've shocked her with his reaction at Ankerwycke, but he certainly hadn't taken advantage. She'd been the one who'd kissed him. She'd pulled him close. She'd given no hint that she changed her mind. He'd even had enough self-control to pull away before they went too far. Barely.

No, Eli hadn't erred. So why was she avoiding him?

He couldn't pass three more days this way. Knowing there was some problem, but not knowing how to fix it.

He forced himself to stop looking at Jane and turned instead to her brother. "Tell me, Edmund, who's favored to win the races today?"

"Bloomsbury for the Ascot Stakes," the boy replied immediately, all trace of his usual reserve gone. "He won at Epsom three weeks ago, and his dame foaled St. Giles as well."

Edmund went on like this for a few minutes. Eli tried to listen politely, but his attention slid back to Jane. She'd parted ways from Miss Danby, but before she could return to his side, she was intercepted by a well-dressed man of about twenty-five or thirty. He looked vaguely familiar, though he had the sort of face that could be mistaken for a hundred other men.

Isn't that the same fellow who came to call the morning after Lady Kerr's rout?

If Eli had been a hunting dog, the hackles on his neck would have risen.

He led their group in Jane's direction, though it took long enough to reach her that she'd had time to laugh twice (*twice!*) at something the gentleman had said.

"Here's my party," Jane announced as they drew near. "Mr. MacPherson, please allow me to present my friend, Miss Williams, and her brother, Lieutenant Williams."

"How do you do," Eli replied automatically, though inwardly he chafed at the introduction. Hannah's brother, she'd said. Not *her* friend. It seemed a deliberate snub.

"Not the Lieutenant Williams from the papers?" MacPherson drew back in surprise.

"Yes, the same," Eli confirmed with a sigh.

"I didn't realize you knew each other," MacPherson began, but caught himself a second later. "Oh, but that's right, you were engaged to Lady Kerr, weren't you?"

"I was."

"Terribly sorry about that. It must have been quite a shock for you to come back and find her married."

What an annoying man.

"Not really," Eli said flatly. "I was presumed dead for nearly two years. It was to be expected."

"Yes, I suppose a pretty young lady never stays unmarried for long." He cast a glance to Jane, presumably to include her in this category.

Where had this hanger-on even come from?

"Are you here with someone?" Eli asked. Maybe he could be encouraged to go back to them.

"Oh, just some chums from Eton. I consider my present company much more pleasing."

He was flirting with her. Right under Eli's nose.

Not that he could assert any claim over Jane. He wasn't her suitor. He'd been nothing at all to her until yesterday, and now he wasn't sure where he stood. But even so, if she had some other admirer waiting in the wings, she might've mentioned it. She hadn't kissed him like she was a woman with another attachment.

Then again, it shouldn't come as a surprise that someone else might see past Jane's occasionally stern exterior to find the virtues beneath. She was lovely, intelligent, and refreshingly straightforward. He couldn't be the only man who appreciated her worth.

Mr. MacPherson continued to smile at Jane, unaware of Eli's frustration. "Are you attending the Ashbys' *conversazione* this evening? The theme is to be the classics, I hear."

"No, we have a quiet supper planned at the Lindens' home tonight."

"How unfortunate for the rest of us! You always find something witty to say. Well, what about Thursday, then? Lord and Lady Pearson are having a ball after Ladies' Day. You mustn't disappoint me twice in one week."

"I believe we're attending that." Jane smiled. "Though Lady Kerr is the one maintaining our social calendar. I'll need to check with her."

Enough of this.

"Shall we go up to our seats?" Eli cut in, extending his arm to Jane. "It must be almost time for the procession. I'm sure your uncle and cousin are waiting on us."

In fact, Mr. Bishop was laughing over something with Mr. Linden a few feet ahead, while Lady Kerr held a necklace up to herself in a mirror. Neither of them looked particularly bothered over the time. No matter. They would be happy to go up once he suggested it.

MacPherson blinked in surprise. "Oh. Yes. I suppose we should all find our places. I'll see you later, Miss Bishop. I hope you enjoy the races." He lingered over his goodbye long enough that Eli made a point of looking at his watch and clearing his throat midway through.

Once they were finally rid of the man, they gathered up the others and climbed the stairs to the balcony.

"How do you know Mr. MacPherson?" Eli asked in what he hoped was a nonchalant tone as he led Jane up the first flight.

"He's simply a friend." She pursed her lips and offered no further insight on the subject, where a few more words might have been welcome. Something like, *I think of him as a brother I'm not fond of,* or, *Terrible shame about his festering syphilis.*

As they came out on the balcony, Jane clutched his arm tightly, pressing against his side. The unexpected contact made his blood pump a little faster, until he realized what had prompted it. The view from up here was a dizzying sight. No roof shielded spectators from the sky, nor did anything much in the way of rails or walls protect those on the upper- and outer-most levels from a fall.

That's right. She's afraid of heights.

"I've got you," Eli assured her, placing his hand atop hers for good measure. "There's my father near the middle. We won't be on the edge. Will you be all right?"

"I—of course." Jane looked up at him in surprise, a nervous laugh escaping her lips. "It's silly of me."

"Not at all," he murmured.

She continued to hold him tightly as they navigated the crowd to their seats, and then she released him all at once, pulling her hands back into her lap as though they'd never touched. Eli swallowed. He supposed it made him a bit of a bastard to have enjoyed the contact when it was born out of fear. But he couldn't help it after the way she'd kissed him. He could smell her scent again. Lilacs and something more essential that was only her. He wanted to bend his head down to rest on Jane's hair and inhale until she filled his lungs. And after that, he wanted to do several things that would require a good deal more privacy.

Instead, Eli waited until she stopped twisting her hands in her lap and some of the tension left the set of her shoulders. She seemed to have settled into her place and gotten over her nerves at being on the balcony now.

He leaned toward her ear and spoke in a low pitch that wouldn't carry in the hum of the crowd.

"I still intend to talk to you."

Jane tensed at the words. His voice was too inviting. It did things to her. Not to mention, she'd been clinging to Eli for dear life only a moment before. It was terribly inconvenient, her natural tendency to turn toward him when she should be pushing him away.

She replied a good deal more loudly than Eli had. "Certainly. Do you have any favorites for the races, Lieutenant?"

What a stupid question. She knew he didn't. They'd already talked about this. Her brain seemed to have stopped functioning.

"That's not what I meant, and you know it." The muscle in his jaw was working, which Jane found irrationally attractive.

She didn't reply.

Eli persisted in a whisper, without any regard for the crowd. "If you won't speak with me at the house, then I'll have to do it here. I only ask you to have the decency to put an end to my confusion. One minute you seem to hate me, the next you...don't. What are you playing at, Jane?"

"It's Miss Bishop," she hissed. No one seemed to have overheard them, but even so. Cecily flanked his other side, in conversation with her husband. What if she were to turn her attention back this way? "The procession is starting. You'll miss it."

Eli burned her with his gaze before he turned back toward the heath, where several landaus were rolling slowly out in parade before the eager crowd. The guard came first, followed by the royal kennel master with his hounds, the royal stable master, and all manner of other royal persons in the coterie, all very finely dressed.

Jane's thoughts were racing loud enough to swallow the murmurs that rose up from the stands. How was she to answer Eli?

I have no idea what I'm playing at. The feelings he provoked in her were very different from hatred, but in a strange way, they weren't different at all. When he hurt her, it stung fiercely. When she kissed him, it ached. Either way, it pierced straight through her.

The Queen passed below them, resplendent in her finery. Her dark hair was parted down the middle into ringlets, and she wore an elaborate gown of emerald green with silver lace and a matching silver hat. Jane couldn't see her jewels from here, only that she wore some, and they sparkled. Her mother sat beside her, looking out upon the crowd imperiously.

From somewhere several rows behind them, a lady's voice called out, "Mrs. Melbourne!"

It was clear enough to carry. The smattering of applause that had been building died off, replaced by a hiss, then another.

"Mrs. Melbourne!" A deeper voice picked up the taunt, though he was quickly shushed by a companion.

Eli twisted in his seat to find the source of the jeers before he turned back to Jane. "What's this about?"

From the other side of him, Cecily answered. "Not everyone approves of the amount of time our new queen spends with her prime minister."

"Is he still the prime minister?" put in Sir Thomas. "It's difficult to keep track these days. I thought Peel was going to form government."

Cecily patted her husband on the knee. "He didn't, darling."

"But that's ridiculous," said Eli. "She's barely more than a girl, and Melbourne must be at least sixty."

"Exactly." Cecily pressed her lips together in a knowing way. "Her Majesty should hurry up and take a husband. It would put a stop to speculation."

The poor thing. Even a queen couldn't escape the pressure to marry.

The procession reached their destination—the royal box which stood adjacent to the grandstand—without further incident. In another few minutes, the opening race would be underway.

Eli was silent while the standard was raised to signal Her Majesty's presence inside her box, but as the horses took their marks and the crowd began to cheer once more, he leaned toward her ear. The heat of his breath on her neck made her shudder. "I'm not asking you for much. Only don't toy with me, Miss Bishop."

There was no avoiding it. She was trapped here, at least while the horses ran their circuit.

"Fine, we'll talk." Perhaps they could do this in a secret language, as she had with Della. She tried to keep her voice light. "It was a lovely picnic, but I wouldn't expect to return to that spot. We've a very full schedule between now and Friday."

"But...you did enjoy the picnic?" Eli's voice was still pitched low enough to hum inside the core of her being. There was a compelling mix of eagerness and trepidation there. As if he both needed and feared to hear her reply.

It would have been too cruel to lie to him.

"I did," she admitted, her voice catching.

He sucked in a breath. "Good. So did I." Another breath, and then he added for good measure, "Very much."

"Nevertheless," she continued, "it was the sort of event one doesn't repeat."

"You're embarrassed." At Jane's stern look, he added softly, "About...your gown being ruined by the mud. But I don't think ill of you for it."

"I don't mind what you think of me," she said swiftly. This wouldn't pass for an innocent conversation any longer, but she couldn't let him believe she was hanging on the hopes of his affection, eager to lap up Cecily's scraps.

At least the horses were rounding the halfway mark, and the crowd was cheering for their favorites. Their words must be lost in the din.

"Well, I mind what *you* think," Eli admitted. "It pained me to lose your good opinion. I should like to earn it back."

"Earn it back?" she echoed. "How might you do that?"

"I was hoping you could tell me. Say what I might do to please you."

She was flushing again. There were certainly acceptable responses she could make to that request. She could tell him to introduce her to some connection she might like for her gambling club, or even to leave her alone forever. But the first thing that came to mind was the sensation of his arousal pressing urgently against her sex as she'd drawn perilously close to climax.

It couldn't happen again, but it *had* pleased her.

Maybe Della had a point. Jane couldn't trust Eli with her heart, but that didn't mean she couldn't enjoy a...what had she called it? An *adventure*. Something to give her a taste of passion before she settled into spinsterhood.

Just so long as she didn't do anything that could be found out.

Eli seemed to read her thoughts on her face, for his gaze fell to her lips, lingered long enough to make it clear he wanted to kiss her, and then slid lower, to her breasts. He was staring openly, though everyone around them watched the race.

When he dared to speak again, his voice was hesitant. "I haven't been able to stop thinking about the view from the priory."

It was her turn to suck in a breath. Were they really doing this? Here?

But she was every bit as incorrigible. Her nipples tightened into peaks beneath his stare. She wanted him to keep looking at her like she was a particularly delectable tart he planned to devour. And to keep talking this way.

So she encouraged him, her heart hammering in her chest. "Haven't you?"

He swallowed and sat a little straighter, as if his chair had suddenly grown uncomfortable. "No. In fact, it's almost the only thing I can think of. It's quite distracting. I don't know that I'll have peace unless I can set my eyes on it again."

His voice was rough. The sound was doing as much for her as his hands twisting at the fabric of her gown had yesterday.

"That's presumptuous," she retorted, "as I've just told you we won't be returning." But it was hard to keep Eli in check when she couldn't keep herself in check. A moment later, she added, "If we *did* have occasion to make the journey to Ankerwycke again...would you do anything differently?"

Jane couldn't bear to look at him while such a question escaped her lips, so she kept her gaze riveted straight ahead. But she could feel his eyes on her body, lingering on all the places he'd like to touch. She heated in response.

Eli didn't answer right away. For a long moment the air between them was filled only by the sound of his breathing, unnaturally quick. Finally, he spoke, measuring each word. "I think that if I were so fortunate as to have the opportunity for such an outing a second time, I should take particular care to ensure that my fellow visitors enjoyed their day thoroughly and saw every sight they wished to."

Oh my. Jane grew worried that she might finally know what it was to faint.

Suddenly people were cheering. Why were they cheering? Who'd won? She squinted at the horses on the track below, but it was too late.

"I think we've missed it," Jane remarked.

Eli cupped his hands over his mouth and shouted a very unconvincing, "Hurrah for Bloomsbury!" He was quite flushed, though she'd never seen him color before.

Beside him, Cecily rose to her feet. "We're going to go downstairs to find something to drink before the next one starts. Back in a moment."

She took Sir Thomas by the arm and disappeared. Jane realized she was thirsty as well. The lemonade the people in front of them were enjoying looked delicious.

"Shall we go down with the others?"

Eli shifted uncomfortably at this suggestion. "I can't," he said tightly.

"What do you mean?"

"I'm sure you can reason it out."

Jane bristled at his clipped tone, until understanding finally reached her. Her gaze fell immediately to Eli's lap, but he'd set his program in such a way as to shield himself from her view.

"Oh." She didn't quite know where to look. "How long does it take to...?" She couldn't believe she'd asked him that. She was learning all sorts of new things. This *was* an adventure. Della would be proud.

"Faster if we talk about something else. Or don't talk at all."

"Very well." Jane opted for the latter choice, as she didn't have the presence of mind to manage a normal conversation right now. Instead, she stared out over the heath and reflected on the occasional advantages of having been born without that sort of equipment.

Eleven

AFTER THE ASCOT STAKES THERE CAME SWEEPSTAKES, DERBY
stakes, Saint James palace stakes, and various other stakes that Eli
lost track of. He watched them all pass before his eyes with the sort of
polite attention one mustered for the long-winded stories of a kindly
relative: only the appearance of interest.

His thoughts were fixed on Jane and the way she'd been talking
to him. She hadn't said anything filthy. Not really. But the way she'd
been beckoning him on, her voice low and husky…

She'd *wanted* to hear what he'd like to do to her. Just as much as
he'd wanted to say it.

God, what he wouldn't give for an hour alone with her.

She sat beside him for the next two races, but he could barely
manage an intelligent remark. Every time he glanced over at her, his
eyes slid back down to her breasts of their own accord, no matter how
he tried to stop. His blood was pumping through his veins with the
sort of urgency he'd only known on deck when a storm was coming.
It wouldn't let him sit still. If he started talking again, he didn't think
he'd be able to cloak his language in their pretense anymore.

You're going to scare her off.

Jane had proven herself unbelievably bold since yesterday, but Eli couldn't quite forget how cold she'd been before then. If her feelings could change so quickly, how much faith could he put in them?

He was going to make some misstep. He could feel it. He was going to say the wrong thing or prove himself too eager, and then Jane would go right back to hating him, the door slammed shut on this brief interlude.

When the last race was done, everyone wandered back downstairs to the promenade, where the crowd had grown so thick they had no hope of reaching their carriage anytime soon. As Jane joined her cousin in conversation with some mutual friend, Eli found his parents. They stood on the edges of the group, turned away from one another. His father's face was pulled into a deep scowl, the lines of his face taking on the shape of crevices in stone after so many years spent in the same expression. His mother examined her hands with great interest, her eyes bright.

There was no point in asking what happened, for he already knew this story. It could be any number of things, and yet it was always the same thing. They were ill-matched, both in temperament and principles. It was as simple as that.

It could easily be his own fate, despite escaping a doomed marriage to Cecily with his flight to sea. Once, he'd believed he and Jane might be compatible enough to find happiness. Now, he wasn't so sure. Perhaps the memory of his betrayal would always hang between them, resentment poisoning the affection they could have shared.

What future can we have together, after that?

Eli turned to his sister. Perhaps she could provide a little distraction for everyone. "Hannah, how was your day?"

"Fine." She, too, stared glumly at nothing in particular.

"Did you like the races?"

Her puffed sleeves rustled and shifted as she shrugged.

"Is something the matter?"

"No."

Not very convincing. He might have pressed further, but the crowd had finally cleared enough that they could inch toward the exit. Eli took position near the head of their group, keeping an eye out for pickpockets as he led the way. They were nearly at their carriage when a gentleman stopped him.

"Lieutenant Williams?" He was about fifty, with graying hair and sad, watery eyes. His wife stood at his side, their arms linked together. Both of them looked a bit lost.

"Yes, sir?" Eli didn't recognize the pair.

"Oh, it *is* him. You see?" The woman squeezed her husband's forearm, a nervous smile flickering over her face for only a second before it vanished again.

"My name is Hugh Meredith, and this is Mrs. Meredith. I believe you served with our son, Owen, on the *Libertas.*"

Eli's heart sunk. He remembered Owen Meredith. He'd been a gunner with a hearty laugh and a quick temper. He'd also been one of the last onboard, alongside Eli, when the ship went down.

He knew what the Merediths were going to ask; it was written in the mixture of hope and desperation on their faces.

"We saw your story in the papers," Mrs. Meredith began, her voice wavering, "about how you were abducted when everyone thought you'd drowned. And we wondered..."

"I'm sorry, madam," Eli interrupted, not wanting to hear the words. "I didn't see any sign of your son after the wreck."

She swallowed, exchanging a look with her husband. "But if *you* made it out, and no one knew until now..."

"I'm sorry," Eli repeated gently. "I do wish I had something better to tell you."

She looked as though she might say more, but her husband took her by the shoulders and inched her away. "Come along, Ann. We have our answer." Mr. Meredith nodded to Eli as he withdrew. "Thank you, Lieutenant."

No one else said anything the rest of the way back, but Eli could feel their eyes on him the whole time, smothering him with the weight of their muted concern.

$$\mathcal{J}\kern-0.4em\sim$$

Eli washed and dressed for supper quickly once they returned to the Lindens', breathing a sigh of relief when he could dismiss his valet. Being alone felt easier than being around other people at the moment.

How many times would he have to discuss the shipwreck before the story exhausted itself? He couldn't shake the feeling he'd handed the Merediths the second-worst news of their lives. Broken their hope all over again. Would there be more like them, other families seeking some miracle for their drowned sons with that same, bleak look in their eyes?

Supper, he reminded himself, adjusting his cravat in the mirror. The Lindens had been gracious enough to host them. The least he could do was summon up some good humor and make polite conversation for the evening.

But when he strode out into the hall, a sound from behind Jane's door gave him pause. It sounded suspiciously like a lady's sobs.

Eli froze.

This was it. He'd known he would make a misstep. Jane had seemed to encourage his talk on the balcony, but he'd gone too far, and now she was terrorized.

Going in might make it worse, but he couldn't walk on as if he hadn't heard anything. He would try to apologize, if she allowed it. Eli rapped softly on the door, then pushed it open.

It wasn't Jane crying, but Hannah. She sat on her bed, her face red and blotchy.

"Oh!" She hastily wiped her cheeks. "You startled me."

"What's happened?" He crossed the threshold and shut the door behind him.

"Nothing. It's silly. Go back downstairs." She sniffed wetly. "I still need to change this awful dress before supper, and you'll make us both late."

"I'm sure it isn't silly if it's made you this upset."

Eli sat down on the bed next to Hannah and swung his arm around her shoulders. She'd only been twelve when he'd left England on the *Libertas*. He couldn't say that he knew much about her life now, who her closest friends were, how she enjoyed passing her time. But she would always be his little sister. It was his job to look out for her, and he'd clearly been remiss.

Distracted.

"You can tell me," he prodded. "I can keep a secret."

This was true in the extreme.

"It really is stupid." Hannah sniffed. "There...there were two gentlemen at the Ascot today whom I overheard talking about me. What they said...wasn't flattering."

"They weren't gentlemen, then," he observed darkly. "What did they say?"

"That I looked like an oversized flamingo in my frock." Hannah's lower lip began to quiver and another tear slipped out.

"That's cruel and entirely untrue. You look beautiful." The gown in question was a bright, sunny pink with an excessive amount of ruffles on it. Perhaps a bit loud, but that didn't give anyone the right to talk about his sister that way.

"My nose *is* too long. Everyone notices it."

"You look beautiful," Eli repeated firmly. "Who said this about you? I'll give him a sound thrashing."

A half smile played at Hannah's lips, though it didn't reach her eyes. "You can't go around hitting people. It's ungentlemanly."

"Then I shall challenge him to a duel and run him through with a rapier. A very gentlemanly way to exact revenge."

Hannah played along. "What if he killed you?"

"He couldn't possibly. I'm very good at swordplay. I've fought pirates, and I'm sure they're much stronger than this nameless oaf."

"I don't want you to make a fuss." But there was a spark of amusement in Hannah's eyes that contradicted her words. "No duels."

"No duels," he agreed. "And I promise the utmost discretion."

"Very well." Hannah bit her lip. "It was John MacPherson."

"The same MacPherson that was flirting with Jane half the morning?"

The bastard. He'd known there was something off about him.

Hannah looked startled, and he realized his mistake. He tried to set his features back into a detached sort of concern. "Miss Bishop, I should say."

"I don't know if they were flirting." She was still watching him a bit too closely as she spoke. "But he was talking to her earlier, yes."

"I see." They might be back to the possibility of a thrashing again.

Hannah seemed to read his thoughts, for she frowned. "What are you going to do? Now I wish I hadn't told you."

"Don't worry, don't worry," he said absently. "I'll just have a little talk with him."

It was one thing to flirt with Jane right under his nose, quite another to drive his sister to tears. MacPherson had made an enemy.

"You know…" Hannah hesitated for a long moment, then finally pressed on. "You shouldn't be minding who Jane flirts with. She doesn't like you anymore."

Eli winced.

"Thank you, Hannah. I've gathered."

"You could try apologizing to her."

"I'm the one helping you with *your* problem," he reminded her. "Let's not upend things." Eli withdrew his arm and rose to his feet, bending to kiss his sister atop her head. "And I have tried apologizing. It's not so simple."

"You really shouldn't have proposed to Cecily."

Eli froze in his path to the door.

He hadn't confided his feelings to anyone. It was too much of a mess to sort out. And besides, who would he tell? No one could know that he'd only proposed to Cecily because he'd compromised her, unless he wanted to shatter her reputation.

But Hannah stared right through him. Well, she always had been a clever child.

"No," he agreed with a sigh. "I shouldn't have. But one can't take back the past."

"Did everyone enjoy the opening day?" asked Mr. Linden over their meal that evening. The cook had prepared an impressive array of spring greens and small carrots, roast chestnuts, bread and butter, a joint of beef, chicken, poached eels, and several cheeses. "Are you feeling better now, Jane? You looked well this morning."

"I'm much better," she assured him. "It was a lovely day."

She was able to make conversation without blushing or stammering, which was a marked improvement over last night. She could even look at Eli for short periods of time, so long as she didn't let herself linger.

When she lingered, her thoughts grew confusing. She recalled the way she'd had him trapped on the balcony this morning, the thrill it had given her to reduce him to helplessness without lifting a finger. It made her long for a moment alone with him. But then she thought of what had happened later— the look of grief on Eli's face when that young man's parents had found him—and all she wanted to do was take him into her arms and help shoulder the burdens he carried.

Pure foolishness. If she let her passions run away with her, it would only end in heartbreak. Eli would return to a dangerous life at sea, just as he had before, and she would be left to wonder what became of him.

She'd already known the pain of losing her parents. She wouldn't chase after a man whose safety could never be assured.

"I'd still feel better if you go straight to bed after the meal." Uncle Bertie looked at her so gravely she felt a touch of guilt at deceiving him the night before. Turning to Mr. Linden, he added, "That's how my poor brother passed, you know. Took a chill one morning, and within a few days he and his wife were gone."

"Our parents caught typhus, Uncle Bertie," Jane reminded him.

"It started with a chill, though."

"Do you know what I was thinking?" Mr. Linden had a certain talent for keeping the subject on its proper course. "It might be nice to go to Bath again. It was so healthful. Do you remember that summer that you and Cecily came along with Doris and me? How long has it been now?"

"Seven years," answered Eli. Everyone looked at him. "That was the summer Miss Bishop and Edmund came to stay at Ashlow Park and we first made their acquaintance."

Well. He remembered.

Does he think back on it fondly, or with regret? Jane couldn't recall the early days of their friendship without a touch of embarrassment over the way she'd clung to Eli. She'd been like a lost puppy, using any excuse to trail after him. But if Eli had found it tedious to spend his entire summer with a sixteen-year-old girl, he'd been too kind to give any sign.

"Seven years," Mr. Linden echoed. "I'd say a return visit is in order. What if we dashed down for a week or two after Ascot? What do you say, Bishop? Would you like to come along and take the waters with us?"

Bertie hesitated, with a regretful look to Jane and Edmund.

"You needn't worry about us," Jane assured him. "I can manage our social calendar for a little while if you'd like to go." It would probably do him good to have some time alone with the Lindens.

But Cecily jumped in before her father could reply, her voice crisp. "How could you manage the social calendar when you haven't asked what I have planned? We're already promised at half a dozen events in June, and Papa was supposed to sit with us for our family portrait on the fourteenth."

The disappointment in Mr. Linden's eyes was quickly concealed, but Jane had seen it.

"Perhaps later," Bertie agreed with his daughter, an apology written in his smile. "Once the season is ended."

"Of course." Mr. Linden returned his attention to the greens on his plate and was a bit quieter for the rest of the meal.

After they'd had their dessert of cherries and cream, and the men had retired to smoke for a short time and discuss whatever it was they discussed when no ladies were in earshot, they all reconvened in the drawing room.

Cecily hopped down on the divan in the center of their circle. "What game shall we play?"

"Play?" Jane inclined her head. "We could simply talk."

"Games give one something interesting to talk *about*. Be a bit more diverting."

More diverting, indeed. She was half-tempted to tell them all what she'd been up to these past two days with Eli. No one would think her dull then.

On the other hand, she'd be forced to marry him, and Cecily would spend the rest of her days reminding her that no one liked an encore as much as the original show. No, that wouldn't do. The most diverting thing she'd ever done would have to remain a secret from all but Della.

"Let's play something for forfeits," Cecily continued.

Jane suppressed a groan. Not forfeits. They were Cecily's favorite, almost certainly because she could always find a way to put all the attention on herself.

"Isn't that more appropriate for a different set?" she tried.

"Jane *disapproves* of forfeits," Cecily said too loudly. "She thinks they're just an excuse for everyone to kiss."

"She isn't wrong, though, is she?" observed Mr. Linden with a chuckle.

Jane favored him with a smile. *Dear Mr. Linden.*

"They aren't *always* about kissing," Cecily protested. "We can make them whatever we want. Don't be such a wet blanket, Jane."

Again with this insult. She itched to teach Cecily a lesson. Something to put her in her place.

"Very well," she relented. "Let's play for forfeits. The game will be vingt-et-un."

That would show her. In a few hands, she'd have beaten Cecily and would have the right to make her do whatever she wanted.

Not speaking for the rest of the visit, perhaps. Or dunking her head in a cold basin.

But Cecily merely arched an eyebrow. "I suppose you think you'll have an advantage over us, what with all the practice you get at your club."

She cast Jane a haughty look before turning her attention toward her father. Her intentions were clear—she'd never been able to pass up a chance to tattle to Uncle Bertie.

Jane was too shocked to utter a word. *How could she have found out?* She and Della were careful never to talk about their work openly.

"What club?" Bertie pressed, looking from his niece to his daughter. "What do you mean?"

"It's nothing, Uncle." Jane tried to stave off the disaster that Cecily had brought down upon her head. "You know I play cards with a few friends on Monday evenings—"

"Friends like Lady Eleanor Grosvenor?" Cecily cut in, undeterred. "I hear she lost four pounds last week. It seems you and Miss Danby don't limit your guests to penny wagers."

"Is this true?" asked Hannah. "How exciting! Jane, why didn't you say? May I come?"

"You may not!" her mother replied, looking scandalized. "Losing four pounds in a single night? That's not the sort of behavior gentlemen look for in a wife, Hannah."

This censure from a respectable matron of the ton struck the final nail in Jane's coffin. Uncle Bertie assumed a frown, so unpracticed that it looked like it had wandered there from some sterner man's face by mistake. "I'm surprised at you, Jane. People can lose entire fortunes gambling. You know better than to risk your future this way."

Horrid Cecily.

"It's not really gambling, Uncle. If you adopt a consistent strategy based on the odds, you'll always win over a long enough string of hands."

Bertie clucked his tongue. "*All* gamblers think they'll win, though, don't they? We shall speak on this more in private, mark my words. For now, let's try to enjoy our evening."

What did that mean? He couldn't forbid her to play, could he? If only she could have broken the news on her own terms, with detailed records of her winnings to prove just how thoroughly she'd tuned their betting strategy to maximize profits. But she'd lost her chance to present things in the right light, and there might be no repairing the damage.

Everyone had grown uncomfortable at the exchange except for Cecily, who seemed perfectly satisfied with the results of her revelation. She wore a bright smile as she asked, "Shall we still play then? I'd love to experience your card club firsthand."

"I can't wait," Jane agreed. Forget making Cecily dunk her head in a cold basin. When she won her forfeit, she would make her cousin pack up her things and return to London this very night.

"I'll join," said Eli. A spark of mischief lit the deep brown of his eyes with amber hues. His lips looked ready to jump into a wicked grin.

Perhaps this hadn't been such a good idea. If she lost to Eli, she would have to do whatever he wanted. Might he be tempted to misuse the opportunity?

Then again, if Jane won, she could force him to tell her everything about his disappearance. *That certainly justifies a little risk, especially when I have more practice than him.*

Very well. She would just have to play her best and hope she didn't regret it. They'd see soon enough what it brought.

Twelve

ELI HELPED THE LINDENS PULL A CARD TABLE TO THE CENTER of the room and set the chairs around it, his blood humming. They were four players—himself, Jane, Lady Kerr, and Hannah.

He wasn't worried about losing to Jane. She might have acquired some skill at her club, but skill wasn't enough.

Jane didn't possess a card face. He could always tell when she was angry or worried about something. Even when she was trying to appear indifferent to him, there was an undercurrent of annoyance or, more recently, attraction.

He'd know when she was bluffing, and by the end of the evening, she would owe him a forfeit.

He didn't know what he would use it for, but the temptations were many.

Cecily brought the stationary and pencils out. "Everyone shall write three notes with their name on it, which they may bet. If you win someone's note, they owe you a forfeit, which you may keep or bet again in the next hand if you don't want it. We shall play until everyone has a chance to deal, or until we're out of forfeits, whichever comes first."

Three chances to get Jane's name. He could do this. Eli scrawled his own down with a rushed hand and placed his notes before him.

"Agreed." Jane set her hand upon the deck. "Let's begin."

"Ah-ah-ah, dear cousin. Dealer has quite an advantage. We'll cut for it."

They cut, and Cecily won. She dealt out two cards to each player, then turned to Hannah, who sat to her left. "Would you like another card, darling?"

"That isn't how the game works," Jane interrupted. "You were supposed to deal *one* card, then everyone places their stakes and dealer can double, then the second card is dealt. You're doing everything out of order."

"Well, that isn't going to work unless we write out more forfeits. I can't very well double the stakes when we only have three tokens apiece. Let's just play this way."

"Fine. We can do away with doubling stakes, if you like, but you still have to place your wager *before* you can deal additional cards." Jane wore an expression of long-suffering impatience. "The game doesn't work otherwise."

Eli glanced at his cards. He had a ten and a three.

Everyone wagered a single note, and Cecily turned to Jane once the stakes were placed. "*Now* can I deal the extra cards?"

"Yes, Cecily."

"Does anything special happen if the dealer has a natural, though?"

Damn. There went his hopes for this hand.

"The dealer isn't supposed to *tell* us if she has a natural until the end." Jane spoke through gritted teeth.

"I haven't told you anything. It was only a question."

Cecily dealt out the cards to those who asked for them—which was everyone, for they had nothing to lose now that she'd let slip she was already at twenty-one. No one managed to tie, and Cecily collected her winnings with a squeal of glee and passed the remainder of the deck to Hannah.

Jane buried her face in her hands.

Hannah dealt with a good deal less chatter, though she paused at the end to murmur to Jane, "I would make an excellent dealer at your club, I should think," in a longing tone. Everyone wagered a single note again, save Cecily, who passed the round.

One of Jane's notes already gone, and the second before him on the table. Eli wished they'd written more. At this rate, it wouldn't be his turn to deal before Jane was out of forfeits. Eli beat Hannah and took her second forfeit, though Jane overdrew and had to relinquish hers.

The deal passed to Jane.

She dealt out the cards with efficiency, glancing at her hand before they all put in their stakes.

"Pass," said Cecily.

"You've passed the last hand as well." Jane frowned. "What are you doing?"

"I won a forfeit from everyone and I haven't lost any of my own. What else could I want? I won't bid unless I get a natural again."

"You can't *do* that." Jane's pique was such that she'd raised her voice. "If you're playing the game, you have to play the game."

"I'll retire then, if you like."

"No, that's not—"

But it was too late. Cecily pushed her cards back toward the center of the table, gathered up her winnings, and went to sit on the divan beside her husband.

Jane stared after her, a vein at her temple throbbing. She was bewitching when she was murderously angry.

"I believe it's still your deal, Miss Bishop," Eli reminded her.

"Very well," Jane snapped. "Lieutenant, another card?"

He'd thought he would be able to read Jane's hand upon her face, but he couldn't. She was angry at her cousin for leaving the table. There was no clue there as to how she might rank against him. Whether he should take or stand. Perhaps she wasn't so easy to read as he'd thought.

"Content," he said, though he was not.

Jane drew, then turned her cards up. Twenty, besting both him and Hannah. *Damn.* This wasn't going nearly so well as he'd hoped.

Eli tried to slide the forfeit he'd earned from Hannah across the table, but Jane brought her hand down to halt his progress.

"That's the one Hannah gave you. You should only be able to wager your own, or the game might never end."

"We didn't agree to that before we started," Eli protested. But the pressure of Jane's grip upon his wrist told him she wouldn't back down easily.

She has plans for my forfeit.

After the way she'd kissed him at Ankerwyck and their conversation this morning, what might Jane do if she could have anything from him? Her cheeks were flushed, her eyes bright—she had the look of a huntress in pursuit of her prize. How could he turn down the chance to be at her mercy when she looked at him that way?

"Very well then." Eli reclaimed Hannah's forfeit and passed Jane one of his own in its stead.

"If that's how we're playing, I suppose I'm out." Hannah looked crestfallen as she turned over her final forfeit. "But be kind to me when you cash in, Jane, for I still have one of yours if I need to seek revenge."

It was Eli's deal. In spite of every eye upon them, their game seemed suddenly intimate, with only the two of them left at the table. The rasp of the cards in his palm mingled with the rise and fall of

Jane's breath. He dealt her two cards, then hazarded a look at his own. An ace and a seven. This was his best chance to claim a forfeit from her.

Eli slid the last paper with his name on it into the center of the table. "You won't pass on the last hand, I trust?"

Jane straightened in her seat, venturing a sideward glance toward her cousin. "Of course not. I committed to play, and I won't turn tail and run." She slid her own forfeit out to touch his.

"Would you like another card?" Eli studied Jane, studying him. It was a strange feeling, to find himself reflected in her scrutiny, reaching for the same goal. The air seemed to hum between them.

"If you please." Jane let out a breath as he turned up a jack, and some of her spirit seemed to leave with it. *Most promising.* "Yourself?"

"I stand." Eli revealed his hand.

Jane turned over her cards to reveal thirteen in her hand, plus the jack before her. "I've overdrawn."

It was all Eli could do not to whoop with delight as he scooped up her forfeit. Instead, he settled for a very restrained, "Thank you for the game, Miss Bishop."

He would make excellent use of this.

ϑ

"Well! It looks like I won more forfeits than any of you," Cecily observed, as if they were all unable to count. "I thought you were meant to be good at cards, Jane."

"For the last time, it's based on probabilities. You need more than four hands to—oh, never mind." Jane abandoned her explanation in favor of a good glare. There was no point in trying—Cecily's education had included more pianoforte than maths.

"Stop frowning!" snapped Uncle Bertie.

Cecily drew herself up in her seat. "Anyway, let's cry the forfeits."

Eli cast an uncomfortable look to the stack of papers before her. "It's getting late. Perhaps we should do that another evening."

"Yes," Jane added swiftly. "It seems we'll have to save them." She was more likely to get the full story out of Eli if she used his forfeit when they were alone. Though she might have to reckon with the forfeit she'd lost to him, it would be worth it if she finally learned the truth.

"I shall use mine, at least." Undeterred, Cecily began unfolding papers until she came to the one she wanted. "Eli."

Oh dear. This was sure to be dreadful. And it was her own fault for encouraging play. Why did she keep making such reckless decisions? It wasn't like her at all.

Eli didn't seem any happier about the prospect than she was. "Nothing excessive, please."

"For shame, Lieutenant," Cecily replied with a gay laugh. "An officer crying mercy before the battle has even started? I cannot believe it." She paused for a long moment and folded her hands upon her chin. Probably for effect. "I have it. You must kiss the lady in the room that you admire the most, without any of the others knowing who it is."

Eli groaned. "I've heard this one before. It's not terribly original."

Jane hadn't heard it before, and her heart began to race. Was Eli going to kiss her, or someone else? And either way, how would he do it this evening without anyone knowing?

"My dear Cecily," said Uncle Bertie reproachfully. "You are only proving Jane's point that forfeits are always about kissing."

Cecily pouted at his criticism, but gave no quarter.

"As you wish. But I'll have that back first." Eli stood and plucked the paper from her fingers and tossed it toward the fireplace with a certain gusto. "Now. Would you all please do me the service of closing your eyes?"

"We shall not," Cecily replied immediately. "You aren't entitled to any assistance from the audience."

He shot her a dark look. "I see you're determined to make me kiss everyone then."

Oh, of course. Not that this was any better, really. They were going to have to kiss in front of the entire room.

"Well, only the ladies," said Cecily. "And on the *lips*, if you please."

"I'm related to half the ladies."

"Excepting those."

Eli seemed to contemplate a moment before turning to Miss Linden.

"I'm terribly sorry about this, madam," he said with particular gallantry. "But you can see that I have no choice in the matter."

"Oh, you're forgiven, Lieutenant." Miss Linden laughed, though she was blushing to the roots of her hair. "When I tell all my friends I've been kissed by a dashing officer, I believe I'll leave out the part where it was in a game of forfeits."

Eli dropped down to one knee and brushed his lips lightly over Miss Linden's, who struggled not to laugh.

It was down to her and Cecily.

Eli looked at Jane for a second, and she felt his selection like a current of energy. She stood up as he crossed the floor, not wanting him to have to kneel at her feet as he had for Miss Linden.

"My apologies for this, Miss Bishop," he said softly. She didn't know where to look, so she fixed her gaze on Eli's chin.

He leaned in slowly. Too slowly. Had it taken this long for him to kiss Miss Linden? Though she tried her best not to move, she tilted her head back in spite of herself.

It was a chaste kiss, very different from the one they'd shared before. He didn't coax her lips apart with his tongue or clutch at her gown now. It was only the barest touch of his mouth upon hers.

She knew a hint of his taste and warmth—enough to make her long desperately for more—and then it was over. She held herself rigid, hoping it wasn't obvious how badly his touch affected her.

Once he withdrew, there was nothing left but to watch Eli kiss Cecily.

She would have liked very much to look away, but a self-punishing compulsion held her gaze steady. Eli completed the task in good time, kneeling down at Cecily's feet (of course she would enjoy that part) to peck her lightly and retreat to his place again, the forfeit finally complete.

Cecily looked thoroughly pleased with herself. "Well, now you've kissed the one you admire the most, whomever she may be."

It was clear from her tone that she was confident of the lady's identity.

Cecily set her sights on Hannah next, who was forced to perform what turned out to be a very passible impersonation of Lord Melbourne, to general amusement. As their laughter died off, more than one guest hid a yawn behind their hands. It was nearing midnight, and Uncle Bertie called for an end to the evening. "We have another full day tomorrow."

Jane was happy to oblige. But as she withdrew from the room, she couldn't help but think about the one paper Cecily hadn't used yet, with her own name written upon it. Not to mention Eli, whose stack remained untouched.

Those would be waiting for her on another night. Hopefully her creditors would be merciful.

Thirteen

ELI COULDN'T FIND SLEEP THAT NIGHT. WITHOUT ANYTHING to distract him, he fell quickly back into memories of his encounter with the Merediths, their faces pleading with him every time he closed his eyes. The rise and fall of Edmund's breath from across the room made him feel like an intruder. He didn't belong here, surrounded by people so at ease in their own lives.

He padded out into the hall and down the stairs to the ground floor of the Lindens' house, the creaking floorboards his only company. He might have walked the grounds to tire himself out, but the low rumble of thunder spoke of rain to come. He settled on the library instead.

But when he arrived, he found it already occupied. Jane was curled up in an armchair, a book on her lap, lit by the soft glow of an oil lamp.

"Oh!" She gave an indelicate squawk when she spotted Eli.

"I didn't mean to disturb you. I couldn't sleep."

Jane didn't reply, her eyes wary. Eli was suddenly conscious of the position they were in. Alone together, in the middle of the night, in a state of undress.

Jane's hair tumbled in soft waves around her shoulders, appearing more black than brown in the darkness. From the top of her head to the hollow of her throat, she was unguarded. At her collarbone, a heavy wrap took up the charge of shielding her body from the threat of his gaze. Of course she would have a wrap, even when she'd thought herself alone. There was something reassuring about her prickliness. In his present spirits, Eli wasn't sure he could have brought himself to pursue their flirtation, even if she'd been open to it. But he craved her company. Her steady presence.

Eli chose the seat opposite her—far enough to maintain a veneer of respectability, in the circumstances—and sunk into the over-stuffed cushions. He half-expected Jane to order him out, but she didn't. The way she looked at him made him think she knew exactly why he was roaming the halls at night.

Time for a safer topic. "What are you reading?"

She held up the volume to display the leather-bound cover. *Traité élémentaire du calcul des probabilités*, read the gold leaf lettering. Eli had to smile at her choice.

"How relaxing."

"It is," she protested. "Nothing will make me relax as well as heaps of pounds in the bank and a thorough understanding of probabilities is the foundation to that."

"I commend you," he reassured her. "It looks far more complicated than anything we covered in our study sessions at your uncle's house. You've come a long way."

"Oh, please don't remind me of that. I feel silly for taking so much of your time." He couldn't tell if Jane was blushing, or if it was only the lamp's flame that sent a red reflection along the curve of her broad cheekbones.

"Nonsense. I was happy to help."

It was strange to think back on it now. At sixteen, he hadn't questioned Jane's request to receive a gentleman's education. He'd enjoyed having a pretty girl huddled beside him as they read, hanging on his explanations. But with the benefit of some maturity, Eli saw her choices in another light. What must it have felt like, to assume the burden of her brother's future at such a young age? No doubt it explained why she'd turned out so serious and proper. She'd never had the luxury of a carefree life.

He would have liked to tell her that he could help lighten her burdens, if she let him. But it would be a false promise. Until Eli advanced his naval career, he didn't have the funds to offer her marriage or security, and she'd already rebuffed his attempts to help with her club. So he settled on a more measured assurance. "You don't have to do everything alone."

Even so, it changed something in the air between them.

Jane seemed to sense it too, for she shifted under his gaze. "I could say the same to you. You can..." She shrugged an apology as she trailed off, as if afraid her words were somehow gauche. When she continued, she spoke with greater conviction. "You can talk to me, if you want to. About whatever is bothering you, I mean."

Jane closed her book softly. The sight of her gloveless hands upon the leather reinforced the sense of intimacy between them. This felt more real than any conversation they could have in the daylight, with the demands of propriety penning them in.

Perhaps that was why Eli began to speak, though he hardly knew what he would say. "I know it's not my fault the *Libertas* was wrecked. It just feels..." He searched for the right words to describe it, and found nothing. "I suppose I didn't care for the way they were looking at me this morning. The Merediths, I mean."

Jane made no reply, but she watched him without blinking, as if she were absorbing every word and holding it deep in her heart. Her eyes had darkened to storm clouds in the lamplight.

"They must have been asking themselves, why me and not their son?" he whispered. He'd asked a similar question while he was in captivity. *Why am I a prisoner when everyone else made it to a lifeboat? Why wasn't I just a bit faster, a bit luckier?*

Pure selfishness. He should have been thinking of those like Owen, who hadn't made it out at all.

"I'm sure they don't blame you."

Eli shrugged, unconvinced. "I wish I could have offered them more than another heartbreak, all the same."

Jane reached across the space between them and touched her hand to his. They were at enough of a distance that she had to stretch to maintain this contact, and she withdrew again a moment later. "I'm sorry. I wish I knew what to say to you, but anything I can think of seems inadequate."

"It's all right." He offered her a faint smile. Whether she knew it or not, it did him good just to be near her like this, without any suspicion or challenge between them. Like the old days. "Thank you for listening. Why don't you go back to your book? I'd like to just sit a while, if you don't mind."

"Of course." Jane opened her text again, now and then glancing up to check on him. She flipped the pages so slowly she might not really be reading anymore.

They stayed like that for another quarter hour, Eli breathing in the silent comfort of the room while Jane pretended to be absorbed by her probabilities. He could still feel the warmth of her touch upon his hand, a reminder that some tender sentiment survived everything that had passed.

The next morning, they all repeated the routine to get ready for Ascot, but something was different. When Jane tried to help Hannah get dressed as she had the day before, the girl had no enthusiasm for it. She poked and prodded her gowns, unable to select anything.

"They all look ill on me."

Though Jane tried to cheer her up, she refused to be comforted, nor would she reveal the cause of her poor spirits. Finally, Jane abandoned the effort. She would find another solution.

"What if we played truant this morning?" she suggested. "We could do some sightseeing and be back in time to join the others for supper."

This produced the first smile of the morning, and the plan was set.

When they went down to join the others, Jane found Eli and Edmund framed by the golden light of the window, deep in conversation on the relative merits of the army and navy.

"Of course everyone will tell you it's more gentlemanly to buy a commission, but those waxing poetic on the system are generally not the ones being led into battle by a captain with nothing more to recommend him than a few thousand pounds to spare. Besides which, the navy has the advantage of prize money."

Edmund wore a look of concentration that was normally reserved for racing. Was he considering a career for himself?

It would make sense. He needed an income, if Uncle John's baby was a boy. Still, she didn't like to think of him vanishing from her life for years, just as Eli had. He'd never confided such a plan to her.

Now that she thought of it, she'd probably heard Edmund say more in these past two days than in the past two months. Part of it was being in his element, certainly, but there was more to it than that. Part of it was Eli.

He had an easy manner with people that she would never possess, even with her own brother. People felt comfortable around him. And it wasn't because he employed charm or flattery either. Those things might be pleasing, but they demanded no honest consideration on the part of the speaker. No, Eli was genuine. He cared whether others were comfortable and sought to make them so where he could.

In spite of herself, Jane suffered a pang of regret. She would miss him when he left, even if she'd never held any illusions about their time together.

"Hannah and I have decided to go sightseeing today instead of attending the races," Jane announced, interrupting their discussion of warships. It seemed easier to present her plans as a fait accompli than to ask permission.

Though she'd expected Eli might protest, he merely studied them a moment and replied, "All right."

It was Edmund who adopted a critical tone. "Why come all the way here if you don't even want to see the races?"

"We watched the stakes yesterday and we'll see the Golden Cup tomorrow. Those are the important ones."

"They're *all* important." Edmund might have been a father asked to name his favorite child. "You're going to miss the Swinley Stakes and the Albany Stakes. Women have no appreciation for racing."

"Careful now," Eli warned him, his tone grave. "One should never make a dismissive remark about the fairer sex. You never know when you might find yourself at their mercy."

Truer words were never spoken. Jane favored Eli with a smile, thinking about when she might catch him alone again. Though she hadn't had the heart to confront him last night, when he'd been in such low spirits, she still intended to solve the mystery of his absence.

Jane and Hannah rode up toward Winkfield and Maiden's Green, stopping several times to view the grounds of the historic manor houses in the area at their leisure. Hannah enjoyed being out of doors, and she was in her element here, without any pressure from her mother to meet an eligible gentleman. With her shoulders set back and a bright smile on her face, she looked like a new person.

"I've decided how I want to use my forfeit," she confided to Jane as they rested in the shade of a tree to take some refreshments. "I want an invitation to your card club. Only don't tell my mother. She thinks it too scandalous. You don't mind, do you?"

She passed the little note toward Jane, who hesitated. She didn't like to get involved in a quarrel between Mrs. Williams and her daughter, but it might be a good idea to have Hannah on her side. Aside from the fact that Jane liked the girl, she also needed her help. "We'll be happy to have you," she finally replied.

She studied Hannah for a long moment as the branches above them danced shadows across her face. Jane had a forfeit of her own burning a hole in her pocket, and only one thing she wanted. But how would Hannah take it if she enlisted her help against her own brother? She didn't want to abuse their friendship.

Best to just come out with it. Fortune favors the bold.

"I'd like to use my forfeit too. I'm going to ask you for something a bit odd, but I trust I can count on your discretion." She fumbled with the slip of paper as she searched for the right words. She needed to be delicate. "I would like you to tell me straight away if you ever learn something unexpected about Eli's absence."

"Unexpected?" Hannah repeated. "Are you...saying you think he's hiding something from us?"

Oh dear. It would do no good to cause offense, nor to create a rift between the siblings when she had no greater proof than her own intuition. There was no doubt that Eli had suffered in the shipwreck. She felt quite wretched, poking about after how he'd finally opened up to her last night.

But he still hadn't told her anything about his captivity, where all her questions lay.

"I don't doubt the lieutenant is an honorable man," she said quickly. Thoughtless, but honorable, if his engagement to Cecily had proven anything. "But he says so little about that time, and what he does say is…"

Unsatisfying? Vague? Has the air of dissimulation?

Better to adopt the kindest interpretation she could. "Perhaps he only has difficultly talking about his experience, and you'd be doing him a favor to share his troubles with a friend he can trust. I promise anything you tell me will remain strictly between us."

Hannah gave her the most incredulous look she'd ever seen, but she took the note and tore it up. "I suppose I can't refuse, but I hope you know what you're doing."

"I'm sorry to put you in an uncomfortable position." Jane meant it. "But look at it this way, maybe there will never be anything to tell."

Hannah gave her the second-most incredulous look she'd ever seen.

They decided to head back toward the Lindens' house around three o'clock and wash up before everyone else returned from the races. The tip of the redbrick clock tower on the Sunninghill Church jutted up above the trees as they drew near.

When they arrived back at the house, they found it still empty. Jane let Hannah have the bath first, while she wandered around in search of something to do until her turn. She found baby Tommy in the study, which had been converted into a makeshift nursery for the duration of the visit. He wriggled on the carpet while his wet nurse dangled a bauble for him to flail at with his tiny fists.

"Hullo, Miss Bishop." The woman quickly ceased her game and rose to her feet.

"I don't want to disturb you," Jane said. "I just thought I'd come and play with Tommy for a bit before it's time to get dressed for dinner. Is it a good time?"

"Perfectly fine, Miss." The wet nurse smiled. She was a kindly young woman of about twenty years. "If you don't mind sitting with him, I'll pop downstairs and take some of his laundry to the maids."

Jane picked up the bauble in the wet nurse's absence and dangled it for Tommy as she'd seen the other woman doing. He was a cute little thing. He had enormously fat cheeks, which she was partial to in babies.

Jane picked him up and walked about the room, testing out the feeling. He rested his head on her shoulder and gurgled.

"I don't dislike you, you know," she explained. "It's only the way other people act around you that's bothersome. I worry it will go to your head."

Tommy cooed.

He wasn't so bad, really. It wasn't his fault that his mother was dreadful.

"I'll make you a deal. If you promise not to become conceited, then I shall promise to be a good aunt to you—I'm not your real aunt, but you don't know that, and you don't *have* a proper aunt. Anyway, I'll be a good aunt and teach you important things like how to annoy your parents. We could be great friends."

Tommy did not reply, which she took to be an assent.

"I'm glad we've had this talk, Tommy. You're a nice baby, aren't you? Such a nice baby."

"Ma-ma-ma," said Tommy.

The little drate-poke!

"You did *not* just say that. After I was being so kind to you! Don't you dare do that in front of the others, or it will be all we hear about for the rest of Ascot. Have the decency to wait until we're back home."

A low chuckle from the doorway made her jump. It was Eli, leaning against the frame.

Had he been listening this whole time?

"When did you get back? It's very rude to eavesdrop," Jane scolded, her face growing hot. "I was having a private conversation with Tommy."

"So I see. And we just arrived five minutes ago."

"Did you hear him say 'mama' just now?"

"I heard nothing of the sort."

"No," Jane agreed. "A three-month-old cannot say 'mama.' It's impossible."

"Quite so." Eli sauntered into the room to where she stood. Close enough to make her skin prickle with awareness.

"Would you like to hold him?"

"I don't want to interrupt. How was your outing with Hannah?"

"It was lovely. I think she needed a bit of a break from the crowd."

"Hmm." Eli nodded, though he paused to make a wide-eyed face for Tommy. Once the baby looked away and slumped his head back on Jane's shoulder, he continued, "It was kind of you to take her out this morning. I haven't been here to watch over her the way I should have. I'm glad she has friends she can rely on."

"I didn't do it for you," Jane said. The mantle of his praise was too heavy for her comfort, particularly when she was plotting to unearth his secrets.

"I didn't presume you had. But I'm thanking you all the same."

She pretended to be very interested in Tommy so that she could avoid Eli's gaze. But even without looking at him, she could feel his nearness. Catch his scent of cedar. She wished she'd cleaned up first instead of giving Hannah the bath. She was still in her riding habit, and her hair was probably a mess.

As if reading her mind, Eli reached over and brushed a stray strand from Jane's temple, his touch so light that it made her want to tilt her head toward it in chase of the contact like a cat. She held still with great effort.

"May I kiss you?" he murmured. His voice was like a kiss itself, slow and sensual. "I've been thinking about it since forfeits last night. I want a real kiss this time."

"We can't. I'm holding a baby."

He laughed. "What does that have to do with it?"

"You'd scandalize him. What if he grew up to be a rakehell? We'd always wonder if we were the cause."

"I think I can live with the guilt. It's only a kiss, nothing more. Besides, he's almost asleep."

Sure enough, Tommy's eyelids were drooping closed, his mouth agape.

"Well..."

Eli must have heard the hesitation in her voice, for he hooked his thumb under her chin and tugged her mouth gently toward his. Her reserve gave way, and she let it happen. His kiss was gentle, but not chaste. Not like last night.

He sampled first her upper lip and then her lower, tasting her at leisure. He held himself back, true to his word, but there was a tension in his every move. As if the effort cost him. When Jane dared to slip the tip of her tongue into his mouth, Eli groaned.

How she loved that sound.

He pulled away, his eyes still fixed on her lips as if he wasn't quite finished with them. Neither of them spoke.

Finally, he said, "Why don't you let me take him back to his nurse?"

Tommy had gone entirely limp by this point, and Jane's arm was starting to ache. She gave her assent and gently tipped the infant into Eli's arms without waking him.

"I think she's downstairs."

There was something very endearing about watching Eli settle
Tommy onto his shoulder and glide toward the door, taking great
care not to upset him. It wasn't that she was mad for babies. It wasn't
that she was picturing him as a father either, or herself as a wife and
mother. She couldn't place it at first, but then she had it.

Men were so rarely tender.

Or perhaps they were, at some time she didn't see. But in public
they were often too busy being brusque or stoic or angry about something. Eli was tender now, with his hand hovering over the peach fuzz
on Tommy's bald head, utterly focused on his goal.

He glanced up at her with a sheepish smile, as if he wasn't sure
he was doing it right.

You're doing very well, she wanted to tell him. *You're doing everything too well.*

From listening to her ideas to fetching her in the rain to beating
her at cards. He quietly mastered her without seeming to try. And
she was losing her will to resist.

Eli disappeared from the doorframe and his slow stride took him
down the hall.

If she waited here, he might come back and seize the opportunity
to continue that kiss. There would be no need to stop, save the ever-
present risk of discovery. He might even put his hands on her. Might
press his hips against hers, as he had at Ankerwycke.

Jane sucked in a shaking breath. It frightened her, how much she
wanted this.

What am I doing?

She was letting herself get swept up in the temptation of Eli's
affection again, while there was a house full of people downstairs
who might walk in and discover them at any moment. Then she
would be ruined, bound to Eli irrevocably, until he left her all over
again. No. She couldn't let that happen.

She was so caught up in his spell, she was forgetting that *she* should have the upper hand here. Jane drew a long breath to steady her nerves and reached into her pocket to find the forfeit with Eli's name on it. She had to keep her focus.

Let him come back then. He would find a very different challenge awaiting him.

Fourteen

ELI TOOK THE STAIRS TWO AT A TIME AFTER HE'D DEPOSITED Tommy with his nursemaid, who'd plunked the child quickly into his pram and gone outdoors. There was a mass of noise and movement on the main floor, with everyone coming in from the carriages and Miss Linden calling instructions to the cook and housekeeper for the supper preparations. His parents and the Kerrs were taking tea in the parlor. No one should have reason to hunt for Jane in the study-turned-nursery.

She was still there when he returned, but the flush had left her cheeks, and she'd smoothed down the loose hairs that had been creeping free of her chignon a moment before. She looked a good deal more businesslike.

"Please shut the door behind you."

Eli obliged, his heart kicking into a gallop. His feet carried him across the room quite without any forethought on his part—it seemed only natural to retake his place at Jane's side—but she held up a hand to still him. A piece of paper was perched between her fingers.

"My forfeit?" This was more direct than he'd expected, but he wouldn't complain. "I'm at your mercy then. What will you have of me?"

They would have to be quiet, with so many people in the house. But he could kiss her quietly. He could touch her quietly. The only challenge would be holding himself in check. This newfound confidence of hers was entirely to his liking.

"I want you to answer my questions with complete truthfulness. First, were you really abducted by—"

"Wait." Eli held up a hand, as much to get his bearings as to forestall the interrogation. "You're using your forfeit to question me? I thought you might use it for something more..."

"Something more *what?*" The edge in Jane's voice could have cut glass cleanly, but it was making messy work of his pride.

"More...amiable," he persisted. "Are you still fixated on my abduction? I thought we'd moved on from this."

"I have no idea why you would leap to such a conclusion. I've made my doubts very clear from the start."

"You've been kissing me for the past three days!"

"Not true," Jane replied. "I only kissed you once on the journey here. Yesterday and today, *you* kissed *me.*"

"I didn't hear you protest."

She dropped her gaze. "I may have...allowed certain liberties in order to indulge my curiosity, but you shouldn't have interpreted this as a sign that I've accepted everything you've told me."

To indulge her curiosity? She made him sound like a new parlor game she'd tried out. Hadn't the moments they'd shared meant anything?

"Yes," Eli muttered. "I see that now."

"My questions." Jane folded her hands before her waist, the forfeit still perched between her fingers like a miniature war flag. "There's no one here but us, Lieutenant. If you are truly a man of your word, surely you will honor your debt and give me truthful answers. If you're worried about the risk that I'll ruin your good name, I promise you, I'm not seeking to stir up gossip. I only want to set my own doubts to rest."

Would that he could set her doubts to rest. Perhaps he should just take the opportunity to tell her everything. If they kept kissing like this, he would have to tell her eventually. He wanted honesty between them, not secrets and half-truths. How would it feel to unburden himself to someone without any judgment or consequence?

But it was a hopeless fantasy. Hadn't Jane just admitted that whatever they'd shared recently was a fleeting whim? She wouldn't understand his choices. She might even hate him. And her promise not to spread gossip wasn't much to stake his career on, in light of how easily her opinion of him might change. It wasn't only his own future he would be risking, but Geórgios as well.

Still, Eli couldn't refuse her outright. The way she'd issued her challenge, a refusal to honor his forfeit would appear an admission of guilt.

"I've told you already, I don't like to talk about it. You have one forfeit, so I'll answer one question. That strikes me as fair payment."

She would probably ask him whether he was really held captive by pirates, and he could say yes and end this conversation. All the essential elements of his story were true. The odds that she would hit on one of the few details he didn't want known in only one question were slim.

Jane furrowed her brow in dismay but didn't protest. Though she contemplated for long enough that Eli began to grow nervous. She was too shrewd. He was playing games with a master strategist.

Finally, she spoke, her voice careful and deliberate. "Have you lied to me about anything you said happened during the time you were presumed dead?"

Pure relief. She'd cast her net wide, but he'd never lied to her outright.

"No," Eli said firmly, his eyes never flinching from hers. "Everything I told you was true. I went under in the shipwreck, I was taken by pirates, they held me captive for a time, and I eventually escaped and came home. I swear it on my life."

Jane's eyes took on a wounded look, and the flush returned to her cheeks. When she spoke again, she could barely meet his gaze. "Then I'm sorry I doubted you. You must think me horrid."

"I assure you, I don't." Now it was Eli's turn to suffer the creeping weight of shame. "I know that my reluctance to speak of my experience must create suspicion. It's only natural you would have some doubts."

He felt like he was lying to her even now. If not in word, then in spirit. But what other choice was there?

Eli couldn't risk telling her everything. Not when he had no assurance she felt any loyalty to him, and it might give her the power to destroy not only his own life, but also his friend's.

"Maybe one day I'll be in a position to answer all your questions at length." The words did little to assuage his guilt when Jane still looked so downcast. "Until then, I hope you can be patient with me."

He wanted to say more, but there were no magic words to solve this puzzle. Instead, he watched the regret play over Jane's face in a way that matched his own sentiments until the sound of footfalls on the stairs below reminded him they'd lingered here long enough.

⸎

"How has everyone enjoyed the first two days of the races?" Miss Danby asked over supper that evening.

She was seated to the right of Eli, while her younger sister and brother flanked his left. Jane, Edmund, and Hannah were across from them, while the married members of the party were all at the upper end of the long table, engrossed in their own conversation.

Looking to Jane, Miss Danby added, "I didn't see you in the crowd this morning."

"Hannah and I went up to explore Winkfield instead. But we'll be back for Ladies' Day tomorrow."

"Oh. Did anyone else go?" Miss Danby cast a sidelong glance toward Eli that lasted a second too long.

What did Jane tell her?

"Only Hannah and I."

"Hmm." Miss Danby cast her eyes back down to the slice of pigeon pie in the middle of her plate. "Well, you didn't miss much. The Queen didn't attend today, and quite a few people left early when they saw she wasn't there."

"You missed both the Swinley and the Albany," Edmund insisted. "Which were far more exciting than the chance to catch sight of the Queen."

"You'll have to forgive my brother, Della." Jane took a sip of her punch. Eli tried not to let his gaze linger on her full, pink lips. "Racing is a sensitive subject. We must find something else to talk about."

Edmund glared at her, then fixed his attention pointedly on his meal. They might have lost him for the evening.

Fortunately, Miss Danby was sociable enough to fill the gap. She had a bright, cheery voice and a tendency to flit from subject to subject the instant there was a lull in the conversation. "Lieutenant, what are your plans after Ascot? How long are you with us?"

"Just until the business with my death certificate is sorted out. I was granted leave to regularize my situation, but once that's taken care of, I'm to report back for duty and I'll be assigned to another ship."

"How long do you expect that will take?"

"I don't know." Eli shrugged. "I'll send the letters of support to our family solicitor as soon as we're back in town. I expect it shouldn't take more than few weeks for the registrar to reply."

"And afterward? Do you have any notion where you'll be sailing?"

"I don't have any orders from the navy yet, but given everything that's going on in China, it seems likely that's where they'll need men."

His tone must have betrayed some dismay, for Jane asked, "Don't you want to go?"

Eli glanced up the table before he replied to make sure his father was still deep in conversation. He had strong views on what he termed Eli's "lack of patriotism." "I'm happy to serve my country, but I wouldn't choose that particular conflict, if the choice were mine to make. It was one thing to support rebels wanting freedom from the Ottomans, or to hunt down pirates. It's quite another to prepare for war simply because the Chinese don't want us turning their people into opium eaters."

"You could ask to be discharged, couldn't you?" Did his future hold special interest to Jane, or was she only making conversation? He probably shouldn't hope for more, given what she'd said to him earlier.

"It's not as simple as that."

Regret must have leaked into his tone, for Jane watched him intently. "Why not?"

Eli felt suddenly exposed under her gaze. She could be too observant at times, like when she'd questioned his story or noted her doubts about the ransom in front of Captain Powlett. But even so, a part of him wanted to open up to her. Maybe he only wanted to atone for not confessing everything earlier. Or else the prospect of Jane's interest in him, her understanding, was simply too strong a pull.

So he tried his best to answer her question despite his discomfort.

"I've pledged my service. If I were to request a discharge while I'm still able-bodied, people would assume I was a coward, too shaken by my captivity to return to duty." It was bad enough that everyone in town knew him as the man who'd returned from the dead. He wouldn't become the man who'd run from his duty as well. "Then there's the need to secure an income. I prefer to keep a measure of independence, and one needs funds for that."

He wouldn't say it directly at a crowded supper table. That he couldn't stand to return to his parents' arguing. That his savings had not survived him, Jacob being in need of a grand tour to lend him some polish and a little joy after a year of mourning, and the family having no better use for the money he'd left behind. But Jane seemed to see right through him.

"Yes," she said gently, as if he weren't someone who'd made it through a shipwreck and an abduction and more than one skirmish in the years he'd been away. As if he needed gentleness. "It's a practical solution for one in your position."

She'd no doubt chosen her words deliberately. His position—the firstborn son of a landed family—didn't normally require a vocation. She was referring to his parents, though she was thoughtful enough to couch her language in a way that would escape the others' notice. She'd dined with them often enough in Devon to have observed several unguarded moments.

"Would you still choose it?" Jane pressed, after a pause. "If you had no need of an income and no concern for your reputation?"

"I don't know." He didn't have the luxury of dwelling on such questions. He'd joined mostly to escape home and the specter of his own doomed match, and now it was too late to turn back.

But Jane's question made him pause to examine his sentiments.

"It's hard to compare. Life at sea is like another world. And it's no small thing to walk away from a path you've been on for five years. I promised myself to Her Majesty's service."

He'd made a promise to Lady Kerr too. Bound himself to the

wrong woman because it was the right thing to do. He'd escaped by a quirk of fate, but that didn't mean he could make a habit of running from his obligations. Once he did, where would it stop? He wouldn't disappoint his family again.

"We all make the best choices we can." Jane's eyes were so clear, he couldn't look away. "You must follow whatever obligation places the highest demand on your conscience."

Regret caught Eli unawares, sharp and unexpected as a bee's sting. This was what he'd missed the most while he was gone. The Jane who cared about what he wanted, and whose cool assessment of a situation often helped him orient his own views. There was no one else whose judgment he trusted quite so well.

He'd thought he might never be graced with that communion again. Its reappearance stilled him, lest a careless word send her retreating back behind the battle lines. Their truce was still so fresh; he was scared to upset it.

"What are you talking about over there?" Lady Kerr jarred the moment with her voice.

Just like that, the connection was broken. Jane dropped her eyes to her plate, and Eli turned to shield their newfound fellowship from scrutiny. He needed a distraction. "We were talking about baby Tommy, it so happens." With an apologetic smile to Jane, he added, "I believe I heard him say 'mama' earlier."

Fifteen

THE THURSDAY OF ROYAL ASCOT, ALSO KNOWN AS LADIES' Day, saw some of the most important races (notwithstanding Edmund's insistence that they were all important). It began with the Royal Procession again, then the Gold Cup—a two-and-a-half-mile circuit that boasted the largest stakes of the event: over 200 sovereigns.

Edmund screamed himself hoarse when his favorite, Caravan, won by a length. Many of the other spectators shared his jubilation, though some cursed or hung their heads, perhaps thinking of the sums they owed. By the time they piled back into their carriage to get ready for the evening, Edmund could barely speak, but he still recounted the races to Jane and Uncle Bertie the whole way back, as if they hadn't seen it all with him.

He looked much younger when he was excited. But he was nearly a man, heading off to Oxford in the fall. While Jane would be...where, exactly? She'd been so distracted the past few days, she'd neglected her efforts to recruit more ladies to her club.

This was the biggest night of Ascot. She should focus on what was attainable: improving their connections in fashionable circles until their club was well established. Building a name for themselves.

No matter how thrilling this little dalliance with Eli might be, it couldn't last. He would sail to the ends of the world soon, and she would be left behind.

The only person she could count on was herself.

Jane pushed away her regret and tried to focus on the task at hand. She dressed in her most flattering gown, a violet and silver damask with a wide V-neckline that exposed her shoulders and significant decolletage. Biddy styled her hair better than she could have on her own.

When she came downstairs, Uncle Bertie approved of the results. "I've always said purple is your color."

Though she told herself it shouldn't matter, it was Eli's reaction that pleased her the most.

"You look lovely, Hannah. And you, Miss Bishop." He addressed them in a measured tone, without any trace of impropriety. But his eyes clung to every inch of exposed skin, and he swallowed hard as he looked at her. As if he would have liked nothing more than to devour her on the spot.

That, more than any trinket or ribbon she might decorate herself with tonight, made her feel beautiful.

After the carriage ride over to the Pearsons' house, Eli managed to position himself to be the one to lead her in.

"I can't stop staring at you," he murmured.

"You must. I don't want talk."

"I'm trying, but it's quite beyond my control. That gown seems meant for me to run my mouth over you from neck to shoulder."

Jane shivered, her skin rising to goosebumps as if he had already kissed her flesh. It didn't help matters that he brushed the nape of her neck as he took her cloak to give to a footman.

As they walked into the parlor together to join the other guests before the meal, Eli used the opportunity to whisper, "You know, there's no one at the Lindens' house."

"Of course. We're all here," she said hesitantly. This conversation couldn't be leading where she thought it was.

Then it did.

"If we were to slip away early, we'd have the place to ourselves." Jane tripped on the hem of her own gown and stumbled. "Careful, Miss Bishop," Eli said as he righted her. Then, more softly, "Just think on it. If your night grows dull, I'm sure I can provide you with another sort of entertainment."

They entered the parlor. Other guests rose to their feet to greet her, and Eli was gone from her side, passing through the crowd to shake hands and exchange a word with friends.

But what he'd said stayed with her.

At supper, Jane was seated at the opposite end of the table from the Williamses. By some stroke of chance (or possibly a word from Uncle Bertie) Mr. MacPherson was to her left.

"I'm so glad to see you tonight, Miss Bishop," said MacPherson. "I suppose I have Lady Kerr to thank for including this supper in your busy schedule." He smiled, displaying a piece of spinach stuck between his teeth.

It wasn't fair to compare him to Eli. Really, it wasn't. Most men wouldn't come out well by that standard. There was nothing *wrong* with MacPherson. He had average, bland looks, good manners, and an income of two hundred a year. He was, in every respect, a modest catch. But then, so was she. They suited that way.

"It's a good thing I did," Cecily put in. "I think my father and cousins would be content to stay in every night if I didn't give them a little push from time to time."

"It's not really staying in when we're visiting friends," Jane protested. But no, she shouldn't get drawn into an argument with Cecily now. She should say something gay. She'd grown so used to saying exactly what she thought with Eli these past few days, she'd forgotten to mask her opinions with a polite veneer. "In any event, I'm happy we're here. I'm sure it will be a lovely evening."

And if it isn't, you can always find out what entertainment Eli has planned.

She shouldn't be thinking about that. It was the most indecent suggestion she'd ever heard. What, did he expect that she would just agree to be carried off to his bed for the rest of the evening? She wasn't that sort of lady. It was insulting, really.

But she couldn't quite find the determination to stay insulted. Her imagination was painting a rather heated portrait of what the evening could be, if she so chose.

Mr. MacPherson was still talking to her, though she'd missed a segment of the conversation while indulging in lurid fantasy. "...Always impressed by the showing on Ladies' Day. You look lovely this evening, by the way."

He was flirting with her. She couldn't seem to make herself reciprocate as she normally did. She'd always viewed the task as an obligation to Uncle Bertie, but it felt *wrong* now. She would never marry MacPherson, nor any of the other uninspiring prospects that stumbled across her path at these parties. Why pretend? Cecily had already spilled her secret. Perhaps it was time she gathered her courage and told her uncle of her plans.

When they finally finished dessert, the gentlemen went off to smoke. As the ladies filed out of the room, servants began clearing away the table and chairs to convert the large space for dancing.

More guests began arriving after the meal, and Della was among them. She immediately ushered Jane into a space near the window where they might speak privately. The sky outside was already black. "I scarcely got to talk to you at the Lindens' the other night. Do you have any news to share?"

"I do not."

Della looked at her as though she'd just kicked a puppy. "Because you can't tell me now, or because there's nothing to tell?"

"Both." After a moment's consideration, she amended, "What I have to tell is more of the same, at any rate."

"I still feel as though I haven't heard the first story properly."

"We'll be back at home tomorrow evening. Come by the house and you'll have it then." It would be a relief to shut the door to her room and have a heart-to-heart with no fear of eavesdroppers.

Perhaps it was this longing to confide in Della that made her say what she did next. Or perhaps she had a lapse in judgment, for there was certainly no chance that her friend would guide her down the proper path.

"I think I might easily acquire some news to share this very evening, if I wished it."

Della's eyes grew bright with hope. "And do you wish it?"

There was only one answer that wouldn't disappoint. If only things were that simple.

"You know I'm not the sort of woman to put aside consequences and live for the moment."

"If we're talking about what I think we are, there are certainly ways to avoid unintended consequences."

"I'm not sure my knowledge of the practical details extends that far."

"I have a lovely book I would've brought you, if I had any idea we would find ourselves here. I wish you'd given me a little notice." Della seemed quite put out.

"There was no notice to be had, I'm afraid." Jane couldn't believe she was even considering this. Discussing it. Worse, she wasn't sure that she could possibly make Della understand the nature of her objections when they couldn't speak openly. "It isn't only the risk of...of indisposition," she finished clumsily. "There are social consequences. Emotional ones. It might...change me, I suppose. I'm nervous about that."

"Perhaps I'm not the one you should turn to for reassurance on that point," said Della gently. "And if you remain unsatisfied there, you should do what you think right. But I stand by the view that I have always expressed, which is that such adventures are what make life worth living, provided you're careful about it."

It always sounded so easy when Della said it. She made it look easy too. With her impulsive nature, "adventures" materialized in her life with alarming frequency, but she always skipped ahead of the consequences, outpacing discovery. It helped that Della's parents were rarely home and her siblings had a mutual interest in secret-keeping.

Jane didn't lead such a charmed life. Even if she were lucky enough to avoid detection, could she really throw herself into a love affair with Eli and say goodbye when the time came, unaffected by the loss? But the alternative—to say her goodbyes now without ever knowing what she'd missed—seemed just as bleak.

I never should have kissed him that first time. It's muddled my judgment ever since.

Jane was still struggling to find a reply for Della when their hosts announced that the dancing was starting.

Sixteen

Supper passed very unpleasantly for Eli. He was seated next to Lady Pearson and across from Mr. Bishop. The result was that he found himself obliged to recount the story of his capture and imprisonment for his hostess at great length, with helpful suggestions from Bishop whenever he seemed to lag.

"Two *years* trapped with pirates," Bishop said with a sympathetic look that made Eli shift uncomfortably in his chair. "Can you imagine it?"

Eli could imagine it very well, as one year, eight months trapped with pirates had been close enough to the mark. He wasn't really lying so much as rounding up. People rounded up all the time. Even so, a hot flush of guilt crept up his neck.

"Were they very barbaric?" Lady Pearson asked. Her eyes carried a certain hint of excitement, as if she hoped Eli's answer would be the stuff of penny novels.

"Forgive me, Lady Pearson," Eli replied. "I don't like to talk about it."

He had repeated the phrase so many times, it had become automatic. No one ever pushed further afterward. Except for Jane.

He recalled the way she'd looked at him in the nursery yesterday, her blue-gray eyes lit with a steely challenge that hardened her gentle features. Why did she have to ask for what he couldn't give when he would happily grant her anything else?

"Of course, Lieutenant. I understand completely." Lady Pearson schooled her features into sympathy, though her tone betrayed some disappointment.

Down the table from him, out of earshot but well within sight, MacPherson flirted shamelessly with Jane.

He'd promised Hannah he wouldn't make a scene, but if his temper was the sole captain of the ship, he would've thrown his trifle directly at the man's head by the end of the meal. MacPherson kept leaning toward her when he talked, no doubt for a better view of that tantalizing neckline. The most vexing part was that his attentions didn't seem to be unwelcome. Jane tilted her head in invitation and smiled at MacPherson's address, her habitually stern expression banished from sight. Why was she being so warm with him? She was treating him like a suitor.

What am I then?

When the men retired to the smoking room, Eli spent most of the time glaring at MacPherson from the corner of his eye.

He was going to have a word with the man as soon as he had a chance to get him alone. It wasn't because he was jealous over Jane—that would be overstepping his bounds. No, it was entirely because of Hannah. The churl had reduced his little sister to tears. Eli would react the same way to anyone who committed such a sin.

He had his opportunity shortly. As new additions joined their number for the evening, he spotted a familiar face in the crowd.

"Hal," Eli called, moving to join his friend. "It's good to see you again." They'd only had time for a brief visit before he'd left London, where he'd shared the broad details of his story.

"Ah, Williams." Halsey clapped him on the shoulder. "Do you know I can't go anywhere this season without hearing your name? The town matrons have been asking my mother if we can secure them an introduction. I'm afraid you'll have to make an appearance at our house for supper when we get back, or we'll never be rid of them."

"Only if you promise to limit the guest list." Eli leaned in as he lowered his tone. "Do you think you could help me with something tonight? There's a gentleman here who offended my sister."

"Hannah?" Hal's brows shot up in alarm. "Do you intend to call him out?"

"Nothing so drastic as that. I merely want a word alone to set the matter straight. I thought you might ensure no one disturbs us."

"Ah." Halsey relaxed at this. "Much less life-threatening. In that case, I'm happy to help."

By now the servants had finished clearing the furniture out of the great dining hall and couples had already begun dancing to the lively notes of a string quartet. It took several minutes of searching to find MacPherson twirling about the floor, arm in arm with Jane.

She'd given the first dance to him.

Why would she do such a thing? She should be able to see through his false charm.

With supreme will, Eli kept a pleasant smile on his face as he walked over. MacPherson had already released Jane by the time he reached her side.

"Good evening, Miss Bishop."

"Good evening, Lieutenant." She cast her eyes down as she greeted him, a good deal more demure than her usual mood. He might have thought her cold, but for the blush that lit her cheeks.

She's nervous.

That might be a good thing or a bad thing, depending on the cause.

"I wondered—" She broke off, as if she didn't quite know what she intended to ask. "That is, I thought we might talk more about… what you mentioned earlier. I have some questions."

Eli's heart nearly stopped in his chest.

It had been a rash proposition, uttered when the blood flow to his brain was greatly reduced because it was occupied elsewhere. He'd known the moment he said it that she would never accept.

But she had questions.

He struggled to keep his voice calm, as though he didn't mind what she decided. The choice needed to be hers. "I'd be happy to, Miss Bishop. Perhaps you would dance with me?"

"I'm promised to Sir Thomas now, and then to Lord Pearson. I could give you the dance after."

She pushed her card toward him hesitantly. Eli scribbled his name in the empty space before she could change her mind.

"I'll see you again presently."

Sir Thomas had been waiting quietly to the side until then, so Eli gave up his spot and let them make their way to the floor.

MacPherson was only a few feet away, speaking with another young lady. Halsey lingered farther off, observing the scene with a question written on his face. Eli jerked his head in a swift nod.

Time enough to take care of this, if they were quick.

"Mr. MacPherson, might I have a private word?"

MacPherson blinked several times in rapid succession, no doubt wondering at the request. "I suppose so." He hesitated, then followed Eli in search of a more secluded location.

They walked down a hall, where several ladies clustered before the door to what must be their powder room, so Eli turned off to an adjacent space that stood empty for the moment. It was intended as a retiring room, perhaps, for there were refreshments on a sideboard, but no servant manned the place yet. It would do. He motioned for MacPherson to follow him, while Hal stood guard outside.

Eli came straight to the point.

"You said something unkind about my sister."

"Who?" MacPherson's face screwed up in confusion. "I'm sure there's been a mistake. I don't even know your sister."

"Miss Hannah Williams. Dark hair, seventeen, about so tall." He raised a hand to the level of his nose. "She was wearing a pink gown with a lot of flounces on opening day of the races. You didn't think it flattering."

"*Oh.*" MacPherson had the decency to look abashed, his eyes dropping to some spot on the floor. "Listen, I'm terribly sorry if I gave offense, old boy. I didn't expect her to hear me."

"I'm not your old boy. We don't even know each other, nor do I care to."

This brought the man's eyes sharply back up. "Pardon me?"

"You aren't pardoned. Not yet, at least."

MacPherson looked about the room as if he expected to find someone to stand witness to this rudeness. "Now, see here," he said. "It was just a little joke, that's all. It's most unfortunate she got offended, but I didn't *intend* any harm. We've all gotten on a lady's bad side at some point, hmm?"

"I'm quite sure I've never been deliberately cruel."

MacPherson barked out an incredulous laugh that ended as abruptly as it started. The silence that followed grew very uncomfortable. "This is absurd. I've already said I'm sorry for it. There's nothing else I can do."

"Yes, there is." Eli leaned in a bit, waiting until MacPherson squirmed in his tailcoats.

"Will you be satisfied if I make my apologies to your sister?" His manner indicated that this would be a great imposition, and that he thought quite well of himself for suggesting it.

"No. I don't think she'd want to see you. I will only be satisfied if you retire for the evening, so that she can enjoy the rest of the ball without being reminded of you."

That Eli would also enjoy getting the man away from Jane was a happy accident.

"What?" MacPherson scoffed. "This is the biggest night of Ascot. The evening's only just started."

"Then you'll easily be able to find some other party to attend," Eli said smoothly. "Oh, and one more thing. Stay away from Miss Bishop, as well."

"What has she to do with any of this?" MacPherson shook his head in disbelief. "She's a friend. I haven't insulted her."

"She's a friend of my sister's. I'm sure she'd want nothing to do with you if I repeated your words, though I'd prefer to simply let the matter drop. Which I'm willing to do if you leave now and avoid both ladies in future. Those are my terms."

MacPherson seemed to have lost the power of speech. His mouth worked silently, as though he still couldn't quite believe Eli's gall. Perhaps he should give the man a bit of time to stew.

Besides, he didn't want to miss his dance with Jane.

"I'm going back outside," Eli said. "I'll expect you gone within ten minutes."

He turned his back on his enemy, but MacPherson hadn't finished after all. He clapped Eli on the shoulder, holding him firm. "Wait just a minute, you—"

He never got the chance to finish. Before he was even fully aware of his own actions, Eli had shoved him into the wall and braced his forearm across the man's shoulder, pinning him in place. They stayed like that, MacPherson's eyes rolling wildly from side to side, while Eli's heart hammered in his chest.

"Williams." Hal was at his side, his tone sharp enough to cut through the pounding in Eli's ears.

What was he doing?

This wasn't an enemy in the midst of a battle. Nor a serviceman used to resorting to his fists when tempers got high on a long voyage. He was a toad. An odious gentleman who'd given insult to Hannah, nothing more. MacPherson was quite beneath him.

"I'm sorry," Eli said quickly, stepping back to let him free. "You shouldn't grab a man from behind like that."

MacPherson staggered to one side, adjusting his waistcoat with trembling hands, and edged toward the door, all without taking his eyes off Eli. Only once he was nearly at his escape did he turn and run. A high-pitched shriek from outside indicated that he'd collided with some lady on her way to apply more powder.

"Steady there?" Hal was watching him with concern.

Eli drew a long breath. He might have been almost as shaken as MacPherson. He'd intended a stern lecture, not to use brute force on the man. Only it had set off something he'd been pushing away, to find himself held back that way. Just like when the pirates clapped irons on his wrists.

"A good thing we weren't dueling," Eli said lightly. "I don't think I've ever seen a man run so fast except on a cricket pitch." He adjusted his cravat to give himself somewhere else to look.

It was no matter. MacPherson hadn't been hurt. He was sure to leave the fête now, and with a bit of luck, Eli might never see him again. Nothing had happened, really.

Hal cleared his throat, not quite looking at Eli as he spoke. "You know, I had a bit of trouble getting back into my old life when I first came home. Not just my hand. It felt strange to be doing ordinary things again."

Strange didn't describe the half of it. He seemed to be out of step with everyone, never quite at peace.

"It gets easier with time," Hal assured him.

He hoped so.

Where is Eli?

Jane was so nervous awaiting their dance, she barely remembered to smile at her other partners.

She didn't know why she was overset. Nothing extraordinary would happen once he appeared. A little conversation, that's all.

But she felt the lie in her own thoughts. An unmarried lady couldn't have a conversation about going back to an empty house with a gentleman for an evening of lovemaking. The only acceptable response was to be horrified by the suggestion. Having failed in that, she'd already crossed a line.

The next dance had started by now. Eli was late. Though she knew he wanted to see her, Jane suffered pangs of doubt. What if he'd changed his mind? She'd made a fool of herself for nothing.

But a moment later, Eli hurried to her side, his hair a bit disheveled.

"I'm so sorry. Is it too late?"

"No, they've only just started."

As they rushed to take their place, Jane was acutely aware of Eli's hand upon her waist, and of how he loomed over her when they were so close. Though Jane was only a little smaller than average, she felt tiny beside the broad expanse of his shoulders.

"You have questions," he prompted.

"If—" She stopped herself, her whole body trembling. She couldn't do it. But he was looking at her so intently, his brows drawn together in a slight furrow, waiting on her signal. The hunger in his eyes pulled the rest of the words out. "If I said yes, what would we...do?"

She was lost already. The question was only one step from a concession, and they both knew it.

Eli swallowed.

"Anything you want, and nothing that you don't." The ghost of a smile played across his lips, torn between amusement and longing. "It is Ladies' Day, after all."

Oh dear. He was already good looking. This was simply too much.

"I need you to be more specific than that."

"More...?" Eli cast a glance around the floor to the other couples. "You must enjoy having me at your mercy, but I don't think I can pretend we're talking about a picnic this time."

"I...want to know exactly what I'm getting myself into before I agree to it," she explained. "I don't normally do this sort of thing. If you want me to trust you with my reputation and my person for the rest of the evening, I need the expectations to be clear from the outset."

"Oh." Eli seemed to relax a bit. "I suppose that's fair. But I meant what I said. If you let me take you back to the house, it will be your pleasure tonight. Anything you want."

Her pleasure. The offer was enticing, but also frightening. Not because she didn't trust Eli. He would keep his word.

No, what made it frightening was the sheer, overwhelming possibility of it. What *was* her pleasure? She knew what she liked in the privacy of her own thoughts and her own room, but she'd never shared that with a partner. She'd never even kissed a man before Eli.

What did lovers *do* together? Jane understood the mechanics of it, but not the finer details. She couldn't imagine herself listing her desires for Eli, or telling him how to touch her. What if he thought her slatternly?

Jane's struggle must have shown plainly on her face, for Eli squeezed her hand in reassurance. "What about this? If you can't decide what you want yet, then tell me what you *don't* want, and I'll give you my word not to do it."

That *was* easier. There were lines they couldn't cross.

"You can't—" she stumbled, reluctant to say the words in a crowded ballroom. Finally, she leaned in a bit and whispered, "You can't actually bed me. I wouldn't want to... That's too much." She knew how women found themselves in a family way, and that wasn't going to be her fate. "I'm sorry if that disappoints you—"

"Agreed," Eli interrupted. "And you are absolutely not disappointing me."

"Good," she said. That had been easier than she expected. Once the words were out and Eli reacted well, the embarrassment faded quickly. Maybe she could do this.

"What else?"

"I—I wouldn't want you to do anything that hurts." Several of her married friends had reported to her on the substance of the wedding night, and their experiences ranged from delightful to grueling. Even if Eli wasn't going to perform the conjugal act, and even if everything they'd done thus far had felt extremely pleasant, she harbored her doubts.

"Jane, of course not. That goes without saying." At her look, he added, "You're welcome to say it if you need to, of course. Only I hope you know I would never hurt you."

She didn't care to think on that too much. It wasn't strictly true. Not if one counted injuries of the heart.

"One last thing," she continued briskly. "No one can know. No matter what." She didn't think Eli would be cruel or foolish enough to go bragging to his friends, but there were other ways for a secret to get out. "No unnecessary risks. I expect the utmost discretion."

"You have my word."

She was out of caveats, at least for now. It seemed that she'd agreed.

They'd come to the part of the dance where they switched partners. As Jane turned about Lord Pearson, the gravity of what she was about to do hit her like a lead weight. She pushed the feeling away with all her might. She was doing this. No point in frightening herself.

"What's our plan then?" Jane murmured when they were reunited. "How do we both make our exits without anyone suspecting?"

Surely people would notice them leave together.

"You're still feeling under the weather from being out in the rain on Monday. I'm just seeing you back to the Lindens' safely." The words sounded almost reasonable when Eli said them.

"Wouldn't Hannah be a more natural choice to accompany me?"

"We didn't want to spoil her evening. Or we couldn't find her in time. You felt poorly very suddenly. We tell one person only to pass on the message, then we go. Before anyone can offer to replace me."

That would serve.

"It should be Miss Danby."

Eli blinked twice at this. "Are you sure? I presume she'll know you aren't really ill."

"I trust her discretion."

Anyone in their immediate circle might offer to take Eli's place. Anyone outside it might gossip about the two of them leaving together. Only Della was certain not to commit either sin. She had enough experience covering up her brother and sister's mischief that she should be an old hand, though it would be the first time Jane needed to make use of her talents.

They found her in the retiring room, and Eli stood discretely to one side while Jane explained that a sudden malaise took her away, and would she please convey her regrets to Uncle Bertie and the others in a half hour or so. Della listened to the short speech while the dawning light of pure and unbridled joy shone through her face.

"I *shall* convey your regrets," she agreed, clutching Jane's hands so tightly they began to smart. "What terrible news. Please go straight to bed and feel better. I shall send you a basket of remedies in the morning."

"Thank you, but just the message will suffice."

Jane took her leave and hurried out the door with Eli before she could change her mind.

The entire walk down the approach, he kept shooting her uneasy glances.

"Don't worry," Jane assured him, "she won't still be smiling like that when she tells the others."

"No. Of course not," Eli said quickly, though his stride was a little easier as he signaled the coachman to bring round her uncle's carriage.

Jane took Eli's arm and let him hand her inside.

Seventeen

THIS COULDN'T REALLY BE HAPPENING. HE WAS IN A COACH with Jane, alone, on his way to an empty house where he was to pleasure her at their leisure.

When the coachman shut the door behind him, Eli thought his heart might stop in his chest.

"Come here," he invited her.

It was dim inside, but he could see Jane well enough to tell her eyes had widened.

"Where?"

"On my lap."

He couldn't wait until they got back to their bedrooms. He needed to touch her. To know she was really here and willing to have him.

"But what about...?" She jerked her head toward the coachman's seat out front.

"We'll keep the window closed and be very quiet. He won't know."

Jane stayed in her seat for a long minute. Long enough for him to suffer a keen disappointment. It was too much. He shouldn't have asked.

Then, with a rustle of her skirts, she crossed the gap.

Eli's hands were trembling as he caught her by the waist and settled her onto his lap. He couldn't help it. He was fairly certain he'd had this exact fantasy one evening when he'd been abusing himself.

He pulled her tight, until her hip and buttocks pressed firm against his growing arousal.

"Oh." She wiggled in surprise, which made him groan. "Is it always hard? I thought it only got that way after a man had been kissing a lady or—"

He started kissing her then, too eager to let her finish her question. There was something unbearably exciting about hearing Jane talk about his cock in that matter-of-fact tone of hers.

She tasted warm and sweet. He was starving for that taste. He slid his tongue between her lips, wishing desperately that it was his cock sliding into her quim. He would keep his promise not to bed her, but his mind was determined to do everything his body couldn't.

Jane tugged her gloves off and slid a hand into his hair. Her nails grazed his scalp in passing, and it felt like every nerve in his body jolted to life.

"Do that again," he begged. Not five minutes, and she'd reduced him to this.

"Do what again?"

"With your nails."

She obliged, and he groaned with pleasure.

"Shhh!" Jane stopped what she was doing and placed a finger over his mouth. "You said you'd be quiet."

"I was quiet."

"You *weren't*. You keep making noises. He'll hear us."

There was no real danger of the coachman hearing them. Even if Eli made a noise, it wasn't loud enough to carry outside and then compete with the clacking of the horses' hooves and the jingling of their harness.

But Jane was nervous. And nervous ladies didn't enjoy themselves. Her pleasure, he'd said.

"Don't worry," Eli whispered, "I'll be quiet. I'll be very, *very* quiet."

He leaned his head on the seatback and closed his eyes, drawing a long breath. It was impossible to cool down while Jane was still pressed against him, but he couldn't summon the will to send her back to her seat. When would he have a chance like this again?

So he tried to hold very still, savoring the weight of her body atop of his without pressing things any further, only winding his hands gently up and down her back, from the nape of her neck to the delicious curve above her rump. She shivered under his touch, which he took to be a good sign.

That's it. Slow. Don't rush her.

This was torture, but of an exquisite variety.

"To answer your question earlier," he murmured, "it isn't always hard, but you produce a very distinct effect."

"Oh."

Maybe he'd gone too far. He couldn't judge from just one syllable. Eli opened his eyes to find Jane watching him intently.

"Does it bother you?" he asked. "That you arouse me this way?"

"No," she said hesitantly. "I just... Well, I suppose I'm not really sure what to *do* with it, that's all. It's very...different."

Eli momentarily lost the power of speech.

He had several suggestions as to what she might do with his cock that would remain within the terms she'd set, but he was still struggling to form a coherent sentence with them when Jane bolted off his lap and back over to her side of the carriage.

No. He hadn't been ready. He'd barely had ten minutes to enjoy the feel of her perched atop him.

"What—"

"*Shhh!*"

She was slipping her gloves back on. It was only then Eli realized the carriage had stopped.

They were at the Lindens' house.

He quickly adjusted himself into the waist of his trousers to hide the evidence of his arousal. He'd barely pulled his hands free when the door opened to reveal the coachman waiting on the ground below. Eli couldn't seem to slow his breath to an even meter, but hopefully it would escape notice.

He and Jane filed into the entrance, where the butler awaited them. Once inside the house and surrounded by lamps, it was evident how flushed Jane was, from her cheeks straight down to the top of her breasts. That was fine. It fit with the story that she wasn't feeling well. The problem was how plump and full her lips looked. As if he'd been kissing them for most of the ride back.

The other problem was that he couldn't tear his eyes away.

The butler broke the spell. "Back for the evening?"

"Yes," Eli managed. "Miss Bishop was feeling unwell. Please send her maid up to help her. And I'll take some tea in the library, whenever you have a moment." Turning to Jane, he said formally, "Good night, Miss Bishop. I hope you feel better soon."

"I'm sure I shall." Her eyes lingered on him for a bare moment, and then she turned and climbed the staircase to the upper floor.

It was an effort for Eli to drag his feet to the library, feign interest in a book, and await his tea. But it had to be done. Servants talked, and he'd promised not to risk Jane's reputation. She'd trusted him.

Besides, he could use some time to reflect. He'd promised Jane that this night would be about her pleasure. And if the coach ride here had proven anything, it was that he found it exceedingly difficult to hold himself in check once he got within two feet of her.

He needed to be back in control of himself before he went upstairs. The evening needed to be perfect.

It was a housemaid who brought Eli's tea in. "Will you be wanting your valet soon, sir?"

"No, thank you," he replied. "Tell him not to wait up for me. I'll manage for myself once I'm ready to go up."

Would Jane be undressed yet? Would her maid be safely away? Eli sipped his steaming tea and counted the minutes before he could slip upstairs.

After Biddy came to undress her, and Jane complained of imaginary ailments for a few minutes and sent her away again, she hid in her bed with the covers drawn up to her chin. This was clearly not going to be a position she could maintain for the rest of the evening. Jane knew that, logically. Yet she couldn't seem to throw back the covers and pose in some come-hither way for Eli.

She felt utterly naked. Her linen shift was marginally less transparent than her soaked yellow gown had been (though only marginally, as it wasn't a thick weave), but it was still one layer between her and the world. One layer between her and Eli. And underneath, it was her natural form, without anything to tuck or shape her into an hourglass silhouette.

Perhaps she should go put something else on.

As soon as the thought came to her, it was interrupted by a creak on the stairs. He was coming up. Should she put out the lamp, or leave it burning? She didn't like that he should see her so clearly, but she *did* want to see him. On then.

Oh goodness, what was she doing?

The footsteps reached her door. He rapped softly, so softly that she wondered if she had imagined it, and then he came in.

He was still fully dressed in his evening attire; the only signs of informality were a few disheveled hairs Jane longed to smooth from his firm brow.

"You look like you're still at the ball. I feel underdressed."

As Eli shut the door behind him, he tugged on the end of the knot and turned his cravat back into an ordinary length of silk, pulling it free of his collar. "Better?"

His smile exuded warmth, but it was subdued. Like smoldering embers rather than a roaring fire.

"Somewhat."

Her palms were clammy, and she tried to wipe them on the covers without it being obvious.

Eli slipped out of his coat and set it on her commode beside the tie. He approached her bedside and sat on the edge; very near her but not quite touching.

"Would you mind helping with the cufflinks?" He held up a wrist, and Jane took it gently. She was close enough to watch his pulse flicker as she undid the little gold links.

"Am I to be your valet for the evening?" Her voice came out breathless. She wished she could stop her heart racing.

"If you like."

Once she had both cufflinks, she pressed them into Eli's palm. He leaned over her to set them on the bedside table, his hair brushing Jane's cheek, as if it were perfectly normal to be this close.

When he returned to a sitting position, Eli took a long moment to study her.

"You look nervous. Have you changed your mind?" He'd failed to keep the regret from his tone, but it was gentle. "If you don't want this, tell me now."

"I am nervous, but I haven't changed my mind."

"Maybe we should do something to help us relax then." Eli slid a hand behind the base of her skull as he leaned in to kiss her. His lips brushed over hers lightly at first, but it didn't take long before he deepened the kiss, drinking her in. There was no one to interrupt them now. The servants were all downstairs, and most were asleep. None of their friends and family would be home before two or three in the morning, if this was a typical ball. They had hours.

Eli's tongue slid inside her mouth, and she met it with her own. She'd never been kissed like this. Passionately and thoroughly. Even the other times, they'd always been rushed. Stealing a few bare minutes before someone came in. This was its own unique art.

It made her open up. Her mouth, of course, but also something deeper. Her most intimate parts ached for him. And deeper still. An aching in her heart to pull him closer than two bodies could ever be.

He broke away from her mouth to pay his attentions to her jaw. Her ear. His breath was hot as he whispered. "Say what you want and it's yours, Jane."

Oh, but it was hard to think when he did that.

"I'd rather you told me what you want," she confessed.

"Why?" Eli drew back to look at her. "That isn't what we talked about."

"I know. It's just I'm a bit shy to speak so…explicitly to you. Maybe I'll warm up to the idea if you go first."

Eli sat back on the bed and appeared to study her. "Perhaps I'm shy too. Or, not shy, exactly. I'm worried I'll scare you off if I tell you what I've been thinking."

That was promising. She remembered the rough edge to Eli's voice when they talked about their picnic while overlooking the races on Tuesday. It had seemed to scrape away her restraint.

"You said I could have whatever I wanted," she reminded him. "This is my first request."

He shrugged in surrender, but didn't follow the gesture with any confession. Why didn't he say something?

"Well?" Jane prompted.

"I'm trying to pick one that isn't too filthy."

Trying to pick one. That implied there were many. That he'd thought of this frequently.

Jane felt a rush of pleasure at the notion.

"All right," Eli finally said. Sure enough, his voice had gone rough again, just like on the balcony. "I want to look at you. *All* of you."

It sounded deceptively easy. Looking wasn't even touching. She didn't have to worry if she was doing something wrong.

But "all of you" sounded like it meant...*all*, all.

Eli must have read her face. "That was too much. You don't have to do it if you don't want to."

"I didn't say no." She could do this, surely. She *wanted* to do this. But now that it was before her, it seemed too great. Like stepping off the edge of a cliff.

Don't think too much about it.

Jane let the cover drop from her chin, and the change that came over Eli's face as he took in the sight of her gave her courage. His eyes were riveted to her hands as she pulled at the laces on her collar. When the shift gaped open, she hesitated again.

"What about you?"

"What?" Eli tore his eyes from her chest with some difficulty.

"Fair is fair."

"Right. Of course." He pulled the buttons open and had his crisp white dress shirt off in an impressive time, his eyes still locked on her.

Oh my.

He was perfect. Infuriatingly, impossibly perfect. The muscles of his chest and arms had been shaped by his time at sea, as surely as a sculptor shaped Apollo or Hercules from the clay. She wasn't going to live up to that.

But she'd agreed to it, and she'd feel foolish going back now. Jane slid the gaping neck of her shift first from one shoulder, then the other, until the linen fluttered down her skin to land about her waist with the lightness of a moth's wing. Her nipples hardened to peaks in the cool air. The way Eli looked at her then made her feel perfect, too.

They explored each other silently, the only sound in the room their shaking breaths, coming more rapidly now. It made her wonder, to see how differently they were made. He was firm when she was soft. But the heat of their skin, and the pleasure touch brought, that was the same. Eli leaned closer, claiming her mouth again as his hands cupped her breasts. She arched her spine, curving into his grasp. The skin there was so sensitive, he seemed to set her alight.

"Press yourself against me," she pleaded. "The way you did at the priory. It felt so good."

"The way *I* did at the priory?" He laughed. "That was all you, love. But I'm happy to oblige."

Jane scarcely had time to register his words before Eli eased her back onto the bed and lowered himself on top of her, groaning as their most intimate parts came together. With only the thin linen of her shift and his trousers between them, it felt different. Better.

Much better.

Eli began to rock against her slowly, the head of his cock sliding over her mound.

"Good God," he gasped.

"Yes."

Jane wrapped her arms around Eli's neck and down his back, scratching lightly with her nails. He'd liked that in the carriage. Every muscle was tense, shaking with strain.

He bent his face down to kiss her, though it was rougher than before. More desperate. He grazed his teeth over her bottom lip, and when she returned the gesture, he groaned so loudly she feared a servant would hear.

"Shhh!"

"I—I can't help it," he ground out. "A few inches lower, and I'd be inside you. You're driving me mad." To emphasize his point, he slid a hand under Jane's rear and tilted her hips up to fit better against his.

It was so good, she could hardly bear it.

"Don't stop."

He groaned again, his hips finding a faster rhythm. She moved in time with him, gasping at the sensation that his shaft produced as it rubbed against her through the thin linen.

"Jane." His mouth traced her neck, her jaw. "Forgive me. I can't."

He pulled away, fumbling with the buttons on his breeches. A moment later, he'd pulled his cock free and begun to stroke, his face contorting as Jane watched, stunned. He tugged faster, and faster still. Another instant, and he gave a sharp cry. He spilled his seed into a handkerchief that he'd summoned from his pockets, still gasping as his pleasure moved through him.

"I'm sorry," he rasped, his breath uneven. "I couldn't hold back any longer. Let me do something for you."

Eli kissed her again, though the edge was gone from it now. He was gentler, more measured. But his hand found that same spot where his cock had been pressed only a moment before, rubbing the heel of his palm over her.

"Oh." The only sound that came out of her was a weak little cry of shock. How did this feel so good? She couldn't have stopped him now for anything. "Oh, please."

"I know what you need," he murmured. He broke off from his ministrations to bunch her shift up about her waist and slip his fingers through the slit in her drawers. When he touched her again, it was his bare skin upon her most intimate parts.

Her former shyness had melted away. She felt wanton and very beautiful.

She rocked her hips toward Eli's touch, and he seemed to understand how deep her need went, for he pressed his hand more firmly against her, his pace increasing. Jane wriggled against him, a whimper sliding free of her lips. She felt as though she would burst.

"There you are," he breathed. "That's it."

"Eli," she gasped. This was torture. "Eli, *please*."

He rubbed the heel of his palm downward at the same moment his fingers inside her pressed up. With a cry, Jane clenched around him, her release wracking her with pleasure that seemed to stretch on and on. When she'd finally finished, Eli gently withdrew to stare at her in wonder.

"I could feel you when you climaxed," he explained. "Squeezing my fingers."

"Well yes." Jane laughed, embarrassed. "That's what happens."

"I didn't—" He broke off suddenly, looking flustered.

"Have you not...done this before? With other women?" He seemed so sure of himself when he'd touched her. She'd just assumed.

"I didn't really have much experience before I joined the service," he confessed. "I'd kissed a few girls, but not much more. And then I was a prisoner, so..." Eli shrugged apologetically. "Does it bother you?"

"Why should it bother me? I should think it's much better than the alternative. I wouldn't like to learn that you have a string of illegitimate children scattered across England and Greece."

He laughed with her, the tension broken. "No danger of that." When the amusement had passed from his face again, he added, "It's different for a man, you know. The ladies will look down on a rakehell, but men look down on you if you're not one. They presume you're incapable or something. There's no way not to be wrong on some count."

"I suppose I never thought of it that way." She spent so much time worrying about her reputation as a woman. If the gambling club took off and became widespread knowledge, would the ton decide she was too risqué? What would happen if anyone suspected her affection for Eli? Had she appeared too forward in speaking her mind, or too reserved? The list was both endless and exhausting.

It seemed so easy for men in comparison. It had never occurred to her that they might feel societal pressure just as keenly.

"At least men cannot be ruined," she observed.

Eli eased himself slowly down to lie beside her on the bed, studying her face as if to read her thoughts. There wasn't much room on the narrow mattress, and he was so close that his breath stirred the hairs at her temple. She froze, trapped in the swirl of copper and amber flecks that lit the deeper brown of his eyes.

"I wouldn't ruin you, Jane."

"I believe you already have."

"No," he maintained, his tone gentle but certain. "No one is ruined by a kiss or a touch. It's the act of being discarded and gossiped about that does it. I would never treat you that way."

Jane said nothing, though her heart picked up speed. She wasn't quite bold enough to ask what he meant. Instead, she lay silently in Eli's arms, her heart equal parts contentment and wonder.

Eighteen

THEY LAY THERE FOR A TIME, AND ELI SAVORED EVERY SECOND. This was true freedom. The house was perfectly still, save the occasional creak that all old buildings made, and the distant sound of revelers at another ball tonight, somewhere down the street. Jane was in his arms, mostly naked, and every inch of her skin on his was a balm. He wanted to make this last all night. To stay here instead of sneaking back down the hall to his own bed, alone.

It was a comfortable silence, but after a few minutes Jane spoke again. "Was it…what you hoped it would be?"

He should say yes. It was everything, just being this close to her. But somehow, the real answer was no.

He was greedy enough to want more. He was getting hard again just lying here beside her.

"If I'm being honest, I must admit I'm not satisfied with my performance."

"What? Why?" She laughed, a question in her eyes. "It felt quite nice."

Nice wasn't enough. Nice was a shadow of what he wanted her to feel.

"I told you I was going to devote the evening to your pleasure," Eli explained, "and then I got so excited I couldn't even wait until after you'd finished. It doesn't feel like I kept my word."

He'd been too aroused to hold back. Another few seconds, and he would've spent himself in his trousers. Hardly the seduction he'd planned for her.

Jane's laugh came more easily this time. "The order doesn't matter as long as we're both content, does it?"

"I'm certain you could be *more* content than you presently are, if I were given another chance." Eli watched as she sucked in a breath. It did quite enticing things to her breasts. "What do you say? We still have hours before the others get back."

Please say yes.

Who knew when they might be alone again. He wanted it to be memorable.

Jane nodded, and Eli bent to kiss her again. While his mouth worked on hers, his hands skirted up her thighs. Her skin was so soft, particularly here. So different from his own. Eli's hands were worn from years of rough work. But she was silk everywhere.

Lust welled up in him again, his cock aching for attention as he slid a hand back inside her drawers, quickly finding that little nub inside her that was softer than silk. She was so wet. He wanted to make her clench around his fingers again. Better, around his cock this time. The thought had him hard as an oak.

No. That wasn't what you agreed.

He stamped the urge down firmly. He had to focus on Jane. What would she like?

She liked this very much, it seemed, for she made a lovely whimpering sound when he caressed her. But he wanted more than very much. He wanted to show her ecstasy.

Eli released Jane's lips and let his mouth explore the rest of her.

Her jaw first, then the hollow of her throat, then finally her breasts. He took one dark nipple into his mouth and teased it with his tongue. At Jane's answering moan, his cock pulsed.

God, she was beautiful. He couldn't get enough. Though his eyes lapped up the sight of her, he was frantic to look everywhere at once, touch everywhere at once, lest some precious inch of her be neglected. Jane twisted the sheets beneath her grasp and arched her hips to bring his fingers deeper. She was getting close again. He could tell this time.

Eli slowed his touch, toying with her. She squirmed impatiently. "Don't stop."

"I won't stop," he assured her. He would do this for eternity if he could. But he slowed his pace even further, bringing Jane back from the edge. She was unbearably beautiful this way, her face flushed and her breath coming in halting gasps. Just the sight of it drove him wild.

"You're like a puzzle box," he breathed, humming the words against her belly as his mouth moved lower. "You start off all closed up. Tense. But once I find the trick to you, you open for me."

He would have given anything, anything at all, to be able to slide his cock inside her. Even just for a minute. Instead, he did the next best thing.

Eli tugged Jane's drawers off her hips and slid them down her legs. Then he parted her thighs and looked at her, as he'd wanted to from the beginning. He'd seen his fair share of filthy drawings. Probably more than his fair share, while he was at sea. But it was nothing at all like having a real woman in bed before him.

Not any woman. Jane.

"What are you doing?" Her voice was thick and heavy, as if she was speaking from a deep dream.

"Tasting you," he said. "May I?"

Her eyes widened in shock, but she didn't say anything. If Eli had to guess, he'd wager she didn't have any response at ready for such a request.

Slowly then, and she could decide if she liked it.

Eli bent his head over the thatch of curls and parted her with his tongue. He inched inside carefully, savoring the taste and smell of her. He felt utterly depraved.

"Oh," Jane gasped. "*Oh.*"

That's it.

He slid his tongue deeper, and Jane's hands found his shoulders, her nails digging in. "Eli," she gasped.

He loved his name on her lips. As if he belonged to her.

He reached his hand up to find her mound and tease it with his thumb. She gripped him so tightly it hurt, but that only urged Eli on. He applied his tongue in the manner he desperately wished he could've applied his cock, pushing her closer and closer to release. Jane moaned and twisted beneath him, until finally she came, bucking against his mouth. She cried out as climax took her, loud enough that they should have worried about waking a servant, but Eli couldn't summon the concern for it. If anything, the idea that someone might walk in to find him with his face buried between Jane's thighs had a perverse appeal. He *was* depraved.

Eli gently withdrew to drink in the sight of Jane sprawled across the bed, gasping for breath.

Yes. That was much better. Much more than *nice*.

But when Jane finally raised her head to look at him, there was suspicion in her eye. "I thought you said you hadn't much experience. How on earth did you think to do such a thing?"

"Men talk," Eli replied with a sly grin. "And at sea, with no women about for months on end, the talk is known to turn quite ribald."

"Oh." She relaxed a bit, seeming to ponder this. Then her gaze slid down to the evidence of his arousal. "You're hard again. From... from kissing me there?"

"I did mention you had an effect on me."

She didn't know the half of it. How often his thoughts wandered to her when he took himself in hand. How long he'd been praying for this. But he wouldn't embarrass himself by confessing all that.

"Do you mind if I look at you, while I...?"

He was almost painfully aroused, and he needed the release. It had been difficult to hold back this long. Still, Eli wouldn't make himself unwelcome if Jane didn't like the idea.

But her eyes lingered on his erection with open curiosity, and she replied, "I could help, if you like."

"Help?" his voice had gone completely hoarse.

She traced her fingers down the line of his abdomen and ran them lightly over his cockstand. Pleasure lanced through his core, both at the sensation and at the sight.

"You'll have to tell me if I'm doing it wrong." Jane wrapped her slender hand around his shaft, stroking up and down hesitantly. He thought he might combust on the spot.

"I promise you," Eli gasped, "there is no wrong way for you to touch my cock."

He couldn't stop staring. Her hand on him. And God, but she *was* like silk. When her palm brushed against the sensitive head, he had to bite his tongue to keep from shouting.

"You like it faster, don't you?" Jane quickened her stroke. "That's how you did it."

"Hmm." Eli tried to say yes, but he couldn't form words anymore. She'd been watching him pleasure himself earlier, and she hadn't been shocked or disgusted. No, she'd been paying attention. So that she could be the one to do it.

He was unbearably close. Eli arched his hips as he spilled his seed into her hand, and the sight brought him a primitive pleasure. He still couldn't believe she was really here, willing to touch him this way.

After they'd cleaned up, Eli eased himself down beside Jane on the bed. It was too narrow to fit two without some maneuvering, and he should have been uncomfortable, but he was used to cramped quarters. It felt good, having her beside him. He rested his head upon her shoulder, a heaviness coming over his limbs.

It must be well past midnight by now. He should go back to his own bed. He would, in just another minute.

Jane stared at the ceiling, listening to Eli's breath growing slower. She should ask him to go, before they nodded off, but she couldn't quite break the spell. She was still taking it all in.

Eli had been still for so long that she thought he'd fallen asleep, and it startled her when he spoke.

"Do you know something?" he asked softly. "You called me by my name tonight. That's the first time you've said it again since I've been home."

"No, it isn't," Jane protested. Surely she'd used his given name at Ankerwycke, or when they were talking during the race.

"I'm very sure," he insisted. "You've always called me 'Lieutenant' until right then."

The implication made her uneasy. As did the notion that he'd been keeping track, waiting for some sign that she'd lowered her guard.

"I've missed you, Jane," he murmured, brushing a hair from his eyes as he lifted his head. "I've missed talking to you like this. I meant what I said at the races. I want your good opinion back. I want us to be able to confide in one another again."

"I—I should say you have my good opinion," she stammered. "Or else we wouldn't be here now."

"You know what I mean."

She did, and she didn't. If she was still angry with Eli, it meant this was just temporary. An adventure.

If she forgave him, then what were they doing?

Marriage was impossible. Even if she were willing to give up everything she'd planned for her future, all of London knew he'd been engaged to her cousin only a few years before. A doomed love, as the papers had deemed it. Add the resemblance between her and Cecily, and it was obvious what they would all think. Second choice. His consolation prize. She couldn't bear the pity that would be in everyone's eyes.

Not to mention, it still felt as though Eli's absence from her life was a blank slate where anything might have happened. She might have been wrong to presume the worst, but that didn't mean his ongoing silence was right. How was she to feel close to him again, if his time apart from her remained a secret?

Why wouldn't he trust her?

Eli took her silence as permission to press even further. "You haven't let me apologize. Not properly."

Jane felt very bare, suddenly. Too exposed. She wasn't ready for this.

She sat up, slipping her arms back through the sleeves of her shift and working on the laces. "This sounds like a conversation for another day. It's very late, and the others might come back soon. Let's not press our luck."

"Jane."

"You said you wanted to make me happy," she reminded him. "You were doing an excellent job of it until a minute ago. Let's not ruin things."

Eli watched her for a long time before he stood and retrieved his shirt, slipping it on and closing the long line of buttons without a word. Then he picked up his tie and tailcoat, slung them over one arm, and padded from her bedroom as silently as he'd come into it.

It was only after the door clicked shut in its frame that Jane realized she couldn't quite swallow the lump in her throat.

Nineteen

JANE WAS STILL IN HER SHIFT AND CORSET WHEN THERE CAME a knock on the door that next morning.

Biddy, arrived in time to help me dress for once. But it wasn't Biddy. It was Cecily.

"I *must* talk to you."

Without waiting for a response, she marched straight past Jane and into the middle of their bedroom. She was already dressed for the day and fully decked in jewelry. In contrast, Jane and Hannah had only just risen.

Cecily took in the disarray surrounding her. "Would you mind giving us a moment alone, please, Hannah?"

"It's *our* room," Jane protested.

"She doesn't mind," Cecily insisted. "You don't mind, do you darling? You must tell me at once if you do. The last thing I'd want is to cause inconvenience."

"It's fine." Hannah tugged a frock over her head and struggled to do up the buttons behind her neck without any assistance, so Jane walked over and finished the row. With a last, curious look, Hannah left the room.

"You didn't ask me if *I* minded." Jane placed her hands on her hips. "I'm not dressed yet either."

"But we're family." Cecily waved her objections away like a plume of smoke. "I can help you dress if you like. Oh, not *that* one, please. It doesn't do much for your color."

"What would you like to talk about, Cecily?"

As with most of life's trials, the only way out was through.

"You've been keeping secrets from me, you wicked thing."

Jane fought to keep her face at neutral. *Don't panic. Don't give yourself away.* The others hadn't come back to the house until nearly an hour after Eli left her room. She couldn't possibly know.

"What can you mean, Cousin?"

"You and Eli."

Jane knew a split-second of utter horror, where her heart lurched in her chest. She saw her future unfold before her, bleak and inevitable. A forced marriage. A husband who hadn't chosen her, and left her for the sea the moment he could. A life of gossip and pity.

Before she could make any answer, Cecily continued. "And John MacPherson."

"I...beg your pardon?" Jane was too shaken to piece these names together into anything like an explanation. What had Mr. MacPherson to do with anything?

"Don't you know?"

"Know what?" She hated to beg, but Cecily would draw the news out until she did, and this was giving her a nervous fit. "*Please* tell me what you're talking about."

"Eli came to blows with MacPherson last night. Over you."

"That's impossible." Jane shook her head. "Lieutenant Williams would have told me."

"But Mr. MacPherson wouldn't have? How interesting."

A misstep. Perhaps a fatal one.

"I hardly saw Mr. MacPherson," she replied, thinking quickly. "Except for our dance."

"Why would they have cause to fight over you? Have you been up to something you shouldn't?" Her cousin's eyes were ravenous. "Did Eli use his forfeit for something naughty?"

"Of course not. I told you, this can't be true. Where did you hear it?"

"From Mrs. Gladstone, who heard it from Miss Berry, who saw it with her *own eyes*."

"It would have been difficult to see with someone else's eyes."

"You're so droll. But you must have some idea why they were fighting over you. I won't rest until I have it."

There must be a way out of this. There had to be. "What did Miss Berry see, exactly?"

"She was on her way to the powder room, and she saw them in the next room with a third fellow. She said Eli and MacPherson were in fisticuffs, and she distinctly heard your name mentioned."

Gossip could distort things, but this wouldn't have come from nowhere. There must be some kernel of truth to it.

Even if there wasn't, it hardly mattered now. It was being talked about, which was more dangerous than truth. What had Eli done? He'd *promised* her that no one would know about them. This was the perfect opposite.

Cecily was watching her carefully. "Do you love him? You can tell me, darling. I'm the soul of discretion."

This was so outrageous that Jane almost laughed, but she managed to keep herself in check. Cecily had the power to hurt her if she spread the rumor any further. It wouldn't do to inflame tempers.

"Who, Lieutenant Williams or Mr. MacPherson?" She squinted, as if both men were texts written in a sloppy hand.

"Either one."

"Neither one," Jane returned. "I can't tell you why they came to

blows, if it truly happened, but I'm sure I didn't do anything to provoke it. You know me, Cousin. Have I ever been the sort to inspire
men to grand gestures?"

"Not in the least," Cecily said, a bit too emphatically.

Never mind, she would let that one pass. It suited her purpose
at present.

"Exactly. There must be something else at issue. Perhaps they
already had some grudge. A gambling debt or an insult. Who knows
why men fight."

"I suppose." Her cousin watched her through hooded lids. Like
a lizard. But a moment later, she switched back to her usual, sunny
pitch. "Anyway, I'm glad to hear it. I wouldn't want you to get your
hopes up. I think Eli will always be a bit heartbroken over me. He
certainly kissed me the other night like a man still in love."

"When you cried your forfeit and made him, you mean." Jane
couldn't help herself. It stung, and she wanted to sting right back.

But Cecily only smiled smugly. "Call it what you like. He seemed
to enjoy it."

"Isn't your *husband* missing you? You should probably get back
to him."

"Don't worry about Sir Thomas. He knows my devotion, and
unlike some, he doesn't fuss over a little harmless fun."

They faced off across a tense silence until Cecily finally said, "I'd
best let you get ready for the closing race then. I'll send Biddy in to
see if she can do something about your hair."

$$\mathcal{J}\!\!\sim$$

The only race left on Friday was the Wokingham Stakes. Eli would
have been just as content to begin the ride back to London after
breakfast, but Lady Kerr was adamant that they should take the

occasion to see everyone off in their finery, and Edmund wouldn't miss the last race.

No matter. It meant more time with Jane before they returned to sleeping under separate roofs. He'd gotten used to having her near, to talking to her as he used to when things were still easy between them. It felt like more than four days had passed, but it was also too short.

It was going to be harder to steal time alone with her once they were back in town.

He still couldn't believe what they'd done. It felt like a dream. She'd been so responsive to his touch, her strict demeanor forgotten.

No one else knew that side of her. To the rest of the world, she was upright and proper. The other Jane, the one that came out when she finally let her guard down, that was only for him. The notion gave him almost as much pleasure as he'd felt last night.

When they got to the races, Eli took a seat at her side, as he usually did. Once the crowd started cheering, he might have another few minutes in which they could actually talk without fear of anyone overhearing. But Jane kept her face turned out toward the Royal Procession as if she hadn't seen it twice before. She sat stiffly in her seat, inclined slightly away from him.

Is she embarrassed again?

"How are you this morning?" he tried. Innocuous enough if anyone was listening.

"Very well. I'm focused on the race, though." She kept her gaze straight ahead as she spoke, never looking at him.

That wasn't a good sign. Eli pushed down a growing unease.

Perhaps she was waiting until the crowd started cheering to tell him something. He tried to be patient, but his mind jumped between various possibilities. She'd enjoyed herself. He was sure of it. Why had the frost returned overnight?

The pistol rang out, and the horses charged forward. The crowd began to cheer. Still, Jane didn't favor him with a word, nor a look.

Eli touched a fingertip to her wrist, the delicate warmth of her skin making him wish he could dare more contact. "Is something wrong?"

She jerked her hand away.

A definite yes. What had he done? He'd left her room last night when she'd wanted him to. Was he to be punished just for saying that he missed her? Or did she regret everything in the light of day?

"Not here," she whispered.

Where then? It was impossible to get a moment alone. At least at the races, there was enough noise to cover their words.

Seeing he was about to protest, Jane added, "Cecily is watching."

Eli managed not to turn and look. Instead, he pretended to shield his eyes from the sun and follow the course, while stealing glances toward Lady Kerr from the corner of his vision. She was a few places down from him today. Sure enough, either she had a terrible crick in her neck, or she was straining to watch them.

Could she have learned he'd spent last night with Jane, somehow? They'd been careful. No one had seen him come or go from her room.

The rest of the race was all tension. He and Jane sat silent as two statues, fixed in the same tableau, but never bending toward each other. Eli didn't see who won. He was too busy thinking about what it would mean if they'd been uncovered.

Marriage, certainly. One didn't spend half the night in a lady's bedchamber and escape with no consequences. He would have to propose, and she would have to accept.

Regardless of what she wanted.

Good God, how did I manage this twice? He must be the unluckiest bastard alive.

If someone had asked Eli to describe what he looked for in a woman, the response would match Jane well. Intelligent, forthright, steadfast, and hiding a deep well of passion beneath the surface.

But all that was meaningless if they were only together because they'd been trapped. Eli barely knew how to imagine the life he wanted with her, only that it should look nothing like what he'd seen between his parents, or what he'd almost been forced to share with Cecily. He was wandering without a map.

There was a wall between them, and not only because Jane closed up every time he tried to talk about his past with her cousin. It was also a question of all the things she didn't know. If she found out that he could have come home sooner, she would feel betrayed.

Jane valued her independence above all else. By seducing her last night, he might have robbed her of the chance to build the life that she wanted, without him in it. She would hate him for it. *God, let there be some mistake. Let Cecily not know.*

As they descended the balcony back to the grand floor, Lady Kerr tried to sidle up to Eli in the crowd.

"You look tired this morning, Eli. Were you up late last night?"

"Not at all," he said a bit too sharply. "I took tea and retired early, as any of the servants could tell you." He was in no mood for her games.

She started to ask, "Was Jane very unwell when you left? She seemed fine this—" But Eli didn't let her finish the interrogation.

"You'd have to ask Miss Bishop how she feels; I couldn't say. Now if you'll excuse me, I've seen someone I must say goodbye to before we set out."

It wasn't strictly a lie, for he'd spotted Captain Powlett in the crowd. He left Lady Kerr's side, suppressing the urge to run. This was a damned mess. She was the last person he wanted poking around.

Had Jane been subjected to a similar intrusion this morning? That explained her ill humor.

Captain Powlett must have seen him at nearly the same moment, for he crossed the crowd to meet him. "Williams. So you *are* here. I heard you attended the Pearsons' ball last night, but I couldn't find you."

"I had to leave early. Have you enjoyed Ascot?"

"Very much. I'm glad I saw you before we left, though. I've been wanting to talk to you about something." Powlett's face took on a serious air.

"Yes, Captain?"

"I've been trying to write that letter of yours, but I keep thinking about what Miss Bishop said the other night, about the pirates not ransoming you. It *is* odd. And we had no word of you for so long. It didn't sit right with me." Powlett had always been a direct man. When he had a problem with an inferior on board the *Libertas*, they knew about it. This was no different. He reached into his coat and produced a folded sheet of paper. "This is a copy of a letter I've written to the lords commissioners to inform them of my concerns."

Not to Somerset House. This wasn't anything to do with annulling his death certificate.

The lords commissioners of the admiralty handled naval crimes.

Eli kept his voice perfectly neutral as he replied. "I see."

Captain Powlett shifted his posture but didn't avoid Eli's gaze. "I thought it only fair that you should see exactly what I've said. I'm not one to go behind a man's back."

"I appreciate your honesty, Captain, but I'd much prefer the opportunity to settle this between us, if possible. Could I call on you in town tomorrow to discuss it?" He wasn't sure what he would say to persuade Powlett not to take the matter any higher up the chain, but he would have the coach ride home to come up with something.

"You're welcome to call if you like, but the letter is already in the post. I have a duty not to hide my suspicions from the navy. It will be for the lords commissioners to decide if they'll convene a court-martial, not I. If you have nothing to hide, I'm sure they'll be satisfied with your explanations and the matter will end there."

This would have been more reassuring if Eli didn't have a great deal to hide. He couldn't make any explanation to the lords commissioners without committing perjury, which would only add to his charges.

Well, he would face this with dignity, whatever it brought. His solicitor had warned him, hadn't he? He couldn't claim he hadn't known. And anyway, there was no need to panic. It was only a letter. Nothing more.

Eli took the envelope reluctantly. He both wanted and dreaded to open it. But not here, with half the ton about.

"Do you still have your McArthur?" Captain Powlett asked.

The manual of court-martial procedure was commonly read to the crew at sea along with the articles of war, so that they might know their duties. Eli knew how courts-martial worked. He'd even witnessed a half dozen. But it was one thing to sit in silent observation, quite another thing to conduct his own defense, if matters should come to that.

"I can easily get one."

"Well, you should be set then." Captain Powlett nodded brusquely, their business concluded. "It's nothing personal, Williams. Only I must follow my conscience and my duty, retired or no. I hope this is all a misunderstanding and everything turns out well for you."

"Thank you, sir."

Powlett walked away from him. The whole conversation had taken less than five minutes, yet it had shot a cannonball through the center of his life. Had his greatest problem only a moment ago been whether Lady Kerr suspected his affair with Jane? Now it was whether he would find himself tried for desertion.

Twenty

THEY SAID THEIR GOODBYES TO THE LINDENS AT THE GRAND-stand and set out for London directly from Ascot. There was no picnic this time, thank goodness. Jane didn't think she could endure a return to the scene of her original fall into temptation. They'd taken a light luncheon at the Lindens' house before the last race to tide them over until they reached home.

In spite of this happy plan, the horses still needed to be rested and watered, so it would be impossible to avoid Eli and Cecily forever.

Until then, Jane would enjoy two hours of respite in the family carriage. Or so she'd thought.

"We never did have a chance to talk about this gambling club of yours, Jane," Uncle Bertie began the moment they set off. His manner was almost absurdly serious. "Don't think I've forgotten."

That's right, the fight between Eli and MacPherson wasn't the only damning secret Cecily had on her. In the chaos of this morning, Jane had almost forgotten she still had to face a reckoning for her club.

"I know you think it's all in good fun," Bertie continued. "But you must see how it could threaten your chances of making a match. Surely it's not worth the risk."

A match. The idea seemed laughable now, if indeed it had ever been otherwise. There were few men who wanted a lady with no dowry, and even fewer who wanted the mistress of a gaming hell, but she'd now added a dalliance with another man to the list of points against her. No, the door had firmly closed on the possibility of marriage. It was a relief, really. She could stop pretending.

"I'm not concerned with that, Uncle." Jane drew a long breath and girded her loins for the task ahead. It was past time. "The truth is, I don't expect to marry."

"Nonsense, my dear. You mustn't get discouraged just because you've had a few seasons. Sometimes we find the right match a bit later in life, but that doesn't make love any less sweet."

"No," she said firmly. "It isn't a matter of finding the right person. I don't *want* to marry."

Her pronouncement was shocking enough that even Edmund put down his racing journal to observe the exchange.

"But you must!" Uncle Bertie appeared utterly bewildered, as if Jane had announced that she no longer wished to wear clothes, or breathe air. "What will become of you? Someone must provide for you, Jane. You know that you'll always be welcome in my home, but I won't live forever. I want to know that you'll be safe once I'm gone."

"A husband won't keep me safe," Jane protested. "I'm not likely to marry into a wealthy family, and if my husband gains his income from a living or a profession, it will die with him. How can I rely on that?" She couldn't. It was too great a risk.

"But there's no reason to presume the worst. One hopes your future husband will live to a ripe, old age—"

"I want to build my *own* future. With the club. With Della."

"I can't understand what you mean. Are you saying you wish to become a professional gambler?" Poor Bertie was evidently bewildered.

"Not a professional gambler," Jane corrected hastily. "The proprietress of a profitable establishment." How to explain so that it would make sense? She'd intended to do this with her records all laid out for him, but she could summon the numbers from memory. She'd gone over them so many times, they were like old friends. "We've made over fifty pounds this season, which isn't even over yet. We kept the bids low and used to average only a few pounds a night when we first began, but we've more than doubled our membership since April, and last week we took home fourteen. I know that may not seem like much if you don't put it into context, but you have to remember that it's a new venture. These are only the people we've found so far. If we rented out some assembly rooms, we'd have enough space to—"

Uncle Bertie held up a hand to ward off this proposal. "What will happen when your luck runs out and your debts catch up to you? Cecily said Lady whoever-she-was lost four pounds on a single hand. That's too rich for our blood, Jane."

"Cecily has no business meddling!" Jane snapped, finally at the end of her rope. Must her cousin ruin *everything*? She'd poisoned the well with Bertie before Jane even had a chance to make her case. "She's only trying to cause trouble for me."

"Nonsense," Bertie said. "She's worried about you because she cares. Just as I do."

Worried about me? Ha! Cecily would probably watch her drown without lifting a finger to save her if she had the chance.

"Besides," her uncle continued, "I think she was a bit hurt that you kept all this a secret. It would have been kind of you to invite her along, you know."

This was simply too much to bear.

"I didn't think she would want to come," Jane managed to force the words out through gritted teeth. "Anyway, there's no need for either of you to worry about me. I assure you I know exactly what I'm doing."

"Throwing away your future." Bertie shook his head sadly. "All for the thrill of the game. And once you have cause to regret it, it will be too late to salvage your reputation."

"It's not a thrill, it's a sound plan of business. I can show you my ledgers once we're home—"

"No, Jane. I...I *forbid* it." Bertie had straightened himself in his seat for this announcement, which was issued in a weighty tone. It was hard to say which of them was more surprised.

"Forbid it?" she repeated. He might never have forbidden her anything, really. Oh, Jane had been scolded when she'd done something naughty, of course, but those days were so long behind her she could scarcely remember them. She'd always been a rule-abiding child. To have the gavel come down upon her now, when she was a grown woman and only trying to provide for herself—it was ridiculous! "Uncle, you *can't*. Della is counting on me. And besides, all our guests are expecting us on Monday. It would be humiliating to let them down."

All her work, wasted! Just when they were meeting with real success. But what was she to do—defy her uncle while she lived on his charity?

Tears stung Jane's eyes, and she bit her tongue, too frustrated to continue her protests. At the sight of her distress, Uncle Bertie's resolve fell apart like a sandcastle crumbling beneath the tide.

"Perhaps I could let you finish up this next week," he amended, "as you've already issued your invitations. So long as you promise not to place any extravagant bets."

"I never do." Jane sniffed.

"Well, one last time then. To say goodbye."

Jane looked out the window, unable to bring herself to thank him.

They fell silent for a long stretch. The carriage rattled as the coachman drove the horses quickly through Hounslow Heath, where the risk of robbery was greatest, and continued on Bath Road.

"I don't do this to make you unhappy," Uncle Bertie said gently, after a time. "You shall thank me one day, once you realize how close this might have brought you to ruin."

They continued on until Osterley Park, where they found a crofter's cottage overlooking the manor house to provide them with fresh-baked bread for a collation. The footmen set out blankets and ginger beer while the coachmen (and Edmund) watered the horses.

Jane took some refreshment, but didn't join the others, pleading the need to stretch her legs. She wouldn't risk being trapped in conversation with anyone in her current spirits, least of all Cecily or Eli.

But Eli didn't sit either. Nor did he take any bread. Instead, he paced the hillside, staring over the grounds without seeming to see them.

"How long until we depart again?" he asked.

"About a quarter hour, I think," replied Cecily.

Eli turned to Jane abruptly. "Would you accompany me on a walk down to the lake, Miss Bishop?"

"I'm quite comfortable here," she declined.

Eli produced a slip of paper from his breast pocket and handed it to her without a word.

"You're using your forfeit?" she asked, incredulous. "To make me walk with you?"

"If I must." He seemed tense, his tone slightly clipped. His usual, casual air had vanished.

"Very well." She certainly wasn't going to argue in front of everyone, even if she didn't appreciate being singled out. It might do her good to have a private talk with Eli. She had a few choice words for him. And the others were mostly absorbed in cooing over Tommy again, whose wet nurse had brought him out to lay on the blanket.

Jane accepted Eli's arm and they walked down toward the lake together. It wasn't far, and once they got past the initial stretch of farmland, there were enough trees lining the path to the manor house that they were shielded from the rest of their party.

"We don't have much time," Eli began. "What did Cecily say to you? Does she know about us?"

"I should think everyone knows about us," Jane snapped. "Or should I say, everyone knows about you and Mr. MacPherson fighting over me at the Pearsons' ball last night."

"What?" Eli halted his step, coming up so suddenly that she nearly lost her footing. Jane pulled her arm free, turning to face him.

"Am I not meant to have learned of that?"

"I—" Eli closed his mouth without finishing the thought. Clearly, she wasn't. "How did Cecily find out?"

"Does it matter? Someone saw you, and now we're the ton's latest piece of gossip." Her heart was pounding in her ears. "How could you, Eli? I trusted you. You promised no one would know."

It seemed her whole life was falling down about her ears. Bertie was taking away her club to protect a reputation that could soon be in shambles anyway. Without the slightest warning, she was losing everything.

This is what happens when you take foolish risks. She should never have kissed Eli in the first place.

"It isn't what you think," Eli protested. "I wasn't fighting with MacPherson over you. He insulted Hannah on the first day of the races, and I asked him to leave the ball so she wouldn't have to see him. It wasn't supposed to be more than that, only he—" Eli broke off here, gesturing heavenward with one hand. "He grabbed me from behind as I was about to leave, and I pushed him against the wall. I didn't mean for it to happen. He caught me by surprise, and I apologized afterward. It was hardly a fight."

Was that why Hannah hadn't wanted to go back to Ascot on Wednesday? The revelation took some of the wind out of her sails. Mr. MacPherson didn't deserve much sympathy, if he'd bullied a debutant.

"Why did Miss Berry think I was the cause then?"

Eli's gaze slunk away from hers. "I might have mentioned you briefly at the end."

"Do tell."

"I...advised him to stay away from you as well as Hannah." At Jane's look, he held up his hands in surrender. "I'm sorry. I know I shouldn't have done it. It just slipped out."

"It just slipped out?" she repeated. "You had no right to decide whom I talk to."

"He wanted more than just talk from you," Eli muttered darkly.

"And what if he did? It's still not your place to interfere. We're not—" She stopped herself without completing the thought, but it was too late.

Eli was watching her carefully. His features looked suddenly sharp, and his eyes had lost their usual warmth. "Go on. We're not what?" Although he hadn't raised his voice, there was an edge to his tone. "Speak to me plainly, as I asked you to from the outset."

She didn't want to. But it was too late to go back now.

"You and I haven't...promised each other anything." She'd been careful of that.

"We haven't promised each other anything," he repeated. A humorless laugh escaped his lips.

"Well, we haven't." It had been four days. An eyeblink in the span of her life. Surely neither of them thought it would last.

"What am I supposed to say to that?" His voice was still even, but Jane could tell that Eli was well and truly angry. The muscle in his jaw was working furiously, and he paced the green. "Am I supposed to make you an offer, Jane? Because I would if I thought it would solve everything, but I know it won't change how you feel."

Jane's mouth tried to form words, but no sound came out.

"It's obvious you still haven't forgiven me," Eli continued, "and I'm meant to just resign myself to it because there's nothing else to do. You won't hear me out. You won't let it go. I can't decide if you actually care for me or if this is just the most exquisite punishment you could devise."

"I'm not punishing you," Jane managed. Her mind had screeched to a halt at what he'd said about an offer, and she was still struggling to catch up. Had he really meant it? "Of *course* I care for you."

"Do you?" he returned. "It doesn't always feel that way. As soon as I get too close, you push me away again."

She couldn't handle this right now. She was still reeling at the loss of her club, fumbling for the grace to add the loss of Eli to the wound, even if she'd known it must happen eventually. What alternative was there?

"It isn't fair to make me feel guilty for needing some time to sort out how I feel about all this. It's been...confusing." The word seemed woefully inadequate.

"That's not what I'm trying to do." Eli sighed. "If you need time, that's one thing. But I don't know how long we have together, and I don't want to go back to sea knowing that you're still holding a grudge over something I did five years ago. Otherwise, you *are* punishing me, whether you mean to or not."

"You've been gone from my life since you joined the navy," she reminded him. "You've only been back two weeks. I can't just resume our connection as though none of that ever happened."

He acted as though it were as simple as snapping one's fingers. As if, merely by coming back to England, he'd erased all her pain.

"I didn't ask to be shipwrecked or captured," Eli protested. "But I'm here now, and we have a chance to be together. Isn't that what matters?"

"No!" Jane cried. The words were coming out too fast now; they shocked her as much as they shocked Eli. "What matters is that I thought you were *dead*. I thought you'd drowned somewhere far from home so that they couldn't even find your body to give you a proper funeral, and I'd never get to talk to you again. And I couldn't even tell anyone how much it hurt me, because you were someone else's fiancé."

She drew a shaking breath, raw as if the grief were still fresh. Eli stared at her with regret in his dark eyes, looking as lost as she felt. He lifted a hand toward her, but she took a step back.

"And if I start to care about you again now"—Jane fought to keep her voice steady—"you're going to leave me in a few weeks to fight in Lord Melbourne's ridiculous war and get yourself killed over some opium profits, only it will be real this time. *That's* what matters, Eli."

"Jane, I—" Eli's voice broke, and he drew a long breath before he continued. "I'm sorry. I'm so sorry. I didn't know I put you through all that. I didn't think—" He ran a hand over his brow, his hair falling out of place. "I didn't realize that you cared so deeply."

Jane didn't say anything to that. What could she say? It was humiliating to admit how deeply she'd cared, when he'd chosen Cecily.

They stared each other down across a long silence, neither of them knowing how to move forward. Finally, Jane mumbled, "We should head back to the others or they'll come looking."

"You can't expect me to leave things like this. Tell me what I can do to make it right."

"Are you planning on leaving your service?" She tried to keep her voice neutral, but it carried an accusation all the same.

"It isn't as simple as that. My family put everything I set aside into Jacob's tour of the continent when they thought I was dead. If I request a discharge, it will leave me with no income." His eyes seemed to plead with her for understanding. "I can't build any kind of life for myself while I'm living with my parents."

No, he couldn't. Anyone who knew Mr. and Mrs. Williams could see how miserable they were together. It was no wonder that he wouldn't want to spend decades under their roof. But neither could Eli build any kind of life with her if he was to sail back to the ends of the earth.

"Then there's nothing for it," she said softly. "We're simply ill-matched."

"Don't say that."

"I don't blame you," she assured him. "It wasn't your fault you were captured, as you say. But it changed everything, and it can't be undone."

She'd meant the words to lighten the burden that Eli must carry for compromising her, but if anything, he only looked more upset. Something in his eyes hardened, and his thoughts were closed off to her. After a long silence, Eli offered his arm and led her from the woods, back into the open field. She fell into step without a word.

"And your cousin? What shall we do about the gossip over my argument with MacPherson?"

"The only thing we can." Jane squinted at the carriages ahead, trying to distinguish the figures against the sunlight. Cecily was watching them again. "We ignore any talk and hope it blows over."

What choice did they have? She wasn't going to be pressured into a marriage she didn't want just because Eli couldn't control his temper.

"It would probably be best if we didn't see much of each other in town," she added. "It will only add to speculation."

Eli stiffened slightly. "If that's what you want."

"It is."

No good could come of prolonging the inevitable. Eli would sail back out of her life in a few weeks. The more she let herself grow attached to him, the greater her heartbreak would be when he left again. Better not to rely too much on anyone.

They walked the rest of the way in silence.

"*There* you are," said Cecily as they approached. "You took your time."

"It's a longer path than it looks from here," Eli replied.

"What did you talk about that whole way?"

"Nothing of any import." Without a backward glance, he walked to his family's carriage and stepped inside.

Cecily turned immediately to Jane, but she spoke first, leaving Cecily with her mouth set in the "O" of a gasping fish. "Let's get back on the road then. We want to be home by supper."

She stepped into the clarence, and her family followed close behind. Jane pulled back the curtain and watched the farmland roll by as they left Osterley. In less than two hours, they should be back at the town house and the Williamses would be back at theirs. They wouldn't need to see each other again.

She hadn't said goodbye. Not properly.

Jane swallowed hard, but the lump in her throat didn't go away.

To the attention of the Lords Commissioners,
The Admiralty, London

I have the honor to address your Lordships in accordance with
the obligation that my conscience lays upon me regarding the
return of Lt. Eleazar Williams to British soil a fortnight ago. Lt.
Williams served on the Libertas, late under my command, which
was wrecked in pursuit of pirates in the Adriatic Sea on the 5th
of June, 1837. I logged his death myself, having seen him pulled
under with the ship.

The Lt. informs that he was held captive by the pirates
for two years and made his escape only recently. However, I
remained at Corfu until October of 1837 and never heard of
any demand for ransom. Further, the pirates who plundered this
coast were not known to take prisoners.

I trust their Lordships will undertake such verifications as
they deem necessary to satisfy themselves of the cause of Lt.
Williams's absence from service, with all due respect for his
rank and person, and the good character I observed during
his time aboard my ship. I bring this to your attention in
keeping with my highest sense of duty toward Her Majesty's
Royal Navy.

Your loyal servant,
Capt. Richard Powlett

Eli continued to stare at the paper long after he'd finished reading. The words jumped and shuddered before his eyes with every bump of the carriage over their path.

How was he going to explain this?

The lords commissioners would call upon him to answer Powlett's suspicions. Perhaps they had done so already, and a letter would be awaiting him at the town house.

But he couldn't answer them completely. If they asked the wrong questions, he'd find himself in worse straits than he already was, and Geórgios would find himself in a hangman's noose.

I'm going to be court-martialed. The knowledge swallowed him up like a plunge into ice water.

"What are you reading?" his mother asked. "You've been staring at it the whole way."

He hesitated. How could he protect her from this? She was sure to panic, and his father would do nothing but complain, as if Eli's problems were a horrid inconvenience. But he couldn't very well leave them to hear the news from another source.

"A letter from Captain Powlett to the lords commissioners of the Admiralty." There was no use putting it off. He would have to prepare them for what was to come. "He's written to express his concerns about my absence."

Eli passed the page across the carriage. His heart pounded as his mother read.

"But this makes it sound as though you've done something wrong." She handed the letter to Eli's father. "It's hardly your fault the pirates didn't ransom you! Why should this captain be writing to anyone about it?"

"He's simply doing his duty, as he sees it."

"What's going to happen?"

"First the lords commissioners will probably want to investigate, and then they'll decide whether the matter should end there or I should be tried by court-martial."

"But why should they want to hold a court-martial when you were captured? It isn't your fault!"

It might not be his fault he'd been captured, but Eli certainly felt responsible for the fear in his mother's eye now. And Jane. He couldn't stop thinking about her face back on the grounds of Osterley Park.

I couldn't even tell anyone how much it hurt me, because you were someone else's fiancé. A sick feeling coiled in his guts. He'd done that. It didn't matter that he wanted nothing more than to make her happy. He'd wounded Jane so deeply, he could likely never make it right.

"It's not so bad as it sounds," he tried to reassure his mother. "A court-martial often clears the officer of any wrongdoing. Besides, it might not even get that far."

Eli spent most of the ride back explaining the next steps in the most reassuring manner he could muster as the scenery rolled by, unnoticed.

"Please don't spread the news to anyone else. I'll ask the lords commissioners for the same courtesy when they summon me. Perhaps we can keep it out of the papers." They might succeed, though it was too much to hope they could keep it secret if his case went to trial.

Would Jane learn of it? The thought was like a wrench twisting his guts one turn too tight.

Should he pay her a call in town to warn her before she heard it somewhere else? But no, she'd asked him to stay away.

She'd made her wishes clear. He wouldn't go to her with his hat in hand, begging for sympathy now that he faced a reckoning for his mistakes.

Maybe all this worry was for nothing. It was only a letter, after all.

But when they arrived at the house, Eli found there was a message from the lords commissioners already waiting for him. He was informed, in the most respectful but definite terms, that he was to report to the Admiralty immediately, and that they would soon be convening a court of inquiry to look into Captain Powlett's concerns.

"What does that mean?" asked his mother, fluttering nervously at his elbow as he read.

"It just means they don't know what to do about the captain's letter yet," he explained. "An inquiry is a bit like a grand jury. They'll appoint judges who will look at all the evidence and decide whether it's enough to support a court-martial or not."

"Why should they hold one trial just to decide if there should be another trial?" his father complained to no one in particular. "If you ask me, all this nonsense was dreamed up by judges and barristers to give themselves more ways to make money."

It would do no good to tell his father there were no barristers in naval proceedings, only captains and admirals with more than enough to occupy them.

"It could be worse." Eli attempted a joke. "At least I'm not in the Court of Chancery."

After some further lamentation, all futile, his parents accepted that there was nothing more to be done tonight and disappeared into the house to give instructions to the housekeeper and change for supper. It was already eight in the evening.

Only Hannah lingered, watching him quietly when he put away the letter.

"I should like my forfeit back," she said.

"Pardon?" He couldn't have heard right. What importance were forfeits now?

"You still have mine. I bet you think you can make me do something horrible like darn all your socks, and I'll feel too sorry for you over this court-martial business to protest, but you're mistaken."

Eli chuckled in spite of himself. Which he suspected had been his sister's intent. "Very well. Let me think a moment. I won't make it too awful."

"You won't make it anything." Hannah dropped her voice to a lower tone. "I have something of yours. You're going to trade me my forfeit to get it back, and to buy my silence."

"Your silence?" Was this still a joke? He hadn't a clue what she could mean.

Hannah pulled a fist from her reticule and extended it into the air between them, opening her fingers to display, upon her open palm, a pair of gold cuff links.

The ones he'd been wearing the night of the Pearsons' ball.

"You forgot these in our room."

Damn.

Eli pocketed the cuff links without a word. How could he have missed them? If one of Jane's family had found them before Hannah, his fate would have been sealed.

"My forfeit, if you please."

The little monger. Eli fished out the note and passed it to her. "You won't tell anyone," he warned.

"Of course not." She tore up the forfeit with a look of satisfaction. "But you should really stop ruining women."

Ruining women, indeed. She made it sound like he was a rakehell. How he'd managed to be caught out twice for compromising a lady without even losing his virginity was quite a feat.

"Hannah," he began. "I didn't—"

"Tut-tut. Don't scandalize me with the sordid details. I'm at a tender age. If you really want to convince me that you have honorable intentions, you'll marry her. I expect I could earn a standing invitation to her gambling club if Jane were my sister. It sounds much more fun than balls."

Eli sighed. "It's not as simple as that."

"Manage your own affairs then. But I hope you'll take more care not to leave behind evidence next time."

There won't be a next time. Jane had made her wishes plain. Whatever he meant to her, it wasn't enough to overcome their past.

He opened his mouth to tell Hannah as much, or at least an abbreviated version of it, but it was too late. She'd already turned and left the room.

Twenty-One

UNCLE BERTIE WAS WAITING WHEN JANE JOINED THEM AT breakfast the next morning, a spark of excitement in his eyes. The scent of fresh bacon warmed the air.

"Ah, you're awake. Eat quickly, please. I want you dressed and looking your best for callers by ten o'clock."

His hopes for her future were verging on delusional, given how badly she was mucking it all up. Hadn't they settled this yesterday?

"But, Uncle—"

"Yes, yes, I know. You've decided not to marry. But you can still sit in the drawing room for twenty minutes with your hair curled nicely and talk to any visitors who happen by, can't you?" He paused for a sip of his tea. "It's only good manners. And if one gentleman in particular makes you see how stubborn you're being, so much the better. There is someone out there for everyone, my dear, even if you haven't found him yet."

Was there no end to Bertie's optimism? Jane was fairly certain she'd exhausted every prospect in London by now. Even dependable Mr. MacPherson, who'd provided her uncle with a source of speculation all season, must have been scared off by Eli.

Besides, none of them would hold any interest for her. None of them had the expressive brown eyes she'd grown to admire, or the attentive manner, or the spark of animation that lit him when he spoke.

If there was someone out there for Jane, she'd found him years ago, and the chance had passed unclaimed.

Fortunately, Della came to call shortly after breakfast and saved her from wallowing in self-pity any longer.

"I can't wait to hear everything," Della whispered as they scurried away from her family's prying eyes to the safety of the library.

"You don't know the half of it," Jane said miserably. "Something else happened. Cecily told Uncle Bertie about our club, and now he's forbidden me to continue."

"What?" Seeing Jane's anguish, Della pulled her into a quick hug. "Don't fret, I'm sure we can find a solution. Might we change his mind?"

"I don't think so. He's convinced that gambling will ruin my reputation for marriage. You know how he is about finding me a match. He's said that I may only attend one last time to close things down."

"I suppose he leaves us no choice then." Della drew in a long breath, as if steeling herself for disappointment. But when she continued speaking, it wasn't the voice of a woman defeated. "After this meeting, we'll take a break to divert suspicion, and then we'll think of something more proper to occupy you. A charity, perhaps? Your uncle could accompany you once or twice to see that it's real, then once he drops his guard, you'll start coming back to my house again. We'll have to move the dates around. We mustn't be *too* obvious. And we might consider having our members swear an oath of secrecy from now on..."

Jane blinked in amazement. "You didn't even need to think about it!"

How had she conjured all of that so easily? It was incredible, really.

"What is there to think about? Surely you don't intend to give up now! You love our club."

"I do, but I can't lie to my uncle."

"Why on earth not?" A pucker appeared in Della's chin as she struggled to make sense of this. "You get to keep doing what makes you happy, and he's happier too, for not knowing about it. It's what's best for everyone."

Could it really be so easy? The image of Bertie's hopeful face hovered in her mind's eye, the way he walked on pins and needles when he nudged some hapless gentleman in her direction. Misguided, yes, but only because he wanted the best for her. How crushed he would be if he knew that she'd gone behind his back.

Jane's reluctance must have shown plainly, for Della shook her head in disappointment. "Never mind. You can think on it a bit longer and tell me when you're ready to acknowledge my genius. I still want to hear the rest of what happened at Ascot, if you please."

Jane poured the story out, though it took nearly a quarter hour to recount properly. She began with the kiss she'd shared with Eli at the Ankerwycke Priory, hurrying over the rest of their visit with the Lindens until she arrived at the evening of the Pearsons' ball, where she provided Della with a general outline of how the night had unfolded after they parted ways.

"With his *tongue*?"

It seemed Jane had, at long last, found an adventure to impress her friend. Her cheeks grew hot. "Never mind that, the problem is what happened the next morning."

She relayed Cecily's interrogations and her ensuing row with Eli, complete with her analysis of the inflection of each word. By the time she'd reached the end, Jane was feeling morose once more.

"...And then I told him we shouldn't see each other."

"Why would you do such a thing?" Della exclaimed crossly.

"Because it will only fuel more talk." Surely this was obvious. "He fought with Mr. MacPherson over me." Seeing Della about to protest, she continued quickly, "Or near enough to it. If people see us often together, they'll conclude it's true. And once Uncle Bertie hears of it, he'll expect Eli to marry me, just as he did with Cecily."

"Don't you want to marry him?"

"No!"

"Truly?" Della squinted, as if expecting a different answer to reveal itself under closer scrutiny. "You've always said you were choosing the club instead of marriage, but Lieutenant Williams knows what we're doing and didn't mind one whit. He's an officer, he has an income to support you, and if he gives you his permission to continue running the club, your uncle can hardly interfere. What are you looking for that he lacks?"

"Someone who wasn't with Cecily first." The words tumbled from her lips without any need to think about them. "And who won't spend most of our marriage across the world from me," she added. She probably should've opened with that part.

"Jane..." Della's voice carried a note of fatigue. As if she were addressing a beloved but stubborn child. "At some point you may need to decide whether your competition with Cecily is more important to you than your own happiness."

"*My* competition with Cecily?" Jane repeated, stunned. "I'm not competing with her. *She's* the one competing with me. You see how she is."

Competing wasn't even the word for it. Sabotaging, more like. The continual barbs and snide remarks—Jane never did anything to warrant that.

"Oh, she's quite beastly to you," Della agreed. "But that's her decision. You don't have to give in to it. You could walk away."

"I avoid her as much as I can." It would never be possible to remove Cecily from her life, but Jane gave her as wide a berth as could be managed.

"I suppose I mean more than just physically walking away. You let it bother you. Let it determine whether you want to marry a man, for goodness' sake. She's directing your life, even when you're not in her presence."

Jane didn't answer this. It gave her a very uncomfortable feeling.

"Are you in love with him?" Della asked.

"We only spent four days together. That's too short a time to fall in love unless one has a theatrical disposition, which I do not."

"You've known him far longer than four days," Della pointed out. "And you talk about him all the time. Most importantly, you didn't deny it."

"I'm denying it now," Jane said sternly, though she wished she'd said it straight off.

She couldn't be in love with him. That would be foolish. She'd known from the outset they had no future together.

"If you want my advice, you'll go talk to him."

Della made it sound so easy—just talk to him—but what could she say that hadn't already been said? It wasn't about competing with Cecily, no matter what Della thought. The real obstacle was in wanting to be first in his eyes instead of merely good enough. Wanting to matter so much that he would stay.

Eli might have every attribute she could want in a match, but what was it worth if he didn't see her the same way? Any assurance he might give her would speak less than his actions. He'd had the chance to be with her years ago, and he hadn't taken it.

Hadn't wanted her.

And anyway, Della had no proof that he would be the answer to all their problems. A marriage was quite different from a passing flirtation. For all they knew, he might share Uncle Bertie's view that

Jane should pull back from her club to protect her reputation, if he ever thought of making her his wife.

"My uncle is still hoping some callers might turn up this morning. I don't think he'll let me get away." Jane avoided the accusatory look in her friend's eyes.

"You should do it soon," Della persisted. "While you can still mend things. Don't be stubborn."

"Hmm."

"I mean it," Della pressed. "You'll regret it later if you don't."

Jane changed the subject. "What are our numbers like for Monday? Is Lady Eleanor coming again?" She was on safer footing here. She knew how to gauge the odds of victory on a given hand or fill out the room with the right people, whereas Eli left her feeling baffled and wounded.

If it was to be her last time in her own element, she would make it an evening to remember.

"What did they say?"

Eli returned home from the lords commissioners' office the next morning to find his entire family waiting in the parlor for him.

"Shouldn't you all be out on morning calls?" he asked, taking a seat as the maid served him tea. "We should try and behave as though all is well." It might take another week or more before the court of inquiry had selected the judges and was ready to hear him. They needed to project a strong facade in the meantime.

"Yes, but what did they *say*?" his mother insisted.

"Only what I expected. They've assured me they have no interest in leaking the proceedings to the papers, though once the actual inquiry is held, it will be difficult to prevent the ship's crew from spreading the story. With some luck, it will be over before anyone hears of it, and we can weather any talk."

"Why can't you just tell them to drop the whole thing?" his father grumbled.

"I'll certainly try at the inquiry," Eli replied. "Regardless, the best thing we can do now is carry on with our lives." He would reach out to a few officers he could trust to exert favorable influence on his behalf. Perhaps Halsey could help. Didn't he say he was secretary to one of the naval lords now?

Beyond that, it would be better not to stir up gossip.

"I suppose you're right." His mother rose to her feet and fetched a pile of calling cards from the sideboard. "These all came while we were at Ascot. I shall make a schedule for the return calls. If we hurry, we might still get an offer for Hannah before anyone learns of this court-martialing business."

Hannah shot Eli a desperate look as Mrs. Williams began listing off names.

"Lady Hastings should be first on our list. Mr. Cooke can wait... Oh! What on earth is this?" She held up a scrap of paper, about the same size as the other cards but thinner, as if cut from a letter or a flyleaf. On it, a messy hand had scrawled, *To Eli, from Geórgios,* followed by an address.

Eli's heart stopped in his chest. He snatched the "card" from his mother's grip, but it was too late. She'd already seen it. Far worse, Geórgios had already left it.

This wasn't possible. How could he be in England? More importantly, how could he have found him?

"Oh, that's right," his father said. "Cuttle mentioned that an odd-looking fellow came by the house this week without any card. When Cuttle sent him away, he came back the next day with *that.*"

"Odd-looking how?" Hannah peered at the card in Eli's hand.

"And the address is in Spitalfields! Who do you know who lives *there*?"

"No one. Just a friend from when I was overseas."

"Sounded foreign, Cuttle said." Mr. Williams wrinkled his nose.

His mother and sister were staring at him. Eli tried to keep his voice light, as if this weren't a perfect disaster. "I'll look in on him presently. Don't think of it any further."

Good God, what am I going to do?

The address Geórgios had left was for a doss-house in a very questionable neighborhood in the East End. A worn sign out front proclaimed beds for five pence a night, and Eli judged that to be a poor bargain given the state of the building. He looked at the card again on the faint hope he'd misread. No luck. Well, whatever Geórgios was doing in England, it was safe to assume he was out of money.

Eli would happily give him some if it meant that his friend would leave town quietly before he came to the attention of anyone in the navy.

A sour old clerk at the entrance informed Eli that he couldn't enter without the evening's ticket, so he paid five pence for a little brass chip and went upstairs to search the common rooms where a resident might pass the waking hours. There were a few working men in the kitchens and a smoking room upstairs, speaking in French and several languages Eli didn't recognize. He found Geórgios in a cramped room with grease-smudged walls, his hulking form bent over a game of draughts.

"Eli!" Geórgios boomed when he caught sight of him. He rose to his feet so quickly that he upset the game and drew a curse from his opponent. "You've come at last!"

"Hello." Eli crossed the room and clapped his friend on the shoulder. "Might I ask what the devil you're doing here?"

"I thought you'd be happy to see me," Geórgios replied, disappointment taking his voice down to a more intimate volume. "I've come a long way."

"I'm sorry," Eli said quickly, with a look around the room. Surely the other residents weren't *really* staring. It was only his imagination. "Of course, I'm glad to see you again. This is just a delicate time for a reunion."

He should be on the continent, where Eli had left him. Far from any inquisitive naval court judges.

"Is there someplace more private we could talk?" Most dosshouses like this didn't rent rooms, only beds, but it was worth a try.

But Geórgios shook his head no, so they would have to tolerate the company. There were only three other men here anyway, and two of them were playing a heated card game. Certainly none of them were likely to have ties to the navy, this place being decidedly below that class.

"Why have you come to England?"

"To see you, my old friend!" Geórgios might look a bit rough at first glance, with his thick, untamed black hair and beard, but his easy smile betrayed his true nature quickly enough. "You told me so much about London, I wanted to see it myself."

"But how did you know my address?"

"You are in the papers," he explained. "Everyone I ask knows who you are."

"I—" Eli tried to digest this statement, but found it too large to bite off at once. "When you say 'everyone,' how many people did you ask about me, exactly?"

"Not so many. Maybe twenty people?" Geórgios gave his response with enthusiasm, as if this were an amusing diversion and not the difference between life and social death. "They say in the papers you were at a party at Lady Kerr's house in Berkeley Square, so I went there, but she was away for some horse race. Her butler told me where your house is, but you were away too."

"You were at Lady Kerr's?" Eli had more than enough to deal with, without adding this to the mix. "Did you tell anyone how you knew me? Who did you say you were?"

"Your friend from Greece, come to see you. Don't worry, don't worry. I wouldn't talk about anything important."

Eli folded his hands over his face, offering up a silent prayer. Though it was increasingly clear that if any guardian angel was following the events of his life, they were having a grand time at his expense.

"Geórgios." Eli had kept his voice low since the start of this conversation, but now he dropped it even further, so that his friend had to lean in to hear him. "I'm in a spot of trouble with the navy at the moment, and I need you to stop going about town talking about me. If you say the wrong thing, it might give people the notion that I deserted."

"What is this?" He frowned at the unfamiliar word.

"Running away from my post," Eli explained. Geórgios had acquired his English with impressive speed, but there were still a few gaps in his vocabulary. "It's very important that you not tell *anyone* about the time I spent with you on the continent. You could get me in a lot of trouble."

"Ah. I see." Geórgios assumed a grave expression for the first time since Eli walked in. "But you know you can trust me. How many times have we helped each other? I won't say anything to make problems, and no one here knows who I am."

He meant the words, no doubt. But even if Geórgios would never intentionally put Eli in harm's way, his very presence was bound to stir up interest. With his towering stature and his foreign mode of speech and dress, he cut a figure one didn't easily forget.

"Any chance you're planning to go back to the continent soon?" Maybe he would say yes, and put Eli's mind at ease.

"Oh no." Geórgios grinned, a spark of mischief in his eye. "I want to see all the sights, and besides, I can't go back. There was some trouble with a woman, and I'm also out of money."

Lord help me.

Even if he promised not to make any more "social calls" now that he'd found Eli, Geórgios couldn't be left to roam free, where anyone he'd already told of their friendship might spot him and decide to ask questions. Sooner or later, the wrong person would take notice of their connection, and word would get back to the naval court judges.

It would be the end of them both. He couldn't let that happen.

"I insist you stay with us at my aunt's town house, as my guest," Eli announced. He would keep Geórgios under tight watch until the inquiry was over. It was the only way to contain this threat. "Do you need to collect any of your things before we leave?"

"Ah, thank you, Eli. And no." Geórgios picked up a leather satchel from the floor near where he'd played checkers earlier. "I carry everything with me. This place is full of thieves."

The irony didn't escape Eli, but better to let it slide.

"Good. Let's go." His parents weren't going to like this, but that was a problem to sort out an hour from now.

Twenty-Two

"STOP FUSSING WITH THOSE," DELLA SCOLDED. "EVERYTHING IS perfect."

Jane set the namecards back in their places and tried to keep her hands from alighting on everything in sight. It was Monday evening and their guests would arrive any minute, but she couldn't seem to settle herself.

Her last night. How could it end this way, with a rebuke from Bertie instead of the triumph she'd planned? She'd staked everything on this, telling herself it didn't matter if she never married, it didn't matter if Cecily laughed at her spinsterhood, so long as she had her club.

Now she would have nothing.

"Did anyone ask you about Eli and MacPherson fighting over me?" Jane asked. "Do you suppose they all know?"

If she had to say goodbye, she would have liked to do it with a clear heart instead of worrying about potential gossip. But Della only smiled and squeezed her hand.

"That story isn't as bad as you think. It makes you sound exciting.

I should *love* to reduce a pair of men to fisticuffs. You're rapidly out-pacing me as the daring one in this friendship."

"Until Uncle Bertie hears of it," Jane reminded her. "We've already established that he has a hair-trigger when it comes to forc-ing marriage proposals."

"It may reassure you to learn that I have an emergency plan in case anyone says anything to upset you." Della took a glass of cham-pagne from the row her servants had prepared for their guests and enjoyed a long sip. "I shall knock over a lamp and set the tablecloth on fire, bringing an end to the evening and giving everyone some-thing else to talk about."

Jane wasn't sure whether to laugh or protest, for there was a chance Della was serious; she'd had worse ideas. Before she could decide, the butler announced Miss Williams's arrival.

"Good evening," Jane hurried forward to greet her, pushing her emotional tumult aside. "You're a bit early. No one else is here yet."

"I know," Hannah explained. "I wanted to talk to you about something before the others arrived."

Perhaps she wants some betting tips. But a closer look at Hannah's face revealed that this was a more serious matter. Her brow was drawn, and she cast an uncertain glance toward Della, as if hesitant to discuss the matter before her.

Eli wouldn't have told his sister anything about them, would he? Jane could still picture his face clearly, as he'd looked when they'd parted. *I didn't know I put you through all that. I didn't realize that you cared so deeply.*

He'd looked so wounded, it twisted her heart even now. Had Hannah noticed and decided to involve herself?

But when she spoke, she turned the subject in quite another direc-tion. "It's about my forfeit."

Her promise to share anything unexpected about Eli's absence.

Jane had all but forgotten it after Eli swore that he was telling the truth. He'd seemed so sincere. But what was this then?

"Della, would you mind giving us a moment?" Jane murmured.

"Of course." Della exited the room swiftly, though not before one last look over her shoulder.

Hannah poured out her secret the moment the door was closed. "Eli's moved a strange man into our house and hardly lets us talk to him."

"Pardon?" Whatever she'd been expecting, it wasn't that.

"He knows Eli from his service, but he isn't in the navy. I think he's Greek, though every time I try to learn anything about him, Papa threatens to send me to stay with my aunt in Bath, and then Mama starts crying about my marriage prospects." Hannah heaved a long sigh. "It's been the worst few days you can imagine."

"My goodness." Had this man assisted Eli during his mysterious absence? He must be someone important, to have been moved into the house. "We have to learn more about him. Do you think I could call on you tomorrow?"

"Oh no, we're not receiving now because Eli's so worried someone will see him. We're all pretending Papa's ill. And I'm sworn to secrecy, so you must *promise* not to tell. I haven't told anyone about your forfeit, and I wish you hadn't put me in this position." Hannah scowled at her, which she probably deserved. "Oh, and Eli's also being court-martialed for desertion."

"*What?*"

"No, maybe not court-martialed. Court inquired? I'm not sure exactly how it works. Don't worry, though, he's assured me they'll find him innocent. And that's a secret too."

"Why wouldn't you tell me about that part first?" Jane demanded. It took all her self-control not to shout.

A court-martial!

The navy must share her doubts about what really transpired during Eli's captivity. But where Jane's concerns had little consequence, a court-martial could mean infamy, disgrace, and harsh retribution.

Were men shot for desertion? Whipped?

The thought struck her like a hole in her chest.

When Hannah spoke again, Jane could scarcely make sense of her words. "Trust me, the strange man living in our house is *much* more interesting than this legal business. It's all just a lot of waiting around for something to happen."

"But Hannah, if he's found guilty, who knows what they might do to him!"

"He won't be found guilty, of course." Hannah looked at Jane as if she'd suggested it might rain toads tomorrow. "My brother's not a coward. He was *captured.*"

Perhaps she was right. Eli wasn't a coward, and besides, why would he come back and reveal himself to half of London if he'd run from his service? But he *was* keeping secrets about his absence, something he hadn't been willing to share with her. Would he share it with the court-martial? Surely he must, if his life were at stake.

He had to. The alternative was too frightening.

"Anyway, you must swear to me you'll keep all of this to yourself," Hannah interrupted her thoughts. "My family will never forgive me if they find out I told you, but I thought you had a right to know."

Jane tossed her a sharp look, wondering again what she might suspect. Hannah added hastily, "Because of the forfeit, I mean."

"I see."

Without quite meeting her gaze, Hannah added, "And you tend to give good advice, which Eli could probably use at the moment. I'm not persuaded he knows what he's doing."

I don't know what I'm doing, either, Hannah.

"Let's call Della back before the guests arrive," Jane murmured.

Her thoughts were still whirling, but lingering over what she'd learned wouldn't help Eli. The best thing they could do now was to put on a brave front for the crowd. One battle at a time.

Della may as well have had a giant question mark written over her face when she returned, but she was good enough to save that for later and focus on the evening. Though, as their guests arrived, she must have noticed Jane wasn't holding up her end of the small talk very well.

"My, we're a large number tonight," Mrs. Muller commented once she'd settled in next to Jane. "If we keep this up, we'll need a second room!"

It was true. Besides Hannah, there were a number of new faces in the group. Della must have continued her recruitment efforts in spite of the trouble with Uncle Bertie.

She should be happy. Even if Jane had to bow out, there was no reason Della couldn't enjoy their victory. But it pained her to think of her friend going on without her, savoring all the triumphs they were meant to have enjoyed together.

"We're so glad to have you with us, Mrs. ..." Jane read the name-card across the table, perched before a young lady she didn't know. "Mrs. Alan. Tell me, how do you know Miss Danby?"

"Oh, Lieutenant Williams introduced us the week before last. He's a friend of my husband, Commander John Alan."

Jane's thumb slipped and she made a mess of her shuffle. She scrambled to right the cards back into an orderly block. "Did he? How kind of him."

He'd been helping her. Back before she'd even started being friendly to him again. And he hadn't said anything to take credit.

She'd always thought that a suitor would threaten her plans. But Eli had done more than she'd dared to hope for. Believed in her, even when she'd offered him nothing in return.

Jane was having trouble focusing on the cards she dealt. They were six at the table instead of their usual four, and she couldn't for the life of her manage any calculations to adjust the odds, though it should have been simple.

What if Eli was convicted, and they actually sentenced him to death? Why hadn't he *told* her he was facing a court-martial? Yes, she'd asked him to stay away, but that was before she'd realized his life might be in danger. This was the sort of thing you told someone you cared about, even if you'd had a recent falling out after threatening a rival at a party.

And Jane did care about him, no matter how much simpler things would be if she didn't. She'd thought rejecting Eli would keep her from hurt if he were in danger, but here they were anyway. She hadn't protected her heart. She hadn't kept her feet on the ground. She'd fallen hopelessly, foolishly in love with him, and now he might be in grave danger and there was nothing she could do to help.

The realization could have knocked her off her feet, if she hadn't already been sitting.

"Oh, that reminds me, Miss Bishop, I asked a few of my husband's friends about our good lieutenant." Mrs. Muller startled her from her thoughts. The request Jane had made at their last meeting seemed like years ago. "The stories they told me about the shipwreck were simply *ghastly*. I spoke to a rear-admiral who knew the midshipman from the *Libertas*. He said the poor man still had nightmares about drowning, even now. It's so tragic, isn't it? I can't imagine what the lieutenant must suffer."

"Nor can I," Jane managed.

She wished she'd never asked. She'd been so thoughtless in her pursuit of the truth. She felt quite wretched. Then again, there was still the matter of the mysterious Greek man at Eli's house.

She would pay him a call and get the truth from him directly, as she should have done from the start instead of poking around with others. Surely, he wouldn't refuse to see her. Maybe she could still convince him to tell her what was going on if she swallowed her pride and begged.

She had to try. They played for an hour, Mrs. Muller betting more extravagantly as the game continued, until she'd driven up the others and they had twenty pounds sitting on the table. *Twenty pounds!* Jane kept her card face on, as if she were accustomed to seeing such a sum laid out like pocket change. She was just reaching out to collect her winnings when a frantic knocking at the door halted her hand.

Heavy footsteps tracked down the hall as the butler answered, followed by muffled voices. Della was already on her feet, and Jane signaled the players at her table to wait as she moved to join her.

The butler poked his head in the room, murmuring to his mistress "I'm terribly sorry, miss, but it's Lieutenant Williams for his sister. I've told him you were occupied, but he won't be put off. He said it was urgent."

Has something happened with his court-martial? Della was already motioning the butler to let her pass, and Jane shadowed her, fully intending to come along.

"Lieutenant Williams?" Mrs. Duff peered eagerly at the door. "What a wonderful surprise."

The whole room began to buzz.

"Please stay at your places, ladies," Jane said, though it was anyone's guess whether they were listening. "The lieutenant won't be joining us this evening; he's only come to collect his sister. We'll return in just a moment."

She motioned to Hannah, whose face slid into a pout. She set down her cards and followed Jane and Della from the room, muttering, "It's not fair. I hardly got to play."

When they met Eli at the entrance, he looked tousled and out of breath as if he'd raced here. "We don't have long," he began without any greeting. "My mother's found out Hannah isn't at Miss Parker's house as she said, and now my father's on his way here to search for her. He's in a state."

He glanced at Jane only once, preferring to keep his attention on Della and Hannah. She couldn't say she blamed him. She wasn't sure how to behave as though he didn't make her knees weak either.

"What did they do, go there to check on me?" Hannah's voice rose in indignation. "Is there no trust in our house?"

"Why didn't you think of a better lie?"

"He has a point." Della came between the siblings with a knowing tone. "If you're going to use someone else as your excuse, you must bring them in on the plan first. It's just good sense."

"Can we please focus on what to do?" Jane interrupted. "Eli, can you take Hannah home directly and head him off? We can pretend she was never here."

"I can try, but I'm not sure what route he took. I slipped out to warn you while my parents were still talking."

He'd helped her again, though he had far greater problems of his own to worry about. "Thank you," she managed. Eli only nodded, his dark eyes catching hers for a long moment. She would have given a small fortune for his thoughts, if only they were alone.

Hannah hadn't even managed to get her cloak over her shoulders when they heard the jingling of a horse and carriage outside.

Eli muttered an oath. "If he comes in, he'll make a fuss in front of your guests. I'll try to head him off."

"I'm in so much trouble," Hannah wailed, covering her face with her hands. "They'll never let me go anywhere fun again. I'll be trapped in stuffy old ball jail."

"Wait." Jane held up a hand to stop Eli from opening the door. "What if she weren't gambling?" She might let the siblings face

their father alone and pray their punishment wouldn't be audible
to the ladies sitting in the drawing room, but that seemed a cold
fate. Besides, there was no guarantee Mr. Williams wouldn't pound
on the knocker and hold her and Della to account. The man had
a temper. "We'll let him walk in on us doing something perfectly
acceptable, and Hannah won't be in any trouble."

The girl would still have to explain to her parents why she wasn't
at her friend's house, but she could sort that out afterward. At least
Jane could offer what help she was able.

"My quilting supplies!" Della exclaimed. "I'll bring them down.
Hannah and Jane, you go prepare the others. Eli, tell my butler to
stall your father. Don't worry, he's an old hand. You can hide in the
kitchens until he goes, and we'll pretend you were never here. Hurry
everyone!"

Della was gone in a flash, raising her skirts to leap up the stairs
two-by-two. Jane barely had time to exchange a look with Eli before
she darted back to the drawing room with Hannah. It was all done
in the span of two minutes, Jane explaining the threat of discovery quickly as Della handed out scraps of fabric to cover evidence
of card play. The ladies rose to the occasion without complaint;
several of them had endured the trials of an overbearing father or
husband, and Hannah provoked sympathy as the youngest in their
number.

"There aren't enough!" whispered Mrs. Duff, as the last of the
fabric went to the lady beside her. A knock sounded at the door, and
they all listened to the footsteps of the butler.

"Don't worry," Della said. "I brought a few odds and ends in
case we needed them." Without missing a beat, she produced a half-
finished watercolor for Mrs. Duff, followed by a sheet of pressed fern
fonds for Miss Anwar. "There, now. All set."

She took her seat with a serenity Jane envied. Clearly, their subterfuge was nothing remarkable for Della. "Everyone talk about something," she hissed. "Act natural."

They managed a few hasty words, and then Mr. Williams was upon them, bursting through the door with the promise of fire and brimstone in his eyes. He had his mouth open to speak, but froze as he took in the sight.

"Oh, Mr. Williams," Jane exclaimed, feigning surprise as she rose to her feet. "How good to see you up and about. Hannah told us you were feeling under the weather."

He blinked, having obviously forgotten all about this in his haste to catch his daughter. "I—er...yes, Miss Bishop. Much better." After a beat, he added quickly. "Though I think I might take ill again soon. It, uh...it comes and goes."

"What are you doing here, Papa?" Hannah asked. She'd put on a wide-eyed expression, and had actually run a needle through the fabric before her, working on a seam as she spoke. She was the only one in the room who'd thought to do so. Hopefully Mr. Williams wouldn't notice.

"I—but I thought this was a gambling club?" He was red in the face as he looked about the room, the color holding steadfast as chagrin replaced anger.

"A gambling club?" Della laughed. A few of the ladies joined her, though none quite matched her talent for acting. "Of course not, Mr. Williams. This is a quilting circle, as you can see."

"But..." He was quite confused by now, his wrath entirely gone. "But I thought Miss Bishop admitted it. That you..." He trailed off again, squinting at the sight before him.

"We play cards on *Tuesdays*," Della supplied. "Though I would hardly call it gambling. More like a friendly match. Mondays are quilting." Seeing Mr. Williams's gaze alight on Mrs. Duff, she added, without missing a beat, "And watercolors. We find they complement each other well."

"I see." Mr. Williams cleared his throat. "But you told your mother you'd be at Miss Parker's house this evening, Hannah."

"I'm *sure* I said I was going to Miss Danby's," she replied. "Mama must have misheard me."

A tense silence followed, in which Mr. Williams seemed to debate whether he would press the argument in front of an audience. Propriety finally won out. "In that case, I—I'm sorry to have intruded. I'll see you back at the house."

No one dared to breathe until they'd heard his steps retreat down the hall and the door shut firmly in place behind him, then they all erupted in breathless whispering.

"Did you see how confused he was?" Miss Anwar laughed. "Poor fellow! We'd make excellent spies."

Jane was already leaving their congratulations behind, hurrying out the door to find Eli. But there was no sign of him in the kitchens, where Della had told him to hide.

"The lieutenant has already left, Miss Bishop," the butler explained, finding her staring at the empty butcher block as though it held the answer to her questions. "He said he didn't want to intrude any longer."

Jane's breath escaped her in a sigh. Thanks to Eli, her club was out of danger—but what about him? Not even the prospect of the twenty-pound bet still waiting for her on the table beneath a heap of quilting fabric could distract her from that.

Twenty-Three

"A CALLER AT THE DOOR FOR YOU, SIR." CUTTLE MADE THE announcement with the same look of disdain he'd been wearing since Eli had brought his guest home four days ago.

He and Geórgios were in the guest bedroom at the furthest possible corner of the house from the rest of the family, plotting Geórgios's escape from England. Or rather, Eli was plotting. Geórgios was squinting at a book entitled *A Discerning Gentleman's Guide to London*, selecting places he absolutely had to visit before he left.

It had been a trying week.

"What do they mean here, when they say 'house of ill-fame'?" Geórgios asked in a booming voice more suited to a busy ship than a tiny bedroom. "Is that a bordello?"

"Do you remember our little talk about not going out in public?" Eli replied before turning to the butler. "Cuttle, could you please tell them we aren't receiving callers?" They'd been over this.

"I told them, sir, but they were most insistent I inform you it's Miss Jane Bishop and her uncle on a matter of great importance."

What could that mean? Had Jane's uncle got wind of his fight with MacPherson and come to force an engagement after all? Or did this have something to do with the brief appearance he'd made at her club yesterday? He'd violated her request to stay away, but it had seemed the lesser evil.

"Is this the Jane you told me about when we were at sea?" A sudden spark of interest lit Geórgios's face. "Let me meet her."

"No!" Eli rushed to place himself before the door. "You stay here, please. I'll deal with this and be back in just a minute."

Geórgios's enormous shoulders slumped a touch, and Eli suppressed a twinge of guilt as he left him behind and followed Cuttle out into the hall. His friend hadn't received the warmest welcome in this house. Eli's father had forbidden the women from speaking to him and muttered darkly about "foreign invaders" whenever he saw him coming. But it was safest for everyone if Geórgios stayed out of sight, at least until the court of inquiry was over.

Soon he would resolve this whole business and they could return to their normal lives.

A moment later, Eli was settled with Jane and her family in the parlor, along with Hannah, who'd peered in to see what the commotion was about.

"What a pleasant surprise. How are you?" Eli began. The question was addressed to the room, but it was Jane he couldn't turn away from. It was almost painful to see her like this, dressed up for a morning call as though he were an ordinary acquaintance and nothing had passed between them. But her eyes betrayed her. A dozen emotions battled for space there.

"Very well, thank you." Jane smoothed down her skirts nervously. "Er...Cuttle will have told you that we aren't receiving visitors, as my father is ill. I believe you said there was a matter of importance to discuss?"

"Oh, but it's that," her uncle explained. "That your father was ill.

We were worried he must have caught Jane's cold at Ascot, and we've brought you some broth from our kitchens to speed his recovery. It was Jane's idea. Isn't she thoughtful?" He produced a large jar of amber liquid from a basket, the glass fogged with steam, and set it on the end table.

"Most thoughtful," Eli agreed with a helpless look to Jane.

It was plain that Mr. Bishop knew nothing of his fight with MacPherson, nor his visit to Miss Danby's house yesterday, so what was the meaning of this?

She had a sort of urgency written on her face, but all she said was, "We just wanted to make sure you were all right, and to invite you to call on us if there's anything at all we can do."

A chill worked its way down Eli's spine as understanding set in. She looked truly worried.

Could she know of the court-martial? There had been nothing in the papers.

"Why don't we all take a walk about the gardens?" Hannah suggested. "Our aunt has some rosebushes that are... Well, they aren't in bloom yet, exactly, but they have some very promising buds."

"How wonderful," Jane agreed too quickly.

Eli stared at his sister, dumbstruck. Was *she* behind this? The traitor! Were oaths of secrecy meaningless these days?

She countered his fury with a shrug and led them down the hall toward the back door.

Well, at least he might have a chance to steal a word or two with Jane while they walked. He fell into step beside her, deliberately lingering as the others drew ahead.

"What is this really about?" he whispered.

"I told you, we were worried," she returned.

"Worried about what?"

"I was hoping you would tell me that."

They were passing the kitchen, which was set at the rear of the town house overlooking the gardens, when a deep voice carried out to them from the other side of the door.

"Eli, is that you? Have your friends gone yet?"

Jane gasped at the sound, peering toward the kitchen with interest. "Who is *that*?"

"No one," Eli barked. "Never mind."

Hannah was a little ways ahead, at the back door of the house already. Judging from the panic written on her face, she'd heard Geórgios too. "Right this way," she urged their guests. "Pay no mind to our new cook."

"You go ahead," Eli told Jane. "I'll catch up with you in a moment. I'll just...get us some refreshments. We can take tea outside."

"I'll help you carry everything," Jane said happily.

"No, you won't," Eli shot back. "I'll ring a servant for that. You go on."

"I insist." She had an eager glint in her eye that said she knew exactly what she was doing. "Go ahead without us, Uncle Bertie. We'll catch up in just a moment."

With that, she flung open the door to the kitchen and dove inside, leaving Eli no choice but to race after her, slamming it shut in their wake. Geórgios sat at the table, a spread of cold meats and pasties before him. At their entrance, he rose to his feet and bowed.

"I asked you to stay upstairs!" Eli hissed.

"I got hungry." Geórgios's smile was all innocence, but the timing was too coincidental for Eli to be quite persuaded this was an accident.

Perhaps it's not too late to explain him away somehow.

But no, one glance at Geórgios revealed how impossible it would be. He cut a figure that would have been out of place anywhere. Aside from his imposing size and his long hair, his mode of dress marked him immediately as a foreigner. He still wore the traditional fustanella popular in his homeland, but he'd added a waistcoat in the French style overtop, plus a smattering of rings and a gold pin.

In short, he looked like he'd wandered through an assortment of fashion plates and travel illustrations, picking up whatever item struck his fancy.

"So this is Jane!" he exclaimed, looking altogether too pleased with himself for securing the introduction. "Ah! So beautiful."

"Oh, but you know me?" She appeared delighted where she should have been apprehensive. "I wish I knew your name as well, sir."

"That won't be necessary—" Eli began, but they both ignored him.

"Geórgios Diamantopoulos," he replied, adding another bow for good measure before he reclaimed his seat, even though Jane was still standing. "You may call me Geórgios. I feel like we are old friends, because Eli says so much about you."

I'm doomed.

"It really isn't appropriate to use someone's Christian name without a long-standing acquaintance," Eli interrupted. "Regardless, *Miss Bishop* needs to get back to her family before—"

"Oh no, I'm definitely staying here." Though no one had pulled out a chair for her, Jane did it herself and plucked a pasty from the plate to underscore her point. "Is that a Greek name?"

"Yes." The grin hadn't left Geórgios's face the whole time they spoke.

"So you must have met Eli while he was stationed there."

"Yes. We are like brothers!" Geórgios gestured to Eli. "It is he who teaches me English."

"*Jane.*" Eli loomed awkwardly over them both. If he sat down, it would mean this was really happening. "Geórgios is leaving England soon, and he has a lot to prepare. He really doesn't have time for this. I'd be happy to tell you everything myself if you would give me a moment in private."

Jane ignored him pointedly, her hungry gaze lapping up each revelation. "Why don't you start by telling me how you first met Eli? I'd love to hear all about it."

"Ah, well…" Geórgios hesitated, turning to Eli with a question written upon his face.

"You needn't worry," Jane pressed before he had a chance to say anything. "Eli and I are particular friends, and his secrets are safe with me. Besides, he's just said that he plans to tell me everything himself, hasn't he? Unless he didn't mean it?"

She shot Eli a look that dared him to reverse course.

"I meant it," Eli promised. "Only—"

"Then there's no harm in hearing it from your friend's own lips, now is there? Unless you're worried about what he might tell me."

What a mess. It was increasingly obvious Jane wouldn't leave the room unless he hauled the chair out from under her, an option that wasn't likely to put him back in her good graces. And if he silenced Geórgios now, she would be suspicious of anything Eli tried to explain.

There was no help for it. The truth would come out, and he would have to face the consequences.

"Go ahead, Geórgios," Eli said, resignation heavy in every word. "As Jane said, we are particular friends, and I trust her with my secrets."

Hopefully she won't judge me too harshly.

Geórgios spoke without further hesitation. But then, he'd always loved a good sailor's yarn. "We found him…how do you say it? Shipwrecked! His ship was wrecked, his men left without him, and we found him all alone. He was very thirsty."

"What about the pirates?" Jane continued. "Eli mentioned there were some pirates about?"

"But this is me!" Geórgios said, his booming voice full of mirth. "I am the pirate!"

"You're...a pirate."

Really? Jane looked him up and down with a critical eye. He would certainly be useful in a fight, with that physique. And he was wearing nearly as much gold as a British dandy, from a tooth that glinted when he smiled to the rings on his fingers. But he didn't look...well, *evil* enough. And shouldn't he be Eli's enemy, not his friend?

Was *this* what Eli had been hiding: that he'd secretly become a pirate sympathizer?

"Yes." Geórgios laughed. "Do you know, we have the same word in Greek? *Peiratēs!* But we are not criminals, beautiful Jane. No, no. We are like the man in the story. Eli, what is the story you told me? About the man who steals but is good?"

"Robin Hood."

"Yes," Geórgios shouted. "We are like Robin Hood!"

"Robin Hood gave the money *away*, though, Geórgios," Eli said with a glance out the window to the gardens where the others strolled. "You kept it all."

"Robin Hood gives to the poor," Geórgios replied. "But *we* are poor, so..." He spread his great hands wide as if to say, *What choice did I have?*

"I see," said Jane. He wasn't nearly as fearsome as she would've expected, for a pirate. And as he was proving so talkative, she could hardly leave. Perhaps this was how the sympathizing began.

"After the *Agonas*—" He stopped abruptly and turned to Eli. "Tell me how to say the *Agonas* in English."

"The Greek revolution against the Ottomans."

"Why is this twice as long?" Geórgios frowned. "But you under-stand. The *Agonas* brought us many years of war and hardship. Peloponnisos and Athína were freed, but those in Kōnstantinoúpolis, Kríti, and many other places, they had to leave their homes or they died. We had nothing. So." He shrugged broadly. "We had no choice but to be *peiratēs*."

Jane wasn't sure she was following all of this, but they were getting off track. "And so you found Eli," she prompted. Let them stick to that part.

"Yes." Geórgios nodded. "We took him to our ship. We wanted to sell him to England. But then our men got sick, many died, so…" Geórgios spread his hands in that same gesture. "We needed more men to sail the ship."

"You see?" Eli looked indignant. "I told you all that."

"So you just…kept him on your ship for two years. Without ever seeking a ransom."

Eli appeared supremely uncomfortable at this turn in the conver-sation, as though he would have liked to interrupt, but he clenched his jaw shut and let them carry on. "Two years?" Geórgios repeated. "Oh no, we escaped before that and went to *Gallía*."

"*Gallía?*" Jane blinked in confusion. "Where's that?"

"May *I* tell this story?" Eli offered. "I think I could offer some important nuance that Geórgios is lacking."

"You had your chance," Jane protested. "And anyway, I like the way he tells it. We're covering a lot of ground."

Happily, Geórgios seemed the type to keep talking once he'd started. "Ah, what do you call it in English? The place where they pray to the *pappās* Gregorios."

"Do you mean the pope?" Jane squinted at him. "Ireland?"

"No, no," he amended. "Where they eat many cheeses."

"France?"

"Yes!" he exclaimed, triumphant. "France. *Gallía.*"

She turned to Eli. "You've been in France for the past…how long, exactly?"

He sighed. "Three months, more or less."

"Why didn't you come straight home? What were you doing all that time?"

But Eli addressed Geórgios rather than answer her. "I think Jane must be satisfied she's heard the most damning parts of the story now. Would you mind going back upstairs to leave us in private a moment?"

With a final bite of his food and a wink toward Jane, Geórgios rose to his feet and lumbered away.

"I wanted to tell you," Eli began, taking a seat beside Jane at the table. It seemed important that she believe him, though there was no way to prove his intentions. If only Geórgios had stayed out of sight. He could've delivered the story with greater delicacy himself. "I hated keeping things from you, Jane, only I couldn't risk anyone else hearing of it."

"Oh?" Jane's eyes had taken on the hue of a brewing storm. She'd been a good deal warmer when Geórgios was still here. Maybe he shouldn't have sent his friend away quite yet. "I seem to recall spending quite a bit of time alone with you at the Lindens' house, where you might have unburdened yourself of any important secrets you were hiding, if you weren't otherwise occupied."

"It wasn't just a question of whether we were alone," he tried to explain. "How was I supposed to tell you that I'd befriended a pirate who'd helped me escape and hidden me in France for three months? If you said anything to your uncle, and he'd told Lady Kerr, the whole town would know. I'd be charged with desertion, and Geórgios would be executed. The navy isn't terribly forgiving toward pirates, even the ones who think themselves to be Robin Hood."

This seemed to mollify Jane somewhat, though her brows were still drawn in a furrow as she replied, "I could have kept a secret if you'd asked me to."

"I know you're able to keep a secret for a friend, I just didn't know if you'd be willing to do it for me," he admitted. "It...hasn't been easy to know where we stand since I came back."

Jane's expression softened at this, though it was still reserved. "It might have been easier to sort that out if you'd been honest with me from the start."

Very well. Maybe he'd gotten everything wrong, but he could do his best to put it right from here on in. He had little to lose at this point. She already knew enough to destroy him, and she was still here, listening. That was a good sign.

"I didn't mean for any of this to happen. Those first few months with the pirates, when the crew took ill, I thought I was certain to die without anyone ever knowing what had become of me. I wanted nothing more than to get free, or to get word back to my family, but I couldn't do anything. I was trapped.

"Geórgios often kept watch over me, and over time we became friends. He was kinder than the others. He was interested in learning English and hearing stories about my home. As we talked, I persuaded him that things might be better for both of us if he helped me escape. The life of a pirate was dangerous, and the Ottomans had retaken his village, so he had no place to return to. He agreed to help me get back to the continent. My escape was much as I've said. We took a chance when we were near Corinth and jumped overboard while he was on the evening's watch, then found passage with some merchants bound for France."

Jane had been silent while he spoke, but she interjected now. "Why didn't you present yourself to a British ship in the region?"

"I owed Geórgios my life. I couldn't abandon him, but he might have been recognized if we'd stayed nearby." It had been a nerve-wracking time, with no promise of safety ahead.

Eli hesitated. Up to this point, he'd behaved in keeping with his conscience as best he could under the circumstances. He had no cause for shame.

But then came the rest of the story.

"By the time we reached France, and I could part ways with Geórgios without putting him in any danger, I'd already been gone for over a year and a half. I knew that everyone I cared about must think me dead. Not only that, but that all of you must already have mourned me and come to accept my loss."

Was there any way to explain it so that she could understand? He felt like a liar, trying to make her see things as he had. Perhaps he'd lied to himself when he'd chosen to believe that the worst of the damage was already done. What difference would a little more time make?

"I'm starting to wish Geórgios were still telling this story," Jane muttered. "He'd have told me what you did in France by now."

"I waited." Waited when he could have pressed on. Cost Jane and his family another three months of thinking him dead, when they might have instead known the truth. "Geórgios stayed in Marseille and I went on to Paris and earned a bit of money as an English tutor while I tried to get news from home. Eventually, I discovered that my brother was in the city on his grand tour and I found him—"

"I don't understand. Why couldn't you just go back?"

He drew a long breath. "A gentleman can't end an engagement."

He studied Jane as comprehension dawned, dreading the next emotion that would cross her face. Would she judge his choice? Would she be disgusted with him?

"You'd rather hide in France than be married to Cecily?"

"I knew we would have made each other miserable." They would've been like his parents, constantly arguing while their children pretended not to hear. Decades of that stretched out before him, with no escape. "I couldn't refuse the match, having been caught in a compromising position." At least his service had given him an excuse to postpone the unhappy event, but it had always lingered in the background. "Then the shipwreck came, followed by my captivity. And I got to thinking…if I've been dead this long anyway, I may as well wait to have news of her situation before I return. I didn't think it likely that she would mourn me too deeply."

"Oh, you'd be surprised." Jane's tone betrayed her annoyance. "She cost Uncle Bertie a fortune in crepe, and she used to burst into tears anytime someone mentioned your name. I think she liked the attention. But never mind. So your brother knew where you were? What about Hannah and your parents?"

"I swore Jacob to secrecy. Promised that I would go home as soon as Lady Kerr was safely married. He knew that she'd formed another engagement but didn't know the date, so I had him write home to ask after her and await their reply before I could come back." Knowing nothing of her feelings for Sir Thomas, he wasn't willing to risk the possibility that she might give her first engagement priority over her second. As it turned out, his time in France had been for nothing. Cecily was long-since wed and expecting her son when they'd docked at Marseille, and he might have avoided a great deal of trouble if he'd known it was safe to go straight home.

If only he could do it over. He would've returned to England with nothing to hide, no secrets to divide him from Jane. Maybe she would've been willing to let her guard down, if only she'd sensed his sincerity from the start.

Jane's face remained still as she took this in. He wished she would say something.

"Tell me what you're thinking... Do you hate me for it?"

"No," she assured him, reaching out to press a hand to his forearm. The whole of his consciousness narrowed to that tiny point of contact. "I could never hate you. To be perfectly honest, I'd probably have hidden in France for three months too, if it meant avoiding a marriage to Cecily. I just...I still don't understand why, if *you* felt that way, you went out to the gardens with her in the first place?"

"I'm sorry I did. I can't tell you how often I regretted it." He gave her a moment to take in the apology before he continued. "I could say I'd had too much to drink that evening or that it was a rash decision, but nothing I say will excuse my behavior. I made a selfish and impulsive choice, and I paid the consequence. But at the time, it seemed such a small thing, to kiss a woman in the gardens at a house party. It was ten minutes of my life, at most. I never thought it would lead further than that."

The explanation didn't seem to have the effect he'd hoped. It was torture to come this close and find forgiveness still just beyond reach. And there was no one to blame but himself.

"Is there anything I can say to make things right?" he asked softly. "I hate that I've hurt you, Jane. If there's something else you need from me, tell me so that I can give it to you."

Jane ran her finger along the rim of the plate Geórgios had left behind, avoiding Eli's gaze. "I suppose...I don't understand why you picked *her*. Instead of...well, me." The last part came out little more than a murmur. "It made me wonder, why wasn't I good enough?"

"Oh." Eli sat up a bit straighter. This was an unexpected gift one he hadn't dared hope for. "I didn't think you felt that way about me. At least not then."

"I spent *all* my time with you."

"Yes, but you also kept saying what a good friend I was," Eli pointed out. "I wish you'd kissed me under a secluded archway instead. It would have saved us an enormous amount of trouble." He would never have sailed out of England if Jane had been his match. Never would have lost all that time.

Jane finally managed to look him in the eye, some of the tension broken. "I don't think I was courageous enough yet. And anyway, isn't it supposed to be the gentleman's job to take the first step?"

"I might have done if I'd known how you felt. I was afraid it would be unwelcome."

Eli's smile faded as he reached out a hand to cup her face, his voice suddenly serious. "Jane. You must know how I feel about you. How I've always felt about you."

He leaned in and brushed his lips over hers, wishing it were five years earlier and this were their first kiss. To think how much happiness they'd missed! Maybe it wasn't too late to set things right after all. There must be a way forward. He wouldn't lose her again.

Eli coaxed her lips open, pleading shamelessly for more of her warmth, more of her touch. Finally, he traced his mouth along her jaw, spreading a trail of heat to her ear, where he whispered, "You *are* good enough, Jane. You're the very best. There's no one else I want."

Jane clutched Eli tightly, finding his mouth again. A groan escaped his lips, mingling with the tapping sound outside.

Wait, why is there a tapping sound outside?

Eli broke off the kiss and whirled toward the window. There was a face there, his brows drawn together in outrage as his fingers rapped against the glass.

It was Jane's uncle.

Twenty-Four

OH NO. NO, NO, NO.

The face had already vanished, most likely because its owner was racing back indoors to confront them at any second.

This was a nightmare. Eli had suffered it before, more than once. Some men on the *Libertas* had been haunted by the battles they'd fought or storms they'd barely survived. Eli relived the moment where Herbert Bishop had caught him compromising Cecily and forced him into an odious engagement.

Eli pinched himself discreetly beneath his shirt cuff. No improvement.

"Quick!" Jane cried. "You hide under the table, and I'll say he imagined it."

But Mr. Bishop was already upon them, flinging open the door with a clatter.

"Lieutenant, *really*." His expression was a dangerous mix of shock, outrage, and what might have been glee. "I cannot believe you would accost Jane in such a manner!"

"I'm not accosted," said Jane, panic rising in her voice. She jumped to her feet to meet her uncle as he descended upon them, and Eli followed suit. "I'm not sure what you think you saw, Uncle, but you must be mistaken. That window is very foggy. Lieutenant Williams only leaned over to brush a crumb from my hair, and—"

"I shall not be hoodwinked, my dear. I saw it very clearly." Yes, that was definitely glee. "You are compromised. Ruined beyond repair. Do you deny it, Lieutenant?"

Jane looked at him with murder in her eyes. *Deny it,* that look said. But how could he lie to Bishop's face, when the man had caught them in the act? It would be pointless.

"I would prefer not to use that description, but I will own that I kissed your niece, sir." If only there were a lever he could pull to slow time. Gain a few minutes to think and to talk to Jane. But Bishop barreled forward like a post chaise.

"Taking advantage of the trust we placed in you." He clasped his hands together as if in prayer. "But even so, I hope you are still a man of honor and will fulfill your duty."

"This is absurd," Jane insisted. "He kissed me last week at the Lindens' house before an entire room, and you had no objection. Miss Linden as well. Perhaps he should marry her."

"You know perfectly well it isn't the same thing. We were playing forfeits, and that 'entire room' served as your chaperone. Here I find the lieutenant has contrived to get you alone, and only my arrival prevented further surrender to temptation. It will be impossible to find you another match if this should be known."

"How could it be known?" Jane's voice continued to rise, though whether in frustration or fear was hard to judge. "If you forget it ever happened, so shall we. Uncle, be reasonable."

If Mr. Bishop's shock had been tempered by other sentiments at the outset, it stood alone now. His eyes had formed enormous circles to match his open mouth. "Forget it ever happened? Jane, do you consider stealing kisses with a gentleman to be something I could sweep under the rug for you? What were your intentions, if not to be married? I thought I raised you better than this."

She was making things worse. They needed to change course.

"That's enough," Eli said. "Let me speak."

The Bishops turned to him in unison. It would have been a more inspiring moment if he had any idea what to say. This still felt unreal, yet his next words would determine the rest of their lives.

He had to marry Jane.

There was no other course. If Mr. Bishop knew the half of what had passed between them, he would be making the same speech with the aid of a pistol. And then there was Hannah's meddling, and Cecily hounding about for rumors. This had already gone past the point where it could be kept quiet. There were too many parties to their secrets, and Jane was the one who stood to lose everything if they were exposed.

He'd promised her on Ladies' Day that he would protect her reputation, and he'd failed miserably. It was his duty to fix this. Eli squared his shoulders and met Mr. Bishop's eyes.

"I'm sorry that I betrayed your trust, and Jane's. I can't imagine what you must think of me, but I want you to know that this wasn't something I did for sport. I care deeply for your niece, and I intend to make her my wife."

Bishop's pique vanished like rain clouds parting to reveal the sun. "I knew you were a good man, Lieutenant."

"Do I have any say in this?" Jane's cheeks were dotted with red.

Is she angry with me, or only her uncle? He hadn't expected her to weep tears of joy at such a rushed proposal, but surely Jane could see he was trying to set things right.

"Certainly not!" Bishop rounded on her. "Your say was in allowing the kiss."

"If I may, Mr. Bishop?" Eli cut in. "I must inform you both of an important matter that may impact your decision. The navy has expressed some concerns about my absence that they wish to clear up before they can assign me a new post."

"Concerns?" Bishop echoed. "What sort of concerns?"

"They wish to conduct an inquiry to confirm my whereabouts during that time. I'll settle the whole thing presently, but you understand why it might not be in Jane's best interest to announce a formal engagement to me until after I clear my name. I suggest we keep the offer a secret for now. You know my intentions, and you have my word as a gentleman. If the inquiry reaches a conclusion which tarnishes my reputation, I would expect Jane to release me with no one the wiser. It wouldn't be fair to tie our futures together when mine is uncertain."

There. It would buy Jane time to think, at least. And it was all quite true. How *could* he promise any life for her when he didn't know if he would find himself branded a deserter?

Jane grew quiet, appeased by this strategy, perhaps. But he couldn't entirely forget her initial reaction. She had protested a bit *too* strenuously. Not the best beginning for a marriage.

"I see." Mr. Bishop paused for a moment. "You're quite right to think of it. Most considerate. But once you *are* found innocent, you must be married before you return to sea. I don't wish Jane to be waiting for years as Cecily did. Not that I expect you to be captured by any more pirates, of course, but one never knows. If we could obtain a special license directly after the inquiry, that would reassure us all."

Married before he returned to sea. Even if he was cleared, it didn't guarantee them an easy life. He would barely be able to enjoy the wedding night before it was time to leave Jane again. She'd made her objections plain, but what other choice did he have? He needed an income if he was to support a wife.

It was no worse than what all navy wives endured. The important thing now was to appease Mr. Bishop until they could talk further. Eli replied, "I'm sure we can make some arrangement."

"Perhaps Sir Thomas could be of assistance. He is a knight, you know."

"Oh, yes, I'd nearly forgotten," Eli murmured with a faint smile toward Jane.

She didn't quite smile back, but her eyes held a grudging resignation.

It was probably the best he could have hoped for, given the circumstances.

Jb

Engaged. Promised to Eli, whether either of them liked it or not.

"We must have you fitted for a new gown straightaway and start planning the celebrations. Would you prefer a brunch or a supper after the wedding? We should start our guest list now, even if we can't send out invitations until this inquiry is done..." While Uncle Bertie laid out the Herculean series of tasks before her over breakfast the next morning, Jane pushed her sausage and eggs around her plate and wondered at the quirk of timing that had ensnared her. Every time she looked up, Bertie added a new detail to his plans. She hadn't seen him this happy since Cecily secured her proposal from Sir Thomas.

Jane loved her uncle dearly, but he was putting her to the test with this business.

She hadn't even said yes, and it was already arranged, right down to the timing of her nuptials. Before Eli returned to sea, he'd said. If he was cleared by the inquiry next week, she might be a married woman by the one that followed. And then what? They would say their goodbyes and he would sail away from her, leaving nothing but letters to remember him by. She would hold her breath each time the post came, dreading the one with black sealing wax that marked a tragedy.

She wasn't suited for such a future. She still remembered how it felt to receive the news of Eli's supposed death two years ago. Cecily reading each word slowly until she'd broken down into hysterics and Jane had to finish it herself. He hadn't even been hers then, and still it had torn her apart.

She couldn't lose him again.

Thankfully, the footman brought in a letter from Mr. Linden after breakfast to distract Bertie from his list. Jane savored the silence for an entire five seconds.

"I can't believe you're marrying Eli," Edmund said once their uncle had withdrawn to attend to his correspondence. "You didn't even tell us he was courting you. Are you moving out then?"

"I suppose so," Jane replied. "They don't keep their own town house, so I shall probably live at his parents' estate in Devon." The idea made her heart sink. She would have to leave her club behind, and she wouldn't see her family or Della unless she came back each year for the season. It was exactly the situation she'd hoped to avoid.

Would Bertie and Edmund miss her as much as she would miss them?

"Could I have your room?" asked Edmund, spoiling her tender reflections.

Shortly past noon, Eli turned up, looking sheepish as Bertie ushered him in with a great fuss.

"I received word from the court of inquiry this morning. They've summoned me to appear before them next Tuesday."

Somehow, it seemed simultaneously so far away that Jane would die of impatience and so close that they had no time to prepare. "Is there anything we can do to help? May we attend?"

"These types of proceedings are held onboard ships, and it will only be the judges and crew present. I'll call on you afterward to tell you how it goes." His expression softened as he took in her distress. "Don't worry. I'll sort this all out."

Jane was not persuaded that a charge of desertion was the type of thing that one simply "sorted out," but she held her tongue in front of Uncle Bertie. Seeing her sideways glance, he rose to his feet. "I imagine there might be things you two wish to discuss in private. I'll give you a few minutes, though I trust you both understand there will be *no more kissing* until you're married."

Bertie attempted to muster a stern gaze, but he was so obviously overjoyed to have Jane spoken for, it failed to inspire any fear in their hearts.

Once he was gone, Eli gave up his chair and came to sit beside Jane on the divan, taking her hands into his. "I know this must be frightening for you, but these sorts of proceedings end all the time with no blame apportioned to the officer. It's standard practice to investigate any complaint or irregularity. It doesn't mean they'll charge me with anything."

"But what's the punishment for desertion? Don't they—" She bit back her words, struggled for a moment, then judged them worth saying. She had to know what he was facing. "Don't they execute men for that?"

"Only in wartime, really," said Eli. The reassurance didn't help much. Jane bit the inside of her cheek, wishing she could shield him from danger. "The important thing is, it won't get as far as charges of desertion, because they need to have some evidence before they can recommend a court-martial. As far as I can tell, they don't have anything but a letter from my former captain voicing some vague suspicions."

"But those suspicions are *true*," Jane whispered, even though they were quite alone. It seemed too great a secret to trust to an audible pitch. "What if they find out you were in France for three months?"

"The only person who knows that besides us is Geórgios, and whatever his faults, he would never testify against me. He'd be putting his own neck in the noose if he admitted to piracy, for one thing, and he's also loyal."

Jane's head was swimming. How could he sound so confident when everything was an unknown?

"Anyway, I have a friend at the naval lords' office I'll call on next. With any luck, he might tell me if the judges know more than they've let on." At least that was something, though it didn't stop the pounding of Jane's heart. Eli squeezed her hands tightly. "Trust me. This will all be over in a few days, and then we can put it behind us."

"All right," she murmured. What else could she do? But despite Eli's optimism, their worries wouldn't end once his name was cleared. It would only put him that much closer to leaving her again.

Jane's doubt must have shown on her face, for Eli's brow furrowed in concern. "What's the matter?"

"It's only...I'll still worry for you, even if the inquiry goes well. You'll be out across the world from me, and I'll spend every day waiting for news. What will happen if Lord Melbourne takes us to war with China?"

Eli drew a long breath, his face grim. "I wish I could stay, but what choice do I have? Without my income, I won't have any way to support you. A lieutenant's pay might not be a fortune, but if you live modestly, at least I could rent you a house in town where you can live as you please. And if I can get my hands on enough prize money, it needn't be too long. Five or ten years at most."

Five or ten *years*? She knew officers often served longer, but even that was an eternity. "I don't need you to rent me a town house. I'd expected that we'd live in Devon."

"And give up your club? I can't let you do that."

She might have been grateful if the circumstances had been different. All she'd ever wanted was the freedom to manage her own affairs. Her independence. But it meant nothing if Eli wasn't safe.

"I'd rather give up my club than risk losing you again. I don't mind living in the country."

Jane had never imagined she would say those words. Her club had meant the world to her a few short weeks ago. It still did. But nothing was worth the cost of Eli's life. She'd thought that she could protect herself from the grief she'd felt when her parents died if she didn't depend on anyone, and he'd snuck his way into her heart despite her efforts to keep a distance between them. Offered her a glimpse of what it would feel like to have his full support and affection. She didn't want to go back to a life without him. She wanted him *here*, safe at her side, as a true partner through everything.

"You don't know how hard it is to listen to my parents fight all day," Eli said. "And you'd be so far from your friends and family in Devon, you might come to resent me in time. I couldn't bear that, Jane."

He looked so troubled by the idea, Jane's protest died on her lips. She noticed the shadows under his eyes for the first time. Had he slept since yesterday? He had enough to deal with before Uncle Bertie had forced him into proposing, it wasn't fair to add to his burdens. Perhaps he hadn't wanted any of this. "You should be focusing on your defense. Let's wait to discuss this after the inquiry is over. I don't want to keep you from your friend any longer."

Eli hesitated, searching her face. "Are you certain? I thought you might want to discuss the wedding. Everything happened so quickly yesterday, we hardly had a chance to speak."

"It will keep," she assured him. "You wouldn't have to plan a wedding and a court inquiry in the same week if Uncle Bertie hadn't forced your hand. I'd hate to be a distraction for you. You can call on me directly after the hearing on Tuesday. Until then, you should devote all your energies to your preparations. That's what matters most."

"If you're sure…" He placed a chaste kiss upon her cheek and rose to his feet, still looking to Jane as he retrieved his hat, as though expecting her to call him back. When she didn't, he nodded and saw himself out.

Twenty-Five

ELI SCARCELY NOTICED THE NEIGHBORHOOD PASS BY HIM ON the way to Halsey's town house. Everything seemed to move in a blur.

I'd hate to be a distraction for you. It had all the appearance of a kindness, if one could forget that he and Jane had been pressed into a surprise engagement only yesterday, and she'd barely spoken to him since. Distraction was inevitable. The only question was: Did she plan to release him the moment the inquiry was over?

He would greatly prefer to know the answer before Tuesday.

When Hal received him in the sitting room and offered him a drink, Eli took it without hesitation.

"Feeling nervous, are you?" Hal was good enough to pour himself a bit of whiskey to match Eli and not comment on the fact that it was barely one in the afternoon.

"That's an understatement." His nerves at the prospect of the inquiry could be managed. He'd been preparing himself as best he could, and all he'd told Jane was quite true. He liked his odds of coming out clear if they had nothing more damning than a letter.

His engagement, though. That was more complicated.

Was Jane only distant because she was worried about him, or did she regret being trapped in a marriage she hadn't chosen? There was little hope of assuaging his fears anytime soon. Even if she didn't want to marry him, Jane wasn't the sort to kick a man while he was down. He wouldn't know her true thoughts until he was out of danger.

"I was hoping you might have heard something about my case from the naval lords," Eli began. At least this was one problem he could address. "Do you know if they have any evidence against me beyond Captain Powlett's letter?"

"I have good news for you there. I understand there's nothing else. Admiral Ward came to me himself when he realized I'd served with you on the *Libertas*—strictly an informal discussion, of course—and I told him that all of us saw you go under, and that there were pirates in the region at the time." Hal smiled, lifting his glass in a toast. "To your imminent exoneration."

"Let's not celebrate the victory before it's won."

The greatest danger lay not in the letter, but in what the judges might extract from his testimony if he gave the wrong answers.

"Do you think they'll ask a great many questions about my absence?"

"What should it matter if they do?" Hal still wore a smile, but the corners were beginning to droop as he contemplated this question. "No one is trying to trap you, if that's what you're worried about. You need only reassure them this is all a misunderstanding and they'll be happy to send you on your way, I'm sure."

It would have been as easy as Hal made it sound, if only he didn't have Geórgios to protect and his own delay in France to conceal. What if they asked for the exact date he'd arrived there? He could lie, but if someone turned up to expose him later, it wouldn't matter that the inquiry didn't have enough evidence to charge him with desertion. They would have him up for perjury.

"What's wrong?" Hal asked. "I thought you'd be happier at this news."

"I am happy," Eli said swiftly.

"No, you aren't. Your face is stuck in an expression I can only describe as" —He considered a moment before settling on—"like you're expecting a horse to kick you in the balls."

"I'm just eager to have everything over with."

Hal stared at him until it became uncomfortable. His dark eyes seemed to bore holes in Eli's facade. "You're hiding something."

"That's absurd!"

"It's the truth. We may not have seen each other in two years, but I still know when you're bluffing."

"Leave it, Hal." Eli shot him his darkest look.

If his friend had read him this easily, it didn't bode well for his chances at the inquiry.

But Halsey was undeterred. "I won't turn you in, you know. I wouldn't betray a friend. Did you truly desert?"

"No!" Seeing that this would be an insufficient explanation, Eli added, "The truth is a touch more complicated, but I assure you, I never intended to shirk my duty. It's best we forget this. I wouldn't want to put you in a difficult position."

"I might be able to help, if you let me."

The offer was tempting. Halsey had always been a decent fellow not the sort to go back on his word. But even so, it was an outrageous risk to run.

Perhaps he could trust his friend with a half-truth. Enough to understand the situation Eli was in, but not enough to put anyone in danger.

"Very well. There is something I've left out of the story," he admitted. "Someone helped me get free of the pirates, but I cannot discuss the circumstances of his assistance or the path I took back to England without putting his life in danger. You can see the dilemma I'll face if they ask for too many details at the inquiry."

"Ah." Hal required a moment to digest this news, his face grave. "That is a bad spot. What are the odds that anyone could catch you out if you hide your friend's involvement from the judges?"

"I wish I knew. I don't think anyone currently in England could expose me, but I can't say with certainty that no one with knowledge of my actions will ever *return* to England." The crew on the merchant ship to France had seen Geórgios and knew when he'd really arrived at port. He'd tried to stay out of sight in Paris, but his landlady or a handful of others could undo him so long as their memories remained fresh, and the British navy were everywhere. "You know how travelers love to talk about any shared connection they can find."

"Hmm." Hal ran a thumb across his beard. "Perhaps the safest option for you is not to testify at all."

"Refuse to answer?" Eli knew the judges had no power to compel him to give evidence at the inquiry, but he'd dismissed the possibility as likely to invite a court-martial. "Won't that make me look guilty?"

"Not if you go about it the right way." Hal jumped to his feet and strode toward the door. "Back in a moment. Let me get some papers."

He returned with a stack of leather-bound volumes tucked under his arm, which he soon had splayed across the tea table between them.

"I'm certain I've seen a case where the accused refused to testify at the inquiry and came out well. Let me just find it…"

Eli craned his neck, struggling to take in the stream of words that flashed before him as Halsey flipped the pages in search of the correct record.

"Ah, here we are. You see? The accused claimed it would be unfair to answer at an inquiry before he even knew what the charges against him would be. The judges accepted this was a valid reason not to testify."

Eli read over the transcripts, searching the judges' words for signs of doubt. The case was from quite a few years ago, and he didn't recognize their names. Still, at least Hal had provided him with an idea. A way to escape a court-martial and save his career without putting Geórgios in danger. "Do you really think this will work?"

"It's better than committing perjury, isn't it?"

Eli had to own that it was.

Jane had expected Bertie to pounce on her the moment Eli departed with questions about their progress on wedding plans, but he was curiously absent.

Perhaps he's hoping that if he leaves us alone long enough, I'll ruin myself too completely to back out of this engagement. In spite of her uncle's warnings about the dangers of kissing, Jane had to wonder if he'd somehow contrived this outcome when they'd visited Eli's town house yesterday. Why else had he been peering in the kitchen window at precisely the right moment?

She decided to go in search of him to better demonstrate that Eli's call had ended with her frock still in perfect order.

Bertie occupied two adjacent rooms on the upper story of the house, overlooking the street below. She found him seated at his desk, engrossed in papers. He jumped at her greeting, and when he looked up, his eyes were bright and rimmed with pink, as if tears threatened.

What's happened? Jane's heart pounded against her ribs.

"What is that you're reading? Have you had bad news?" Bertie might be a tad excitable, but she'd never seen him weep except for a death.

He rose to greet her.

"Pardon? Oh no, nothing to trouble you with. Why have you come to see me? Did you and your lieutenant discuss your preference for a wedding date, by any chance? You recall that Cecily is on the committee of arrangements for the ball on the twelfth, so it will have to be afterward..."

"Tell me what's troubling you before we talk about that. Now I'm worried."

Bertie managed a faint laugh. "There is no cause for it, I assure you. I only had a letter from Mr. Linden that put me in bad spirits."

"Is he hurt?" Though Mr. Linden had not stood as a parent to her in the same way Uncle Bertie had, he was near enough to it.

"Oh, perfectly fine. He's only a bit cross with me. It's nothing that won't mend." Seeing Jane's worried expression, Bertie sighed and returned to his chair. She followed suit, occupying a leather armchair that squeaked as she settled into it. Bertie continued. "You recall that he invited me to visit Bath with him when we were there for the races? Well, I suppose he took it a bit personally when I declined. He feels that I'm...neglecting our friendship."

Jane took a moment to absorb both what Bertie said and what he left unsaid.

"Anyway," he said briskly, "our quarrel doesn't concern you. We always sort things out."

Jane normally would have let the matter end there, for she was of the view that Uncle Bertie could decide for himself how much he wished to share with her, but this felt different. He might have gone with Mr. Linden if only he weren't so caught up in his charges' lives.

Cecily was married now, Jane was engaged to Eli, and even Edmund was nearly an adult. Yet Bertie still devoted himself wholly to their various concerns. No doubt her recent engagement would only add to the responsibilities that kept him from following his own heart.

"Forgive me," Jane pleaded. "I fear we've been terribly thoughtless."

"What can you mean, my dear?"

"You should go to Mr. Linden. He needs to know that he's a priority in your life, and if it weren't for me and Cecily, you could have gone to Bath with him as he wanted instead of fretting over our plans for the season. When was the last time you had a chance to pay him a visit that didn't center on all of us?"

"My dear Jane." Bertie laughed, blushing slightly at her declaration. "I couldn't possibly rush off to Bath now. Lieutenant Williams is facing an inquiry! And then there's your wedding to think of, once he's cleared. I'm sure once I explain all that's transpired since we left Sunninghill, he'll understand."

"If someone is important to you, you have to show them," she insisted. "I know you're trying to care for me the way you've always done, and I'm grateful, but I'm old enough now that you can trust me on my own. Cecily and Edmund too. At the very least, you should go down to visit for a few days and tell Mr. Linden that you'll take that trip with him as soon as my wedding is done with. It would show him that you're taking his feelings to heart. It isn't far, and you can be back before Eli's inquiry on Tuesday. I can manage the house until then."

Bertie stared at the letter for a long moment without reading it.

"I know you can," he said at last. "You're a very capable young lady. I'm quite proud at how well you've turned out. It's only that…I don't know. I suppose I feel guilty if I'm not there when you might need me. As if I'm being selfish."

"You aren't," she assured him. "You never could be."

With a slow nod to himself, Bertie seemed to decide. "Very well then. I'll pop down to Sunninghill tomorrow, and I'll entrust things here to you. Only you mustn't entertain any gentleman callers while I'm away. You don't have the protection of a husband quite yet."

"Of course not. The only gentleman caller is likely to be Eli, and I've told him he should put all his focus on preparing for the inquiry anyway, so he won't come again until afterward."

Regret hit her the moment she'd said it. She didn't relish waiting alone here for news, but she would have to manage. Eli needed to focus on his defense, and Bertie needed to call on Mr. Linden.

"But what about all we have to *do*? You must allow me to take you to the dressmaker today, at the very least. I won't have you wait until the last minute and risk looking shabby."

"Let's not worry about that yet," Jane pleaded. "Even if the lieutenant is cleared, there's so much to sort out before we can finalize any plans."

"What is there to sort out, aside from the special license?"

Jane dropped her gaze, suddenly shy. Bertie was so happy to see her engaged after all this time, she hated to complain. "Only the usual things, I suppose," she mumbled unconvincingly. "I'm sure every bride needs a little time to plan for married life."

The creases on Bertie's forehead grew deeper as he scrutinized her. "I fear we may be long overdue for a good talk. Are you cross with me for pressing your engagement? I know it might not have been the most illustrious manner of achieving a match, but there's no reason that should bode ill for your future happiness. The important thing is that he shall make you a fine husband, and you shall be settled in comfort."

"It isn't that." She sighed.

"Then what?"

"It's only that I hate to think of him returning to the navy when there might be a war soon. What's the good of a fine husband if he puts himself in danger?"

"Hmm." This seemed weighty enough to finally dampen Bertie's enthusiasm. "Have you asked your lieutenant whether he intends his naval career to be a long one?"

"I think things might be different if he didn't have need of the income, but there's no other way for us to afford a house in town. He doesn't wish for me to live in the country with his parents."

"I must say I agree. Devon is entirely too far from me." Uncle Bertie gave her a playful wink, but his countenance grew somber afterward. He passed a long moment in deep thought, then seemed to shake it off as quickly as it had come. "But enough of this. You must take your own advice, my dear. Don't search for reasons to put off happiness. You and Lieutenant Williams care for one another and you're both people of good character. I'm sure we shall find a solution to everything."

He made it sound so simple, as if happiness could be assured by wishing alone.

Even so, Jane hoped he was right. She was certainly wishing hard enough for it.

Twenty-Six

Eli was not quite sure how he found himself sneaking into Jane's courtyard in the dead of night that Monday.

He'd intended to focus on preparing for the inquiry, as she'd advised. But once he and Hal had determined that the whole of his plan was to keep his mouth shut and hope for the best, it had left a great deal of free time to stew about his engagement. He'd finally concluded that his only choices were to drive himself mad with wondering, or to talk to Jane.

He'd tried a morning call—a more respectable, conventional option—but the butler had coolly informed him that Mr. Bishop was absent and Jane would not be admitting gentlemen until his return.

She'll forgive the intrusion once I explain, Eli told himself as he scaled the gate behind Jane's town house with no small concern for the state of his trousers and dropped to the earth below. It might not be the most respectable means of entry—and yes, one busybody neighbor with an owl's vision was all he needed to sound the alarm—but what was the worst that could happen? He could hardly be forced to propose a second time.

It wasn't a particularly difficult climb up the side of the house, as the ground-floor windows were framed with decorative brickwork that jutted out from the face of the building and gave him easy purchase. Certainly no worse than scaling a ship's mast. The hard part was in contemplating what would happen if she didn't answer his tapping at the window.

When Jane's lamplit face finally appeared at the pane, inches from his own, she gave a little shriek.

"Shh!" he said, quite uselessly.

She rushed to undo the latch and threw the window wide to admit him to the safety of her chambers. "What are you *doing*?" She whispered, jerking the curtains back in place to hide them from sight the moment his feet were safely upon the floorboards.

"Your butler refused to admit me this morning." Eli removed his hat, which had miraculously retained its perch atop his head the whole time. "I needed to see you. This was the only way."

"Did you consider throwing pebbles at my window until I came down to unlock the door, like an ordinary prowler?"

"It was an easy climb," Eli protested.

Jane stared at him in wonder for another minute, then took the hat from his hands and plopped it on her vanity. It seemed a concession. Eli's eyes had adjusted to the lamplight by now, and he absorbed the gentle form of Jane's curves beneath her nightgown. She hadn't put on her wrapper before she came to the window, and the thin muslin didn't do much to preserve modesty.

"I woke you," he murmured.

"It's all right." She must have realized what he was looking at, for she folded her arms across her chest and blushed, the faint color barely visible in the lamplight. "Has something happened? Have you decided to make a run for it instead of facing the inquiry?"

"Make a run for it?" Eli smothered his laugh, a reflex prompted by surprise more than amusement, before it could wake the household. "Why would you think such a thing?"

"What other reason could you have to creep into my room in the dead of night the evening before your hearing?"

"To talk to you, of course."

"You should be sleeping so that you're at your best tomorrow!" Jane's eyes flashed in the lamplight, but her pique didn't mollify him in the least. She worried because she cared. It was something to hold on to.

"I couldn't sleep. I kept thinking about how if I'm cleared tomorrow, your uncle will want to announce our engagement straightaway even though we haven't discussed things properly. This felt like my last chance to speak to you while you can still tell me what you truly want." Eli brought a hand to rest against Jane's cheek, cupping her face in his palm.

The air felt heavy between them, the scent of crushed grass on the soles of his shoes mingling with the faint, acrid smoke of the lamp, and something else. The tension of what neither of them had said aloud yet.

Jane parted her lips, but Eli spoke first, half-afraid that she might put him off again before he got out what he'd come to say. "No, let me finish. I need to tell you this. We were rushed into a match before you'd had a chance to think about anything I'd told you. I hate to think you only agreed because your uncle forced your hand."

Everything up until this point could still turn out to be a dream. Jane could still tell him that she'd thought on it further and couldn't forgive his mistakes. She could still release him. Worse, if she *didn't* release him, he might spend a lifetime wondering how much of the choice was hers.

"Would you let me try again?" Eli dropped to his knee, fumbling in his breast pocket for the ring he'd purchased yesterday, a delicate amethyst teardrop surrounded by seed pearls. "A proper proposal this time. As you deserve."

Jane sucked in a swift breath, her eyes dark pools in the shadows.

"Will you marry me?" Eli asked softly, half-afraid of the answer in spite of their current circumstances. "I know I've been foolish, and it isn't fair to ask anything of you with the inquiry hanging over my head, but I want you to know that there's no one for me but you, Jane. If I come out of this unscathed, I'll give you everything I have. But if you don't want that, tell me now, and we'll think of some excuse to put off your uncle before this goes any further."

"I know that," she whispered, holding out her hand to accept his ring. "Uncle Bertie didn't force me into anything, Eli. I want this. I want *you*."

Eli rose to his feet to claim Jane's lips, giddy with the thrill of her acceptance.

She kissed him deeply, tracing the plane of his chest as her hands came up to hold him. He shivered at her touch, though the air in her room was warm.

"Jane," he breathed. Eli's heart was hammering.

But she didn't pull back. Nor did she tell him again that he should go home to sleep.

He slid his thumb across her collarbone, pushing the muslin gown lower. It was like opening a present. The buttons were hard to make out in the darkness, barely the size of his fingernail, and he undid each one with methodical care. Jane had his shirt off with greater efficiency, bending to kiss his chest as she stripped off the fabric.

"Are you sure?" he whispered.

This still didn't feel real. He could measure the time since their first meeting in the library in weeks, when she'd walked out on him with only a few cold words. Everything seemed to have unfolded at a breakneck pace since then. But at the same time, it felt like this had been building forever. For all the time they'd spent together, and the time they'd been apart, when she'd haunted his thoughts. It was all for this.

In answer, Jane pulled him closer, her grip telling him she didn't intend to let go.

Eli kicked off his shoes and trousers and pulled Jane to the bed, naked skin against naked skin. The sensation had him swelling rapidly against her hip. She kissed him, opening her mouth to invite him in. He slid his hand down over her belly to find her sex. She was already wet, but not enough. He teased her with his fingers until her breath turned shaky. There, that was better.

"I don't want to hurt you," he murmured, pulling back from their kiss long enough to speak. "Do you want to stay on top, so that you have more control?"

In answer, she braced her weight on his shoulders to bring her legs around and straddle him. But instead of settling back down on him, she remained with her body suspended, the tip of his cock barely touching her.

Eli whimpered, rocking forward to press into her by the barest degree. It was the smallest movement, and it was everything. He groaned, desperate for more.

"Please," he managed. "God, Jane, I want you so much."

"Go slowly," she instructed, humming a sigh as she inched herself slightly lower on his cock. "Like that."

Good Lord. She was going to kill him with wanting. She was so tight and wet around his shaft, it took every ounce of control to obey. *Slowly.* Eli squeezed his hand in between the place where their sexes joined and pressed against her the way she'd liked it before. He was rewarded for his efforts with a little mewl of pleasure.

I'll never get tired of that sound.

He stroked her in time to the languid pace of their lovemaking, every muscle in his body straining with the urge to go faster, deeper. But there would be other chances for that. Decades, he hoped. He only had one chance to make sure Jane's first time was what she deserved.

Time was suspended as he fell into the rhythm of their pleasure, and he lost himself in it. His patience paid off, for Jane gradually grew bolder, arching her back as her body tensed. She was getting tighter around his cock, and it drove him wild. Eli dared to thrust a bit deeper, groaning as she rode him. He could feel her getting close.

"I love you," he whispered, skirting the edge of his own release. He couldn't climax yet. But God, it was hard to hold back.

"I love you too," she replied between halting gasps. She pressed herself against his hand as she found her pleasure, her features contorting as a cry escaped her lips.

It was enough to push him past the limit of his self-control. He pulled out, barely in time, and spent himself against her thigh.

Jba

Afterward, Jane lay inside the protective circle of Eli's arms and contemplated her situation. A few weeks ago, she would never have imagined herself here. Giving herself freely to Eli before they were married, particularly when she only needed to wait another day to learn how the inquiry would unfold. But it felt right.

She didn't want to be able to release him if he were disgraced. They were bound together now irreversibly. Whatever happened, she would face it by his side.

"You should go back home," she said reluctantly. "Get some sleep before it's too late."

"What about the rest of it?" His eyes were somber in the darkness. "Where we'll live, and all that? I still feel the same way I did before.

I intend for you to have a house in town, even if it means I have to remain in the navy for a time. I won't let you give up your life for me."

Jane bit her lip, not trusting herself to speak.

It felt as though everything she'd ever wanted was just inside the window to a cheery little house, the curtains flung back to display the scene to her covetous eye, and she was trapped outside in the cold. To have her happiness so close at hand, and yet be unable to touch it!

There must be a solution. She could calculate the odds to determine her best chance at a profit in a hundred scenarios in vingt-et-un; surely she could find an answer to this. The problem was only a lack of funds, and hadn't she been trying to secure her financial security from the very start?

It was obvious, really. She'd just been too cautious to see it.

"What if there were a way we could have everything? A steady income without you returning to sea. Would you be willing to leave the navy, if money were no issue?" The excitement of an idea was taking root. "I don't want to force you to give up your career if that isn't what you want for yourself."

"I don't understand how it could be possible." He studied her, his eyes two fathomless pools in the darkness. "Of course I want to be with you, but I don't want to feel ashamed at how we must live."

Hmm, that might still be an issue. But it was the best solution she could find, so she would forge ahead.

"I have an idea, but I'm worried you might laugh." Jane felt shy suddenly. Who was she to plan their finances? She was an orphan with next to nothing in her name. A woman who couldn't hope to earn anything. Yet she did hope.

"I won't laugh. I respect your judgment."

"Why couldn't our income be my gambling club instead of your pay?" The words tumbled out of her mouth before she could talk herself out of it. Uncle Bertie might have forbidden her, but she would soon answer to her husband, not her guardian. And Eli had already proven himself to be more understanding. "We turn a good profit, and I know we could do better. If we rented rooms to expand our membership and added more games, we could make enough to support ourselves without your pay. I know we could."

"Jane…" The regret was thick in his voice. Jane knew what he would say before he even said it: that it was his job to support them. That this was a fine little hobby for pin money, but not a real business. She steeled herself for the condemnation to come.

But Eli didn't say any of that. He stroked his hand along her arm, firm and reassuring.

"You know I believe in your idea, but if we're to stake our livelihood on it, we need a large sum to invest in the expansion you're planning. We don't have that."

If she hadn't already promised to marry Eli, she would do so again just for that. His faith in her.

"Della and I have earned nearly seventy pounds from the club this season, and there's another four hundred in Edmund's bank account that are all our savings since our parents died. I've been contributing here and there over the years."

"Would he agree to invest some of it in your club? Four hundred should be more than enough to rent rooms, buy tables, and hire a few dealers to get started."

If Della wished to remain an equal partner, she might match their contribution. They wouldn't need much at first. The most important thing was a good location, not the size. They could start scouting now and be ready to open by next season.

"I don't see why he shouldn't. The money was supposed to be for his studies, but he won't need all of it upfront. We could repay him after we're established."

At least some was her rightful share. Jane could lay a claim to half without any guilt, though she would take less if it meant obtaining Edmund's blessing.

Even a hundred pounds would make all the difference.

"All right then." Eli's voice was full of wonder, as though he couldn't quite believe what he'd agreed to. Before she could ask if he was sure, he leaned over and brushed his lips over her brow, the heat of his breath lingering after the kiss ended. It felt like a benediction. "If you're up for the challenge, so am I."

"What about the navy? Will they allow you to leave?"

He hesitated now. "I've seen them grant men my age an honorable discharge when there was some good reason to cut short their service. But they might just as easily decide to issue a dishonorable discharge as punishment if they aren't satisfied with my answers tomorrow. You understand what that could mean for us? It would follow me for the rest of my life, and you'd be tarnished by association. I can't know how the judges are inclined until I have a chance to speak with them. That's why I wanted you to have the chance to release me if things take a bad turn."

"I'm not sure the reputation of the proprietress of a ladies' gaming hell needs much protecting," Jane returned. "We'll be a well-matched pair. Scandalous together." Eli was tense beneath her touch. Her words hadn't reassured him as she'd hoped. After a pause, she added softly. "I still want to try, if you do. Unless you don't believe the club can turn a profit?"

"No. It will work." Eli drew a long breath. "I feel it. But even if I'm wrong, I'd rather know we tried everything to build a life we could both be happy with than accept defeat without a fight."

Jane kissed him with everything she had. She would never forget how lucky she felt in this moment.

"Tell me what you need to begin," Eli murmured, as though it weren't the middle of the night and he didn't have a court hearing to threaten his future in the morning.

A million details spread over Jane's thoughts like a spiderweb. It would take days to examine each one—what neighborhood was the best to set up shop, whom they would hire to deal and serve refreshments, what games should be offered, how to price entry and membership—but for the moment, she had all she needed. A good idea, and someone who believed in her.

Twenty-Seven

Jane went to see Della directly the next morning.

"Of *course* I'll remain an equal partner," her friend assured her, bouncing in her seat as Jane laid out her intentions. "This is so exciting! I *knew* you wouldn't really bow out. I'm sure I can persuade my parents to free up a portion of my dowry for an investment if we go to them with a plan in hand. We should secure a lease straight away, preferably one that needs to be snatched up before it's gone. They respond best to a little urgency. Do you suppose we could find something on Saint James's Street, to match White's?"

"Let's not get ahead of ourselves until I have a chance to speak to Edmund about withdrawing my share of the money in his account." Jane was a little taken aback by how rapidly this plan was unfolding. A lease on Saint James's Street would bankrupt them! But then, Della had a tendency to get carried away. It often fell to Jane to bring her back down to earth. "We can start looking for premises after I know how much he's willing to part with."

"But shouldn't half the inheritance be yours? I'm sure your brother won't refuse you. Why don't we just take a little carriage ride over to Pall Mall and see if we spot any vacancies along the way?"

"I need to be back home before Eli's inquiry ends." Jane shot a glance at the clock on the mantel. It was only a quarter to ten. Had they begun the proceedings yet? She had no idea how long it might take, but she couldn't risk missing his call. She'd only ventured as far as Della's because she knew it would be quick, and she needed to distract herself. "I'll talk to Edmund about the funds as soon as I return."

"Of course, of course," Della amended. "We'll begin our hunt tomorrow then, once all this other business is settled."

Like as not, she'll go without me the moment I'm out the door. But Jane had neither the time nor the energy to argue. There was no real harm in Della's enthusiasm, so long as nothing went wrong.

And things *couldn't* go wrong. She'd convinced Eli to risk everything on this plan. It had to work.

Della saw her to the door, still humming with excitement. "If Edmund gives you any trouble about the investment, might I suggest a spot of blackmail? It works wonders when I need a favor from Peter or Annabelle."

"I...don't think I have the same type of relationship with my brother as you have with your siblings."

Della's brow puckered at this. "Do you mean to tell me you don't know any of his secrets? Jane, however can you get away with trouble of your own if you've nothing to bargain with?"

"I *don't* get away with things," Jane returned. "As you may recall, I'm presently engaged because I kissed Eli in view of a window."

"You enjoyed a few interesting diversions before you were discovered, though," Della reminded her, suppressing a smile.

Once Jane had made the journey back home with a hurried step and reassured herself that Eli hadn't come in the short time she was out, she went in search of Edmund. Happily, he was reading in the study and not out riding.

"Has Uncle Bertie come home?" He looked up at her approach.

"No, though I expect he'll arrive any moment. I was hoping to speak with you alone first." Edmund blinked in surprise, and Jane decided to press on before she could lose her nerve. "I've decided to expand my gambling club into a proper business, and I'd like to withdraw some funds from our bank account for an initial investment. I wouldn't need much. A hundred pounds should be enough to rent—"

"It's *my* account, not ours," he corrected.

Oh dear. This wasn't the beginning she'd hoped for.

"The only reason your name is on it is because I'm a woman," Jane said, her tone clipped. The bank's refusal to serve female clientele still rankled. "But you know the funds from Mama and Papa are mine as much as yours. And I've been adding my extra pin money and my club winnings."

"You always told me that was for my education," Edmund observed.

"W-well, yes, I did say that. But that was before I'd formed more definite plans for my future. And besides, I'm not proposing to clean you out. We're discussing an equitable share."

Why was he being difficult? She'd expected that they might quibble a bit over the exact figure, not that he would behave as though everything were rightfully his. Edmund could be stubborn, but he wasn't cruel.

"If you're worried there won't be enough for your studies, I'm willing to repay whatever I can in a few years, once my club is established," Jane offered. "You know I don't live extravagantly. You'll have the money back before you even need it."

"I need it now," Edmund said, his tone grim. "You didn't see the letter that came this morning, I take it."

"No..." Jane hesitated. She'd been too preoccupied with her plans to check. Had Bertie written? "Why? What's happened?"

"Aunt Nora had her baby. A boy."

"Oh no." Some of the wind went out of her sails. No wonder Edmund was worried about his finances. His status as a future land-owner had just gone up in smoke. "I'm so sorry, but we knew this day might come." The prospect of another heir to supplant him had always lurked in the background.

"I need to make some other provision for myself," he continued without missing a beat. "I've decided to join the army."

"The army?" Jane echoed hopelessly. "With things in China being what they are? That's madness! You'll get yourself killed."

She couldn't blame her brother for wanting the same financial independence she did—but to choose such a dangerous course! Even if he escaped injury, he would pass his life going from one battle to the next on the orders of a Parliament more concerned with lining its pockets than any sense of justice. It was unthinkable.

"Most of my friends without an inheritance have joined the army or the navy. It's the best option for me."

"What about the church? It would be a much more sensible way to establish yourself."

"With what living? Uncle John already sold the one at Ashlow, and we don't have a wealthy patron."

"If you attend Oxford, you might make connections that could assist you. At least take a year or two to think about it before you make any rash decisions."

"What good will a few more years studying Latin and Greek do me? Oxford won't help me earn an income; I'll come out in the same position I'm in now, only a little older and a lot poorer." Edmund cut through her suggestion as swiftly as an ax splitting wood. "If I buy my commission now, I might use that time to build a name for myself and save funds for advancement. My mind is made up."

He must have been considering this even before the letter came. Why hadn't he said anything? The headstrong adolescent before her was a stranger, so different from the child she'd tried to protect after their parents died. Jane didn't know how to talk to him. He had an answer for everything.

"Very well," she conceded. "I don't agree with your choice, but if you're determined to risk your life for no good reason, you're old enough that I can't stop you. But you can't decide my future. Let me do as I please with my share."

"Ensign-level commissions start at four hundred pounds. I'll need our entire inheritance to cover the expense. I'm sorry to set back your project, but it can't be helped." Edmund was perfectly calm as he explained his reasoning, which only made Jane more furious.

Set back her "project," indeed! As though all her dreams were nothing more than an idle fancy that couldn't be allowed to interfere with his grand plans.

"Who's to say that your goals matter more than mine, just because you're a gentleman?"

"It isn't because I'm a gentleman," Edmund replied easily. "It's because I have the greater assurance of success. The army is a respectable career. You're proposing to sink a hundred pounds into a gaming house for ladies, with no guarantee that you won't be met with scorn and censure from the ton. It's only logical that if we don't have enough for both of us, we prioritize the one with better prospects."

He said it with such assurance, it was plain he thought her a bit foolish for expecting otherwise.

"Oh, I could just—consider yourself lucky I can't blackmail you!"

"Beg pardon?"

"Never mind," she snapped, "but I don't accept this. I need that money, and you have no right to deny me a share. If I have to take this up with Uncle Bertie when he returns, that's what I shall do."

Jane wasn't proud of the threat, nor did she relish the idea of running to their uncle with her tale like a child, but there was no other choice. Their legal guardian was the only one liable to carry any weight with the bank.

Even so, Edmund didn't seem bothered by her threat. "You really think he'll consider a gambling club to be a better idea than a military commission? You know he disapproves." He didn't smirk, exactly, but there was a muted sympathy on his face that Jane could've done without.

"I haven't the faintest idea what he'll say to my plans," she admitted. "But I'm confident he'll agree that my offer to take a hundred pounds for myself and leave you with three times that amount is a generous one."

It was the first time her brother actually hesitated. Perhaps cold numbers didn't provide him as much opportunity for excuses as her explanations had.

"Let's not draw Bertie into it." He backtracked without a trace of shame. "You know I'd be happy to give you your hundred pounds if it would leave me with enough to buy my commission, but it's impossible. You can always save your pin money for a few more years and expand your club later."

"You could always purchase the commission later," Jane returned. "It only seems fair that the eldest go first."

She couldn't give in, not when she'd convinced Eli to stake his future on this. They'd already lost so much time.

Jane thought she saw a trace of fear in the widening of Edmund's eyes. She didn't relish it, but she had to admit it was better to be taken seriously than brushed aside without any real consideration.

He looked around the room as if expecting to find some help there, and grew agitated to see none. He fussed with his cravat, his tone suddenly businesslike once more. "Very well. If we can't settle this reasonably, then I suppose I don't have much choice." He studied her for an instant, seemed to settle on some course of action, and then left the room.

"Where are you going?" Jane rushed after him, struggling to keep up with Edmund's long stride. He walked with a purpose. This wasn't the stomping defiance of a child going to sulk in his room, but the step of a man who knew his destination. He didn't answer, but descended the stairs and went directly to the entrance, where he found his hat and crammed it roughly atop his head. "I said, where are you going?" Jane repeated, tugging at his arm and trying to quell the panic that was swirling inside her.

She was trembling before he even gave his response. Perhaps she already knew how easily her little brother might reduce her dreams to ash with a snap of his fingers, and she didn't want confirmation.

"To the bank." He didn't look at her as he delivered the killing blow, intent upon his coat buttons. "I'm sorry about this, but I won't let you cost me my commission."

"Edmund." She tightened her grip on his arm, but he shook her off with a rough motion. "Don't do this. I need the investment. Eli is counting on me."

"Please don't follow me. It will only make a scene, and it won't change anything."

The truth in that statement was nearly as devastating as the decision unfolding before her. What would the bank managers do if she turned up on their doorstep pleading for her portion of the inheritance? She didn't have a trust to protect her, and the account was in Edmund's name. They would judge her hysterical and send her home without a second thought, and he would still take everything.

There was no way to stop him.

Edmund left her in the entranceway, her thoughts darting helplessly like moths around the flame. What was she supposed to do now? She couldn't ask Della to shoulder the costs of their venture alone and still expect to take half the profits for herself, and Eli didn't have any funds to contribute without his income.

Oh God, the hearing.

He'd said he would broach the subject of a discharge today. Eli was about to sacrifice his career for her—had perhaps already done so—because he'd trusted her so completely that the idea of giving up a stable source of income to start a ladies' gambling club didn't seem ridiculous. And when he came to call on her, she would have to explain that she'd been too hasty. She'd assumed that she could access her own money without obstacle, taking Edmund's assent for granted.

Hadn't she always known that marriage would bring misfortune? Only she'd had it backward. Jane hadn't dared risk her future on a man, and in the end, it was Eli who'd risked his future on her and would lose everything for it.

If only she'd known what her brother was planning!

When the hoofbeats and jangling harness of a carriage sounded outside a short time later, Jane had the urge to hide. She couldn't face Eli. Not without a plan.

But it was Uncle Bertie who entered the vestibule a moment later with Cecily in tow.

"Hello there, my dear." He smiled as he removed his hat and gloves. "Have I missed the lieutenant's call? I meant to arrive sooner, but I wanted to check on Cecily on my way back into town."

"Thank goodness you're home," Jane cried, sweeping her uncle into an embrace that was less of a welcome and more of a clutch for dear life. She should probably have shown more restraint in front of her cousin, but there was no time to worry about that now. Edmund couldn't have more than a ten-minute head start, and the only person who might be able to talk sense into him was standing before her. "I need you to go directly to the bank and try to find Edmund. No time to unpack your things."

"What's happened?" Cecily spoke before her father could. "Does it have to do with your engagement? Imagine how surprised I was to learn of it from Papa. You know how I hate to be the last one to find out!"

Jane ignored this accusation and focused on her uncle. "There's no time to explain. What matters is, I desperately need to withdraw a portion of my inheritance if I'm to marry Eli, and Edmund has gone to the bank to clean house and leave me without a single shilling. If you go after him directly, you might arrive before my portion is spent."

"That doesn't sound like our Edmund." Bewilderment tugged Bertie's eyebrows up toward his hairline. "Why should he do such a thing?"

"He's taken it into his head to purchase a commission." They were running out of time. Every minute brought Edmund that much closer to his goal. "Never mind that. Only *please* go stop him while you still can. We can hash out the details once he's back at home and the funds are safe."

Bertie seemed at last to grasp the urgency of the situation. "Very well. Rest assured that I'll do my best to prevent any irreversible action until we've had a chance to talk this over properly. Are you coming with me?"

Jane hesitated. She might miss Eli's call, but wouldn't it be preferable to salvage her funds than to face him empty-handed?

Cecily filled the silence, her voice bright and helpful, "I can mind the house in case Eli calls while you're out."

Goodness, no. That wouldn't do at all. "I'd best stay here too. You go ahead, Uncle. If you miss him at the bank, you might try—I don't know, where do young men go to buy commissions?"

"I imagine the War and Colonial Office, or the military academy," Bertie supplied, placing his hat back atop his head and opening the door. "I'll check both if he's already left the bank. Don't lose hope."

He was gone a moment later. *Please let him arrive in time.* Jane sent the prayer out into the world, hating how useless she felt to stay behind and wait.

"Well, darling, shall we take some tea until your beau arrives?" A hungry smile tugged at Cecily's lips, though her eyes remained cool. "I daresay you've a lot to tell me."

Twenty-Eight

"I BRING THIS TO YOUR ATTENTION ONLY IN KEEPING WITH MY highest sense of duty toward Her Majesty's Royal Navy. Signed, Captain Richard Powlett." Admiral Ward set down the letter, turning his eyes to Eli with solemnity. "Well, Lieutenant Williams? What answer will you make to these charges?"

The admiral, a white-haired man nearing eighty, was the president of Eli's inquiry. He sat now in the day cabin on the roman HMS *Achilles*, dressed in full uniform and flanked on either side by the two other judges who heard Eli's case. The judge advocate sat at his own table a little further down, scribbling notes in his log as they spoke. It was a large room, lined with windows to let in the sun, and several of the skeleton crew that manned the *Achilles* while she was at harbor had come in to occupy the space, perhaps seeking some novelty in their day.

Though Eli would have preferred no audience at all, it could have been worse. The real challenge would be if one of them decided to alert the papers.

"With the greatest of respect, Admiral, I understand them not to be formal charges, merely concerns."

"True," Admiral Ward amended quickly. "I don't mean to overstate the situation, but whatever information you can provide to us will certainly determine whether we recommend charges be brought or no."

The scribbling of the judge advocate's pen upon the page grated away Eli's concentration. He fought back the urge to tell the man to be quiet. He needed to approach this carefully, just as he'd planned with Halsey. One wrong word could mean his ruin.

"There lies my difficulty, sirs." Eli measured each word. "As no charges have been brought yet, I cannot know what case the Crown will have to prove. You can understand my reluctance to give any evidence at the inquiry which may be used against me later."

He couldn't be forced to lie if he refused to speak. Time to see how the judges would take it.

"You have been summoned here in order to present your side of the story, Lieutenant," said Captain Eden, who sat, frowning, to the admiral's left. "In the hopes that we may avoid a court-martial altogether, if it is not needed. I ask you therefore: Were you a hostage of pirates, as has been reported in the papers?"

All they wanted was a yes. If he gave it to them, this could end now.

But it was a false hope. For once he submitted to examination, another question would follow. And another.

"This court has no authority to compel me to testify." Eli glanced down at his notes. "In the case of Sir John Mordaunt—"

"Yes, yes," Admiral Ward interrupted. "We're all familiar with that matter. But even if we cannot compel testimony, surely you can see that it may benefit you to cooperate with us. I've followed your story with interest, and I'm sure we would all be happy to see this resolved today, if you can only satisfy us that there is a full explanation for your absence."

It could be so easy. Was he making a mistake in refusing to answer?

But if they asked how long it had taken him to get home, what would he say? If they wanted the name of the merchant ship, if they tried to track down its crew to verify details and dates, everything would start to unravel.

No. He'd found his way forward, and he would have to hold to it.

"Thank you for your candor, Admiral, but I must maintain my refusal."

Behind him, a few of the onlookers murmured at his response. Admiral Ward sighed, exchanging a dark look with Captain Eden, who shook his head. The judge advocate's pen scribbled furiously on.

"So you let the letter stand uncontroverted then?" asked Captain Eden.

"I don't consider the letter to provide any evidence against me," Eli replied. "Captain Powlett himself confirms that I am a man of good character, and he has no proof I committed any crime. The circumstances of the shipwreck and my unwilling separation from my crew are well-known. The captain confirms there were pirates traveling the region at the time of the wreck. If the case against me is merely that he thinks it strange they made no demand for ransom, this falls short of the standard required for a court-martial."

"Thank you, Lieutenant." Admiral Ward held up a finger to signal patience while he exchanged a murmur with the others. Eli strained to catch his words, but they were even softer than the splash of the waves against the hull outside. Time seemed to stretch on and on before he turned back to Eli. "You understand that even if we were to accept your argument that the evidence is insufficient to support charges, we would still be within our rights to recommend your demotion or dismissal to the Admiralty in light of your refusal to elucidate matters?"

Any relief Eli felt at the beginning of that sentence had evaporated by its end. Dismissal. It would mean infamy and the censure of the ton, if the story made the papers. Even if he'd told Jane he would ask for a discharge, he'd planned to do so on his own terms, with his reputation intact.

Now that the moment was before him, he hesitated. It was a huge risk he would be taking. What if her club failed and they were left with nothing? He couldn't recover his rank and income once he abandoned it.

But if Jane really believed they could do this, he had to trust her.

"I understand, Admiral, and I accept the consequences of my choice today. I only hope that the lords commissioners will prove understanding of the difficult position I'm in. I would be grateful to receive the courtesy of a discharge, rather than a dismissal, if you're inclined to spare a consideration for my reputation as a gentleman."

"Very well," Admiral Ward replied. "We'll take your request under advisement. If you refuse to be examined, do you wish to recommend any other witnesses to the Court who might have knowledge of this matter?"

"No, sir." Every survivor of the wreck would only say the same thing as Captain Powlett: they'd seen him pulled under and never heard from him again until now.

"Does anyone see a need to hear from Captain Powlett in person?" Captain Eden cast a glance to the other judges. "It seems to me his letter encompasses the whole of his account."

"I agree," Admiral Ward said. "There's no sense in dragging this out. I'd like to confer with my colleagues in private a moment."

Everyone stood to attention as the three judges retired to an adjacent room. The scribbling of the judge advocate had finally stopped, though it was past the point where it could bring Eli any relief. The dice were cast. All he could do now was wait.

They returned after a quarter hour, retaking their seats with solemnity.

Admiral Ward cleared his throat. "After deliberation, this court inquiry is in agreement that there isn't sufficient evidence of any crime to allow us to recommend charges be laid before a court-martial." Eli drew a long breath, trying not to let his relief show. "Though we understand why you might believe it contrary to your interest to testify in the absence of any formal charges, your refusal has left this court with unanswered questions about your where-abouts during the time you were absent from your service following the wreckage of the *Libertas*. In the circumstances, we intend to rec-ommend your other-than-honorable discharge from the navy. We shall inform you once our report is submitted to the lords commis-sioners. That is all, Lieutenant."

It was the best he could have hoped for, given the situation. He'd escaped both a court-martial and a dishonorable discharge. Even so, he felt lost.

He needed to see Jane and reassure himself that he hadn't made a mistake. He needed to hear her good judgment again.

"Thank you, sirs."

With a salute to his superiors, he took his leave and climbed back up to the quarterdeck, then walked the gangplank back to the docks.

*

"I *knew* you were keeping secrets from me." Cecily sipped her tea as if it were the distillation of all her suspicions. "There really was a fight between Eli and MacPherson, wasn't there?"

"Pardon?" It took Jane a minute to recall their quarrel at the Pearsons' ball. How was she expected to focus when Eli might arrive any minute? She wondered if Bertie had reached the bank yet, and if he'd been able to reason with Edmund. It wasn't a long ride. "No, there wasn't any fight. And there's not much to tell. Eli and I care for each other, and we've decided to marry."

If she didn't add fuel to the fire, perhaps they could keep this brief.

Jane glanced at the clock on the mantel, which ticked off the seconds at a pace that seemed to slow the longer she watched it. Did it just go backward?

"I'll have to host a ball to celebrate your engagement, I suppose." Cecily sighed, as if this was an imposition and not her own suggestion. "Do you suppose it will be very awkward for you if I do?"

"Why would it be awkward?"

"Well, surely everyone who sees us together will be thinking of how Eli was supposed to marry me first."

Perhaps it was the headache that had been slowly building at her temples since her quarrel with Edmund, or perhaps she was simply overset by the events of the day, but Jane had reached the limit of her patience. She closed her eyes and steeled herself, drawing in a long breath before she spoke again. "Cecily, I need you to stop doing this if we're to get along for Uncle Bertie's sake."

"Doing what?" She brought a palm to her chest, ready to assume a wounded pose at a moment's notice. "I was only concerned that—"

"This." Jane jabbed a finger at the air between them. "The little barbs, the false concern. I don't have the energy to keep it up anymore, honestly. If you want us to be able to spend time in each other's company, you'll have to be kinder to me."

"*Me*, be kinder to *you*?" Cecily's voice rose a touch. Gone was the injured facade, replaced by more genuine sentiment. "You're the one who dislikes me. I invite you to all my parties and when have you ever returned the favor? You didn't even invite me to your gaming club." Cecily was sitting quite straight in her chair, and the line of her mouth had gone as rigid as her spine. Her eyes, in contrast, were bright and liquid. "I had to hear about it from others. It was humiliating!"

"It—it wasn't personal," Jane stammered. It felt like this

conversation had slid on a wet tile and was now careening toward a sudden fall. "I didn't think you even liked cards."

"If you wanted me there, you would've asked," Cecily insisted. "You've always excluded me."

"I have not." It wasn't as though Jane was in any way the social superior of the two. Her cousin had a sizable dowry, a living parent, a knighted husband, and a healthy son. "What could I possibly exclude you *from*? You've had everything you've ever wanted."

"So you think me spoiled," Cecily concluded. "Is that why? It isn't easy being a society hostess, you know. It takes a great deal of work behind the scenes, which you've *never* underst—Oh, don't you *dare* roll your eyes at me."

An ugly flush mottled Cecily's face.

"I didn't," Jane said swiftly, though she probably had. She hadn't meant to, at any rate. She'd just been offering a silent prayer for the conversation to end, and her eyes had slipped heavenward.

"You don't appreciate anything that I've done for you!" Cecily snapped. "I spent *weeks* planning our trip to Ascot, and you didn't lift a finger to help. Then you spoiled everything the second day by running off to have your own little party with Hannah, as if you're too good for us, and you disappeared from the Pearsons' ball without even saying goodbye."

"I was feeling poorly!"

"You always have some excuse. I know the real reason. You're jealous of me and you're determined to punish me for it, though I've done nothing to warrant such treatment."

"Jealous of you!" That was rich. "And you've done *nothing* to deserve it? You can't think of any time you've wronged me?"

"What have I done then?"

"You know perfectly well."

"Is this about Eli?" Cecily puffed up her chest, the picture of wounded pride. "I can't believe you're still holding on to that, years later. It's not my fault he preferred me to you."

But it didn't hold the same power it once had.

"He didn't prefer you, you threw yourself at him. You *knew* that I fancied him, and you decided to steal him from me for no other reason than to hurt me."

Cecily couldn't have loved him; she'd barely known him then.

"Well *you* stole my father," Cecily cried. "Which is much worse. It serves you right if I dashed your hopes with Eli."

"I beg your pardon?" How could she reply to such a ridiculous accusation? She hadn't stolen Uncle Bertie. He worshipped his daughter. "Are you blaming me for being orphaned and having no other place to go?"

"Poor Jane." It was Cecily's turn to roll her eyes. "You've had such a hard life. Papa's treated you like his own daughter, when he already *had* one, and somehow you're still hard done by."

"I'm very grateful to Uncle Bertie for taking me in," Jane protested. "But I haven't replaced you. He adores you."

"But he doesn't talk to me the way he talks to you!" Cecily was in tears by now, the words punctuated by small hiccups. It must be genuine, for she didn't look pretty while doing it. "You're the one he always goes to for advice. He ran off to Sunninghill because *you* told him to. And neither of you told me of your engagement until today!"

Cecily was obliged to break off to fish a handkerchief from her reticule to smother her cries.

Jane was too stunned to reply. She was forced to listen to Cecily's quiet sobs for the span of twenty seconds as her mind worked to twist all of this into something that made any sense.

"I never knew you felt this way," she finally said.

Cecily sniffed loudly.

"I suppose…I could try harder to include you when we're making plans?" She felt as though she were fumbling for an oil lamp in the dark. "Would that help?"

"It would be a start." Cecily dabbed at her eyes. "I also want a standing invitation to your club."

Ha.

"I'll use my forfeit if I have to," she added, perhaps sensing that she was on shaky ground. She actually began rummaging in her reticule. Had she planned this when she'd come over?

"Oh, put that away."

It was only with supreme effort that Jane kept from refusing her outright. This was her only bargaining chip, really. She and Cecily both loved Uncle Bertie, and were therefore stuck with one another.

"*If* I agree," Jane paused, more to gain her cousin's full attention than to collect her thoughts, "you must promise never to insult me again. No more comments about Eli being engaged to you first, or my taking too long to find a husband, or any of that. And no flirting with him either."

If the deal held, it was worth a lifetime membership to her club. Cecily would only be losing her own money, after all.

To her credit, Cecily didn't pretend not to know what Jane was talking about. She held her gaze, finally answering. "Very well."

"Thank you."

It felt like something they should shake on, but Jane worried it would look silly, so instead she smoothed out the wrinkles in her skirts.

"You are the closest thing I have to a sibling, you know," Cecily said abruptly. "Edmund doesn't count. He never talks to me."

"He's like that with everyone," Jane assured her.

Twenty-Nine

ELI MADE HASTE TO JANE'S HOUSE FROM THE INQUIRY. HE'D expected to be greeted by her uncle, by this hour of the day, but the butler showed him into a drawing room where Jane and Lady Kerr awaited him.

"Good day." He bowed to each of them in greeting and took a seat near the window, trying to hide his surprise at his present company.

"How did everything turn out?" Jane wore a worried line upon her brow that he longed to smooth away, but he glanced to her cousin before he replied. How much did she already know?

"Don't mind me, darling," she volunteered, seeing his hesitation. "Anything you can tell Jane, you can tell me, surely. Congratulations on your engagement, by the way."

"Thank you, dear cousin." The degree of fatigue in Jane's voice told Eli that they'd been waiting together for a considerable time before he arrived. "Perhaps you might spare us a moment in private. I assure you we'll manage without a chaperone."

Lady Kerr looked for a moment as though she might protest, but in the end she merely favored Jane with an indulgent look and withdrew from the room.

"The judges aren't recommending any charges," Eli reported, the moment they were alone. "And I'm to be granted my discharge."

"Thank goodness you've been cleared." He'd expected Jane's face to flood with relief at the news, but it barely seemed to lighten her burden.

This was everything they'd wanted, wasn't it?

"What's the matter?"

"Your discharge, is it already final?"

"The judges will write a recommendation on my case to the naval lords, and I need to await their decision, but it's just a formality." Was she worried that his request could still be denied? "I've no reason to think they'll refuse."

"Oh goodness. I hardly know how to tell you this." Jane looked so bleak, it must be serious. Eli rose from his spot to join her on the divan and take her hands in his. "Edmund has taken it into his head to purchase a commission in the army," she continued, her voice thick with emotion. "He plans to use all our funds for it. My uncle went to the bank to stop him, but he should have returned by now if he'd found him easily. I fear it may be too late, and there'll be nothing left to start the club."

Eli's stomach sank as the implications hit him. Without Jane's investment or his salary, they couldn't afford a house in town. They would be stranded in Devon, far removed from their friends. Worst of all, he would be taking Jane from her dream.

He'd wanted to offer her the freedom to pursue her own goals in their marriage. Something he might even help her to build, for she and Miss Danby were sure to need trustworthy supporters in the initial stages of their endeavor. After the grief he'd put her through, he wanted to give her that.

"Could you go back to the navy and tell them you've changed your mind?" Jane asked, her voice tinged with reluctance. "Before the naval lords make their final decision?"

"No." Eli spoke gently, conscious of her distress. "The judges were dissatisfied with my refusal to provide any details of my absence. The discharge is a courtesy to me, to preserve my reputation as they've no evidence of any wrongdoing, but they won't let me stay unless I answer their questions, which would put both Geórgios and myself in danger."

"I'm so sorry. I never should have encouraged you to risk everything on my club. It was so selfish of me!"

"This isn't your fault. Edmund is the one being selfish. And as to my naval career, there was no way to avoid it, once I accepted the help of a pirate and delayed my time in France. It wasn't because of you." He'd lowered his voice at this last part, with a glance at the door to make sure it was still firmly shut against Lady Kerr's curiosity, but they seemed to be safe.

Jane looked utterly defeated, her shoulders slumped low.

"This doesn't have to be the end," he tried, desperate to lift her spirits. They were supposed to be celebrating their plans for the future, not mourning their loss. "Did Miss Danby agree to partner with you?"

"Yes, but I can't expect to take half the profits if she's the only one contributing an investment. It's worked so well until now because we've always been equally devoted in our efforts."

"Perhaps there's still time to win back some of what you've lost. The season's not over yet, and I can help you drum up more members. I might ask my parents for help, as well." He hadn't wanted to ask them to repay his savings—he could hardly blame them for giving the money to Jacob when they thought him dead, after all—but now might be an appropriate time to raise the subject.

"But the amount we would need—"

Before Jane could finish her thought, a rap on the door signaled Lady Kerr's return.

"Papa's carriage is approaching!" She peered in, her gaze lingering on their entwined hands.

Jane leaped to her feet, hurrying out to meet her uncle on the front steps, and Eli followed.

As Mr. Bishop descended, the coachman began leading the team to the stables. No one else emerged from the carriage. Not a good sign.

"Ah, Lieutenant," he said as he walked up. "You're here. But why are you all out of doors as if the world is falling down about our ears? Come, let's all retire to the drawing room and talk about this sensibly. You must tell me how your morning went."

"Everything is resolved," Eli said. The news had lost its luster on the second telling, but Bishop displayed all the enthusiasm Jane had lacked.

"Marvelous!" He led them down the hall and back to the drawing room with a smile on his face. "I never had a doubt. Then we may finally announce your engagement, I take it? Oh, no one has offered you tea, I see!"

"I would have, Papa," Lady Kerr replied. "But they did not wish to be disturbed."

"But did you find Edmund?" Jane pressed. Who cared about tea at a time like this? "Did you stop him from spending the money?"

Bertie drew a long breath, as if fortifying himself. "Yes, I found him. There is good news and bad news. Which do you want first?"

"The bad."

"I'm afraid the money is gone. He's already bought himself a commission and is now an ensign in the infantry. I tried to get him to come home to talk to you about this himself, but he's being a bit stubborn."

"What's the good news?" Eli prompted, hoping for something to redeem these events.

"The good news is that Edmund is now an ensign in the infantry." Mr. Bishop smiled brightly, as though this were obvious. He took a seat and motioned for the others to follow suit. "Everyone is overreacting. It's a very respectable choice for him. And though he's done you a disservice, Jane, this is nothing we can't resolve."

"But four hundred pounds," she lamented softly, sinking onto the divan.

"Tut, tut," cut in Bertie. "You haven't let me finish. I was hoping to make this announcement under happier circumstances, but I'm giving you two a wedding gift."

Jane exchanged a look with Eli.

"It's the town house," he continued excitedly. "I want you to have it."

Jane was too stunned to speak, so her uncle kept talking. "You needn't worry that it will be too crowded for you to set up your own household. Edmund will be in the army, and I'll be moving to Sunninghill." He let this statement hang in the air a moment before explaining, "I've proposed to Miss Linden, and she's accepted."

"I knew it!" Lady Kerr crowed, triumphant. "I always said you should make a fine match. I have a talent for spotting such things."

"Engaged to Miss Linden!" Jane looked considerably more shocked at the news. Perhaps she'd thought her uncle too old to marry again.

Whatever the reason, Mr. Bishop seemed to understand Jane's confusion, for he addressed her as he spoke. "She and her brother are *both* in agreement that we should all reside at his house in Sunninghill together, as Miss Linden prefers the country to London. It's an arrangement we considered long ago, only we worried about the appearance of things if a bachelor were to live under the same roof as two young girls who weren't any blood relation. But now that you and Cecily are both settled, I may retire to their home with an easy heart."

Jane's smile grew broader at this. "I'm very happy for you, Uncle," she said heartily.

"Congratulations, Mr. Bishop," Eli said. "But such a gift is too much. We couldn't accept it."

"If it makes you feel any better, Lieutenant, I shall have it settled on Jane and her descendants in your marriage contract. Then you needn't feel any sense of obligation."

"That would make me feel better," he conceded with a chuckle. "But...the property isn't part of the entail on your brother's estate?"

"No, no," Bishop assured them. "It belonged to my father free and clear, and he willed it to me. I think he felt a bit badly that John should have everything else." Bishop offered them a kindly smile. "In keeping with this tradition, it seems only fitting that it should go to you, Jane, as I've always felt a bit badly that I had nothing to leave you. Cecily has her mother's country house, and Edmund can build himself a fortune with his military career. I should like you to have this."

"You're too generous, Papa," Lady Kerr said.

It *was* too generous, but Eli wouldn't protest any further if it was Jane's gift to accept. It would be an enormous relief to have a place in town free of any rent. The difference between despair and hope.

"Thank you," Jane managed, her voice breaking. "I don't know how we can ever repay you, Uncle Bertie."

"My dear, you mustn't think of it. I've never been happier in my life." His elated smile confirmed the assessment. "Everything is settled just as I'd wished! There is nothing else I could possibly ask for, except that you should tell me you found time to select your wedding gown while I was away."

Jane Bishop and the former Lieutenant Eli Williams were married on a Thursday—which, though it felt long in coming as they waited for the banns to be read, proved just enough time to arrange everything that mattered.

Under Uncle Bertie's insistent gaze, Jane had a new dress made for the occasion, a lilac crepe that suited her coloring, and they drew up a marriage contract that settled the town house on her and any future heirs. This important business dealt with, she and Eli had only to count the days until they were united, while Bertie began packing for his eventual move to Sunninghill.

They held an intimate ceremony in the morning for their closest relatives, plus Della, followed by a breakfast at Bertie's house.

Though Jane had not quite forgiven her brother, she did her best not to let resentment cloud her joy. Even Cecily was on good behavior, offering her congratulations and complimenting Jane's gown without any veiled insult. She nearly faltered at the breakfast, when she learned that no one else was expected, by announcing, "I could have hosted a larger party at mine if you'd only asked. We hosted seventy after we were married." But a second later she caught herself, adding, "Then again, sometimes a more intimate gathering is called for."

Jane was quite proud of her progress.

Once the celebrations were ended, and the guests had trickled home, Eli spent the rest of the day moving his things into Jane's rooms, which he would be sharing until they could reorganize the house.

"Do you suppose once the club is up and running in the new space, we might be able to find some work for Geórgios? He doesn't want to go back to the continent, and he's out of money. I thought perhaps he might be able to stand watch in the evenings. He's very large."

"You want to entrust our winnings to…a pirate." Jane flashed her husband a skeptical look.

"It sounds silly if you say it like *that*, but I don't think he'll distribute the money to his band of merry men. Just let the idea sit and see how you feel. I don't like to abandon him."

No, Jane didn't like to abandon him either, when he'd saved Eli's life. "I suppose I *have* become a pirate sympathizer," she mused.

"Beg pardon?"

"Never mind," she replied. "We'll make some arrangement."

It seemed the smallest concession when she had so much joy before her. She and Della could scarcely speak of anything but their plans, and they'd already found the perfect location to set up next season—a former chocolate shop on Piccadilly in need of nothing more than a little redecorating. Even Uncle Bertie had forgotten his opposition to the club as soon as he learned that she had her husband's full support. It was a bit frightening, how easily the state of matrimony swayed him.

Eli opened the trunk the footmen had brought up and inspected its contents, which were mostly clothes. "Where should I put these?"

"Is that all you have?" It looked like he hadn't acquired too much since his return from the dead. "They'll fit in my wardrobe until Uncle Bertie gives you the master suite."

"Are you sure you don't mind?" he asked, frowning as he hung his evening jackets into the narrow space beside her gowns. "I could have waited to move in until after your uncle's wedding."

"I'm sure," Jane replied. Once he'd finished with the clothes he was holding, she slipped her arms around Eli's neck and pulled him toward the bed before he could go back for more. "In fact, you might keep on sleeping here even once you take the master bedroom. I want every minute with you. We've spent enough time apart."

As Jane's calves came up against the foot of the bed, she flopped backward to land on the middle of her quilt. Eli observed her for only a second before he followed, his face breaking into a grin.

"You only say that now because you've never spent an entire night with me." He climbed over her, bringing his mouth to her earlobe and nibbling the tender skin before he whispered wickedly, "I snore."

"You do not!"

"I do. Now that you've married me, it's too late to do anything about it."

Jane groaned and smacked his shoulder. "I take back everything I said. You can sleep in your own room. I'll allow you to visit me on occasion only if you're very kind."

"That's fine." Eli paused and brushed a stray hair from Jane's forehead, his smile fading even as he eyes grew more intent. "I plan to be very kind to you, so I expect I'll visit often."

He bent his head low to lay kisses along her neck, shifting his weight to one elbow so that his hand was free to tug at the laces of her bodice.

"Hmm." A contented sigh escaped her, even as her blood heated. She hurried to assist him with the bow on her gown. "How kind?"

"Very kind," he repeated. "I have five years to make up for, and I don't think I'll be able to give you a moment's peace until I've settled the debt."

Acknowledgments

I've been so fortunate to have received encouragement and support from many people to make this book possible. In roughly chronological order: I am grateful to my husband and children for their patience and understanding when I needed time to myself to write. No writer can create anything without this.

A huge thank you to everyone who provided feedback on early drafts of this novel before I took it to the querying trenches—Gabriella Buba, Rosie Danan, Ruby Barrett, Gwynne Jackson, and especially Lisa Lin, who was my mentor as part of the Inclusive Romance Project and helped guide me through revisions.

Thank you to my wonderful agent Rebecca Strauss for believing in this book and for her endless patience both in helping me to make *The Lady He Lost* the best that it could be before we went on submission and for answering several hundred questions as this baby author learned to toddle through the publishing industry without crashing into things.

To everyone in the loon slack and smutfest 2.0, I am so grateful to have you to bounce ideas off of and to hold my hand when things get scary. A special shout-out to Mia Tsai and Eri M. Caro for reading my manuscript and giving me so much advice and encouragement. It can be hard to find a writing community close to home, and I'm so glad that I was able to find one online. You are all such wonderful, caring people and I'm very privileged to call you my friends.

Thank you to everyone at Sourcebooks Casablanca for taking my manuscript and turning it into a real live book. My editor, Deb Werksman, has been so understanding of my vision for this novel and of my limitations when I have to squeeze writing in between a day job and my family. I couldn't be happier to have her heading my team. A big thank-you also to Jocelyn Travis, Susie Benton, Ellie Tiemens, and Rachel Gilmer for all their hard work ushering this book through edits and into its final form, and to Sarah Brody and Brittney Mmutle for bringing their expertise to the art and marketing. I also consider myself very fortunate to be able to thank the incredibly talented and experienced Alan Ayers for this book's cover.

Finally, I'd like to thank you for reading, whether you supported this book by buying a copy or by borrowing it from your local library. I hope you enjoyed it and that I'll see you again next time.

About the Author

Faye Delacour was raised in the Canadian prairies before deciding that she needed a challenge and should move to a place where everybody spoke French. She now lives and works in Montreal with her partner and children, a reformed street cat, and an Australian Shepherd who hasn't yet accepted that he can't herd the cat.

Faye writes historical romance featuring strong, feminist heroines and enthusiastic consent.

WEBSITE: fayedelacour.com
INSTAGRAM: @fayedelacour

To receive newsletter updates,
scan this QR code: